THE LITTLE OTTLEYS

Other Virago Modern Classics published by The Dial Press

ANTONIA WHITE
Frost in May
The Lost Traveller
The Sugar House
Beyond the Glass

RADCLYFFE HALL
The Unlit Lamp

REBECCA WEST
Harriet Hume
The Judge
The Return of the Soldier

F. TENNYSON JESSE
The Lacquer Lady

SARAH GRAND
The Beth Book

BARBARA COMYNS
The Vet's Daughter

HENRY HANDEL RICHARDSON
The Getting of Wisdom

MARY WEBB
Gone to Earth
Precious Bane

EMILY EDEN
The Semi-Attached Couple
*   & The Semi-Detached House*

MARGARET KENNEDY
The Ladies of Lyndon
Together and Apart

MAY SINCLAIR
Mary Olivier: A Life

E. ARNOT ROBERTSON
Ordinary Families

ADA LEVERSON

The Little Ottleys

LOVE'S SHADOW

*

TENTERHOOKS

*

LOVE AT SECOND SIGHT

—

With a new Introduction by Sally Beauman

—

The Dial Press
New York

Published by
The Dial Press
1 Dag Hammarskjold Plaza
New York, New York 10017

Love's Shadow first published London, 1908
Tenterhooks first published London, 1912
Love at Second Sight first published London, 1916
First published in this edition by MacGibbon & Kee Ltd 1962

Library of Congress Cataloging in Publication Data

Leverson, Ada.
The little Ottleys.

Contents: Love's shadow — Tenterhooks — Love at
second sight.
I. Title.
PR6023.E875L5   1983   823'.912   82-25246
ISBN 0-385-27918-3

CONTENTS

———

INTRODUCTION

In June 1894, a year before his prosecution of the Marquess of Queens-berry for criminal libel, and his own subsequent trial at the Old Bailey, Oscar Wilde published a long poem, *The Sphinx*. The following month, in *Punch*, a parody of it (entitled *The Minx*) appeared. It was written by his friend of two years' duration, Ada Leverson; Wilde was delighted by it.

Since the publication of his own poem he had already begun to address Ada Leverson as 'Dear Sphinx' in the constant stream of notes, letters and telegrams he sent her. Thereafter the soubriquet stuck. Wilde himself used it until his death. It was taken up and perpetuated by Ada Leverson's friends, even those, like the Sitwells, who were of a different generation, and who met her for the first time some twenty years later.

The nickname was odd, for two reasons. Firstly, as Colin MacInnes was to remark, in his introduction to the reissue of Ada Leverson's three finest novels (grouped together under the title *The Little Ottleys*, Mac-Gibbon & Kee, 1962) it cemented her relationship with a legend. Ada Leverson was, thereafter, to be celebrated first and foremost as Wilde's friend, the woman he once called 'the wittiest in England', the woman who took him into her house at the time of his trial, when the London society that had so eagerly sought his favours a few months before turned on him, and ostracized him. Ada Leverson, to this day, and despite MacInnes's valuable re-assessment of her work, is still more celebrated as the 'Sphinx', than as a novelist. Her reputation as an adornment of Edwardian drawing rooms has outlived and eclipsed her reputation as a writer. Even those who have perpetuated her memory, including her chief acolyte, Osbert Sitwell, and her daughter, Violet Wyndham, have chosen to emphasize the woman, not her work. For any writer this would be a disservice; for a writer as great as Ada Leverson it is a terrible distortion—certainly not what she would ever have wanted.

But Wilde's nickname for Ada Leverson was odd for a second reason, unrelated to her later reputation. It was, on the face of it, perverse. Wilde used it with apparent negligence. Attached to the messages he sent her it seems purely complimentary, a teasing salute to the feminine mystique. Yet the poem which led to the coining of the name was very far from being a graceful ode to the mystery of the eternal feminine. Rather it had the absinthe flavour of the nineties, the self-consciously *maudit* tones of Dowson's *Cynara*. Florid, overblown, indulgent—the poem is filled with an anguished and overt sexuality. The Sphinx, in Wilde's poem, assumes the proportions of nightmare; she has lain with Anubis, god of the underworld, and survived his destruction. Unsated, she finally pursues the poet, who reacts with violent fear and loathing:

Your pulse makes poisonous melodies, and your black throat is like the hole
Left by some torch of burning coal in Saracenic tapestries . . .
Get hence you loathsome mystery. Hideous animal, get hence.
You wake in me each bestial sense, you make me what I would not be . . .[1]

Odd, after such a poem, to apply the term 'Sphinx' to a friend. Odder still to attach the name to a woman ceaselessly portrayed by her friends as the embodiment of the gentler female virtues, a woman apparently forever poised well above the darker pits of human experience. Odd, unless it were an accident. Or unless Wilde sensed in Ada Leverson something more, something darker and more dangerous than is attributed to her memory. Odd, and worth remembering when one comes to look at what Ada Leverson herself wrote: six novels of increasing technical assurance, whose prevailing tone is comedic, whose atmosphere is slightly rarified; novels so lucidly, so apparently transparently written, that they resemble portraits etched on glass.

They are portraits of marriage, all of them; marriage among the English upper classes at the turn of the century. Jealousy, infidelity shade them; illness, despair, death, and for the most part the lower classes, are excluded. War (the 1914–18 War) is mentioned only marginally. Their tone, unmistakably descended from Jane Austen, with a gift for epigrams as developed as Wilde's, is understated, precise, unsentimental, and satiric. Their pace is mellifluous, so subtly managed by the author that it is apparently effortless, and without seams. Their action, for the most part, takes place in public rooms in which the characters must adopt public faces, and observe the social conventions of their age. The characters themselves are brilliantly observed; their foibles, eccentricities, pretensions and hypocrisies captured almost purely through dialogue. They find (they admit to it, they are intensely

English) it is extremely difficult to speak their hearts. We are, in short, it would seem, in familiar territory; comedy of manners, at its most proficient.

And yet. There are ante-rooms off these salons in which something darker waits. The marriage which provides the central story and momentum of the three best novels is an unhappy one. They chart a long deterioration in the relationship between a spirited, intelligent, sensitive woman and her vain, patronising, foolish, infuriating and ultimately immoral husband. In Bruce, that husband, Ada Leverson created one of the genuine monsters of twentieth-century English fiction, and the poise of her comedy never quite lets one forget that. Into this marriage, inevitably, erupts a love affair, one of passionate feeling and repressed sexuality. That relationship, and its accumulating force, which is charted with great realism, threatens not just the characters, but also the precepts and conventions that underpin the rigid society in which they live. Ada Leverson resolves the clash of those two forces comedically; at the eleventh hour tragedy is averted—or perhaps deliberately excluded, by the author.

But she takes her characters to the brink; they look over into the world of the Sphinx, into a territory normally beyond the bounds of a comedy of manners. She pulls them back, it is true; but still the abyss is there, glimpsed. It is precisely that progressively strong awareness that the characters are perfectly poised on very thin ice that gives the novels their accumulative power.

Wilde's nickname for Ada Leverson was, perhaps intuitively, apter than he knew.

The facts of her life are precise, well-documented, and yet—like her own writing—constantly suggestive of currents beneath the surface calm. She was born in 1862, one of eight children and the eldest of four decorative daughters. Her mother, Zillah, was Jewish, a beauty, celebrated as a gifted amateur pianist; amateurism afflicted women of her class then like a disease, and it was to afflict her daughter also. Ada Leverson wrote no novels until she was in her forties, and separated from her husband. Her father, Samuel Beddington, was a rich property investor and hypochondriac. Ada Leverson's upbringing was lavish, artistic, sheltered, and cushioned from need; she was educated, privately and thoroughly, by a young Girton graduate.

She revolted against her family early, marrying Ernest Leverson against their wishes, when she was only nineteen. He was twelve years older than she, the son of a diamond merchant, working in the City. Shortly after her marriage she discovered he had an illegitimate daughter, who was being brought up in a convent in France. Ernest, undoubtedly the model for Bruce in *The Little Ottleys*, (just as the novels' heroine, Edith, is clearly based on Ada Leverson herself) was a compulsive gambler, an incautious investor, and a philanderer. They had two children, a son and a daughter, the son dying when he was a young child.

Their marriage, too, was an unhappy one. 'She had made the discovery,' her daughter later wrote, 'that she was never to know the happiness of living with someone with whom she was in love; that the rest of her life would have to be a compromise.'[2] Her daughter (Violet Wyndham) does not place that discovery exactly, but clearly the onset of disillusion came early in the marriage.

Little is known about the first ten years of her married life; in a desultory way, Ada Leverson contributed various articles, parodies and sketches to periodicals, most of them anonymous. Her life altered and entered its most celebrated phase through one of those sketches, a parody of *Dorian Gray*, in 1892, when she first met Oscar Wilde. Their friendship grew swiftly; both she and her husband were swept up into the exotic circle of Wilde's friends, the most fashionable in London. Her life, her daughter wrote, 'became a succession of luncheon and dinner parties, first nights and suppers at Willis's Rooms, constantly in the company of the inspiring Oscar and the poet Lord Alfred Douglas.'[3] She began to purchase dresses from Worth and Paquin; hats were sent for inspection from Paris. She became friends with many of the leading artists and actors of the day, including Sickert, Beardsley, Sargent, Mrs. Patrick Campbell, and Herbert Beerbohm Tree. When she and Ernest moved to a smarter address (from Courtfield Gardens to Deanery Street, off Park Lane) the young and newly fashionable Max Beerbohm advised her on its decoration.

Her friendship with Wilde undoubtedly dominated her life at this point; but she had, however, already embarked on a series of relationships with other men of heterosexual tastes. Whether they were platonic, or physically fulfilled is uncertain. Judging from her novels, and the reactions of her heroine in a similar situation, almost certainly the former. The men became that ambivalent figure, the *ami de la maison*; Ernest acquiesced to their presence; the marriage remained intact. When he was cited as co-respondent in a much publicized divorce case, Ada Leverson took care to appear with him the next day, as publicly as possible. Her daughter explains this staunchness chiefly by her mother's detestation of scandal—an emotion strongly present in Edith Ottley. But Ada Leverson was also a passionately devoted mother and that may also partly explain her actions.

After 1900, when Wilde died, Ada Leverson's life began to take a downward turn that was to produce her finest work. Many of her closest friends including Beardsley, Prince Henri d'Orleans (one of the earliest *amis de la maison*) and Kitty Martineau (the model for Hyacinth Verney in *Love's Shadow*, the first of the Ottley trilogy) were also dead. Ernest, having lost most of his money in an unwise investment, was packed off to Canada by his father to start a new life. Ada Leverson did not accompany him; she continued to live in London, though in considerably reduced circumstances. In 1905 she began to write. Her first novel, *The Twelfth Hour* was published in 1907; the remaining five were all written in a ten year period, the last, *Love at Second Sight*, which completes the Ottley trilogy, being published in 1916 when she was fifty-four. She lived another seventeen years, dying at the age of seventy in 1933. She wrote no further books.

Her novels were written, Violet Wyndham recalled, 'in bed, in a confusion of foolscap, newspapers, cigarettes and oranges. A tall gaunt stenographer would spend hours daily being dictated to, typing, and generally assisting the writer, whose amiability and sense of fun seemed to make up for her impracticability . . .'⁴ She was in love with her publisher, Grant Richards, a married man who in her company never referred to his happy family life, and the final novel was dedicated to him, under the nickname Ada Leverson had given him, 'Tacitus'. Her love for him was, her daughter considered, 'a spur to literary creation';⁵ she does not explain, and there is no way of knowing, why, after completing her best book, that spur seems to have been removed.

Her last years were spent much in the company of a younger circle of friends, including William Walton and Harold Acton, and dominated by the Sitwells, with whom she travelled frequently to Italy. She wrote one last fine thing: *The Importance of Being Oscar*, a memoir to her friend. It was published by T. S. Eliot, then editor of *Criterion*, under the title *The Last First Night*, in January 1926.

In 1933, while in Florence, she became ill. She returned to England and died of pneumonia shortly after. Osbert Sitwell has written a vivid account of her in old age⁶—when she had grown plump, was distressingly deaf, and habitually dressed in flowing black clothes topped by a hat shaped like a mushroom—but surprisingly few accounts of her survive to tell us what she was like earlier, in the years of her prime. 'The Egeria of the Nineties movement,'[7] Grant Richards said of her; Oscar Wilde once wrote of being 'caught in the net of her jade eyes';[8] a kind and generous man himself, he praised her as often for her warmth as for her wit. Something of the flavour of that wit still emanates from the stories and anecdotes about her, although it is best enshrined in what she wrote. It was interestingly sharp—Mrs Beerbohm Tree, she once said, was 'one of those women on whom real ermine always looks like rabbit'—but it was rarely cruel. Rather its prevailing tone was droll, and mocking—and she was capable of mocking herself as well as others. One of the extraordinary things about her life was that she chose to remain married to a man who was, by all accounts, utterly devoid of a sense of humour. That divide, mirrored on the first page of *The Little Ottleys* in the first description of Edith and Bruce, widens to a chasm in the course of the three books. It is seen, ultimately, as a moral divide; humour for Ada Leverson, as for her heroine, is an ethical corrective. Bruce, lacking that corrective, becomes increasingly morally blind.

The comedic vision, with its eye for absurdity and untruth, is at base an isolating one; it accounts, perhaps, for the strong undertow of sorrow that can be glimpsed beneath the sparkling surface of these books. 'Joking *apart*,' Ada Leverson once said, taking up a friend on a cliché. 'How dull that sounds! Fancy joking apart, all by oneself . . .'

The three novels, composed at four-yearly intervals, are cyclic in their construction. They begin with Edith and Bruce, a young married couple, seated opposite one another, separated by the width of their dining table in their new white flat. Bruce moves to his writing table to compose a note to his friend, Raggett, and complains that his wife's scrappy girls' education has left her unable to spell the friend's name. The tone for their relationship is established in a few paragraphs: Bruce is querulous, patronizing, and unreasonably reproachful; his wife is good humoured and accommodating; her mockery of her husband, already present, is mild. In the penultimate scene of the final novel, they stand by the same writing table. Their relationship has changed forever. Edith is brimming over with happiness. Bruce's last words, like his first, are of reproach: the inkstand on the writing table is too full.

These are two tiny episodes, but they illustrate the qualities that

underpin Ada Leverson's writing: the resourcefulness of her symbol-
ism, which is always deft, glancing, never overstated, yet omnipresent in
the books; and her iron control over structure, which is disguised with
such grace that the books can appear at first sight to proceed artlessly
and at random, although nothing is further from the truth. Earlier
critics, including members of her family who found her plots 'slight',
and the critic of the *Saturday Review of Literature* who praised her for the
'gossamer froth of her material', were off-course. They missed the
underlying steel—mistook the feint perhaps, or seeing the palpable hit
judged it slight, not realising its aim made it deadly.

The three novels confuse, perhaps, because they begin with a crafty
obliquity. Their main theme, the relationship between Edith and Bruce,
the exploration of a marriage, is not investigated head-on until the
second book. The first, *Love's Shadow*, begins with Edith and Bruce, but
maintains them as sub-plot and counterpoint to the main drama, the
love affair of Hyacinth Verney and Cecil Reeves. It is, deliberately so, a
conventional and banal story, of an immature beauty falling in love with
an unreliable young man. It ends with their reconciliation after mis-
understandings and jealous tiffs and the final chapter bears the ironic
title, 'The Solution'. It is the predictable ending of romance, and the
novel has remorselessly demonstrated that it is inadequate. At the end of
the novel Hyacinth is already exhibiting precisely the same self-
abasement in the face of Cecil's self-righteousness that we have already
witnessed in the relationship between Edith and Bruce. Cecil is, in fact,
a domestic tyrant, a Bruce in embryo; we have seen their future even as
they embrace. On the final page, Hyacinth puts her beautiful head into
the very same yoke Edith has bowed under on the first:

> 'And, oh Cecil, if I'm *never* so horrid and bad-tempered again, will you
> forgive me?'
> 'Well, I'll try,' said Cecil.

It is as light, as gentle, as that. And yet, if one has read attentively,
unbeguiled by the surface wit, there can be no doubt that it is a prison
sentence. Ada Leverson never tells us whether Hyacinth escapes; she
and Cecil Reeves disappear from the story. With the beginning of the
second novel, *Tenterhooks*, the central theme is taken up again, in the
persons of Bruce and Edith, who move at once centre stage.

But before moving on to that novel, it is worth perhaps glancing back
at another character who also disappears abruptly at the end of *Love's*

Shadow. This is Anne Yeo, companion to Hyacinth, and one of the most interesting figures in all three books. Anne Yeo is plain, spinsterish, and as sharp as a knife. Since she is devoted to Hyacinth, perhaps in love with her, she has no inclination—as have all the other young female characters—to subdue her intellect in order to attract a man. Throughout she is dour and direct; she speaks what Edith Ottley clearly thinks, but as yet dare not express; she is, in a sense, her *alter ego*, the woman she could be were she not married to Bruce. Anne's conversation provides the counterpoint to Hyacinth's notions of romance: Here, they are speaking of Cecil:

> 'Anne, really tonight there were one or two little things that made me think he is beginning to like me. I don't say he is perfect. I daresay he has his faults. But there's something I like about his face. I wonder what it is.'
> 'I know what it is. He's very good-looking,' said Anne.

It is wonderfully funny; Hyacinth's self-delusion so uncomfortably familiar, Anne's put-down so refreshing. The twist comes later. It is Anne who contrives the reconciliation between Hyacinth and Cecil, although it means the end of her friendship. Anne, having served as a *deus ex machina*, sets off to Cook's alone, to purchase a ticket to Australia, or America. We are not even told her destination. But the image of her small defiant figure, setting off for a New World haunts the remaining two books. 'I only say what I think,' she has told Hyacinth; Edith Ottley still has to discover that freedom—and the courage to act upon it.

The second novel begins with two incidents, both treated with Ada Leverson's deceptive inconsequentiality. Edith gives birth to a second child, a daughter; Bruce, conducting Edith to a dinner party, goes to the wrong address. The two incidents, four years apart, apparently unconnected except by narrative proximity, are treated with an infectious, effervescent humour, and they set the course for the rest of the book. Edith wants to call her daughter Matilda (Old German: strength in battle); Bruce, who is away in Carlsbad, nursing one of his constant and entirely imaginary ailments, wires that he dislikes the name. 'I would rather she were called Aspasia,' he says. Edith promptly christens the baby Aspasia Matilda Ottley: 'It was characteristic of Edith,' Ada Leverson comments laconically, 'that she kept to her own point, though not aggressively'.

So, a loving mother and a less patient wife than we have previously seen her, Edith sets off with Ernest for a dinner party at his friends, the Mitchells. In a brief, very funny sequence, he takes them twice to the wrong house, and on finding the right one, discovers the dinner was the previous night. Since, for once, he cannot blame Edith for this fiasco, Bruce recovers his spirits with a swiftness he is quick to commend: but the point has been made. Bruce, in more than one sense, is lost; his wife, whose mockery is already sharper, can still curb her tongue, but is less inclined to subdue the independence of her mind.

This is Chapter One; in Chapter Four Edith and Bruce do, finally, go to dinner with the Mitchells. There Edith meets Aylmer Ross. It is an immediate *coup de foudre*, made convincingly so by Edith's extreme reluctance to admit it. During the course of the rest of the book, a great tension is built up, a force field in which Edith is caught between twin poles: Aylmer and Bruce, the dictates of her heart and head and her increasingly passionate commitment to her children. It can be resolved only through her free choice. The conflict of loyalties is, surprisingly for its period, intensified by passionate sexual feeling, increasingly overt between Edith and Aylmer, intensified, as in a crucible, by the conventions of a society that makes it difficult for them to meet alone, and even more difficult for them to speak what they feel. That strength of emotion is brilliantly and even cruelly contrasted by the furtive sexuality around them; by Bruce's intrigues; by Edith's friend, Vincy, the immaculate nineties exquisite, whose encounters with an acquisitive artists' model fill him with post-coital *tristesse* and shame, though more because of her vulgarity than her lack of rectitude. Even in such a situation, convention has a stranglehold. Just as Edith and Aylmer fence about love, substituting 'care' for that dangerous word, so Vincy and the dreadful Mavis Argles fence about lust:

> 'What a frightfully bright light there is in the room,' Vincy said. He got up and drew the blind down. He came back to her.
> 'Your hair's coming down,' he remarked.

He undoes her hair; that is all; there Ada Leverson cuts. But we need no more. We all know what is enacted on that same divan or bed; with economy, with an unflinching precision, in a scene that lasts four pages, we see the reality of clandestine sex; its implications reverberate throughout the book.

In the third, and final novel of the sequence, the finest of the three, with the writer in total control of her powers, the story moves to its final coda. Aylmer returns, wounded in the war in which Bruce's 'neurotic heart' prevents his fighting. Delicately, carefully, Ada Leverson shows the deepening of his and Edith's love. Ada Leverson ends the trilogy in happy and unclouded resolution. She does so masterfully, without contrivance, in a sequence of black farce, and aided by the introduction of one of her finest comic creations, the immensely stupid, immensely benign Madame Frabelle, who fastens onto the Ottley family like a plump limpet. The dip into tragedy, closest in *Tenterhooks*, is averted, and convincingly so. The three novels end on an upbeat; the dragons of conformity, convention and timidity have been well and truly slain. The resulting, liberating happiness, felt by the characters, and gently, unassertively communicated by their author, is infectious.

Edith Ottley resolves freedom, love, and her own very precise code of honour; Ada Leverson, of course, in her own life, was less fortunate. The more impressive, then, that in portraying in art a resolution she never achieved in life, she showed no bitterness. And the more understandable, perhaps that—after completing these books, her *credo*—she chose, Sphinx-like, to remain silent.

Sally Beauman, London, 1982

Notes

1 *Complete Works of Oscar Wilde*, Collins, 1977, p. 833 f.
2 Violet Wyndham, *The Sphinx and her Circle*, Andre Deutsch, 1963, p. 20
3 *Ibid*, p. 29
4 *Ibid*, p. 69
5 *Ibid.*
6 In *Noble Essences*, Osbert Sitwell, Macmillan, 1950
7 Quoted by Wyndham, *ibid*, p. 31
8 *Ibid*, p. 32. See letter to Robert Ross, March 25 1898, *The Letters of Oscar Wilde*, Hart-Davis, 1962
9 Quoted by Wyndham, *ibid*, p. 26

Love's Shadow

Love like a shadow flies
   When substance love pursues;
Pursuing that that flies,
   And flying what pursues.

SHAKESPEARE

CHAPTER I

Hyacinth

'THERE'S only one thing I must really implore you, Edith,' said Bruce anxiously. '*Don't* make me late at the office!'

'Certainly not, Bruce,' answered Edith sedately. She was seated opposite her husband at breakfast in a very new, very small, very white flat in Knightsbridge—exactly like thousands of other new, small, white flats. She was young and pretty, but not obvious. One might suppose that she was more subtle than was shown by her usual expression, which was merely cheerful and intelligent.

'Now I have to write that letter before I go,' Bruce exclaimed, starting up and looking at her reproachfully. 'Why didn't I write it last night?'

Edith hadn't the slightest idea, as she had heard nothing of the letter before, but, in the course of three years, she had learnt that it saved time to accept trifling injustices. So she looked guilty and a little remorseful. He magnanimously forgave her, and began to write the letter at a neat white writing-table.

'How many g's are there in " Raggett "?' he asked suspiciously.

She didn't answer, apparently overtaken by a sudden fit of absence of mind.

'Only one, of course. How absurd you are!' said her husband, laughing, as he finished the letter and came back to the table.

She poured out more coffee.

'It's a curious thing,' he went on in a tone of impartial regret, 'that, with all the fuss about modern culture and higher education nowadays, girls are not even taught to spell!'

'Yes, isn't it? But even if I had been taught, it might not have been much use. I might just not have been taught to spell " Raggett ". It's a name, isn't it?'

'It's a very well-known name,' said Bruce.

'I daresay it is, but I don't know it. Would you like to see the boy before you go?'

3

'What a question! I always like to see the boy. But you know perfectly well I haven't time this morning.'

'Very well, dear. You can see him this afternoon.'

'Why do you say that? You know I'm going golfing with Goldthorpe! It really is hard, Edith, when a man has to work so much that he has scarcely any time for his wife and child.'

She looked sympathetic.

'What are you doing today?' he asked.

'Hyacinth's coming to fetch me for a drive in the motor.'

His face brightened. He said kindly, 'I *am* so glad, darling, that you have such a delightful friend—when I can't be with you. I admire Hyacinth very much, in every way. She seems devoted to you, too, which is really very nice of her. What I mean to say is, that in her position she might know anybody. You see my point?'

'Quite.'

'How did you meet her originally?'

'We were school-friends.'

'She's such a lovely creature; I wonder she doesn't marry.'

'Yes, but she has to find someone else whom *she* thinks a lovely creature, too.'

'Edith, dear.'

'Yes, Bruce.'

'I wish you wouldn't snap me up like that. Oh, I know you don't mean it, but it's growing on you, rather.'

She tried to look serious, and said gently, 'Is it, really? I am sorry.'

'You don't mind me telling you of it, do you?'

'Not at all. I'm afraid you will be late, Bruce.'

He started up and hurried away, reminding Edith that dinner was to be at eight. They parted with affectionate smiles.

When he had gone down in the lift, Edith took an inextensive walk through the entire flat, going into each room, and looking at herself in every looking-glass. She appeared to like herself best in the dining-room mirror, for she returned, stared into it rather gravely for some little time, and then said to herself: 'Yes, I'm beginning to look bored.'

Then she rang the bell, and the nurse brought in a pretty little boy of nearly two, fluffily dressed in white, who was excited at the prospect of his great morning treat—going down in the lift. Speaking of him with some formality as Master Archie, she asked the nurse a few questions, which she mistakenly supposed gave that personage the impression that she knew all that there was to be known about children. When she was alone with him for a minute she rushed at him impulsively, saying, privately, 'Heavenly pet! Divine angel! Duck!' in return for which he pulled her hair down and scratched her face with a small empty Noah's Ark that he was taking out with him for purposes of his own.

When he had gone she did her hair up again in a different way—parted in the middle. It was very pretty, wavy, fair hair, and she had small, regular features, so the new way suited her very well. Then she said again—

'Yes, if it were not for Hyacinth I should soon look bored to death!'

Hyacinth Verney was the romance of Edith's life. She also provided a good deal of romance in the lives of several other people. Her position was unusual, and her personality fascinating. She had no parents, was an heiress, and lived alone with a companion in a quaint little house just out of Berkeley Square, with a large studio, that was never used for painting. She had such an extraordinary natural gift for making people of both sexes fond of her, that it would have been difficult to say which, of all the persons who loved her, showed the most intense devotion in the most immoderate way. Probably her cousin and guardian, Sir Charles Cannon, and her companion, Anne Yeo, spent more thought and time in her service than did anybody else. Edith's imagination had been fired in their school-days by her friend's beauty and cleverness, and by the fact that she had a guardian, like a book. Then Hyacinth had come out and gone in for music, for painting, and for various other arts and pursuits of an absorbing character. She had hardly any acquaintances except her relations, but possessed an enormously large number of extremely intimate friends—a characteristic that had remained to her from her childhood.

Hyacinth's ideal of society was to have no padding, so that most of the members of her circle were types. Still, as she had a perfect passion for entertaining, there remained, of course, a residue; distant elderly connections with well-sounding names (as ballast), and a

few vague hangers-on; several rather dull celebrities, some merely
pretty and well-dressed women, and a steadily increasing number
of good-looking young men. Hyacinth was fond of decoration.

As she frankly admitted, she had rather fallen back on Edith,
finding her, after many experiments, the most agreeable of friends,
chiefly because in their intercourses everything was always taken
for granted. Like sisters, they understood one another without explanation—*à demi-mot*.

While Edith waited impatiently in the hall of the flat, Anne Yeo,
her unacknowledged rival in Hyacinth's affections, was doing
needlework in the window-seat of the studio, and watching
Hyacinth, who, dressed to go out, was walking up and down the
room. With a rather wooden face, high cheek-bones, a tall, thin
figure, and no expression, Anne might have been any age; but she
was not. She made every effort to look quite forty so as to appear
more suitable as a chaperone, but was in reality barely thirty. She
was thinking, as she often thought, that Hyacinth looked too
romantic for everyday life. When they had travelled together this
fact had been rather a nuisance.

'Why, when you call at the Stores to order groceries, must you
look as if you were going to elope?' she asked dryly. 'In an
ordinary motorveil you have the air of hastening to some mysterious
appointment.'

'But I'm only going to fetch Edith Ottley for a drive,' said
Hyacinth. 'How bored she must get with her little Foreign Office
clerk! The way he takes his authority as a husband seriously is
pathetic. He hasn't the faintest idea the girl is cleverer than he is.'

'You'd far better leave her alone, and not point it out,' said Anne.
'You're always bothering about these little Ottleys now. But you've
been very restless lately. Whenever you try to do people good, and
especially when you motor so much and so fast, I recognise the
symptoms. It's coming on again, and you're trying to get away from
it.'

'Don't say that. I'm never going to care about anyone again,'
said Hyacinth.

'You don't know it, but when you're not in love you're not
yourself,' Anne continued. 'It's all you live for.'

'Oh, Anne!'

'It's quite true. It's nearly three months since you—had an attack. Blair was the last. Now you're beginning to take the same sort of interest in Cecil Reeve.'

'How mistaken you are, Anne! I don't take at all the same interest in him. It's a totally different thing. I don't really even like him.'

'You wouldn't go out today if you were expecting him.'

'Yes, but I'm not . . . and he doesn't care two straws about me. Once he said he never worshipped in a crowded temple!'

'It's a curious coincidence that ever since then you've been out to everyone else,' said Anne.

'I don't really like him—so very much. When he *does* smile, of course it's rather nice. Why does he hate me?'

'I can't think,' said Anne.

'He doesn't hate me! How can you say so?' cried Hyacinth.

'Doesn't he?'

'Perhaps it's because he thinks I look Spanish. He may disapprove of looking Spanish,' suggested Hyacinth.

'Very likely.'

Hyacinth laughed, kissed her, and went out. Anne followed her graceful figure with disapproving, admiring eyes.

CHAPTER II

The Anxieties of Sir Charles

L I K E all really uncommon beauties, Hyacinth could only be adequately described by the most hackneyed phrases. Her eyes were authentically sapphire-coloured; brilliant, frank eyes, with a subtle mischief in them, softened by the most conciliating long eyelashes. Then, her mouth was really shaped like a Cupid's bow, and her teeth *were* dazzling; also she had a wealth of dense, soft, brown hair and a tall, sylphlike, slimly-rounded figure. Her features were delicately regular, and her hands and feet perfection. Her complexion was extremely fair, so she was not a brunette; some remote Spanish ancestor on her mother's side was, however, occasionally mentioned as an apology for a type and a supple grace sometimes complained of by people with white eyelashes as rather un-English. So many artistic young men had told her she was like La Gioconda, that when she first saw the original in the Louvre she was so disappointed that she thought she would never smile again.

About ten minutes after the pretty creature had gone out, Anne, who had kept her eyes steadily on the clock, looked out of the window, from which she could see a small brougham driving up. She called out into the hall—

'If that's Sir Charles Cannon, tell him Miss Verney is out, but I have a message for him.'

A minute later there entered a thin and distinguished-looking, grey-haired man of about forty-five, wearing a smile of such excessive cordiality that one felt it could only have been brought to his well-bred lips by acute disappointment. Anne did not take the smile literally, but began to explain away the blow.

'I'm so sorry,' she said apologetically. 'I'm afraid it's partly my fault. When she suddenly decided to go out with that little Mrs Ottley, she told me vaguely to telephone to you. But how on earth could I know where you were?'

'How indeed? It doesn't matter in the least, my dear Miss Yeo.
I mean, it's most unfortunate, as I've just a little free time. Lady
Cannon's gone to a matinée at the St James's. We had tickets for
the first night, but of course she wouldn't use them then. She preferred to go alone in the afternoon, because she detests the theatre,
anyhow, and afternoon performances give her a headache. And if
she does a thing that's disagreeable to her, she likes to do it in the
most painful possible way. She has a beautiful nature.'

Anne smiled, and passed him a little gold box.

'Have a cigarette?' she suggested.

'Thanks—I'm not really in a bad temper. But why this relapse
of devotion to little Mrs Ottley? And why are you and I suddenly
treated with marked neglect?'

'Mrs Ottley,' said Anne, 'is one of those young women, rather
bored with their husbands, who are the worst possible companions
for Hyacinth. They put her off marrying.'

'Bored, is she? She didn't strike me so. A pleasant, bright girl.
I suppose she amuses Hyacinth?'

'Yes; of course, she's not a dull old maid over forty, like me,'
said Anne.

'No-one would believe that description of you,' said Sir Charles,
with a bow that was courtly but absent. As a matter of fact, he did
believe it, but it wasn't true.

'If dear little Mrs Ottley,' he continued, 'married in too great a
hurry, far be it from me to reproach her. I married in a hurry
myself—when Hyacinth was ten.'

'And when she was eighteen you were very sorry,' said Anne
in her colourless voice.

'Don't let us go into that, Miss Yeo. Of course, Hyacinth is a
beautiful—responsibility. People seem to think she ought to have
gone on living with us when she left school. But how was it possible? Hyacinth said she intended to live for her art, and Lady
Cannon couldn't stand the scent of oils.' He glanced round the
large panelled-oak room in which not a picture was to be seen. The
only indication of its having ever been meant for a studio was the
north light, carefully obstructed (on the grounds of unbecoming-
ness) by gently-tinted draperies of some fabric suggesting Liberty's.
'Life wasn't worth living, trying to keep the peace!'

'But you must have missed her?'

' Still, I prefer coming to see her here. And knowing she has you with her is, after all, everything.'

He looked a question.

' Yes, she has. I mean, she seems rather—absorbed again lately,' said Anne.

' Who is it?' he asked. ' I always feel so indiscreet and treacherous talking over her private affairs like this with you, though she tells me everything herself. I'm not sure it's the act of a simple, loyal, Christian English gentleman; in fact, I'm pretty certain it's not. I suppose that's why I enjoy it so much.'

' I daresay,' said Anne; ' but she wouldn't mind it.'

' What has been happening?'

' Nothing interesting. Hazel Kerr came here the other day and brought with him a poem in bronze lacquer, as he called it. He read it aloud—the whole of it.'

' Good heavens! Poetry! Do people still do that sort of thing? I thought it had gone out years ago—when I was a young man.'

' Of course, so it has. But Hazel Kerr is out of date. Hyacinth says he's almost a classic.'

' His verses?'

' Oh no! His method. She says he's an interesting survival—he's walked straight out of another age—the nineties, you know. There were poets in those days.'

' Method! He was much too young then to have a style at all, surely!'

' That *was* the style. It was the right thing to be very young in the nineties. It isn't now.'

' It's not so easy now, for some of us,' murmured Sir Charles.

' But Hazel keeps it up,' Anne answered.

Sir Charles laughed irritably. ' He keeps it up, does he? But he sits people out openly, that shows he's not really dangerous. One doesn't worry about Hazel. It's that young man who arrives when everybody's going, or goes before anyone else arrives, that's what I'm a little anxious about.'

' If you mean Cecil Reeve, Hyacinth says he doesn't like her.'

' I'm sorry to hear that. If anything will interest her, that will. Yet I don't know why I should mind. At any rate, he certainly isn't trying to marry her for interested reasons, as he's very well off—or perhaps for any reasons. I'm told he's clever, too.'

'His appearance is not against him either,' said Anne dryly; ' so what's the matter with him?'

' I don't know exactly. I think he's capable of playing with her.'

' Perhaps he doesn't really appreciate her,' suggested Anne.

' Oh, yes, he does. He's a connoisseur—confound him! He appreciates her all right. But it's all for himself—not for her. By the way, I've heard his name mentioned with another woman's name. But I happen to know there's nothing in it.'

' Would you really like her to marry soon?' Anne asked.

' In her position it would be better, I suppose,' said her guardian, with obvious distaste to the idea.

' Has there ever been anyone that you thoroughly approved of?' asked Anne.

He shook his head.

' I rather doubt if there ever will be,' Anne said.

' She's so clever, so impulsive! She lives so much on her emotions. If she were disappointed—in that way—it would mean so much to her,' Sir Charles said.

' She does change rather often,' said Anne.

' Of course, she's never really known her own mind.' He took a letter out of his pocket. ' I came partly to show her a letter from Ella—my girl at school in Paris, you know. Hyacinth is so kind to her. She writes to me very confidentially. I hope she's being properly brought up!'

' Let me read it.'

She read—

'DARLING PAPA,

' I'm having heavenly fun at school. Last night there was a ball for Madame's birthday. A proper grown-up ball, and we all danced. The men weren't bad. I had a lovely Easter egg, a chocolate egg, and inside that another egg with chocolate in it, and inside that another egg with a dear little turquoise charm in it. One man said I was a blonde anglaise, and had a keepsake face; and another has taken the Prix de Rome, and is going to be a schoolmaster. There were no real ices. Come over and see me soon. It's such a long time to the holidays. Love to mother.

' Your loving,

'ELLA.'

'A curious letter—for her age,' said Ella's father, replacing it. 'I wish she were here. It seems a pity Lady Cannon can't stand the noise of practising—and so on. Well, perhaps it's for the best.' He got up. 'Miss Yeo, I must go and fetch Lady Cannon now, but I'll come back at half-past six for a few minutes—on my way to the club.'

'She's sure to be here then,' replied Anne consolingly; 'and do persuade her not to waste all her time being kind to Edith Ottley. It can't do any good. She'd better leave them alone.'

'Really, it's a very innocent amusement. I think you're over-anxious.'

'It's only that I'm afraid she might get mixed up in—well, some domestic row.'

'Surely it can't be as bad as that! Why—is Mr Ottley in love with her?' he asked, smiling.

'Very much indeed,' said Anne.

'Oh, really, Miss Yeo!—and does Mrs Ottley know it?'

'No, nor Hyacinth either. He doesn't know it himself.'

'Then if nobody knows it, it can't matter very much,' said Sir Charles, feeling vaguely uncomfortable all the same. Before he went he took up a portrait of Hyacinth in an Empire dress with laurel leaves in her hair. It was a beautiful portrait. Anne thought that from the way he looked at it, anyone could have guessed Lady Cannon had tight lips and wore a royal fringe. . . . They parted with great friendliness.

Anne's wooden, inexpressive countenance was a great comfort to Sir Charles, in some moods. Though she was clever enough, she did not have that superfluity of sympathy and responsiveness that makes one go away regretting one has said so much, and disliking the other person for one's expansion. One never felt that she had undersood too accurately, nor that one had given oneself away, nor been indiscreetly curious. . . . It was like talking to a chair. What a good sort Anne was!

CHAPTER III

Anne Yeo

'W o u l d you like me to play to you a little?' Anne asked, when Hyacinth had returned and was sitting in the carved-oak chimney-corner, looking thoughtful and picturesque.

'Oh no, please don't! Besides, I know you can't.'

'No, thank goodness!' exclaimed Anne. 'I know I'm useful and practical, and I don't mind that; but anyhow, I'm not cheerful, musical, and a perfect lady, in exchange for a comfortable home, am I?'

'No, indeed,' said Hyacinth fervently.

'No-one can speak of me as "that pleasant, cultivated creature who lives with Miss Verney," can they?'

'Not, at any rate, if they have any regard for truth,' said Hyacinth.

'I wish you wouldn't make me laugh. Why should I have a sense of humour? I sometimes think that all your friends imagine it's part of my duty to shriek with laughter at their wretched jokes. It wasn't in the contract. If I were pretty, my ambition would have been to be an adventuress; but an adventuress with no adventures would be a little flat. I might have the worst intentions, but I should never have the chance of carrying them out. So I try to be as much as possible like Thackeray's shabby companion in a dyed silk.'

'Is that why you wear a sackcloth blouse trimmed with ashes?' said Hyacinth, with curiosity.

'No, that's merely stinginess. It's my nature to be morbidly economical, though I know I needn't be. If I hadn't had £500 a year left me, I should never have been able to come and live here, and drop all my horrid relations. I enjoy appearing dependent and being a spectator, and I've absolutely given up all interest in my own affairs. In fact, I haven't got any. And I take the keenest interest in other people's—romances. Principally, of course, in yours.'

'I'm sure I don't want you to be so vicarious as all that—thanks

13

awfully,' said Hyacinth. 'At any rate, don't dress like a skeleton at
the feast tomorrow, if you don't mind. I've asked the little Ottleys
to dinner—and I want Charles to come.'

'Oh, of course, if you expect Cecil Reeve!—I suppose you do,
as you haven't mentioned it—I'll put on my real clothes to do you
credit.' She looked out of the window. 'Here's poor old Charles
again. How he *does* dislike Lady Cannon!'

'What a shame, Anne! He's angelic to her.'

'That's what I meant,' said Anne, going out quickly.

'Charles, how nice of you to call and return your own visit the
same day! It's like Royalty, isn't it? It reminds me of the young
man who was asked to call again, and came back in half an hour,'
said Hyacinth.

'I didn't quite see my way to waiting till Monday,' he answered.
'We're going away the end of the week. Janet says she needs a
change.'

'It would be more of a change if you remained in town alone;
at least, without Aunty.'

From the age of ten Hyacinth had resented having to call Lady
Cannon by this endearing name. How a perfect stranger, by marrying her cousin, could become her aunt, was a mystery that she
refused even to try to solve. It was well meant, no doubt; it was
supposed to make her feel more at home—less of an orphan. But
though she was obedient on this point, nothing would ever induce
her to call her cousin by anything but his Christian name, with no
qualification. Instinctively she felt that to call them 'Charles and
Aunty', while annoying the intruder, kept her guardian in his
proper place. What that was she did not specify.

'Well, can't you stay in London and come here, and be confided
in and consulted? You know you like that better than boring
yourself to death at Redlands.'

'Never mind that. How did you enjoy your drive?'

'Immensely, and I've asked both the little Ottleys to come to
dinner tomorrow—one of those impulsive, unconsidered invitations
that one regrets the second after. I must make up a little party.
Will you come?'

'Perhaps, if I arranged to follow Janet to Redlands the next day,
I might. Who did you say was the other man?'

'I expect Cecil Reeve,' she said. 'Don't put on that air of marble archness, Charles. It doesn't suit you at all. Tell me something about him.'

'I can't stand him. That's all I know about him,' said Sir Charles.

'Oh, is that all? That's just jealousy, Charles.'

'Absurd! How can a married man, in your father's place, a hundred years older than you, be jealous?'

'It is wonderful, isn't it?' she said. 'But you must know something about him. You know everyone.'

'He's Lord Selsey's nephew—and his heir—if Selsey doesn't marry again. He's only a young man about town—the sort of good-looking ass that your sex admires.'

'Charles, what a brute you are! He's very clever.'

'My dear child, yes—as a matter of fact, I believe he is. Isn't he ever going to *do* something?'

'I don't know,' she said. 'I wish he would. Oh, *why* don't you like him?'

'What can it matter about me?' he answered. 'Why are you never satisfied unless I'm in love with the same people that you are?'

'Charles!' she exclaimed, standing up. 'Don't you understand that not a word, not a look has passed to suggest such a thing? I never met anyone so—'

'So cautious?'

'No, so listless, and so respectful; and yet so amusing. . . . But I'm pretty certain that he hates me. I wish I knew why.'

'And you hate him just as much, of course?'

'No, sometimes I don't. And then I want you to agree with me. No-one sympathises really so well as you, Charles.'

'Not even Miss Yeo?'

'No, I get on so well with Anne because she doesn't. She's always interested, but I prefer her never to agree with me, as she lives here. It would be enervating to have someone always there and perpetually sympathetic. Anne is a tonic.'

'You need a little opposition to keep you up,' said Sir Charles.

'Didn't I once hear something about his being devoted to some-one? Wasn't there a report that he was going to be married to a Mrs. Raymond?'

'I believe it was once contradicted in the *Morning Post* that he was engaged to her,' said Sir Charles. 'But I'm sure there's no truth in it. I know her.'

'No truth in the report? Or the contradiction?'

'In either. In anything.'

'So you know her. What's she like?' Hyacinth asked anxiously.

'Oh, a dear, charming creature—you'd like her; but not pretty, nor young. About my age,' he said.

'Oh, I see! *That's* all right, then!' She clapped her hands.

'Well, I must go. I'll arrange to turn up to dinner tomorrow.' He took his hat, looking rather depressed.

'And try to make him like me!' she commanded, as Sir Charles took leave.

CHAPTER IV

The Sound Sense of Lady Cannon

LADY CANNON had never been seen after half-past seven except in evening dress, generally a velvet dress of some dark crimson or bottle-green, so tightly-fitting as to give her an appearance of being rather upholstered than clothed. Her cloaks were always like well-hung curtains, her trains like heavy carpets; one might fancy that she got her gowns from Gillows. Her pearl dog-collar, her diamond ear-rings, her dark red fringe and the other details of her toilette were put on with the same precision when she dined alone with Sir Charles as if she were going to a ceremonious reception. She was a very tall, fine-looking woman. In Paris, where she sometimes went to see Ella at school, she attracted much public attention as *une femme superbe*. Frenchmen were heard to remark to one another that her husband *ne devrait pas s'embêter* (which, as a matter of fact, was precisely what he did—to extinction); and even in the streets when she walked out the gamins used to exclaim, '*Voilà l'Arc de Triomphe qui se promène!*'—to her intense fury and gratification. She was still handsome, with hard, wide-open blue eyes, and straight features. She always held her head as if she were being photographed in a tiara *en profil perdu*. It was in this attitude that she had often been photographed and was now most usually seen; and it seemed so characteristic that even her husband, if he accidentally caught a glimpse of her full-face, hastily altered his position to one whence he could behold her at right angles.

As she grew older, the profile in the photographs had become more and more *perdu*; the last one showed chiefly the back of her head, besides a basket of flowers, and a double staircase, leading (one hoped) at least to one of the upper rooms in Buckingham Palace.

Lady Cannon had a very exalted opinion of her own charms, virtues, brilliant gifts, and, above all, of her sound sense. Fortunately for her, she had married a man of extraordinary amiability, who had always taken every possible precaution to prevent her discovering that in this opinion she was practically alone in the world.

Having become engaged to her through a slight misunderstanding in a country house, Sir Charles had not had the courage to explain away the mistake. He decided to make the best of it, and did so the more easily as it was one of those so-called suitable matches that the friends and acquaintances of both parties approve of and desire far more than the parties concerned. A sensible woman was surely required at Redlands and in the London house, especially as Sir Charles had been left guardian and trustee to a pretty little heiress.

It had taken him a very short time to find out that the reputation for sound sense was, like most traditions, founded on a myth, and that if his wife's vanity was only equalled by her egotism, her most remarkable characteristic was her excessive silliness. But she loved him, and he kept his discovery to himself.

'Twenty-five minutes to eight!' she exclaimed, holding out a little jewelled watch, as Sir Charles came in after his visit to Hyacinth. 'And we have a new cook, and I specially, *most* specially told her to have dinner ready punctually at half-past seven! This world is indeed a place of trial!'

Sir Charles's natural air of command seemed to disappear in the presence of Lady Cannon. He murmured a graceful apology, saying he would not dress. Nothing annoyed, even shocked her more than to see her husband dining opposite her in a frock-coat. However, of two evils she chose the less. They went in to dinner.

'I haven't had the opportunity yet of telling you my opinion of the play this afternoon,' she said. 'I found it interesting, and I wonder I hadn't seen it before.'

'You sent back our stalls for the first night,' remarked Sir Charles.

'Certainly I did. I dislike seeing a play until I have seen in the papers whether it is a success or not.'

'Those newspaper fellows aren't always right,' said Sir Charles.

'Perhaps not, but at least they can tell you whether the thing is a success. *I* should be very sorry to be seen at a failure. Very sorry indeed.'

She paused, and then went on—

'*James Wade's Trouble* has been performed three hundred times, so it must be clever. In my opinion, it must have done an immense amount of harm—good, I mean. A play like that, so full of noble sentiments and high principles, is—to me—as good as a sermon!'

'Oh, is it? I'm sorry I couldn't go,' said Sir Charles, feeling very glad.

'I suppose it was the club, as usual, that made you late. Do you know, I have a great objection to clubs.'

He nodded sympathetically.

'That is to say, I thoroughly approve of your belonging to several. I'm quite aware that in your position it's the right thing to do, but I can't understand why you should ever go to them, having two houses of your own. And that reminds me, we are going down to Redlands tomorrow, are we not? I've had a little' (she lowered her voice) 'lumbago; a mere passing touch, that's all—and the change will cure me. I think you neglect Redlands, Charles. You seem to me to regard your responsibilities as a landowner with indifference bordering on aversion. You never seem amused down there—unless we have friends.'

'We'll go tomorrow if you like,' said he.

'That's satisfactory.'

'I can easily put off the Duke,' he said thoughtfully, as he poured out more wine.

She sprang up like a startled hare.

'Put off the . . . what are you talking about?'

'Oh, nothing. The Duke of St Leonard's is giving a dinner at the club tomorrow, and I was going. But I can arrange to get out of it.'

'Charles! I never heard of anything so absurd! You must certainly go to the dinner. How like you! How casual of you! For a mere trifle to offend the man who might be of the greatest use to you—politically.'

'Politically! What do you mean? And it isn't a trifle when you've set your mind on going away tomorrow. I know you hate to change your plans, my dear.'

'Certainly I do, but I shall not change my plans. I shall go down tomorrow, and you can join me on Friday.'

'Oh, I don't think I'll do that,' said Sir Charles, rather half-heartedly. 'Why should you take the journey alone?'

'But I shall not be alone. I shall have Danvers with me. You need have no anxiety. I beg of you, I *insist*, that you stay, and go to this dinner.'

'Well, of course, if you make a point of it—'

She smiled, well pleased at having got her own way, as she supposed.

'That's right, Charles. Then you'll come down on Friday.'

'By the early train,' said Sir Charles.

'No, I should suggest your coming by the later train. It's more convenient to meet you at the station.'

'Very well—as you like,' said he, inwardly a little astonished. as always, at the easy working of the simple old plan, suggesting what one does not wish to do in order to be persuaded into what one does.

'And, by the way, I haven't heard you speak of Hyacinth lately. You had better go and see her. A little while ago you were always wasting your time about her, and I spoke to you about it, Charles —I think?'

'I think you did,' said he.

'But, though at one time I was growing simply tired of her name, I didn't mean that you need not look after her at *all*. Go and see her, and explain to her I can't possibly accompany you. Tell her I've got chronic lumbago very badly indeed, and I'm obliged to go to the country, but I shall certainly make a point of calling on her when I return. You won't forget, Charles?'

'Certainly not.'

'I should go oftener,' she continued apologetically, 'but I have such a great dislike to that companion of hers. I think Miss Yeo a most unpleasant person.'

'She isn't really,' said Sir Charles.

'I do wish we could get Hyacinth married,' said Lady Cannon. 'I know what a relief it would be to you, and it seems to me such an unheard-of thing for a young girl like that to be living practically alone!'

'We've been through that before, Janet. Remember, there was nothing else to do unless she continued to live with us. And as your nerves can't even stand Ella—'

Lady Cannon dropped the point.

'Well, we must get her married,' she said again.

'What a good thing Ella is still so young! Girls are a dreadful responsibility,' and she swept graciously from the dining-room.

Sir Charles took out an irritating little notebook of red leather, the sort of thing that is advertised when lost as 'of no value to anyone but the owner.' It was full of mysterious little marks and unintelligible little notes. He put down, in cabalistic signs, '*Hyacinth's dinner, eight o'clock.*' He enjoyed writing her name, even in hieroglyphics.

CHAPTER V

A Proposal

'I say, Eugenia.'

'Well, Cecil?'

'Look here, Eugenia.'

'What is it, Cecil?'

'Will you marry me?'

'I beg your pardon?'

'Will you marry me, Eugenia?'

'*What?*'

'You heard what I said. I asked you to marry me. Will you?'

'*Certainly* not! Most decidedly not! How can you ask such a ridiculous question!'

The lady who thus scornfully rejected a proposal was no longer young, and had never been beautiful. In what exactly her attraction consisted was perhaps a mystery to many of those who found themselves under the charm. Her voice and smile were very agreeable, and she had a graceful figure. If she looked nearly ten years younger than her age (which was forty-four), this was in no way owing to any artificial aid, but to a kind of brilliant vitality, not a bouncing mature liveliness, but a vivid, intense, humorous interest in life that was and would always remain absolutely fresh. She was naturalness itself, and seemed unconscious or careless of her appearance. Nor did she have that well-preserved air of so many modern women who seem younger than their years, but seemed merely clever, amiable, very unaffected, and rather ill. She had long, veiled-looking brown eyes, turned up at the corners, which gave to her glance an amusing slyness. It was a very misleading physiognomical effect, for she was really unusually frank. She wore a dull grey dress that was neither artistic, becoming, nor smart. In fact, she was too charming to be dowdy, and too careless to be chic; she might have been a great celebrity.

The young man who made the suggestion above recorded was fair and clean-shaven, tall and well-made, with clear-cut feature; in fact, he was very good-looking—good-looking as almost only an Englishman can be. Under a reserved, dandified manner, he tried unsuccessfully to conceal the fact that he was too intelligent for his type. He did not, however, quite attain his standard of entire expressionlessness; and his bright, light-blue eyes and fully-curved lips showed the generous and emotional nature of their owner. At this moment he seemed very much out of temper.

They were sitting in a dismal little drawing-room in one of the smallest houses in a dreary street in Belgravia. The room was crowded with dateless, unmeaning furniture, and disfigured by muddled, mistaken decoration. Its designer, probably, had meant well, but had been very far from carrying out his meaning. There were too many things in the room, and most of them were wrong. It would be unjust, however, to suppose Mrs Raymond did not know this. Want of means, and indifference, or perhaps perverseness, had caused her to leave the house unchanged since his death as a sort of monument to poor Colonel Raymond's erring taste.

'You might just as well marry me as not,' said Cecil, in his level voice, but with pleading eyes. He made the gesture of trying to take her hand, but she took hers away.

'You are very pressing, Cecil, but I think not. You know perfectly well—I'm sure I make no secret of it—that I'm ten years older than you. Old enough to be your mother! Am I the sort of person who would take advantage of the fancy of a gilded youth? And, now I come to think of it, your proposal's quite insulting. It's treating me like an adventuress! It's implying that you think I *would* marry you! Apologise, and withdraw it at once, or I'll never speak to you again.'

'This is nonsense. To begin with,' said Cecil, 'I may be a little gilded—not so very—but I'm far from being a youth. I'm thirty-four.'

'Yes, I know! That's just the absurd part,' she answered inconsequently. 'It's not as if you were a mere boy and didn't know better! And you know how I *hate* this sort of thing.'

'I know you do, and very likely I wouldn't have worried about marrying at all if you had been nicer to me—in other ways. You see, you brought it on yourself!'

'What *do* you mean? I *am* nice. Don't you come here whenever you like—or nearly? Didn't I dine with you once—a year or two ago? I forget, but I think I did.'

'You never did,' he answered sharply.

'Then it must have been with somebody else. Of course I didn't. I shouldn't dream of such a thing.'

'Someone else! Yes, of course; that's it. Well, I want you to marry me, Eugenia, because I want to get you away from everyone else. You see my point?'

She laughed. 'Oh, jealousy! That's the last straw. Do you know that you're a nuisance, Cecil?'

'Because I love you?' he said, trying to look into her sly Japanese eyes.

She avoided his glance.

'Because you keep on bothering. Always writing, always telephoning, always calling! As soon as I've disposed of *one* invitation or excuse to meet, you invent another. But this last idea is quite too exasperating.' She spoke more gently. 'Don't you know, Cecil, that I've been a widow for years? Would I be so ridiculous as to marry again? Why, the one thing I can't stand is being interfered with! I prefer, far prefer, being poor and alone to that. Now what I want you to do is to marry someone else. I have an idea who I should like it to be, but I won't talk about it now. It's the most charming girl in the world. I shan't tell you her name, that would be tactless. It's that lovely Miss Verney, of course. She's much too good for you—an heiress, a beauty, and an orphan! But she's wonderful; and she really deserves you.'

He stopped her.

'How heartless you are!' he said admiringly.

'Really not, Cecil. I'm very fond of you. I'd be your best friend if you'd let me, but I shan't speak to you again or receive you at all unless you promise not to repeat that nonsense about marrying. I know how horridly obstinate you are! Please remember it's out of the question.'

At this moment the servant brought in a letter to Mrs Raymond. As she read it, Cecil thought she changed colour.

'It's only a line from Sir Charles Cannon,' she said.

'What's he writing about?'

'Really, Cecil! What right have you to ask? I certainly shan't say. It's about his ward, if you must know. And now I think you'd better go, if you will make these violent scenes.'

He stood up.

'You must let me come soon again,' he said rather dejectedly. 'I'll try not to come tomorrow. Shall I?'

'Yes, do try—not to come, I mean. And will you do everything I tell you?'

'I suppose it will please you if I dine with Hyacinth Verney this evening? She asked me yesterday. I said I was half-engaged, but would let her know.'

'Yes, it *would* please me very much indeed,' said Mrs Raymond. 'Please do it, and try to know her better. She's sweet. I don't know her, but—'

'All right. If you'll be nice to me. Will you?'

She was reading the letter again, and did not answer when he said good-bye and left the room.

CHAPTER VI

The Little Ottleys

'Edith, I want you to look nice tonight, dear; what are you going to wear?'

'My Other Dress,' said Edith.

'Is it all right?'

'It ought to be. Would you like to know what I've done to it? I've cut the point into a square, and taken four yards out of the skirt; the chiffon off my wedding-dress has been made into kimono sleeves; then I'm going to wear my wedding-veil as a sort of scarf thrown carelessly over the shoulders; and I've turned the pointed waist-band round, so that it's quite *right* and short-waisted at the back now, and—'

'Oh, don't tell me the horrible details! I think you might take a little interest in *me*. I thought of wearing a buttonhole. Though you may have forgotten it now, before I was a dull old married man, I was supposed to dress rather well, Edith.'

'I know you were.'

'I thought I'd wear a white carnation.'

'I should wear two—one each side. It would be more striking.'

'That's right! Make fun of me! I hope you'll be ready in time. They dine at eight, you know.'

'Bruce, you're not going to begin to dress yet, are you? It's only just four.'

He pretended not to hear, and said peevishly—

'I suppose they don't expect *us* to ask *them*? I daresay it's well known we can't return all the hospitality we receive.'

'I daresay it is.'

'It's awful not having a valet,' said Bruce.

'But it would be more awful if we had,' said Edith. 'Where on earth could we put him—except in the bathroom?'

'I don't think you'll look you're best tonight,' he answered rather revengefully.

26

'Give me a chance! Wait till I've waved my hair!'

He read the paper for a little while, occasionally reading aloud portions of it that she had already read, then complained that she took no interest in public events.

'What do you think Archie brought home today,' she said to change the subject, 'in his Noah's Ark? Two snails!' She laughed.

'Revolting! *I* don't know where he gets his tastes from. Not from *my* family, that I'm quite sure.' He yawned ostentatiously.

'I think I shall have a rest,' Bruce said presently. 'I had a very bad night last night. I scarcely slept at all.'

'Poor boy!' Edith said kindly. She was accustomed to the convention of Bruce's insomnia, and it would never have occurred to her to appear surprised when he said he hadn't closed his eyes, though she happened to know there was no cause for anxiety. If he woke up ten minutes before he was called, he thought he had been awake all night; if he didn't he saw symptoms of the sleeping sickness.

She arranged cushions on the sofa and pulled the blinds down. A minute later he turned on the electric light and began to read again. Then he turned it out, pulled up the blinds, and called her back.

'I want to speak to you about my friend Raggett,' he said seriously. 'I've asked him to dinner here tomorrow. What shall we have?'

'Oh, Bruce! Let's wait and settle tomorrow.'

'You don't know Raggett, but I think you'll like him. I *think* you will. In any case, there's no doubt Raggett's been remarkably decent to me. In fact, he's a very good sort.'

'Fancy!' said Edith.

'Why do you say fancy?' he asked irritably.

'I don't exactly know. I must say something. I'm sure he's nice if he's a friend of yours, dear.'

'He's a clever chap in his way. At least, when I say clever, I don't mean clever in the ordinary sense.'

'Oh, I see,' said Edith.

'He's very amusing,' continued Bruce. 'He said a very funny thing to me the other day. Very funny indeed. It's no use repeating it, because unless you knew all the circumstances and the *characters* of the people that he told the story of, you wouldn't see the point. Perhaps, after all, I'd better ask him to dine at the club.'

'Oh no! Let him come here. Don't you think I'm worthy to see Raggett?'

'Oh nonsense, dear, I'm very proud of you,' said Bruce kindly. 'It isn't exactly that. . . . Mind you, Raggett's quite a man of the world—and yet he *isn't* a man of the world, if you know what I mean.'

'I see,' said Edith again.

'I can't decide whether to ask him here or not,' said Bruce, walking up and down the room in agitation.

'Well, suppose we leave it till tomorrow. You can make up your mind then,' she said good-naturedly.

Edith was dressed, when she found Bruce still in the throes of an agitated toilet. Having lost his collar-stud, he sat down and gave himself up to cold despair.

'You go without me,' he said in a resigned voice. 'Explain the reason—no, don't explain it. Say I've got influenza—but then perhaps they'll think you ought to look after me, and—'

'Here it is!' said Edith.

In the cab he recovered suddenly, and told her she looked awfully pretty, which cheered her very much. She was feeling rather tired. She had spent several hours in the nursery that day, pretending to be a baby giraffe with so much success that Archie had insisted upon countless encores, until, like all artists who have to repeat the same part too often, she felt the performance was becoming mechanical.

CHAPTER VII

Hyacinth's Little Dinner

'THE little Ottleys,' as they were called (they were a tall, fine-looking couple), found themselves in a small circle of people who were all most pleasing to the eye, with the single exception of Miss Yeo. And even she, in a markedly elegant dress of a peculiarly vicious shade of green, had her value in the picture. A little shocked by the harshness of the colour, one's glance turned with relief to Hyacinth, in satin of a blue so pale that it looked like the reflection of the sky in water. A broad, pale blue ribbon was wound in and out of her brown hair in the Romney fashion. Of course she looked her best. Women always do if they wish to please one man when others are there, and she was in the slightly exalted frame of mind that her reflection in the mirror had naturally given her.

The faint atmosphere of chaperonage that always hung about Sir Charles in Hyacinth's house did not interfere with his personal air of enjoying an escapade, nor with his looking distinguished to the very verge of absurdity. As to Cecil, the reaction from his disappointment of the afternoon had made him look more vivid than usual. He was flushed with failure.

He talked rather irresponsibly, and looked at Hyacinth, his neighbour at dinner, with such obvious appreciation, that her gaiety became infectious. In the little panelled dining-room which, like all the house, was neither commonplace nor bizarre, but simple and distinguished, floated an atmosphere of delightful ease and intimacy.

Sir Charles admired the red roses, which Anne declared she had bought for two-and-threepence.

'Very ingenious,' said Sir Charles.

'I *am* ingenious and clever,' said Anne. 'I get my cleverness from my father, and my economy from my mother. My father's a clergyman, but his wife was a little country girl—a sort of Merry Peasant; like Schumann's piece, you know. Peasants are always merry.'

'I fancy that's a myth,' said Cecil. 'If not, I've been singularly unfortunate, for all the peasants *I* ever ran across seemed most depressed.'

'Of course, if you ran over them!' said Hyacinth.

'But I didn't exactly run over them; I only asked them the way to somewhere. They *were* angry! Now I come to think of it, though, they weren't peasants at all. It was only one man. He was a shepherd. I got to know him better afterwards, and he was rather a good chap. Shepherds don't have a bad time; they just wear ribbons and crooks and dance with shepherdesses, you know.'

'Oh, then *can* you tell me why a red sky at night is a shepherd's delight?' asked Hyacinth. 'Is it because it's a sign of rain, and he needn't look after the sheep, but can go fast asleep like little Bo-peep—or was it little Boy Blue—if he likes?'

'For you, I'll try to find out; but I'm ashamed to say I know very little of natural history—or machinery, or lots of other interesting things. And, what's far worse, I don't even want to know any more. I like to think there are some mysteries left in life.'

'I quite agree with you that it would be rather horrid to know exactly how electricity works, and how trains go, and all that sort of thing. I like some things just to *happen*. I never broke my dolls to see what they were made of. I had them taken away the *moment* any sawdust began to come out,' said Hyacinth.

'You were perfectly right, Miss Verney. You're an Idealist; at least, you don't like practical details. But still you take a great interest in other people psychologically. You want to know, I'm sure, just how a shepherd really feels, and why he feels it. I don't even care for that, and I'm not very keen on scenery, or places either, or even things. My Uncle Ted's so frightfully fond of Things. He's a collector, you know, and I don't sympathise a bit. In fact, I hate things.'

'You seem rather difficult to please, Mr Reeve. What *do* you like?'

'People; at least, some people. Don't you?'

'Do you like people who talk nonsense?'

'Yes, and still more people who listen to it charmingly,' he answered. 'I didn't know before tonight that you ever listened to nonsense or talked it. I always thought you were the person who solves all the Hard Cases in *Vanity Fair*—under different names.'

'I wonder you didn't think I won all the prizes in the Limericks,' said Hyacinth.

'I have my faults, Miss Verney, but I'm not blasphemous. Will you have an olive?'

She accepted it. He lowered his voice to say—

'How wonderful you're looking tonight!'

'What am I to say to that? I don't think people should make unanswerable remarks at dinner,' she said, trying to look reproving, but turning pink with pleasure.

'If people will look adorable at dinner—or anywhere—they must take the consequences,' said Cecil, under cover of a very animated discussion between Bruce and Miss Yeo on sixpenny cab-fares.

Then for a second he felt a remorseful twinge of disloyalty. But that was nonsense; wasn't he obeying Mrs Raymond's distinct commands? Nothing would please her so much. . . .

And to flirt with Hyacinth was not at all a disagreeable task. He reflected that Eugenia might have asked him to do something a good deal harder.

Under the combined influence, then, of duty, pique, and a little champagne, he gave way to the curious fascination that Hyacinth had always had for him, and she was only too ready to be happy.

He remembered how he had first met her. He had been dragged to the Burlingtons' dance—he loathed all large parties—and, looking drearily round, he'd been struck by, and asked to be introduced to, Miss Verney. She wasn't Eugenia, of course, and could never, he was sure, be part of his life. He thought that Eugenia appealed to his better nature and to his intellect.

He felt even a little ashamed of the purely sensuous attraction Hyacinth possessed for him, while he was secretly very proud of being in love with Mrs Raymond. Not everyone would appreciate Eugenia! Cecil was still young enough to wish to *be* different from other people, while desiring still more, like all Englishmen, to *appear* as much as possible like everybody else.

He did not thoroughly understand Hyacinth; he couldn't quite place her. She was certainly not the colourless *jeune fille* idealised by the French, but she had even less of the hard abruptness of the ordinary young unmarried Englishwoman. She called herself a bachelor girl, but hadn't the touch of the Bohemian that phrase usually seems to imply. She was too plastic, too finished. He admired her social dexterity, her perfect harmony with the charming background she had so well arranged for herself. Yet, he thought, for such a young girl, only twenty-two, she was too complex, too civilised. Mrs Raymond, for instance, seemed much more downright and careless. He was growing somewhat bewildered between his analysis of her character and his admiration for her mouth, an admiration that was rather difficult to keep entirely cool and theoretical, and that he felt a strong inclination to show in some more practical manner. . . . With a sigh he turned to Edith Ottley, his other neighbour.

As soon as Anne had locked up she removed with the greatest care her emerald dress, which she grudged wearing a second longer than was necessary, and put on an extraordinary dressing-gown of which it was hardly too much to say that there was probably not another one exactly like it in Europe. Hyacinth always said it had been made out of an old curtain from the Rev Mr Yeo's library in the Devonshire Rectory, and Anne did not deny it.

She then screwed up her hair into a tight knot, put one small piece of it into a curling pin, which she then pinned far back on her head (as if afraid that the effect on the forehead would be too becoming), took off her dainty green shoes, put on an enormous pair of grotesque slippers, carpet slippers (also a relic), and went into Hyacinth's room. Anne made it a rule every evening to go in for a few minutes to see Hyacinth and talk against everyone they had seen during the day. She seemed to regard it as a sacred duty, almost like saying her prayers. Hyacinth sometimes professed to find this custom a nuisance, but she would certainly have missed it. Tonight she was smiling happily to herself, and took no notice of Anne's entrance.

'I suppose you think it went off well,' said Anne aggressively.

'Didn't it?'

'I thought the dinner was ridiculous. A young girl like you asking two or three friends needn't have a banquet fit for a Colonial Conference. Besides, the cook lost her head. She sent up the same dish twice.'

'Did she? How funny! How was that?'

'Of course, *you* wouldn't know. She and the kitchenmaid were playing Diabolo till the last minute in the housekeeper's room. However, you needn't worry; nobody noticed it.'

'That's all right. Didn't Edith look pretty?'

Anne poked the fire spitefully.

'Like the outside of a cheap chocolate-box.'

'Oh, Anne, what nonsense! Bruce seemed irritable, and fatuous. I didn't envy Edith going back with him.'

'Bruce was jealous of Cecil Reeve, of course. You hardly looked at anybody else.'

'Anne, really tonight there were one or two little things that made me think he is beginning to like me. I don't say he's perfect; I daresay he has his faults. But there's something I like about his face. I wonder what it is.'

'I know what it is, he's very good-looking,' said Anne.

'Do you think he cares for me?'

'No, I don't.'

'Oh, Anne!'

'I think, perhaps, he will, in time—in a way.'

'Do you think if I were very careful not to show I liked him it would be better?'

'No, there's only one chance for you.'

'What is it?'

'Keep on hammering.'

'*Indeed* I shan't! I never heard of such a thing. I suppose you think there's somebody else?' said Hyacinth, sitting up angrily.

'Oh, I daresay he's just finishing off with someone or other, and you may catch him on the rebound.'

'What horrid things you say!'

'I only say what I think,' said Anne. 'Anyhow, you had a success tonight, I could see, because poor Charles seemed so depressed. Why do you have all these electric lights burning when one lamp would be enough?'

'Oh, go away, Anne, and don't bother,' said Hyacinth, laughing.

On his return home, Cecil suddenly felt a violent reaction in favour of Mrs Raymond. Certainly he had enjoyed his evening with Hyacinth, but it was very bitter to him to think what pleasure that enjoyment would have given to Eugenia. . . . He began to think he couldn't live without her. Something must be done. Further efforts must be made. The idea struck him that he would go and see his uncle, Lord Selsey, about it. He knew Uncle Ted was really fond of him, and wouldn't like to see his life ruined (so he put it to himself), and his heart broken, though he also probably would disapprove from the worldly point of view. Decidedly unhappy, yet to a certain extent enjoying his misery, Cecil went to sleep.

CHAPTER VIII

Lord Selsey

T H E mere thought of confiding in Lord Selsey was at once soothing and bracing. He was a widower with no children, and Cecil was
by way of being his heir. Since the death of his wife he lived in
a kind of cultured retirement in a large old house standing a little
by itself in Cambridge Gate. He used to declare that this situation
combined all the advantages of London and the country, also that
the Park that was good enough for the Regent was good enough for
him. He had a decided cult for George IV; and there was even more
than a hint of Beau Brummel in his dress. The only ugly thing
in the house was a large coloured print of the pavilion at
Brighton.

In many ways Lord Selsey was Cecil's model; and unconsciously,
in his uncle's suave presence, the young man's manner always became more expressive and his face more inscrutable.
    Lord Selsey was remarkably handsome; the even profile, well-
shaped head, and blond colouring were much the same in uncle
and nephew, the uncle's face having, perhaps, a more idealistic cast.
The twenty years' difference in age had only given the elder man a
finer, fairer, more faded look, and the smooth light hair, still thick,
was growing grey.

Cecil was not surprised to find his uncle sitting in his smoking-room,
smoking, and not reading the morning paper. He was looking over
his collection of old coins. At a glance he saw by Cecil's excessive
quietness that the boy, as he called him, was perturbed, so he
talked about the coins for some minutes.
    Cecil made little attempt to conceal that fact that Things bored
him.
    ' Well, what is it?' said Lord Selsey abruptly.
    Cecil couldn't think of anything better by way of introducing the

trouble than the vaguely pessimistic statement that everything was rather rotten.

'You don't gamble, you're not even very hard up. . . . It's a woman, of course,' said Lord Selsey, 'and you want to marry, I suppose, or you wouldn't come to me about it. . . . Who is she?'

Cecil gave a rough yet iridescent sketch of Mrs Raymond.

'Of course she's older than I am, but it doesn't make the slightest difference. She's been a widow ever since she was twenty. She's very hard up, and she doesn't care. She's refused me, but I want to make her come round. . . . No, she isn't *pretty*, not very.'

Lord Selsey put his old coins away, and leant back in his chair.

'I should like to see her,' he said thoughtfully.

'I'm sure of one thing, uncle you could never have any vulgar, commonplace ideas about her—I mean, she's so *peculiarly* disinterested, and all that sort of thing. You mustn't fancy she's a dangerous syren, don't you know, or. . . . For instance, she doesn't care much for dress; she just sticks up her hair anyhow, and parts it in the middle.'

'Then it would certainly be difficult to believe anything against her,' said Lord Selsey.

'Besides, she really wants me to marry someone else.'

'Who?'

'She's always trying to persuade me to propose to Hyacinth Verney . . . you know, that pretty girl, old Cannon's ward. . . . She *is* awfully pretty, of course, I know.'

'I should like to see her,' said Lord Selsey.

Cecil smiled. It was well known that Lord Selsey was a collector. Though no-one could have less of the pompous, fatuous vanity of the Don Juan, beauty had always played, and always would play, a very prominent part in his life. It was, in fact, without exception, his greatest pleasure, and interest—even passion. The temperament that gave to beauty and charm a rather inordinate value had, no doubt, descended to his nephew. But Cecil was, in that as in everything else, much less of a dilettante.

'You actually want me to advise you to persuade Mrs Raymond to marry you? My dear boy, how can I?'

'How is it you don't say she's quite right not to?' asked Cecil curiously.

'From her point of view I think she's quite wrong. As you're both practically free and you would marry her tomorrow—or this afternoon for choice—if she cared for you she would probably do it. Where I think she's wrong is in *not* caring for you. . . . Who is it?'

'I don't believe it's anyone. Eugenia's peculiar; she's very independent, very fantastic. She likes to do whatever comes into her head. She's very fascinating . . . but I shouldn't be at all surprised if she's absolutely cold; I mean, really never could care for any man at all.'

'I *should* like to see her,' repeated Lord Selsey, his eyes brightening.

'It's most awfully good of you, Uncle, the way you take it. I mean to say, I'm afraid I'm not at all asking your consent, you know, or anything of that sort, as I ought.'

'You're asking my advice, and it's about the only thing most men of my age enjoy giving. Well, really, Cecil, and frankly, I think it's a dismal little story. It would be humbug if I pretended I was sorry about Mrs Raymond's—a—attitude, and I quite see its absolute genuineness But, if you'll excuse my saying so, what price the other girl?'

'What price? No price.'

'*She* likes you,' said Lord Selsey acutely.

'What makes you think that?'

'Because otherwise you wouldn't be so cool about her. You're a little too frightened of being obvious, Cecil. I was like that, too. But don't give way to it. Hyacinth Verney—what a charming name! . . . What would old Cannon say?'

'I don't think he seems particularly keen on *me*,' said Cecil frankly.

'That's odd. Then he must be very ambitious for her, or else be in love with her himself . . . probably both.'

'Oh, I say, Uncle Ted! Why, there's Lady Cannon! She's a very handsome, gigantic woman, and they have a daughter of their own, a girl called Ella, at school in Paris. She's pretty, too, only a flapper, you know, with a fair plait and a black bow.'

'I should like to see her; what delightful families you get yourself mixed up with, Cecil! If I were you I should certainly cultivate the Verney girl. I know it's no use telling you to do the contrary, as I should if you weren't in your present frame of mind.'

' I should *very* much like you to meet Eugenia,' said Cecil.

' Yes. How shall we arrange it? A dinner at the Savoy or something?'

' No. Somehow that isn't the kind of thing she'd like,' said Cecil.

' I thought not. But if I suddenly go and call on her, even with you, wouldn't it make it too much of a family affair? And I should be so afraid of having the air of trying to persuade her to give you up. I don't want to make a fool of myself, you know.'

Cecil seemed a little stung, though he smiled.

' If she knew *you*, perhaps it would make her more interested in me!'

' Do you think she'd come and hear some music here,' said Lord Selsey, ' if I wrote and asked her?'

' Yes, I think she might. There's no nonsense about her—about etiquette and things of that sort, I mean.'

' Then that's settled. You tell her about it, and I'll write. On Thursday afternoon. The two young pianists, George Ranger and Nevil Butt, are coming, and the little girl, the new Russian singer.'

' A juvenile party?' asked Cecil, laughing.

' No, only two or three people.'

' Two or three hundred, I suppose. Well, I'll get Mrs Raymond to come. Thanks so much.'

They shook hands with more than cordiality. As Cecil went out his uncle said—

' You've been most interesting this morning. But the other girl's the one, you know. Don't neglect her.'

He laughed, for he saw the young man was rather flattered at the notion. Evidently, Mrs Raymond was worth knowing.

CHAPTER IX

The Peculiarities of Raggett

'O h, Bruce,' said Edith, as she looked up from a Sale Catalogue, 'I *do* wish you would be an angel and let me have a little cash to go to Naylor and Rope's. There are some marvellous bargains—spring novelties—there, and Archie absolutely *needs* one or two things.'

Bruce frowned and sat down to breakfast, rather heavily.

'I object,' he said as he took his coffee, 'on principle—purely on principle—to spring sales. Women buy a lot of things they don't want, and ruin their husbands under the ridiculous impression they're buying bargains.'

'I won't ruin you, dear. I want to get Archie a coat—and a hat. I only want'—she watched his expression—'a sovereign—or two.' She smiled brightly, and passed him the toast.

His manner softened.

'Well, dear, you know I'm not a rich man, don't you?'

'Yes, dear.'

'But I should much prefer that you should get Archie's things at a first-rate place like Wears and Swells, where we have an account, and send me the bill. Will you do that?'

'Of course I will, if you like; but it'll cost more.'

She had often marvelled at a comparative lavishness about cheques that Bruce combined with a curious loathing to parting from any coin, however small.

'Then that's settled. And now I want to speak to you about Raggett.'

He paused, and then said seriously, 'I've absolutely decided and very nearly made up my mind to have Raggett to dinner tonight at the Savoy.'

'The Savoy?'

'Yes, yes; no doubt this little flat is very comfortable'—he looked round the room with marked disdain—'and cook, thanks to you, isn't half *bad* . . . but one can't give *dinners* here! And after all I've said to Raggett—oh, one thing and another—I fancy I've given him the impression of a rather luxurious home. It won't matter if he calls here in the afternoon some day, but for a man like that, I'd rather—yes—the Savoy. You look as if you objected. Do you?'

' Not at all. It'll be rather fun. But I'm so glad you can afford it. We haven't an *account* there, you know.'

' I propose to make a slight sacrifice for once. . . . I will engage a table and telephone to Raggett. Women never understand that to do things well, once in a way, is sometimes a—a very good thing,' he finished rather lamely.

' All right. I *am* getting curious to see Raggett!'

' My dear Edith, he's nothing particular to *see*, but he's a man who might be—very useful.'

' Oh, shall you take a private room?'

' I don't think so. Why? You can wear what you wore last night. . . . You looked quite nice in it, and you can take it from me, once for all '—he got up, looked in the glass, and said—' that *Raggett's all right*. Now, tell cook we're dining out. She might have a holiday tonight. A change may do her good; and I shall hope to find the omelette less leathery tomorrow.'

Edith did not point out that Bruce, after specially ordering breakfast punctually at nine, had come down at half-past ten.

' And now I must go. . . . The dinner was charming last night. It was only spoilt by that empty-headed fool—what's his name—Reeve, who was obviously making up to Hyacinth. Anyone can see she only endures his attentions from politeness, of course. He knows nothing about anything. I found *that* out when we were smoking after dinner; and one can't get a word out of old Cannon.'

Edith was putting Bruce's writing-table in order when she found an open letter in the blotting-book, glanced at the signature, and saw that it was from Raggett. So she eagerly read it, hoping to get some further light on the mysterious man in whose honour Bruce was prepared to offer so extravagant a festivity.

It was written on a rough sheet of paper, with no address. The handwriting was small, compressed, and very untidy. It ran—

' DEAR OTTLEY,
    ' Y'rs to hand. I shall be glad to dine with you, as I have told you several times, and I would accept your invitation with

pleasure if I knew when and where the dinner was to be. These two points you have always avoided mentioning.

'Y'rs truly,

J. R. RAGGETT.'

It struck Edith that it was quite extraordinary, after so many descriptions from Bruce—some vivid, some sketchy, others subtly suggestive—how little she could imagine Raggett.

Notwithstanding quantities of words, nothing, somehow, had ever come out to throw the least glimmer of light either on his character, personality, or walk of life. Not bad, all right, useful, rather wonderful, but quite ordinary and nothing particular, were some of the phrases she recalled. She had never been told anything about his age, nor his appearance, nor how long Bruce had known him. She had only gathered that he wasn't athletic like Goldthorpe (Bruce's golf companion), and that he wasn't in the Foreign Office, and didn't belong to Bruce's club. Where, how, and when could he be useful?

If she seemed bored when Bruce was enthusiastic about him, he was offended; but if she seemed interested and asked leading questions, he became touchy and cautious, almost jealous. Sometimes she had begun to think that Raggett was a Mrs Harris—that there was no such person. There, evidently, she had been wrong.

At eight o'clock that evening, on arriving at the Savoy, Edith decided not to take off her cloak (on the ground of chilliness, but really because it was smarter and more becoming than her dress). Therefore she waited in the outer room while Bruce, who seemed greatly excited, and had given her various contradictory tips about how to behave to their guest, was taking off his coat. Several other people were waiting there. She saw herself in the glass—a pretty, fair, typically Engish-looking woman, with neatly-chiselled features, well-arranged *blond-cendré* hair, a tall, slight figure, and a very thin neck. She noticed, among the other people waiting, a shabby-looking man of about thirty-five, who looked so intensely uncomfortable that she pitied him. He had a vague, rough, drab beard, colourless hair, which was very thick in front and very thin at the back, quite indefinite features, an undecided expression, and the most extraordinary clothes she had ever seen. The shirt-front was soft, and was in large bulging pleats. He wore an abnormal-looking big black tie, and the rest of the costume suggested a conjurer who had arrived at a children's party in the country and had forgotten his dress-suit, and borrowed various portions of it from different people staying in the house, who were either taller or shorter than himself. The waistcoat ended too soon, and the coat began too late; the collar reminded one of Gladstone; while the buttonhole of orchids (placed, rather eccentrically, very low down on the coat) completed the general effect of political broadmindedness, combined with acute social anxiety.

He looked several times at Edith with a furtive but undisguised admiration. Then Bruce appeared, held out his hand cordially, and said, ' Ah, Raggett, here you are!'

CHAPTER X

A Musical Afternoon

LORD SELSEY often said he disapproved of the ordinary sub-divisions of a house, and, especially as he lived alone, he did not see why one should breakfast in a breakfast-room, dine in a dining-room, draw in a drawing-room, and so on. Nevertheless, he had one special room for music. There was a little platform at the end of it, and no curtains or draperies of any kind to obscure or stifle sound. A frieze of Greek figures playing various instruments ran round the walls, which were perfectly plain so that nothing should distract the eye from the pleasures of the ear; but he was careful to avoid that look of a concert-room given by rows of chairs (suggesting restraint and reserved guinea seats), and the music-room was furnished with comfortable lounges and led into a hall containing small Empire sofas, in which not more than two persons could be seated. Therefore the audience at his entertainments often enjoyed themselves almost as much as the performers, which is rare.

This afternoon there was the usual number of very tall women in large highly-decorated hats, smooth-haired young men in coats that went in at the waist, a very few serious amateurs with longish hair, whose appearance did not quite come up to the standard of the *Tailor and Cutter*, and a small number of wistful professional feminine artists in no collars and pince-nez—in fact, the average fashionable, artistic crowd. The two young geniuses, George Ranger and Nevil Butt, had just given their rather electrifying performance, one playing the compositions of the other, and then both singing Fauré together, and a small band of Green Bulgarians were now playing strenuously a symphony of Richard Strauss, when Cecil and Mrs Raymond appeared together. Lord Selsey received her as if she had been an old friend. When they shook hands they felt at once, after one glance at Cecil and then at each other, that they were more than friends—they were almost accomplices.

By one of those fortunate social accidents that are always occur-
ring in London, Lord Selsey had met Hyacinth and Anne Yeo at a
party the day before, had been introduced to them, and invited them
to hear Ranger and Butt. Hyacinth, aware she was to meet Mrs
Raymond, wore her loveliest clothes and sweetest expression, though
she could not keep out of her eyes a certain anxiety, especially when
she saw that Cecil greeted her with a slight, cold embarrassment that
was very different from his usual manner. He had not expected to
meet Hyacinth, and resolved to avoid the introduction he knew she
desired. But no man is a match for a woman in a detail of this sort.
In the refreshment-room, where Cecil was pressing coffee on Mrs
Raymond, Hyacinth walked in, accompanied by Anne, and stood
not very far from him. He came up to her, as Hyacinth saw, at
Mrs Raymond's instigation.

'Can I get you anything, Miss Verney? Some tea?'

'Thanks, yes. Isn't that Mrs Raymond? I do wish you would
introduce me to her.'

Mrs Raymond came forward. Cecil murmured their names. They
shook hands. Mrs Raymond looked at her with such impulsive
admiration that she dropped a piece of cake. They spoke a few words
about the music, and Cecil moved aside.

Anne called him back, not wishing to see him spared anything.

'You mustn't,' said Cecil, 'on any account miss the next thing.
It is the wonderful new singer, don't you know—the little girl,
Vera Schakoffsky.'

'Oh, very well,' said Hyacinth. 'I'll go,' and she went on with
Anne. But when they had returned to the music-room she said to
Anne, 'I left my handkerchief,' and went back to the refreshment-
room.

A screen was by the door. Just before she had passed it she heard
Mrs Raymond say—

'What an angel! How can you not be at her feet? Go and talk
to her at once, or I'll never speak to you again!'

'I just shan't!' said Cecil doggedly. 'You make me simply
ridiculous. If you won't be nice to me yourself, you needn't throw
me at the head of other people.'

Hyacinth turned back and went to the music-room again.

Some time afterwards Cecil joined her, Mrs Raymond having

apparently disappeared. The new tenor was singing an old song. Cecil sat down next to Hyacinth on a little Empire sofa.

'Let me look at the programme,' he said. And as he took it from her he pressed her fingers. She snatched her hand angrily away.

'Pray don't do that,' she said in a contemptuous tone. 'Even to obey Mrs Raymond, you needn't do violence to your feelings!'

'Miss Verney! I beg your pardon! But what *do* you mean?'

'Surely you understand. And don't trouble to come and see me any more.'

He looked at her. Her suave social dexterity had vanished. Her eyes were dark with purely human instinctive jealousy. They looked at each other a moment, then Lord Selsey came up and said—

'I'm afraid my attempt at originality hasn't been quite a success. The concert's not as harmonious as I hoped. Come and have tea, Miss Verney.'

Hyacinth did not speak a word to Anne on their way home, nor did she refer to the afternoon, nor answer any remark of Anne's on the subject till that evening, when Anne came into her room to complain of the electric light and make fun of Lord Selsey's guests. Then she found Hyacinth sobbing, and saying—

'I shall get over it. I shall be all right tomorrow. I'm going to cut him out of my life!'

'He'll soon cut in again,' said Anne.

'Indeed he won't! I'm not going to be played with. Preferring an old Japanese who doesn't even *like* him, and then making a fool of me!'

'If she ran after him, and you begged him to stick to her, it would be the other way,' said Anne.

'What do you mean? Hasn't he any real preference?'

'Yes. He's attached to her, fond of her. She's utterly indifferent about him, so he's piqued. So he thinks that's being in love.'

'Then why does he try to deceive me and flirt with me at all?'

'He doesn't. You really attract him; you're suited to him physically and socially, perhaps mentally too. The suitability is so obvious that he doesn't like it. It's his feeling for you that he fights against, and especially because he sees you care for him.'

'I was horrid enough to him today! I told him never to call here again.'

'To show your indifference?'

'I made him understand that I wanted no more of his silly flirtation,' said Hyacinth, still tearful.

'If you *really* made him think that, everything will be all right.'

'Really, Anne, you're clever. I think I shall take your advice.'

Anne gave a queer laugh.

'I didn't know I'd given any, but I will. Whatever he does now, leave him alone!'

'I should think so! Then why did you tell me the other day to keep on hammering?'

'I was quite right the other day.'

'Didn't I look nicer than Mrs Raymond?'

'That's not the point. You talk as if you were rivals on the same platform. She's on a different plane. But he'll get tired in the end of her indifference and remember *you*,' added Anne sardonically.

'Then he'll find I've forgotten *him*. Oh, why am I so unhappy?'

'You're too emotional, but you'll be happy through that too. Please don't make your eyes red. There are other people in the world. Cecil Reeve—'

'And yet there's something so fascinating about him. He's so unlike anybody else.'

'Bosh!' said Anne. 'He's exactly like thousands of other young men. But it just happens you've taken a fancy to him; that's the only thing that makes him different.'

'I hate him,' said Hyacinth. 'Do you dislike him, Anne?'

'Dislike him?' said Anne, turning out one of the lights. 'No, indeed! I loathe him!'

'But why?'

Anne went to the door.

'Because you're a fool about him,' she said somewhat cryptically.

Hyacinth felt somewhat soothed, and resolved to think no more of Cecil Reeve. She then turned up the light again, took her writing materials, and wrote him three long letters, each of which she tore up. She then wrote once more, saying—

'DEAR MR REEVE,

'I shall be at home today at four. Do come round and see me.'

She put it under her pillow, resolving to send it by a messenger the first thing in the morning, and went to sleep.

But this letter, like the others, was never sent. By the morning light she marvelled at having written it, and threw it into the fire.

CHAPTER XI

The Troubles of the Ottleys

'B R U C E ,' said Edith, ' you won't forget we're dining with your people tonight?'

' It's a great nuisance.'

' Oh, Bruce!'

' It's such an infernally long way.'

' It's only to Kensington.'

' West Kensington. It's off the map. I'm not an explorer—I don't pretend to be.' He paused a moment, then went on, ' And it's not only the frightful distance and the expense of getting there, but when I *do* get there. . . . Do you consider that my people treat me with proper deference?'

' With proper *what*?' asked Edith.

' Deference. I admit I like deference. I need it—I require it; and at my people's—well, frankly, I don't get it.'

' If you need it,' said Edith, ' I hope you will get it. But remember they are your father and mother.'

' What do you mean by that?'

' Well, I mean they know you very well, of course . . . and all that.'

' Do you imply . . . ?'

' Oh, no, Bruce dear,' she answered hastily; ' of course I don't. But really I think your people are charming.'

' To *you* I know they are,' said he. ' It's all very well for you. They are awfully fond of *you*. You and my mother can talk about Archie and his nurse and housekeeping and fashions, and it's very jolly for you, but where's the fun for a man of the world?'

' Your father—' began Edith.

' My father!' Bruce took a turn round the room. ' I don't mind telling you, Edith, I don't consider my father a man of the world. Why, good heavens! when we are alone together, what do you suppose he talks about? He complains! Finds fault, if you please!

Says I don't work—makes out I'm extravagant! Have *you* ever found me extravagant?'

' No, indeed. I'm sure you've never been extravagant—to *me*.'

' He's not on my level intellectually in any way. I doubt very much if he's capable of understanding me at all. Still, I suppose we might as well go and get it over. My people's dinners are a most awful bore to me.'

' How would you like it,' said Edith gently, ' if some day Archie were to call us my people, and talk about us as you do of yours?'

' Archie!' shouted Bruce. ' Good heavens! Archie!' Bruce held out his arm with a magnificent gesture. ' If Archie ever treats me with any want of proper deference, I shall cut him off with a shilling!'

' Do give me the shilling for him now,' said Edith laughing.

The elder Mrs Ottley was a sweet woman, with a resigned smile and a sense of humour. She had a great admiration for Edith, who was very fond of her. No-one else was there on this occasion. Bruce always complained equally, regarding it as a slight if they were asked alone, and a bore if it was a dinner party. The elder Mr Ottley was considerably older than his wife, and was a handsome, clean-shaven elderly man with a hooked nose and a dry manner. The conversation at dinner consisted of vague attempts on Bruce's part to talk airy generalities, which were always brought back by his father to personalities more or less unflattering to Bruce.

Edith and Mrs Ottley, fearing an explosion, which happened rather frequently when Bruce and his father were together, combined their united energy to ward it off.

' And what do you intend the boy to be when he grows up?' asked old Mr Ottley. ' Are you going to make him a useful member of society, or a Foreign Office clerk?'

' I intend my son,' said Bruce—' (a little port, please. Thanks.)— I intend my son to be a Man of the World.'

His father gave a slight snort.

' Be very careful,' said Mrs Ottley to Edith, ' not to let the darling catch cold in his perambulator this weather. Spring is so treacherous!'

' Does he seem to show any particular bent for anything? I suppose hardly—yet?'

' Well, he's very fond of soldiers,' said Edith.

' Ah!' said Mr Ottley approvingly; ' what we want for empire-building is conscription. Every fellow ought to be a soldier some time in his life. It makes men of them '—he glanced round rather contemptuously—' it teaches them discipline.'

' I don't mean,' said Edith hastily, ' that he wants to *be* a soldier. But he likes playing with them. He takes them to bed with him. It is as much as I can do to keep him from eating them.'

' The angel!' said Mrs Ottley.

' You must be careful about that, Edith,' said Bruce solemnly. ' I understand red paint is poisonous.'

' It won't hurt him,' said old Mr Ottley, purely from a spirit of contradiction.

' But he's just as fond of animals,' said Edith quickly, to avert a storm. ' That Noah's Ark you gave him is his greatest pleasure. He's always putting the animals in and taking them out again.'

' Oh, the clever darling!' cried Mrs Ottley. ' You'd hardly believe it, Edith, but Bruce was like that when he was a little boy too. He used to—'

' Oh mother, do shut up!' said Bruce shame-facedly.

' Well, he was very clever,' said Mrs Ottley defiantly. ' You'd hardly think so now perhaps, but the things that child used to say!'

' Don't spoil Archie as his mother spoilt Bruce,' said Mr. Ottley.

' Have you seen the new play at His Majesty's?' asked Bruce.

' No, I haven't. I went to the theatre *last* year,' said old Mr Ottley. ' *I* haven't heaps of money to spend on superfluous amusements.'

' Bruce, you're not eating anything,' said Mrs Ottley anxiously. ' Do try some of these almonds and raisins. They're so good! I always get almonds and raisins at Harrod's now.'

Edith seemed much interested, and warmly assented to the simple proposition that they were the best almonds and raisins in the world.

The ladies retired.

' Most trying Mr Ottley's been lately,' said Mrs Ottley. ' Extremely worrying. Do you suppose I have had a single instant to go and order a new bonnet? Not a second! Has Bruce been tiresome at all?'

' Oh, no, he doesn't mean to be,' said Edith.

Mrs Ottley pressed her hand. ' Darling! I *know* what it is. What

a sweet dress! You have the most perfect taste. I don't care what
people say, those Empire dresses are most trying. I think you're so
right not to give in to it as so many young women are doing.
Fashion indeed! Hiding your waist under a bushel instead of being
humbly thankful that you've got one! Archie is the sweetest
darling. I see very little likeness to Bruce, or his father. I think he
takes after *my* family, with a great look of you, dear. Most unfortunately, his father thinks Bruce is a little selfish . . . too fond of
pleasure. But he's a great deal at home, isn't he, dear?'

'Yes, indeed,' said Edith, with a slight sigh. 'I think it's only that
he's always been a little bit spoilt. No wonder, the only son! But
he's a great dear, really.'

His mother shook her head. 'Dear loyal girl! I used to be like
that too. May I give you a slight hint? Never contradict. Never
oppose him. Agree with him, then he'll change his mind; or if he
doesn't, say you'll do as he wishes, and act afterwards in the matter
as your own judgement dictates. He'll never find it out. What's
that?'

A door banged, hasty steps were heard. Bruce came into the
drawing-room alone, looking slightly flushed and agitated.

'Where's your father?' asked Mrs Ottley.

'Gone to his study. . . . We'd better be getting home, Edith.'

Edith and Mrs Ottley exchanged glances. They had not been able
to prevent the explosion after all.

CHAPTER XII

At the National Gallery

IT was with considerable difficulty and self-restraint that Cecil succeeded in waiting till the next day to see Mrs Raymond after his uncle's party. He was of an age and of a temperament that made his love affairs seem to him supremely urgent and of more importance than anything else in his life.

He called on Mrs Raymond at eleven in the morning on the pretext of having something important to tell her. He found her sitting at her writing-table in a kind of red kimono. Her hair was brushed straight off her forehead, her eyes were sly and bright, and she looked more Japanese than ever.

Cecil told her what Hyacinth had said to him.

'Now, you see, I *can't* go on making up to her any more. She doesn't care a straw about me, and she sees through it, of course. I've done what you asked me. Won't you be nice to me now?'

'Certainly not! She's quite devoted to you. Telling you not to go and see her again! I never heard of anything so encouraging in my life. Now, Cecil,' she spoke seriously, 'that girl is a rare treasure. It's not only that she's a perfect beauty, but I read her soul yesterday. She has a beautiful nature, and she's in love with you. You don't appreciate her. If you take what she said literally, you're much stupider than I gave you credit for being. I—I simply shan't see you again till you've made it up. When you know her better you *must* care for her. Besides, I insist upon it. If you don't—well, you'll have to turn your attention somewhere else. For I seriously mean it. I won't see you.'

He looked obstinate.

'It's a fad of yours, Eugenia.'

'It's not a fad of mine. It's an opportunity of yours—one that you're throwing away in the most foolish way, that you might regret all your life. At any rate, *I'm* not going to be the cause of giving that poor darling another moment's annoyance or uneasiness.

The idea of the angelic creature being worried about *me*! Why, it's preposterous! I'm sure she heard what I said to you when she came in behind the screen. I can't bear it, and I won't have it. Now go and see her, and you're not to come back till you have. I mean it.'

' I don't suppose for a moment—'

' Rubbish! A woman knows. She went home and cried; I know she did, and she's counting the minutes till you see her again. Now, I've lots to do, and you're frightfully in the way. Good-bye.' She held out her hand.

He rose.

' You send me away definitely?'

' Definitely. Your liking for me is pure perverseness.'

' It's pure adoration,' said Cecil.

' I don't think so. It's imagination. However, whatever it is I don't want it.'

' Good-bye, then,' said Cecil.

He went to the door.

' You can let me know when you've seen her.'

' I don't suppose she'll see me.'

' Yes, she will now. It's the psychological moment.'

' You shan't be bothered with me any more, anyhow,' said Cecil in a low voice.

' Good. And do what I tell you.'

He shut the shabby door of the little house with a loud bang, and went out with a great longing to do something vaguely desperate.

Lunch produced a different mood. He said to himself that he wouldn't think of Mrs Raymond any more, and went to call on Hyacinth.

The servant told him she was out.

He was just turning away when Anne Yeo came out. She glanced at him with malicious satisfaction.

' Hyacinth's gone to the National Gallery,' she volunteered. ' Did you want to see her? You will find her there.'

Cecil walked a few steps with her.

' I'm going to the greengrocer's,' continued Anne, ' to complain.' She held a little book in her hand, and he noticed that she wore a golf cap, thick boots, and a mackintosh, although it was a beautiful day.

' I always dress like this,' she said, ' when I'm going to complain of prices. Isn't it a glorious day? The sort of day when every-one feels happy and hopeful.'

'I don't feel either,' said Cecil candidly.

'No, you don't look it. Why not go and see some pictures?'

He smiled. They parted at the corner.

Then Cecil, without leaving any message for Hyacinth, jumped into a hansom, giving the man the address of his club in Pall Mall. On the way he changed his mind, and drove to the National Gallery. As he went up the steps his spirits rose. He thought he recognised Miss Verney's motor waiting outside. There was something of an adventure in following her here. He would pretend it was an accident, and not let her know yet that he had called.

He wandered through the rooms, which were very empty, and came upon Hyacinth seated on a red velvet seat opposite a Botticelli.

She looked more dejected than he could have thought possible, her type being specially formed to express the joy of life. It was impossible to help feeling a thrill of flattered vanity when he saw the sudden change in her expression and her deep blush when she recognised him.

'I didn't know you ever came here,' she said, as they shook hands.

'It's a curious coincidence I should meet you when, for once in my life, I come to study the Primitives,' said Cecil.

He then seated himself beside her.

'Don't you think all that'—he waved his hand towards the pictures—'is rather a superstition?'

'Perhaps; but it's glorious, I think. These are the only pictures that give me perfect satisfaction. All others, however good they are, have the effect of making me restless,' said Hyacinth.

'I haven't had a moment's rest,' said Cecil, 'since I saw you yesterday afternoon. Why were you so unkind?'

'Was it unkind?' she asked. Her face was illuminated.

They spent an hour together; had horrible tea in the dismal refreshment-room, and having agreed that it seemed a shame to spend a lovely day within these walls, he said—

'I don't think I've ever met you out of doors—in the open air, I mean.'

'It would be nice,' said Hyacinth.

He proposed that they should do something unconventional and delightful, and meet the next day in Kensington Gardens, which he assured her was just as good as the country just now. She agreed, and they made an appointment.

'How is Mrs Raymond?' she then asked abruptly.

'I don't know. Mrs Raymond—she's charming, and a great friend of mine, of course; but we've quarrelled. At least I'm not going to see her again.'

'Poor Mrs Raymond!' exclaimed Hyacinth. 'Or perhaps I ought to be sorry for you?'

'No, not if you let me see you sometimes.' He looked at her radiant face and felt the soothing, rather intoxicating, effect of her admiration after Eugenia's coldness. . . . He took her hand and held it for a minute, and then they parted with the prospect of meeting the next day.

Hyacinth went home too happy even to speak to Anne about it. She was filled with hope. He *must* care for her.

And Cecil felt as if he were a strange, newly-invented kind of criminal. Either, he said to himself, he was playing with the feelings of this dear, beautiful creature, or he was drifting into a *mariage de convenance,* a vulgar and mercenary speculation, while all the time he was madly devoted to someone else. He felt guilty, anxious, and furious with Eugenia. But she had really meant what she said that morning; she wouldn't see him again. But the thought of seeing Hyacinth under the trees the next morning—a secret appointment, too!—was certainly consoling.

With a sudden sensation of being utterly sick of himself and his feelings, tired of both Hyacinth and Eugenia, and bored to death at the idea of all women, Cecil went to see Lord Selsey.

CHAPTER XIII

More of the Little Ottleys

'FANCY!' said Edith.

'Fancy what?'

'Somehow I never should have thought it,' said Edith thoughtfully.

'Never should have thought what? You have a way of assuming I know the end of your story before I've heard the beginning. It's an annoying method,' said Bruce.

'I shouldn't have been so surprised if they had been anywhere else. But just *there*,' continued Edith.

'Who? and where?'

'Perhaps I'd better not tell you,' Edith said.

They had just finished dinner, and she got up as if to ring the bell for coffee.

He stopped her.

'No! Don't ring; I don't wish Bennett to be present at a painful scene.'

Edith looked at him. 'I didn't know there was going to be a painful scene. What's the matter?'

'Naturally, I'm distressed and hurt at your conduct.'

'Conduct!'

'Don't echo my words, Edith.'

She saw he looked really distressed.

'Naturally,' he continued, 'I'm hurt at your keeping things from me. Your own husband! I may have my faults—'

She nodded.

'But I've not deserved this from you.'

'Oh dear, Bruce, I was only thinking. I'm sorry if I was irritating. I will tell you.'

'Go on.'

'When Nurse and Archie were out in the Gardens this morning, *who* do you think they met?'

56

'This is not a game. I'm not going to guess. You seem to take me for a child.'

'Well, you won't tell anybody, will you?'

'That depends. I'm not going to make any promises beforehand. I shall act on my own judgement.'

'Oh, you might promise. Well, I'll trust you.'

'Thanks! I should think so!'

'They met Hyacinth, walking with Cecil Reeve alone in a quiet part of the Gardens. They weren't walking.'

'Then why did you say they were?' asked Bruce severely.

'It's the same thing. They were sitting down.'

'How *can* it be the same thing?'

'Oh, don't worry, Bruce! They were sitting down under a tree and Nurse saw them holding hands.'

Bruce looked horrified.

'Holding hands,' continued Edith; 'and I can't help thinking they must be engaged. Isn't it extraordinary Hyacinth hasn't told me? What do you think?'

Bruce got up from the table, lighted a cigarette, and walked round the little room.

'I don't know. I must consider. I must think it over.' He paused a minute. 'I am pained. Pained and surprised. A girl like Hyacinth, a friend of yours, behaving like a housemaid out with a soldier in the open street!'

'It wasn't the street, Bruce.'

'It's the same idea.'

'Quite a quiet part of the Gardens.'

'That makes their conduct worse. I scarcely think, after what you have told me, that I can allow you to go out with Hyacinth tomorrow.'

'How can you be so absurd? I must go; I want to hear about it.'

'Have I ever made any objection till now at your great intimacy with Hyacinth Verney? Of course not. Because I was deceived in her.'

'Deceived?'

'Don't repeat my words, Edith. I won't have it! Certainly I was deceived. I thought she was a fitting companion for you—I *thought* so.'

'Oh, Bruce, really! Where's the harm? Perhaps they're engaged;

and if they are I think it is charming. Cecil is such a nice, amusing, good-looking boy, and—'

' I formed my opinion of Reeve some time ago.'

' You only met him once.'

' Once is more than enough for me to form a judgement of any-one. He is absolutely unworthy of her. But *her* conduct I regard as infinitely worse. I always imagined she was respectably brought up —a lady!'

' Good gracious! Anyone can see *that*! She's the most charming girl in the world.'

' *Outwardly*, no doubt, she *seems* all right. But now you see what she is.'

He paused to relight his cigarette, which had gone out, and continued: ' Such behaviour would be dreadful enough in private, but in public! Do you think of the example?'

' The example to Archie, do you mean?'

' Don't laugh, Edith. This is no matter for laughing. Certainly to Archie—to anyone. Now I've only one thing to say.'

' Do say it.'

' That I never wish to hear Hyacinth Verney's name mentioned again. You are never to speak of her to me. Do you hear?'

' Yes, Bruce.'

' It is such a disillusion. I'm so shocked, so horrified, finding her a snake in the grass.'

' Oh, I'm sure she didn't look a bit like a snake, Bruce. She wore that lovely grey dress and a hat with roses.'

' How do you know? Did *Archie* tell you? No; you lowered your-self to question Nurse. A nice opinion Nurse must have of your friends now! No; *that's* over. I won't blame *you*, dear, but I must never hear anything more about Hyacinth.'

Edith sat down and took up a book.

' Why is there no coffee?' asked Bruce rather loudly.

' Oh, you said I wasn't to ring.'

She rang.

While the parlourmaid was bringing in the coffee, Bruce said in a high, condescending voice—

' Have you seen that interesting article in the evening paper, dear, about the Solicitor-General?'

' Which do you mean? " Silk and Stuff "?'

' Yes. Read it—read it and improve your mind. Far better for a woman to occupy her mind with general subjects, and make herself intellectually a companion for her husband—are you listening?—than to be always gossiping and thinking about people and their paltry private affairs. Do you hear?'

' Yes, dear.'

He took his coffee and then said—

' In what direction did you say they were going?'

' Oh, I thought you didn't want me to speak of her again. They were going in the opposite direction.'

' Opposite to what? Now that's the curious difference between a woman's intellect and a man's. You can't be logical! What do you mean by " opposite "?' ·

' Why, Bruce, I mean just opposite. The other way.'

' Do you mean they walked off separately?'

' Oh, *no*! They were going away together, and looking so happy. But really, Bruce, I'm sorry I bothered you, telling you about it. I had no idea you would feel it so much.'

' What do you mean? Feel it? Of course, I'm terribly distressed to find that a wife of mine is intimate with such people—where are you going?'

' I was going to write to Hyacinth and tell her I can't go out with her tomorrow.'

' Why can't you go out with her?'

' You said I was never to see her again.'

' Yes; but don't be in a hurry. Never be impulsive.' He waited a minute; she stood by the door. ' On the whole, since you wish it so much, I will permit you to go out with her this once—for the last time, of course—so that you can find out if she really is engaged to be married to that young ass. What a mercenary scoundrel he must be!'

' I don't think that. Anyone would admire her, and he is very well off himself.'

' Well off! Do you consider that to his credit. So should I be well off if I had relations that died and left me a lot of money. Don't defend him, Edith; his conduct is simply disgraceful. What right has he to expect to marry a beautiful girl in Hyacinth's position? Good gracious, does he want everything?'

' I suppose—he likes her.'

' That's not particularly clever of him. So would any man. What I object to so much about that empty-headed cad, is that he's never satisfied. He wants the earth, it seems to me!'

' Really, Bruce, one would think you were quite—'

' What?'

' Well, quite jealous of him, to hear you talk. If one didn't know that—of course you can't be,' she added quickly.

' This incident is now closed,' said Bruce. ' We will never discuss the subject again.'

' Very well, dear.'

She then went into the little drawing-room and looked longingly at the telephone. She feared there would be no chance of communicating with her friend that evening.

Five minutes later Bruce came in and said—

' And what can old Cannon be about to allow his ward to be tearing about all over London with a man of Reeve's antecedents?'

' What's the matter wih his antecedents? I didn't know he had any.'

' Don't interrupt. And Miss Yeo? Where was Miss Yeo, I should like to know?'

' I can't *think*.'

' A nice way she does her duty as chaperone!'

' Dear, Hyacinth's twenty-three, not a child. Miss Yeo's her companion; but she can't insist, even if she wants to, on following Hyacinth about if she doesn't wish it.'

' She should wish it. Seriously, do you think Sir Charles knows of these goings-on—I mean of this conduct?'

' I shouldn't think he knew the details.'

' Then isn't it my duty as a married man and father of a family—'

Edith concealed a smile by moving the screen.

' To communicate with him on the subject?'

Edith had a moment's terror. It struck her that if she opposed him, Bruce was capable of doing it. He often wrote letters beginning, ' Sir, I feel it my duty,' to people on subjects that were no earthly concern of his. If he really did anything of this sort, Hyacinth would never forgive her.

After a second's concentration of mind, she said mildly—

' Perhaps you had better, if you really feel it your duty. Of course,

I'd rather you didn't, personally. But if that's how you feel about it—'

Bruce wheeled round at once.

'Indeed! Well, I shall not do anything of the sort. Is it my business to open her guardian's eyes? Why should I? No; I won't interfere in the matter at all. Let them go their own way. Do you hear, Edith? Let them do just whatever they like.'

'Yes; I was going to.'

'Mind you, they'll be wretched,' he added rather vindictively. 'If I only saw a chance of happiness for them I shouldn't mind so much.'

'Why do you think they will be miserable if they are married?'

'Of course they will. People who behave in that unprincipled way before—'

'Why, we used to sit in the garden,' said Edith timidly.

'Oh, yes, of course; after your father had given his consent.'

'And once or twice before.'

Bruce smiled rather fatuously. 'Don't compare the two cases. I was a man of the world. . . . I was very firm, wasn't I Edith? Somehow at first your father didn't seem to like me, but I reasoned with him. I always reason calmly with people. And then he came round. Do you remember how pleased you were that day?' He patted Edith's hair.

'Then why be so severe?'

'Perhaps I am a little bit too severe,' he acknowledged. 'But you don't quite understand how it jars on me to think of any friend of yours behaving in a manner that's—are you sure they're engaged?'

'No; I don't know anything about it.'

'Well, of course, if they don't marry after what Archie has seen, it will be a public scandal, that's all I can say. On the other hand, of course, it would be far better not.'

'What do you propose?' said Edith.

'I don't quite know; I'll think it over. Look here, Edith, if you don't mind, I think I'll go for a little stroll. The flat seems so hot and airless tonight.'

Edith glanced at the telephone.

'Oh, don't go,' she said.

He went into the hall and put on his coat. 'I must go, dear. I feel the need of air. I shan't be long.'

' You will only go for a little walk, won't you?'

' I *might* go to the club for half an hour. I shall see. Good night, dear.'

' Good night.'

He came back to say, in a rather mysterious voice—

' What were Nurse's exact words?'

' Oh, she said, " Miss Verney seemed to be carrying on anyhow with a young gentleman in Kensington Gardens," and then she said it was Mr Reeve, that's all.'

' Disgusting! Horrible!'

He went out and banged the door.

Edith went to the telephone.

CHAPTER XIV

Lady Cannon's Visit

LADY CANNON got up one morning earlier than usual and tried on a dress of last season, which she found was a little too tight. For this, naturally, she blamed her maid with some severity. She then dressed rather hurriedly and went all over the house, touching little ornaments with the tip of her finger, saying that the pictures in the drawing-room were crooked, and that nothing had been properly dusted. Having sent for the housemaid and scolded her, and given the second footman notice, she felt better, but was still sufficiently in what is expressively called a bad temper to feel an inclination to do disagreeable duties, so she made up her mind to call and see her husband's ward, and tell her something she would not like to hear. For Hyacinth she always felt a curious mixture of chronic anger, family pride, and admiring disapproval, which combination she had never yet discovered to be a common form of vague jealousy.

Lady Cannon arrived about three o'clock, pompously dressed in tight purple velvet and furs. She thought she saw two heads appear at the studio window and then vanish, but was told that Miss Verney was out.

Prompted by a determination not to be baffled, she said she would get out and write a note, and was shown to the drawing-room.

Anne, in a peculiarly hideous and unnecessary apron of black alpaca, came in, bringing a little writing-case.

'Oh! Miss Yeo, as you're there, I needn't write the letter. You can give Hyacinth a message for me.'

'Certainly, Lady Cannon.'

'How is it that she is out at this extraordinary hour?'

'Is there anything extraordinary about the hour?' asked Anne, looking at the clock. 'It's three; somehow I always regard three as a particularly ordinary hour.'

'I differ from you, Miss Yeo.'

'Anyhow, it happens every day,' murmured Anne.

'Was Hyacinth out to lunch?' said Lady Cannon.

'No—no. She lunched at home.'

'Do you think she'll be long?'

'Oh, no; I shouldn't think she would be many minutes.'

'Then I think I'll wait.'

'*Do,*' said Anne cordially.

'I wanted to speak to her. Considering she's my husband's ward, I see very, very little of Hyacinth, Miss Yeo.'

'Yes, she was saying the other day that you hardly ever called now,' Anne said conciliatingly.

'Has she been quite well lately?'

'Oh, do you know, she's been *so* well,' said Anne, in a high, affected voice, which she knew was intensely irritating. 'So very, very well!'

Anne then stood up.

'Would you like a cup of tea, or coffee, while you're waiting?'

'*Tea?* At three o'clock in the afternoon! I never heard of such a thing. You seem to have strangely Bohemian ideas in this house, Miss Yeo!'

'Do you think tea Bohemian? Well, coffee then?'

Lady Cannon hesitated, but wishing for an excuse to wait, she said—

'Thank you, if it isn't giving any trouble; perhaps I'll take a cup of coffee. I didn't have any after lunch.'

'Oh, yes, do. I'll go and order it at once.'

Anne walked with slow, languid dignity to the door, and when she had shut it, flew like a hunted hare to the studio, where Cecil Reeve and Hyacinth were sitting together.

'Hyacinth,' she said sharply, 'run upstairs at once, put on your hat, go to the hall door and bang it, and come into the drawing-room. Lady Cannon's going to stop the whole afternoon. She's in an appalling temper.'

'She won't wait long,' exclaimed Hyacinth, 'surely?'

'Won't she? She's ordered coffee. She'll be smoking a cigarette before you know where you are.'

'Oh, I'll go,' said Cecil. 'Let me go.'

'Of course you must go,' said Anne. 'You can come back in an hour.'

'But, good heavens, Anne,' said Hyacinth, 'why on earth should we make a secret of Mr Reeve being here?'

'Why, because I said you were out.'

'Well, I'll go and explain,' said Hyacinth.

'Indeed you won't. You're not to go and give me away. Besides, I won't be baffled by that old cat. She's suspicious already. Out you go!'

Cecil took his hat and stick, and went out of the front door.

Anne ran upstairs, brought down Hyacinth's hat, veil, and gloves, and pushed her towards the drawing-room.

'Don't you see?—she'll think you've just come in,' said Anne.

'What about the coachman and footman?'

'Oh, good heavens, *do* you think they're going to call on her and tell her all about it?'

Just as Hyacinth, laughing, was going into the drawing-room, Anne clutched her, and said—

'I don't know that you'd better be at home after all! Charles will be calling directly. Oh, I forgot, he won't come in when he sees the carriage.'

Anne relaxed her clasp and went to order coffee.

Lady Cannon was looking angrily in the glass when Hyacinth came in.

'Oh, here you are, my dear. I'm glad I didn't miss you. I wanted to speak to you about something.'

'Yes, Auntie.'

Lady Cannon coughed, and said rather portentously, 'You must not be offended with me, dear. You know, in a sense I'm, as it were, in the place of your mother—or, at any rate, your stepmother.'

'Yes.'

'Of course you're perfectly free to do exactly as you like, but I heard in a roundabout way something that rather surprised me about you.'

'What is it?'

'We were dining with some friends last night' (it was characteristic of Lady Cannon not to mention their names), 'where we happened to meet that young couple, the Ottleys. You know Mrs Ottley very well, I believe?'

'Edith is my greatest friend,' said Hyacinth.

' Quite so; she seems a very nice young woman. Very devoted to her husband. And I think him a most superior man! He sat next to me at dinner, and I had quite a long talk with him. We spoke of you. He told me something that surprised me so much. He said that you had been seen very frequently lately about alone with a young man. Is this a fact?'

' What did he say about it?'

' Well, he seemed to regret it—he seemed to think it was a pity. Living alone as you do, it certainly is not the right thing for you to be seen anywhere without Miss Yeo.'

Hyacinth became crimson. ' On what grounds did Mr Ottley find fault with anything I do?'

' Merely general grounds, my dear. A very proper dislike to the flighty behaviour of the girls of the present day. As he tells me, he feels it as a father—'

' Father! He has only a little boy of two. I think it's very impertinent of him to talk of me like that at all.'

' On the contrary, I thought it exceedingly nice of him. He sincerely wishes you well, Hyacinth. Oh, *how* well that young man wishes you! Make no mistake about it. By the way, I promised him not to mention his name in the matter. So of course you won't repeat it. But I was really rather upset at what he said. I haven't said anything to Sir Charles yet, as I thought you might give me some explanation.'

' I have no explanation to give. I suppose you know who it is I was walking with?'

' I gathered that it was a Mr Reeve. Now, Hyacinth dear, you know how much I wish you well; if you're engaged, I think your guardian and I ought to know it, and in any case you should be more discreet in your behaviour.'

Hyacinth's eyes flashed.

' Are you engaged?' asked Lady Cannon.

' I must decline to answer. I recognise no right that you or anyone else has to ask me such a question.'

Lady Cannon rose indignantly, leaving her coffee untouched.

' Very well, Hyacinth; if this is the way you take my kind advice and well-meant interest, there's nothing more to be said. Of course, I shall tell Sir Charles what I've heard. From what I can gather from that excellent young man Mr Ottley, Mr Reeve is by no means a person that Sir Charles and I would be glad to welcome with open arms, as one of the family.'

'Cecil Reeve is a friend of mine. There's nothing in the world to be said against him, and you must really allow me the privilege of choosing my own friends.'

'Good-bye then,' said Lady Cannon, going to the door. 'I'm pained, grieved, and shocked at your attitude. I can only presume, however, that you are not engaged to be married, for surely your first thought would have been to ask your guardian's consent; and once more let me tell you, in being reckless as you have, you're simply ruining your future.'

With this Lady Cannon swept from the room.

She returned, however, and said, 'I regard all this as not your own fault, Hyacinth, but the fault of *that Miss Yeo*. From the first I saw she had an evil influence, and I've been proved, as, perhaps unfortunately, I always am, to be perfectly right.'

'The worst of it was,' Hyacinth said, when relating the conversation to Anne a little later, 'that I *can't* tell Auntie that I'm engaged. Isn't it awful?'

'You soon will be,' said Anne consolingly.

'Do you really think so?'

'Yes, and I'm glad Lady Cannon was scored off, anyhow.'

'Edith told me about her having mentioned to Bruce about our meeting the nurse and baby. She was very sorry, but I thought it didn't matter a bit. Why do you think Bruce tried to make mischief in this horrid way?'

'Only because he's a fool. Like so many of us, he's in love with you,' said Anne.

Hyacinth laughed, thinking Anne was in fun.

CHAPTER XV

Raggett in Love

' I F you please, ma'am a gentleman called and left some flowers.'
' Who was it?' said Edith.
' He wouldn't give his name. There's a note for you.'
Edith went into the drawing-room, where she found a large bundle of lilies, violets, and daffodils, and the following letter, written in a cramped, untidy handwriting: —

'DEAR MRS OTTLEY,
  ' I went for a bicycle ride yesterday and plucked these flowers for you, hoping you wouldn't mind accepting them. If you have a moment's time to give me, I wonder if you would let me call and see you one day?

'Sincerely yours,
'F. J. RAGGETT

  'P.S.—I'm extremely busy, but am free at any time. Perhaps tomorrow might suit you? Or if you're engaged tomorrow, perhaps today? I would ask you to ring me up and kindly let me know, but I'm not on the telephone.'

Edith was amused, but also a little bored. Ever since the dinner at the Savoy, now a fortnight ago, Raggett had been showing furtive signs of a wild admiration for her, at the same time hedging absurdly by asking her to tell him when he might call and giving no address, and by (for instance) pretending he had plucked the flowers himself, evidently not knowing that they had been sent with her address written on a card printed with the name of Cooper's Stores in the Edgware Road.

She never knew how Bruce would take things, so she had not said anything about it to him yet. He seemed to have forgotten the existence of Raggett, and never mentioned him now.

She arranged the flowers in some blue and white china vases, and sat down by the window in the little drawing-room. She had before her, until Bruce would come home to dinner, two of those empty hours which all young married women in her position have known. There was nothing to do. Archie was still out, and she was tired of reading, and disliked needlework.

She had just come back from seeing Hyacinth. How full and interesting *her* life seemed! At any rate, *she* had everything before her. Edith felt as if she herself were locked up in a box. Even her endless patience with Bruce was beginning to pall a little.

As she was thinking these things she heard a ring, and the maid came in and said—

'It's the gentleman that left the flowers, and could you see him for a minute?'

'Certainly.'

Raggett came in. He looked just as extraordinary as he had at the Savoy and as difficult to place. His manner could not be said to express anything, for he had no manner, but his voice was the voice of a shy undergraduate, while his clothes, Edith thought, suggested a combination of a bushranger and a conjuror. His tie, evidently new, was a marvel, a sort of true-lover's knot of red patterned with green, strange beyond description. He seemed terrified.

'How very kind of you to come and see me,' she said in her sweetest voice, 'and these lovely flowers! They quite brighten one up.'

'I'm glad you think they're all right,' said Raggett in a low voice.

'They're beautiful. Fancy your plucking them all yourself! Where did you find these lovely lilies growing? I always fancied they were hot-house plants.'

'Oh, I was bicycling,' Raggett said. 'I just saw them, you know. I thought you might like them. How is Ottley?'

'Bruce is very well. Haven't you seen him lately?'

'Not very. I've been working so fearfully hard,' he said; 'at the British Museum chiefly. One doesn't run up against Bruce there much.'

'No. I suppose he hardly ever goes.'

There was a pause.

'Won't you have some tea?' asked Edith.

'No, thank you. I never take it.'

And there was another silence.

Just as Edith was rather at a loss, and was beginning a sentence with—

' Have you been—' he at the same time said—

' Do you know—?'

' I beg your pardon,' said Edith.

' Oh, I beg yours.'

' Do say what you were going to say.'

' Oh, please finish your sentence.'

' I wasn't going to say anything.'

' Nor was I.'

' I was going to ask you if you'd been to the Savoy again lately?'

' No; I've only been there once in my life. It was a great event for me, Mrs Ottley.'

' Really?'

He spoke with more confidence, but in a still lower voice.

' Yes. I met my ideal there.'

He fixed on her an ardent but respectful glare.

She smiled.

' I'm afraid,' continued Raggett, ' that I'm not amusing you much. I suppose you're very fond of wit and gaiety? I wasn't brought up in a very humorous atmosphere. I don't think I ever heard a joke till quite recently.'

Edith laughed.

' My father,' he went on, ' used sometimes to say at night. " Now it's time for Bedfordshire," but I wasn't amused at that after ten years old. My family are really very serious as a whole. I should never dream of asking them even a riddle, because I'm sure they would give it up at once.'

' Did you say you heard one joke recently? What was it?' asked Edith.

Raggett blushed and looked down.

' I'm very sorry, but I'm afraid I can't tell you, Mrs Ottley. Not that I forget it, but it isn't suited to your—well, to your atmosphere ' —he looked round the room.

' Oh! Can't you *arrange* it?'

' Impossible,' he said firmly. ' Quite impossible.'

' Oh well, of course—'

'Impossible,' he repeated, shaking his head.

'Do you go much to the theatre?' she asked conversationally.

'Never. It would interfere with my work.'

'What is your work, exactly?' she asked, with polite interest.

'It's difficult to explain, Mrs Ottley. It takes a great many forms.'

'Oh, yes.'

'Just at this moment I'm a Legitimist—you understand, don't you? We drink to Queen Mary over the water—and put violets on the statue of King Charles the Martyr in February, and so forth.'

'Ah. That must be very hard work.'

'Oh, it isn't only that—I'm a kind of Secretary, you see, to the Society.'

'Really? Really? What fun it must be; I mean how interesting. Can I belong?'

'Oh, dear yes, of course, Mrs Ottley. If you liked.'

'What should I have to do?'

'Well, first of all you would have to pay a shilling.'

'Yes?'

'And then you would be eligible for a year's probation.'

'And what should we do after that?'

'Well, after that, you see, we shall have to bide our time.'

'That doesn't sound very hard,' said Edith thoughtfully. 'Just to pay a shilling and bide your time.'

'I'll send you some papers about it, if you really take any interest.'

'Thanks. Thanks, very much. Yes, do send them.'

'Do you really think you would care to become a member, Mrs Ottley?'

'Oh, yes; yes, I should think so. I always hated Oliver Cromwell.' He looked doubtful.

'Yes, of course—but that alone, I'm afraid, would hardly be . . . you see there might be a revolution at any moment.'

'I see. But—excuse my asking you, what has that to do with the British Museum?'

'I can hardly tell you off-hand like this, Mrs Ottley; but if you let me come again one day—'

'Oh, certainly, do—do come again.'

'Then I'll say good-bye for today,' said Raggett, with an admiring look. 'I—I hope I haven't trespassed on your valuable—'

'Oh, no; not in the least.'

'I've enjoyed our talk so much,' said Raggett, lingering.

'So have I, Mr Raggett. It has been most interesting.'

'I—I felt,' said Raggett, now standing up and looking very shy, I somehow felt at once that there was a kind of—may I say, sympathy?'

'Quite so.'

'Yes? Well, give my kind regards to Ottley, and thank you so much.'

They shook hands, she rang the bell, and he rushed out as if he was in a violent hurry, leaving Edith rather bewildered.

At dinner that evening Edith said—

'Fancy, Bruce, Raggett called today!'

Bruce dropped his spoon in the soup and looked up.

'*Raggett*? He—do you mean to say he came here?'

'Yes. He paid a visit. Why shouldn't he?'

'I don't know, but it seems a very odd thing. He never pays visits. What did he seem to think of the flat?'

'He didn't say. He talked about his work.'

'What did you think of him?' asked Bruce.

'He seemed very vague. He's very good-natured; fancy his sending me all those flowers!'

'He sent you flowers?' said Bruce slowly. '*Raggett!*'

'Surely you don't mind?'

Bruce waited a minute and said, 'We'll talk it over after dinner.'

There was an uneasy pause; then Edith said—

'I saw Hyacinth today. She had just had a visit from Lady Cannon.'

Bruce looked rather guilty and uncomfortable.

'I like Lady Cannon,' he said presently. 'She's a woman of sound sense. She has a very strong feeling of responsibility about Hyacinth.'

'Yes.' Edith and Hyacinth had arranged not to say any more, as it would be useless.

'A very discreet woman, too,' continued Bruce. 'And what news about Hyacinth?'

'None, I think. She seems very happy.'

'Happy! *That* can't last.'

After dinner Bruce followed Edith into the drawing-room, looked angrily at the flowers and said—

'Now what's the meaning of all this? Mind, I'm not jealous. It isn't my nature to be. What I dislike is being made a fool of. If I thought that Raggett, after all I've done for him—'

'Oh, Bruce! How can you be so absurd? A poor harmless creature—'

'Harmless creature, indeed! I think it extremely marked, calling on you when I was out.'

'He didn't know you were out. It's the usual time to pay a visit, and he really came just to ask me to belong to the Society.'

'I don't call Raggett a society man.'

'He's a secret-society man,' said Edith. 'He wants me to be a Legitimist.'

'Now I won't have any nonsense of that sort here,' said Bruce, striking the table with his fist. 'Goodness knows where it will end. That sort of thing takes women away from the natural home duties, and I disapprove of it strongly. Why, he'll soon be asking you to be a Suffragette! I think I shall write to Raggett.'

'Oh, would you, really?'

'I shall write to him,' repeated Bruce, 'and tell him that I won't have these constant visits and marked attentions. I shall say you complained to me. Yes, that's the dignified way, and I shall request him to keep his secret societies to himself, and not to try to interfere with the peace and harmony of a happy English home.'

He drew some writing-paper towards him.

'I'm sure he didn't mean the slightest harm. He thought it was the proper thing, after dining with us.'

'But it isn't like the man, Edith! It isn't Raggett! He's no slave to convention; don't think it. I can't help fancying that there must have been some ulterior motive. It seems to me sinister—that's the word—sinister.'

'Would you think it sinister if he never came again?'

'Well, perhaps not, but in allowing this to pass—isn't it the thin end of the wedge?'

'Give him a chance and see,' she said. 'Don't be in a hurry.

After all, he's your great friend. You're always talking to me about him; and what's he done?—sent a few flowers and called here once. I'm sure he thought you would like it.'

'But don't you see, Edith, the attention should have been paid to me, not to you.'

'He could hardly send you flowers, Bruce. I'm sure he thought it was the proper thing.'

Bruce walked up and down the room greatly agitated.

'I admit that this is a matter that requires consideration. I shouldn't like to make a mountain out of a mole-hill. We'll see; we'll give him a chance. But if he comes here again, or takes any step to persuade you to have anything to do with his Society or whatever it is, I shall know how to act.'

'Of course you will, dear.'

Edith hoped she wouldn't receive a large envelope full of papers about the Legitimists by the first post.

'I hope you know, Bruce, *I* shouldn't care if I never saw him again.'

'Why not? Because he's my friend, I suppose? You look down on him just because he's a hard worker, and of some use in the world—not a dandified, conventional, wasp-waisted idiot like Cecil Reeve! Perhaps you prefer Cecil Reeve?'

'Much,' replied Edith firmly.

'Why? Let's hear your reasons.'

'Why, he's a real person. I know where I am when I'm talking to him—we're on the same platform.'

'Platform?'

'Yes. When I talk to Mr Raggett I feel as if he had arrived at Victoria, and I had gone to meet him at Charing Cross. Do you see? We don't get near enough to understand each other.'

'Quite near enough,' replied Bruce suspiciously. Then he said, 'I feel the want of air. If you don't mind, dear, I think I shall go for a stroll.'

'Oh, don't!'

He went to the hall and put on his coat.

'Just a stroll; or I may look in at the club. You don't understand; a man feels rather cramped in these surroundings, Edith.'

'I quite understand your feeling.'

'I shan't be long,' said Bruce. 'Try and make up your mind to give up Raggett's society altogether. You don't mind making this sacrifice for me, do you?'

'Not in the least,' she answered. 'I prefer it.'

He went out.

CHAPTER XVI

Archie

I t was Sunday afternoon, and Bruce, lunch still pervading his consciousness, found himself reading over and over again and taking a kind of stupefied interest in the 'Answers to Correspondents' in a certain Sunday paper, and marvelling at the mine of extraordinary miscellaneous information possessed by the person who answered them.

'Brief replies:—

'To *Miserable Alfred* (Baldness).—If you comply with the rules, will send private advice.

'*Knutford* (For knee trouble).—My advice is against.' (Bruce vaguely thought this rather harsh. If Knutford liked knee trouble, why shouldn't he have it?)

'*Alter Ego* (Tomato culture).—There's no need to soak the seeds for days. The man who sows in wet soil and then treads down flat foredooms himself to complete failure. This is, however, nothing to go by. If seed be purchased let it be from a trustworthy firm. Personally, I think in the case of outdoor tomatoes the middle course is best.

'*Worried* (Photography).—To avoid curling. The chief trouble with reel films is their tendency to curl. In any case the film should be allowed to soak for five minutes, and I need not dwell upon other methods of treating the latter kind. All my remarks on plate development, etc., apply equally to cut films, as I should almost have thought 'Worried' would have gathered by now.

'*True Blue* (Egg-preserving).—We quite understand your desire to make more headway than you can in a south-coast watering-place ...'

At this moment Edith came in. Bruce looked up a little annoyed at the interruption. He was becoming quite absorbed in the egg-preserving case on the south coast, and morbidly anxious to know what would happen next.

'Bruce, I wonder if you'd do me a very great favour? It really isn't difficult. I've allowed nurse to go out and Bennett is busy, and I wanted to fly over just for a minute or two to see Hyacinth. She telephoned to me. I shouldn't be gone more than twenty minutes.'

'Of course, go. Do go. I don't want you. I'm very busy.'

He took up the paper again.

'It isn't that; but *would* you very much mind looking after Archie while I'm gone? He'll be perfectly good. I'll give him his box of toys, and he'll sit in the corner over there and you'll never notice he's there till I'm back again.'

'Of course, of course. Surely I'm capable of looking after my own son. Do go.'

'Yes, Bruce dear. And if he asks for anything just nod and smile and don't give it to him, and he'll be all right.'

'Oh, don't worry.'

As she was going out he called out—

'And I say, Edith, just give him a hint that I've got some rather important work to do, and he mustn't interrupt me by asking foolish questions.'

'Yes, oh yes. I'm so glad to think you're so sensible, and not ridiculously nervous of having to look after the child.'

'Nervous? What rot! I never heard such nonsense. I say, Edith, what's the doctor's address? In case he has a fit, or anything.'

'Oh, Bruce! As if he would *dream* of having a fit! I shan't give you the address. You'd be telephoning to him on the chance. Good gracious, don't make such a fuss! I shall only be gone a few minutes.'

'I'm not making a fuss. It's you. Fancy thinking it necessary to tell me not to give him what he asks for! As if I should.'

He returned to his paper, and Edith brought in the little boy.

He gave his father a keen glance from under his smooth, fair fringe and sat down in front of the box of toys.

As soon as Edith had gone he held out a card to his father, and said—

'E for efalunt.'

Bruce frowned, nodded, waved his hand, and went on reading.

He had lost the thread of the Egg Question, but became equally absorbed in the following problem.

'*Disheartened.*—You must make a quiet but determined stand against such imposition. It does not follow because you walked out with a young man two or three times, and he now walks out with your friend instead, that . . .'

' X for swordfish,' said Archie, holding out another card.

' Don't talk, Archie.'

' I've got my best suit on,' said Archie.

' Yes.'

' What I was photographed in.'

' Don't talk, old chap. I want to read.'

' This is my bear. It's the same bear.'

' The same bear as what?'

' Why, the same bear! This is a soldier.'

He put the wooden soldier in his mouth, then put it carefully back in the box.

' This is my bear,' said Archie again. ' Just the same bear. That's all.'

Bruce threw away the paper.

' You want to have a talk, eh?' he said.

' This is my best suit,' said Archie. ' Have you any sugar in your pockets?'

' Sugar in my pockets? Who put that into your head?'

' Nobody didn't put it in my head. Don't you put any in your pocket?'

' No. Sugar, indeed! I'm not a parrot.'

Archie roared with laughter.

' You're not a parrot!' he said, laughing loudly. ' Wouldn't it be fun if you was a parrot. I wish you was a parrot.'

' Don't be foolish, Archie.'

' Do parrots keep sugar in their pockets?'

' Don't be silly.'

' Have parrots got pockets?'

' Play with your soldiers, dear.'

' Do parrots have pockets?'

' Don't be a nuisance.'

' Why did you say parrots had sugar in their pockets, then?'

' I never said anything of the kind.'

' What do parrots have pockets for?'

' Do you think your mother will be long?'

' Will mother know about parrots and pockets?'

' You're talking nonsense, Archie. Now be good. Your mother said you would be good.'

' Is it naughty to talk about parrots—with pockets?'

' Yes.'

' Then you're very naughty. You talk about them.'

' Will you stop talking about them if I get you some sugar?' said Bruce, feeling frightfully ashamed of himself, but fearing for his reason if Archie said any more on the subject.

' I'm a good boy. I'll stop talking about parrots if you get me some sugar.'

He put his hand in his father's with a most winning smile.

' I'll show you where it is. It's in the kitchen. It's in the nursery, too, but it's nicer sugar in the kitchen.'

' I oughtn't to give it you. Your mother will be angry.'

' Do parrots have pockets?'

Bruce jumped up and went with the child, and told the cook to give him six lumps of sugar.

She seemed surprised, amused, and doubtful.

' Do as I tell you at once,' Bruce said sternly.

They came back, and Archie was silent and happy until Edith returned.

When she saw traces of sugar on his face and dress she said—

' Oh, Archie! What on earth did your father give you sugar for?'

' For talking about parrots,' said Archie.

CHAPTER XVII

Bruce's Play

'Edith,' said Bruce, 'come in here. I want to speak to you. Shut the door.'

She shut it, and stood waiting.

'Don't stand there. Come and sit down. . . . Now listen to me very seriously. I want to ask you a question.'

'How would you like me to be making about £5,000 a year—at least?'

'Need you ask?'

'And all by my own talent—not by anybody else's help.'

'It would be jolly,' she said, trying not to look doubtful.

'Jolly! I should think it would. Now I'll tell you my scheme—what I've made up my mind to do.'

'What?'

'I'm going to write a play.'

Edith controlled her expression, and said it was a very good idea.

'*Such* a play,' said Bruce. 'A really strong, powerful piece—all wit and cynicism like Bernard Shaw—*but*, full of heart and feeling and sentiment, and that sort of rot. It'll have all sorts of jolly fantastic ideas—like *Peter Pan* and *The Beloved Vagabond*, but without the faults of Locke and Barrie—and it's going to be absolutely realistic and natural in parts—like the Sicilians, you know. However, I don't mind telling you that my model—you must have a model, more or less—*is* going to be Bernard Shaw. I like his style.'

'It's the most lovely idea I ever heard of. What theatre are you going to produce it at?'

'That depends. For some things I should prefer His Majesty's, but I'm rather fond of the Haymarket, too. However, if the terms were better, I might give it to Charlie Hawtrey, or even Alexander, if he offered me exceptionally good royalties.'

' Oh! Are you going to have it put up to auction?'

' Don't talk nonsense. What do you mean? No, I shall simply send a copy round to all the principal people and see what they say.'

He walked up and down the room once or twice.

' The reason I'm so determined not to let Bourchier have it is simply this: he doesn't realise my idea—he never could. Mind you, I believe he would do his best, but his Personality is against him. Do you see, Edith?'

'I see your point. But—'

' There's no reason why it shouldn't be quite as great a success as *The Merry Widow*.'

' Oh, is it going to be a comic opera?'

' Why, of course not. Don't I tell you it's to be a powerful play of real life.'

' Will you tell me the plot?'

He smiled rather fatuously. ' I'll tell you some of the plot, certainly, if you like—at least, I'll tell you how it's going to begin.'

' Do go on!' —

' Well, I must tell you it begins in a rather unconventional way —entirely different from most plays; but that'll make it all the more striking, and I *won't* alter it—mind that—not for anybody. Well, the curtain goes up, and you find two servants—do you see?— talking over their master and mistress. The maid—her name's Parker—is dusting the photographs and things, and she says to the manservant something about " The mistress does seem in a tantrum, doesn't she, Parker?" So he says—'

' But are they both called Parker?' asked Edith.

' Yes—no—of course not. I forgot; it's the man that's called Parker. But that isn't the point. Well, they talk, and gradually let out a little of the plot. Then two friends of the hero come in, and— oh, I can't bother to tell you any more now; but isn't it rather a good idea, eh? So new!'

' Capital! Splendid! Such a lovely original idea. I do wish you'd be quick and do it, Bruce.'

' I am being quick; but you mustn't be in too great a hurry; you must give me time.'

' Will it be ready in time for the season—I mean after Easter?'

' What! in a fortnight? How could they be ready to produce it in a fortnight, especially with the Easter holidays between? It won't be long, that I can promise you. I'm a quick worker.'

He waited a minute, and then said—

'You mustn't be depressed, Edith dear, if I get a little slating from some of the critics, you know. You can't expect them all to appreciate a new writer at once. And it really won't make any difference to the success if my play pleases the public, which I don't mind telling you I know it's sure to do; because, you see, it'll have all the good points and none of the bad ones of all the successful plays of the last six years. That's my dodge. That's how I do it.'

'I see.'

'Won't it be a joke when the governor and the mater are there on the first night? They'll be frightfully pleased. You must try and prevent the mater swaggering about it too much, you know. She's such a dear, she's sure to be absurdly proud of it. And it'll be a bit of a score off the governor in a way, too. He never would have thought I could do it, would he? And Raggett will be surprised, too. You must have a ripping new dress for the first night, Edith, old girl.'

'I think I shall have Liberty satin, dear—that new shade of blue —it wears better than Nattier. But I won't order it just yet. You haven't written the first scene, have you?'

'The first scene? No! Plays aren't done like that. The chief thing about a play like this is to get a scenario.'

'Oh! Isn't that where the people sit?'

'Don't be ridiculous! You're thinking of the auditorium. I mean the skeleton of the play. That's what I shall send round to the managers. They can see what it's going to be like at once.'

'How many acts will it be?'

'Four.'

'And have you settled on the name?'

'Yes, as a matter of fact I have settled on a name; but don't you go giving it away. It's rather an original name. It would do if I developed the comedy interest just the same and just as well as if I made the chief point the tragic part. It's going to be called *You Never Know*. Good name, isn't it?'

'It's a splendid name. But isn't it a tiny bit like something else?'

'How unsympathetic you are! The fact is you don't understand. That's what it is.'

' Oh, I do sympathise immensely, Bruce, and I'm sure you'll have a great success. What fun it will be! Are you going to work at it this afternoon?'

' Why, no! not *this* afternoon. I'm rather tired out with thinking. I think I shall go and look in at the club.'

CHAPTER XVIII

Hyacinth Waits

'H E ' s coming this afternoon, Anne,' Hyacinth said. ' See that I'm really alone today—I mean that I'm out to everyone.'

' You think, then, that he really will propose today?'

' Don't be so horribly explicit. Don't you think his having to go the other day—because of Lady Cannon—would lead to a sort of crisis? I mean, either he wouldn't come here again, or else—'

' I suppose it would,' said Anne. ' At least, it would if he had some glimmering of his own intentions. But he's in such a very undecided state.'

' Well, don't let's worry about his intentions. At any rate, he's coming to see me. The question is, what shall I wear?'

' It doesn't matter in the least. You attach a ridiculous amount of importance to dress.'

' Perhaps; but I must wear *something*. So what shall it be?'

' Well, if you want to look prepared for a proposal—so as to give him a sort of hint—you'd better wear your pale mauve dress. It's becoming, and it looks festive and spring-like.'

' Oh, Anne! Why, it's ever so much too smart! It would be quite ridiculous. Just like you, advising pale mauve *crêpe de Chine* and Irish lace for a quiet visit in the afternoon from a friend!'

' Oh! all right. Then wear your blue tailor-made dress—and the little boots with the cloth tops.'

' Oh, good heavens, Anne! I'm not going for a bicycle ride. Because I'm not got up for a garden-party, it doesn't follow I must be dressed for mountain-climbing. Cecil hates sensible-looking clothes.'

' Then I should think anything you've got would do. Or do you want to get a new dress?'

' Of course I want to get a new dress, but not for this afternoon. It wouldn't be possible. Besides, I don't think it's a good plan to wear something different every time you see a person. It looks so extravagant.'

' Wear your black and white, then.'

' No, it isn't *intime* enough, and the material's too rough—it's a hard dress.'

' Oh! Funny, I had the impression you had more clothes than you knew what to do with, and you don't seem to have anything fit to wear.'

' Why, of course, I shall wear my blue voile. How on earth could I wear anything else? How silly you are, Anne!'

' Well, if you knew that all the time, why did you ask me?'

' Are there plenty of flowers in the studio?'

' Yes; but I'll get some more if you like.'

' No, no; don't have too many. It looks too *arranged*.'

She looked at the clock.

' It won't be five just yet,' said Anne. ' It's only eleven.'

' Yes; that's the awful part. What on earth shall I do till then?'

' Whatever I suggested you would do the reverse.'

' Shall I go for a long drive in the motor?'

' That's a good idea.'

' But it's a very windy day, and I might get neuralgia—not feel up to the mark.'

' So you might. I think, perhaps, the best thing for you would be to have your hair waved.'

' How can I sit still to have my hair waved? Besides, it makes it look too stiff—like a hairdresser's dummy.'

' Ah! there is that. Then why not do something useful—go and be manicured?'

' I'm afraid I shouldn't have the patience today.'

' I suppose what you'd really like,' said Anne, ' would be to see Edith Ottley.'

' No, I shouldn't. Not till tomorrow. I don't want to see anybody,' said Hyacinth.

' Well, all right. I'm going out.'

' Oh, but I can't bear to be alone.'

' Then I scarcely see . . .'

' This afternoon especially, Anne. You must stay with me till about a quarter of an hour before I expect him. The horrible agony of waiting is so frightful! It makes me feel so ill. But I don't want you to stay beyond the time I expect him, in case he's late. Because then I suffer so much that I couldn't bear you to see it.'

' I see. How jolly it must be to be in love! You *do* seem to have a good time.'

' When one has the slightest hope, Anne, it's simply too awful. Of course, if one hasn't, one bears it.'

' And if one has no encouragement, I suppose one gets over it?'

' I have a presentiment that everything will be all right today,' said Hyacinth. ' Is that a bad sign?'

' There are no good signs, in your present state,' answered Anne.

It was about half-past four, and Hyacinth in the blue dress, was sitting in the studio, where she could see both the window and the clock. Anne, by the fire, was watching her.

' You seem very fairly calm, Hyacinth.'

' I am calm,' she said. ' I am; quite calm. Except that my heart is beating so fast that I can hardly breathe, that I have horrible kinds of shivers and a peculiar feeling in my throat, I'm quite all right. Now, just fancy if I had to pretend I wasn't in suspense! If I had no-one to confide in! . . . Do you think he's mistaken the day? Do you think he thinks it's Thursday instead of Tuesday?'

' That's not likely.'

' I'm glad I feel so cool and calm. How ashamed I should be if he ever knew that I was so agitated!'

' Who knows, perhaps he's feeling as uncomfortable as you are?'

' Oh, no, no! There's no hope of that. . . . Will he telephone and put it off, do you think, at the last minute?'

' I shouldn't think so.'

' Are there any little pink cakes?'

' Heaps. Far more than will ever be eaten.'

' Now, don't talk to me, Anne. I'm going to read for a quarter of an hour.'

She took up a novel and read two pages, then looked up at the clock and turned pale.

' It's five. Is that clock fast?'

' No; listen, the church clock's striking. Good-bye.'

Anne went, and Hyacinth kissed her hand to her and arranged her hair in the mirror. She then sat down and resolved to be perfectly quiet.

Ten minutes slowly ticked away, then Hyacinth went to the

window, saying to herself that it was an unlucky thing to do. She
did not remain there long, then walked round and round the room.
Several cabs passed, each of which she thought was going to stop.
Then she sat down again, looking cool and smiling, carelessly holding a book. . . . Each time the cab passed. It was half-past five,
rather late under the circumstances. She was angry. She resolved to
be very cold to him when he first came in, or—no, she wouldn't be
cold, she would pretend she didn't know he was late—hadn't noticed
it; or she would chaff him about it, and say she would never wait
again. She took the letter from her pocket and read it again. It
said : —

'DEAR MISS VERNEY,
    'May I come and see you at five o'clock tomorrow afternoon?
                    'Yours,
                        'CECIL REEVE.'

Its very brevity had shown it was something urgent, but perhaps
he would come to break off their friendship; since the awkwardness
of Lady Cannon's visit, he must have been thinking that things
couldn't go on like this. Then she began to recapitulate details,
arguing to herself with all the cold, hard logic of passion.

At Lord Selsey's afternoon she had given herself away by her
anger, by the jealousy she showed, and had told him never to come
and see her again. Immediately after that had been their meeting
at the National Gallery, where Cecil had followed her and sought
her out. Then they had those two delightful walks in Kensington
Gardens, in which he had really seemed to ' like ' her so much. Then
the pleasant intimate little lunch, after which Lady Cannon had
called. . . . In the course of these meetings he had told her that he
and Mrs Raymond had quarrelled, that she would never see him
again. She had felt that he was drifting to her. . . . How strangely
unlike love affairs in books hers had been! In all respectable novels
it was the man who fell in love first. No-one knew by experience
better than Hyacinth how easily that might happen, how very often
it did. But she, who was proud, reserved, and a little shy with all
her expansiveness, had simply fallen hopelessly in love with him
at first sight. It was at that party at the Burlingtons. She realised
now that she had practically thought of nothing else since. Probably she was spoilt, for she had not foreseen any difficulty; she

had had always far more admirers than she cared for, and her
difficulties had usually been in trying to get rid of them. He
seemed to like her, but that was all. Mrs Raymond was, of course,
the reason, but Mrs Raymond was over. She looked up at the clock
again.

Ten minutes to six. Perhaps he had made it up with Mrs Raymond? . . . For the next ten minutes she suffered extraordinary
mental tortures, then her anger consoled her a little. He had treated
her too rudely! It was amazing—extraordinary! He was not worth
caring for. At any rate, it showed he didn't care for her. . . . If it
was some unavoidable accident, couldn't he have telephoned or
telegraphed? . . . No; it was one of those serious things that one
can only write about. He was with Mrs Raymond, she felt sure of
that. But Mrs Raymond didn't like him. . . . Perhaps, after all, he
had only been detained in some extraordinary way, she might hear
directly. . . .

She went up to her room, and was slightly consoled for the
moment to find the clock there five minutes slower than the one
in the drawing-room. She again arranged her hair and went into
the hall, where she found two or three cards of people who had
called, and been told she was out—an irritating detail—for nothing!
Then she went back to the studio.

Even to be in the place where she had been waiting for him was
something, it gave her a little illusion that he would be here again.
. . . Could he really be an hour and a quarter late? It was just
possible.

She heard a ring. Every sign of anxiety disappeared from her face.
She was beaming, and got back into the old attitude, holding the
book. She could hear her heart beating while there was some parley
in the hall. Unable to bear it any more, she opened the door. It
was someone with a parcel.

'What is it?'

'It's only the new candle-shades, miss. Shall I bring them in for
you to see?'

'No, thank you. . . .'

Candle-shades!

She put her hands over her eyes and summoned all her pride.
Probably the very butler and her maid knew perfectly well she had
been waiting at home alone for Mr Reeve. She cared absolutely

nothing what they thought; but she felt bitter, revengeful to him. It was cruel.

Why did she care so much? She remembered letters and scenes with other people—people whose sufferings about her she felt always inclined to laugh at. She couldn't believe in it. Love in books had always seemed to her, although intensely interesting, just a trifle absurd. She couldn't realise it till now.

Another ring. Perhaps it was he after all! . . .

The same position. The book, the bright blue eyes. . . .

The door opened; Anne came in. It was striking seven o'clock.

CHAPTER XIX

Eugenia

MEANWHILE Cecil had received a note from his uncle, asking him to go and see him. He decided he would do so on his way to see Hyacinth.

For many days now he had not seen Mrs Raymond. She had answered no letters, and been always ' out ' to him.

As he walked along, he wondered what had become of her, and tried to think he didn't care.

' I have news for you, Cecil,' said his uncle; ' but, first, you really have made up your mind, haven't you, to try your luck with Hyacinth? What a pretty perfumed name it is—just like her.'

' I suppose I shall try.'

' Good. I'm delighted to hear it. Then in a very short time I shall hear that you're as happy as I am.'

' As you, Uncle Ted?'

' Look at this house, Cecil. It's full of Things; it wants looking after. I want looking after. . . . I am sure you wouldn't mind—wouldn't be vexed to hear I was going to marry again?'

' Rather not. I'm glad. It must be awfully lonely here sometimes. But I am surprised, I must say. Everybody looks upon you as a confirmed widower, Uncle Ted.'

' Well, so I have been a confirmed widower—for eighteen years. I think that's long enough.'

Cecil waited respectfully.

Then his uncle said abruptly—

' I saw Mrs Raymond yesterday.'

Cecil started and blushed.

' Did you? Where did you meet her?'

' I didn't meet her. I went to see her. I spent two hours with her.'

Cecil stared in silent amazement.

' It was my fourth visit,' said Lord Selsey.

' You spent all that time talking over my affairs?'

His uncle gave a slight smile. 'Indeed not, Cecil. After the first few minutes of the first visit, frankly, we said very little about you.'

'But I don't understand.'

'I've been all this time trying to persuade her to something— against her judgement. I've been trying to persuade her to marry.'

'To marry me?'

'No. To marry me. And I've succeeded.'

'I congratulate you,' said Cecil, in a cold, hard voice.

'You're angry, my boy. It's very natural; but let me explain to you how it happened.'

He paused, and then went on: 'Of course, for years I've wished for the right woman here. But I never saw her. I thought I never should. That day she came here—the musical party—the moment I looked at her, I saw that she was meant for me, not for you.'

'I call it a beastly shame,' said Cecil.

'It isn't. It's absolutely right. You know perfectly well she never would have cared for you in the way you wished.'

Cecil could not deny that, but he said sarcastically—

'So you fell in love with her at first sight?'

'Oh no, I didn't. I'm not in love with her now. But I think she's beautiful. I mean she has a beautiful soul—she has atmosphere, she has something that I need. I could live in the same house with her in perfect harmony for ever. I could teach her to understand my Things. She does already by instinct.'

'You're marrying her as a kind of custodian for your collection?'

'A great deal, of course. And, then, I couldn't marry a young girl. It would be ridiculous. A society woman—a regular beauty— would jar on me and irritate me. She would think herself more important than my pictures.'

Cecil could hardly help a smile, angry as he was.

'And Mrs Raymond,' went on Lord Selsey, 'is delightfully un-worldly—and yet sensible. Of course, she's not a bit in love with me either. But she likes me awfully, and I persuaded her. It was all done by argument.'

'I could never persuade her,' said Cecil bitterly.

'Of course not. She has such a sense of form. She saw the in-congruity. . . . I needn't ask you to forgive me, old boy. I know, of course, there's nothing to forgive. You've got over your fancy, or you will very soon. I haven't injured you in any sort of way, and I didn't take her away from you. She's ten years older than you, and nine years younger than me. . . . You're still my heir just the same. This will make no difference, and you'll soon be reconciled. I'm sure of that.'

'Of course, I'm not such a brute as not to be glad, for her,' said Cecil slowly, after a slight struggle. 'It seems a bit rough, though, at first.' He held out his hand.

'Thanks, dear old boy. You see I'm right. You can't be angry with me. . . . You see it's a peculiar case. It won't be like an ordinary marriage, a young married couple and so on, nor a *mariage de convenance*, either, in the ordinary sense. Here are two lonely people intending to live solitary lives. Suddenly, you—*most* kindly, I must say—introduce us. I, with my great experience and my instinctive *flair*, see immediately that this is the right woman in the right place. I bother her until she consents—and there you are.'

'I hope you'll be happy.'

They shook hands in silence, and Cecil got into a hansom and drove straight to Mrs Raymond's. He was furious.

While Hyacinth, whose very existence he had forgotten in the shock and anger of this news, was feeling, with the agonising clairvoyance of love, that Cecil was with Mrs Raymond, she was perfectly right.

Today Eugenia was at home, and did not refuse to see him.

'I see you know,' she remarked coolly as he came in.

Cecil had controlled his emotion when with his uncle, but seeing Mrs Raymond again in the dismal little old drawing-room dealt him a terrible blow. He saw, only too vividly, the picture of his suave, exquisite uncle, standing out against this muddled, confused background, in the midst of decoration which was one long disaster and furniture that was one desperate failure. To think that the owner of Selsey House had spent hours here! The thought was jealous agony.

'I must congratulate you,' he said coldly.

'Thank you, Cecil.'

'I thought you were never going to marry again?' he said sarcastically.

'I never do, as a rule. But this is an exception. And it isn't going to be like an ordinary marriage. We shall each have complete freedom. He persuaded me—to look after that lovely house. It will give me an object in life. And besides, Cecil,' she was laughing, ' think—to be your aunt! The privilege!'

He seized her by the shoulders. She laughed still more, and put one hand on the bell, at which he released her. He walked away so violently that he knocked down a screen.

' There, that will do,' said Eugenia, picking it up. ' You've made your little scene, and shown your little temper, and that's enough. Sit down,' she commanded.

Cecil sat down, feeling a complete fool.

' Look here. I daresay that it's a little annoying for you, at first, especially as you introduced us; but really, when you come to think it over, there's no law of etiquette, or any other that I know of, which compels me to refuse the uncle of a young man who has done me the honour to like me. Oh, Cecil, don't be absurd!'

' Are you in love with him?'

' No. But I think he will be very pleasant—not worrying and fidgeting—so calm and kind. I refused at first, Cecil. People always want what they can't get, and if it's any satisfaction to you, I don't mind confessing that I have had, for years, a perfect mania for somebody else. A hopeless case for at least three reasons: he's married, he's in love with someone else (not even counting his wife, who counts a great deal) and, if he hadn't either of these preoccupations, he would never look at me. So I've given it up. I've made up my mind to forget it. Your uncle will help me, and give me something else to think about.'

' Who was the man?' Cecil asked. It was some slight satisfaction to know that she also had had a wasted affection.

' Why should I tell you? I shall not tell you. Well, I will tell you. It's Sir Charles Cannon.'

' Old Cannon?'

' Yes; it was a sort of mad hero-worship. I never could account for it. I always thought him the most wonderful person. He hasn't the faintest idea of it, and never will; and now don't let's speak of him again.'

The name reminded Cecil of Hyacinth. He started violently, remembering his appointment. What must she have thought of him?

' Good-bye, Eugenia,' he said.

As he held her hand he felt, in a sense, as if it was in some strange way, after all, a sort of triumph for him, a score that Lord Selsey had appreciated her so wonderfully.

As he left the house it struck seven. What was he to do about Hyacinth?

That evening Hyacinth received a large basket of flowers and a letter, in which Cecil threw himself on her mercy, humbling himself to the earth, and imploring her to let him come and explain and apologise next day. He entreated her to be kind enough to let him off waiting till a conventional hour, and to allow him to call in the morning.

He received a kind, forgiving answer, and then spent the most miserable night of his life.

CHAPTER XX

Bruce has Influenza

A L L women love news of whatever kind; even bad news gives them merely a feeling of pleasurable excitement, unless it is something that affects them or those they love personally.

Edith was no exception to the rule, but she knew that Bruce, on the contrary, disliked it; if it were bad he was angry and said it served the people right, while if it were good he thought they didn't deserve it and disapproved strongly. Bruce spent a great deal of his time and energy in disapproving; generally of things and people that were no concern of his. As is usually the case, this high moral attitude was caused by envy. Bruce would have been much surprised to hear it, but envy was the keynote of his character, and he saw everything that surrounded him through its vague mist.

All newspapers made him furious. He regarded everything in them as a personal affront; from the fashionable intelligence, describing political dinners in Berkeley Square or dances in Curzon Street, where he thought he should have been present in the important character of host, to notices of plays—plays which he felt he could have written so well. Even sensational thefts irritated him; perhaps he unconsciously fancied that the stolen things (Crown jewels, and so forth) should by rights have been his, and that he would have known how to take care of them. 'Births, Marriages, and Deaths' annoyed him intensely. If he read that Lady So-and-So had twin sons, the elder of whom would be heir to the title and estates, he was disgusted to think of the injustice that he hadn't a title and estates for Archie to inherit, and he mentally held the newly-arrived children very cheap, feeling absolutely certain that they would compare most unfavourably with his boy, excepting, of course, in the accident of their worldly circumstances. Also, although he was proud of having married, and fond of Edith, descriptions of 'Society Weddings of the Week' drove him absolutely wild— wild to think that he and Edith, who deserved it, hadn't had an

Archbishop, choirboys, guardsmen with crossed swords to walk under, and an amethyst brooch from a member of the Royal Family at their wedding. New discoveries in science pained him, for he knew that he would have thought of them long before, and carried them out much better, had he only had the time.

Bruce had had influenza, and when Edith came in with her news, she could not at once make up her mind to tell him, fearing his anger.

He was lying on the sofa with the paper, grumbling at the fuss made about the Sicilian players, of whom he was clearly jealous.

She sat down by his side and agreed with him.

' I'm much worse since you went out. You know the usual results of influenza, don't you? Heart failure, or nervous depression liable to lead to suicide.'

' But you're much better, dear. Dr Braithwaite said it was wonderful how quickly you threw it off.'

' Threw it off! Yes, but that's only because I have a marvellous constitution and great will-power. If I happened to have had less strength and vitality, I might easily have been dead by now. I wish you'd go and fetch me some cigarettes, dear. I have none left.'

She got up and went to the door.

' What are you fidgeting about, Edith?' said he. ' *Can't* you keep still? It's not at all good for a convalescent to have a restless person with him.'

' Why, I was only going to fetch—'

' I know you were; but you should learn repose, dear. First you go out all the morning, and when you come home you go rushing about the room.'

She sat down again and decided to tell him.

' You'll be glad to hear,' she said, ' that Hyacinth and Cecil Reeve are engaged. They are to be married in the autumn.'

Guessing she expected him to display interest, he answered irritably—

' I don't care.' It has nothing to do with me.'

' No, of course not.'

' I never heard anything so idiotic as having a wedding in the autumn. A most beastly time, I think—November fogs.'

' I heard something else,' said Edith, ' which surprised me much more. Fancy, Lord Selsey's going to be married—to Mrs Raymond. Isn't that extraordinary?'

'Lord Selsey—a widower! Disgusting! I thought he pretended to be so fond of his first wife.'

'He was, dear, I believe. But she died eighteen years ago, and—'

'Instead of telling me all this tittle-tattle it would be much better if you did as I asked you, Edith, and fetched me the cigarettes. I've asked you several times. Of course I don't want to make a slave of you. I'm not one of those men who want their wives to be a drudge. But, after all, they're only in the next room. It isn't a *very* hard task! And I'm very weak, or I'd go myself.'

She ran out and brought them back before he could stop her again.

'Who is this Mrs Raymond?' he then asked.

'Oh, she's a very nice woman—a widow. Really quite suitable in age to Lord Selsey. Not young. She's not a bit pretty and not in his set at all. He took the most violent fancy to her at first sight, it seems. She had vowed never to marry again, but he persuaded her.'

'Well,' said Bruce, striking a match, 'they didn't consult me! They must go their own way. I'm sorry for them, of course. Lord Selsey always seemed to me a very agreeable chap, so it seems rather a pity. At the same time, I suppose it's a bad thing—in the worldly sense—for Reeve, and *that's* satisfactory.'

'Oh! I think he's all right, said Edith, and she smiled thoughtfully.

'You're always smiling, Edith,' he complained. 'Particularly when I have something to annoy me.'

'Am I? I believe I read in the "Answers to Correspondents" in *Home Chirps* that a wife should always have a bright smile if her husband seemed depressed.'

'Good heavens! How awful! Why, it would be like living with a Cheshire cat!'

Edith warmly began to defend herself from the accusation, when Bruce stopped her by saying that his temperature had gone up, and asking her to fetch the clinical thermometer.

Having snatched it from her and tried it, he turned pale and said in a hollow voice—

'Telephone to Braithwaite. At once. Say it's urgent. Poor little Edith!'

' What is it?' she cried in a frightened voice.

' I'd better not tell you,' he said, trying to hide it.

' Tell me—oh! tell me!'

' It's a hundred and nineteen. Now don't waste time. You meant no harm, dear, but you worried and excited me. It isn't your fault. Don't blame yourself. Of course, you *would* do it.'

' Oh, I know what it is,' cried Edith. ' I dipped it in boiling water before I gave it to you.'

' Idiot! You might have broken it!' said Bruce.

The explanation seemed to annoy him very much; nevertheless he often referred afterwards to the extraordinary way his temperature used to jump about, which showed what a peculiarly violent, virulent, dangerous form of influenza he had had, and how wonderful it was he had thrown it off, in spite of Edith's inexperienced, not to say careless, nursing, entirely by his own powerful will and indomitable courage.

CHAPTER XXI

' Engaged '

LADY CANNON sat in her massive, florid clothes, that always seemed part of her massive, florid furniture, and to have the same expression of violent, almost ominous conventionality, without the slightest touch of austerity to tone it down. Her throat and figure seemed made solely to show off dog-collars and long necklaces; her head seemed constructed specially for the wearing of a dark red royal fringe and other ornaments. Today she was in her most cheerful and condescending mood, in fact she was what is usually called in a good temper. It was a great satisfaction to her that Hyacinth was at last settled; and she decided to condone the rather wilful way in which the engagement had been finally arranged without reference to her. With the touch of somewhat sickly sentiment common to most hard women, she took great pleasure in a wedding (if it were only moderately a suitable one), and was prepared to be arch and sympathetic with the engaged couple whom she expected today to pay her a formal visit.

She was smiling to herself as she turned a bracelet on her left wrist, and wondered if she and Sir Charles need really run to a tiara, since after all they weren't Hyacinth's parents, and was wishing they could get off with giving her a certain piece of old lace that had been in the family for years, and could never be arranged to wear, when Sir Charles came in.

' Ah, Charles, that's right. I wish you to be here to welcome Hyacinth and her fiancé. I'm expecting them directly.'

' I can't possibly be here,' he said. ' I have a most urgent appointment. I've done all the right things. I've written to them, and gone to see Hyacinth, and we've asked them to dinner. No more is necessary. Of course, let them understand that I—I quite approve, and all that. And I really think that's quite enough.'

He spoke rather irritably.

' Really, Charles, how morose you've grown. One would think you disliked to see young people happy together. I always think it's such a pretty sight. Especially as it's a regular love match.'

' No doubt; no doubt. Charming! But I have an appointment; I must go at once.'

' With whom, may I ask?'

' With St Leonards,' he answered unblushingly.

' Oh! Oh well, of course, they'll understand you couldn't keep the Duke waiting. I'll mention it; I'll explain. I shall see a little more of Hyacinth just now, Charles. It'll be the right thing. An engaged girl ought to be chaperoned by a connection of the family—of some weight. Not a person like that Miss Yeo. I shall arrange to drive out with Hyacinth and advise her about her trousseau, and . . .'

' Yes; do as you like, but spare me the details.'

Lady Cannon sighed.

' Ah, Charles, you have no romance. Doesn't the sight of these happy young people bring back the old days?'

The door shut. Lady Cannon was alone.

' He has no soul,' she said to herself, using a tiny powder-puff.

The young people, as they were now called, had had tea with her in her magnificent drawing-room. She had said and done everything that was obvious, kind, and tedious. She had held Hyacinth's hand, and shaken a forefinger at Cecil, and then she explained to them that it would be much more the right thing now for them to meet at her house, rather than at Hyacinth's—a recommendation which they accepted with complete (apparent) gravity, and in fact she seemed most anxious to take entire possession of them—to get the credit of them, as it were, as a social sensation.

' And now,' she said, ' what do you think I'm going to do? If you won't think me very rude ' (threatening forefinger again), ' I'm going to leave you alone for a little while. I shan't be very long; but I have to write a letter, and so on, and when I come back I shall have on my bonnet, and I'll drive Hyacinth home.'

' It's most awfully kind of you, Auntie, but Cecil's going to drive me back.'

' No, no, no! I insist, I insist! This dear child has been almost like a daughter to me, you know,' pressing a lace-edged little handker-chief, scented with Ess Bouquet, to a dry little eye. ' You mustn't take her away all at once! Will you be very angry if I leave you?' and laughing in what she supposed to be an entirely charming manner, she glided, as though on castors, in her fringed, embroidered, brocaded dress from the room.

' Isn't she magnificent?' said Cecil.

' You know she has a reputation for being remarkable for sound sense,' said Hyacinth.

' Well, she's shown it at last!'

She laughed.

He took a stroll round the room. It was so high, so enormous, with so much satin on the walls, so many looking-glasses, so much white paint, so many cabinets full of Dresden china, that it recalled, by the very extremity of the contrast of its bright hideousness, that other ugly, dismal little room, also filled with false gods, of a cheap and very different kind, in which he had had so much poignant happiness.

' Hyacinth,' he said, rather quaintly, ' do you know what I'm doing? I want to kiss you, and I'm looking for a part of the room in which it wouldn't be blasphemous!'

' You can't find one, Cecil. I couldn't—here. And her leaving us alone makes it all the more impossible.'

The girl was seated on a stiff, blue silk settee, padded and buttoned, and made in a peculiar form in which three people can sit, turning their backs to one another. She leant her sweet face on her hand, her elbow on the peculiar kind of mammoth pin-cushion that at once combined and separated the three seats. (It had been known formerly as a ' lounge '—a peculiarly unsuitable name, as it was practically impossible not to sit in it bolt upright.)

Cecil stood opposite and looked down at her.

Happiness, and the hope of happiness, had given her beauty a different character. There was something touching, troubling about her. It seemed to him that she had everything: beauty, profane and spiritual; deep blue eyes, in which he could read devotion; womanly tenderness, and a flower-like complexion; a perfect figure, and a beautiful soul. He could be proud of her before the world, and he could delight in her in private. She appealed, he thought, to everything in a man—his vanity, his intellect, and his senses. The better he knew her, the more exquisite qualities he found in her. She was sweet, clever, good, and she vibrated to his every look. She was

sensitive, and passionate. She was adorable. He was too fortunate!
Then why did he think of a pale, tired, laughing face, with the hair
dragged off the forehead, and Japanese eyes? . . . What folly!

It was a recurring obsession.

' Cecil, what are you thinking about?'

' Of you.'

' Do you love me? Will you always love me? Are you happy?'

He made no answer, but kissed the questions from her lips, and
from his own heart.

So Lady Cannon, after rattling the handle of the door, came in in
her bonnet, and found them, as she had expected. Then she sent
Cecil away and drove Hyacinth home, talking without ceasing during the drive of bridesmaids, choral services, bishops, travelling-
bags, tea-gowns, and pretty little houses in Mayfair.

Hyacinth did not hear a single word she said, so, as Lady Cannon
answered all her own questions in the affirmative, and warmly
agreed with all her own remarks, she quite enjoyed herself, and
decided that Hyacinth had immensely improved, and that Ella was
to come back for the wedding.

CHAPTER XXII

The Strange Behaviour of Anne

I T was a spring-like, warm-looking, deceptive day, with a bright
sun and a cold east wind.

Anne sat, a queer-looking figure, in an unnecessary mackintosh
and a golf-cap, on a bench in a large open space in Hyde Park,
looking absently at some shabby sheep. She had come here to be
alone, to think. Soon she would be alone as much as she liked—
much more. She had appeared quite sympathetically cheerful, almost
jaunty, since her friend's engagement. She could not bear anyone
to know her real feelings. Hyacinth had been most sweet, warmly
affectionate to her; Cecil delightful. They had asked her to go and
stay with them. Lady Cannon had graciously said, ' I suppose you
will be looking out for another situation now, Miss Yeo?' and others
had supposed she would go back to her father's Rectory, for a time,
at any rate.

Today the wedding had been definitely fixed, and she had come
out to give way to the bitterness of her solitude.

She realised that she had not the slightest affection for anyone
in the world except Hyacinth, and that no-one had any for her, on
anything like the same scale.

Anne was a curious creature. Her own family had always been
absolutely indifferent to her, and from her earliest youth she had
hated and despised all men that she had known. Sir Charles Cannon
was the only human being for whom she felt a little sympathy, instinctively knowing that under all his amiable congratulations he
disliked Hyacinth's marriage almost as much as she did, and in the
same way.

All the strength of her feelings and affections, then, which in the
ordinary course would have gone in other channels, Anne had
lavished on Hyacinth. She adored her as if she had been her own
child. She worshipped her like an idol. As a matter of fact, being
quite independent financially, it was not as a paid companion at

all that she had lived with her, though she chose to appear in that capacity. And, besides, Hyacinth herself, Anne had, in a most superlative degree, enjoyed the house, her little authority, the way she stood between Hyacinth and all tedious little practical matters. Like many a woman who was a virago at heart, Anne had a perfect passion for domestic matters, for economy, for managing a house. Of course she had always known that the pretty heiress was sure to marry, but she hoped the evil day would be put off, and somehow it annoyed her to such an acute extent because Hyacinth was so particularly pleased with the young man.

As she told Anne every thought, and never dreamt of concealing any nuance or shade of her sentiments, Anne had suffered a good deal.

It vexed her particularly that Hyacinth fancied Cecil so unusual, while she was very certain that there were thousands and thousands of good-looking young men in England in the same position who had the same education, who were precisely like him. There was not a pin to choose between them. How many photographs in groups Cecil had shown them, when she and Hyacinth went to tea at his rooms! Cecil in a group at Oxford, in an eleven, as a boy at school, and so forth! While Hyacinth delightedly recognised Cecil, Anne wondered how on earth she could tell one from the other. Of course, he was not a bad sort. He was rather clever, and not devoid of a sense of humour, but the fault Anne really found with him, besides his taking his privileges so much as a matter of course, was that there was nothing, really, to find fault with. Had he been ugly and stupid, she could have minded it less.

Now what should she do? Of course she must remain with Hyacinth till the marriage, but she was resolved not to go to the wedding, although she had promised to do so. Both Hyacinth and Cecil really detested the vulgarity of a showy fashionable wedding as much as she did, and it was to be moderated, toned down as much as possible. But Anne couldn't stand it—any of it—and she wasn't going to try.

As she sat there, wrapped up in her egotistic anguish, two young people, probably a shop-girl and her young man, passed, sauntering along, holding hands, and swinging their arms. Anne thought that they were, if anything, less odious than the others, but the stupidity of their happiness irritated her, and she got up to go back.

She felt tired, and though it was not far, she decided, with her usual unnecessary economy, to go by omnibus down Park Lane.

As she got out and felt for the key in her pocket, she thought how soon she would no longer be able to go into her paradise and find the lovely creature waiting to confide in her, how even now the lovely creature was in such a dream of preoccupied happiness that, quick as she usually was, she was now perfectly blind to her friend's jealousy. And, indeed, Anne concealed it very well. It was not ordinary jealousy either. She was very far from envying Hyacinth. She only hated parting with her.

As she passed the studio she heard voices, and looked in, just as she was, with a momentary desire to *gêner* them.

Of course they got up, Hyacinth blushing and laughing, and entreated her to come in.

She sat there a few minutes, hoping to chill their high spirits, then abruptly left them in the middle of a sentence.

At dinner that evening she appeared quite as usual. She had taken a resolution.

CHAPTER XXIII

Bruce Convalescent

'IT'S very important,' said Bruce, 'that I don't see too many people at a time. You must arrange the visitors carefully. Who is coming this afternoon?'

'I don't know of anyone, except perhaps your mother, and Mr Raggett.'

'Ah! Well, I can't see them both at once.'

'Really? Why not?'

'*Why* not? What a question! Because it would be a terrible fatigue for me. I shouldn't be able to stand it. In fact I'm not sure that I ought to see Raggett at all.'

'Don't, then. Leave a message to say that after all you didn't feel strong enough.'

'But, if we do that, won't he think it rather a shame, poor chap? As I said he could come, doesn't it seem rather hard lines for him to come all this way—it is a long distance, mind you—and then see nobody?'

'Well, I can see him.'

Bruce looked up suspiciously.

'Oh, you want to see him, do you? Alone?'

'Don't be silly, Bruce. I would much rather not see him.'

'Indeed, and why not? I really believe you look down on him because he's my friend.'

'Not a bit. Well, he won't be angry; you can say that you had a relapse, or something, and were not well enough to see him.'

'Nothing of the sort. It would be very good for me; a splendid change to have a little intellectual talk with a man of the world. I've had too much women's society lately. I'm sick of it. Ring the bell, Edith.'

'Of course I will, Bruce, but what for? Is it anything I can do?'

'I want you to ring for Bennett to pass me my tonic.'

'Really, Bruce, it's at your elbow.' She laughed.

'I suppose I've changed a good deal since my illness,' said he looking in the glass with some complacency.

'You don't look at all bad, dear.'

'I know I'm better; but sometimes, just as people are recovering, they suddenly have a frightful relapse. Braithwaite told me I would have to be careful for some time.'

'How long do you suppose he meant?'

'I don't know—five or six years, I suppose. It's the heart. That's what's so risky in influenza.'

'But he said your heart was all right.'

'Ah, so he thinks. Doctors don't know everything. Or perhaps it's what he *says*. It would never do to tell a heart patient he was in immediate danger, Edith; why, he might die on the spot from the shock.'

'Yes, dear; but, excuse my saying so, would he have taken me aside and told me you were perfectly well, and that he wouldn't come to see you again, if you were really in a dangerous state?'

'Very possibly. I don't know that I've so very much confidence in Braithwaite. I practically told him so. At least I suggested to him, when he seemed so confident about my recovery, that he should have a consultation. I thought it only fair to give him every chance.'

'And what did he say?'

'He didn't seem to see it. Just go and get the cards, Edith, that have been left during my illness. It's the right thing for me to write to everyone, and thank them for their kindness.'

'But there are no cards, dear.'

'No cards?'

'You see, people who knew you were ill inquired by telephone, except your mother, and she never leaves a card.'

He seemed very disgusted.

'That's it,' he said. 'That's just like life; "laugh, and the world laughs with you; weep, and you weep alone!" Get out of the running, and drop aside, and you're forgotten. And I'm a fairly popular man, too; yet I might have died like a dog in this wretched little flat, and not a card.—What's that ring?'

'It must be your mother.'

Bruce leant back on the sofa in a feeble attitude, gave Edith directions to pull the blinds a little way down, and had a vase of roses placed by his side.

Then his mother was shown in.

'Well, how is the interesting invalid? Dear boy, how well you look! How perfectly splendid you look!'

'Hush, Mother,' said Bruce, with a faint smile, and in a very low voice. 'Sit down, and be a little quiet. Yes, I'm much better, and getting on well; but I can't stand much yet.'

'Dear, dear! And what did the doctor say?' she asked Edith.

'He won't come any more,' said Edith.

'Isn't he afraid you will be rushing out to the office too soon— over-working? Oh well, Edith will see that you take care of yourself. Where's little Archie?'

'Go and see him in the nursery,' said Bruce, almost in a whisper. 'I can't stand a lot of people in here.'

'Archie's out,' said Edith.

There was another ring.

'That's how it goes on all day long,' said Bruce. 'I don't know how it's got about, I'm sure. People never cease calling! It's an infernal nuisance.'

'Well, it's nice to know you're not neglected,' said his mother.

'Neglected? Why, it's been more like a crowded reception than an invalid's room.'

'It's Mr Raggett,' said Edith; 'I heard his voice. Will you see him or not, dear?'

'Yes. Presently. Take him in the other room, and when the mater goes he can come in here.'

'I'm going now,' said Mrs Ottley; 'you mustn't have a crowd. But really, Bruce, you're better than you think.'

'Ah, I'm glad you think so. I should hate you to be anxious.'

'Your father wanted to know when you would be able to go to the office again.'

'That entirely depends. I may be strong enough in a week or two, but I promised Braithwaite not to be rash for Edith's sake. Well, good-bye, Mother, if you must go.'

She kissed him, left a box of soldiers for Archie and murmured to Edith—

'What an angel Bruce is! So patient and brave. Perfectly well, of course. He has been for a week. He'll go on thinking himself ill for a year—the dear pet, the image of his father! If I were you,

Edith, I think I should get ill too; it will be the only way to get him out. What a perfect wife you are!'

'I should like to go back with you a little,' said Edith.

'Well, can't you? I'm going to Harrod's, of course. I'm always going to Harrod's; it's the only place I ever do go. As Bruce has a friend he'll let you go.'

Bruce made no objection. Edith regarded it as a treat to go out with her mother-in-law. The only person who seemed to dislike the arrangement was Mr Raggett. When he found he was to be left alone with Bruce, he seemed on the point of bursting into tears.

CHAPTER XXIV

The Wedding

THE wedding was over. Flowers, favours, fuss and fluster, incense, 'The Voice that breathed o'er Eden,' suppressed nervous excitement, maddening delay, shuffling and whispers, acute long-drawn-out boredom of the men, sentimental interest of the women, tears of emotion from dressmakers in the background, disgusted resignation on the part of people who wanted to be at Kempton (and couldn't hear results as soon as they wished), envy and jealousy, admiration for the bride, and uncontrollable smiles of pitying contempt for the bridegroom. How is it that the bridegroom, who is, after all, practically the hero of the scene, should always be on that day, just when he is the man of the moment, so hugely, pitiably ridiculous?

Nevertheless, he was envied. It was said on all sides that Hyacinth looked beautiful, though old-fashioned people thought she was too self-possessed, and her smile too intelligent, and others complained that she was too ideal a bride—too much like a portrait by Reynolds and not enough like a fashion-plate in the *Lady's Pictorial*.

Sir Charles had given her away with his impassive air of almost absurd distinction. It had been a gathering of quite unusual good looks, for Hyacinth had always chosen her friends almost unconsciously with a view to decorative effect, and there was great variety of attraction. There were bridesmaids in blue, choristers in red, tall women with flowery hats, young men in tight frock-coats and buttonholes, fresh 'flappers' in plaits, beauties of the future, and fascinating, battered creatures in Paquin dresses, beauties of the past.

As to Lady Cannon, she had been divided between her desire for the dramatic importance of appearing in the fairly good part of the Mother of the Bride, and a natural, but more frivolous wish to recall to the memory of so distinguished a company her success as a professional beauty of the 'eighties, a success that clung to her with the faded poetical perfume of pot-pourri, half forgotten.

Old joys, old triumphs ('Who is she?' from the then Prince of Wales at the opera, with the royal scrutiny through the opera-glass), and old sentiments awoke in Lady Cannon with Mendelssohn's Wedding March, and, certainly, she was more pre-occupied with her mauve toque and her embroidered velvet gown than with the bride, or even with her little Ella, who had specially come back from school at Paris for the occasion, who was childishly delighted with her long crook with the floating blue ribbon, and was probably the only person present whose enjoyment was quite fresh and without a cloud.

Lady Cannon *was* touched, all the same, and honestly would have cried, but that, simply, her dress was really too tight. It was a pity she had been so obstinate with the dressmaker about her waist for this particular day; an inch more or less would have made so little difference to her appearance before the world, and such an enormous amount to her own comfort. 'You look lovely, Mamma—as though you couldn't breathe!' Ella had said admiringly at the reception.

Indeed, her comparatively quiet and subdued air the whole afternoon, which was put down to the tender affection she felt for her husband's ward, was caused solely and entirely by the cut of her costume.

Obscure relatives, never seen at other times, who had given glass screens painted with storks and water-lilies, or silver hair-brushes or carriage-clocks, turned up, and were pushing at the church and cynical at the reception. Very smart relatives, who had sent umbrella-handles and photograph-frames, were charming, and very anxious to get away; heavy relatives, who had sent cheques, stayed very late, and took it out of everybody in tediousness; the girls were longing for a chance to flirt, which did not come; young men for an opportunity to smoke, which did. Elderly men, their equilibrium a little upset by champagne in the afternoon, fell quite in love with the bride, were humorous and jovial until the entertainment was over, and very snappish to their wives driving home.

Like all weddings it had left the strange feeling of futility, the slight sense of depression that comes to English people who have tried, from their strong sense of tradition, to be festive and sentimental and in high spirits too early in the day. The frame of mind supposed to be appropriate to an afternoon wedding can only be genuinely experienced by an Englishman at two o'clock in the morning. Hence the dreary failure of these exhibitions.

Lord Selsey was present, very suave and cultivated, and critical, and delighted to see his desire realised. Mrs Raymond was not there. Edith looked very pretty, but rather tired. Bruce had driven her nearly mad with his preparations. He had evidently thought that he would be the observed of all observers and the cynosure of every eye. He was terribly afraid of being too late or too early, and at the last moment, just before starting, thought that he had an Attack of Heart, and nearly decided not to go, but recovered when Archie was found stroking his father's hat the wrong way, apparently under the impression that it was a pet animal of some kind. Bruce had been trying, as his mother called it, for a week, because he thought the note written to thank them for their present had been too casual. Poor Edith had gone through a great deal on the subject of the present, for Bruce was divided by so many sentiments on the subject. He hated spending much money, which indeed he couldn't afford, and yet he was most anxious for their gift to stand out among the others and make a sensation.

He was determined above all things to be original in his choice, and after agonies of indecision on the subject of fish-knives and Standard lamps, he suddenly decided on a complete set of Dickens. But as soon as he had ordered it, it seemed to him pitiably flat, and he countermanded it. Then they spent weary hours at Liberty's, and other places of the kind, when Bruce declared he felt a nervous breakdown coming on, and left it to Edith, who sent a fan.

When Hyacinth was dressed and ready to start she asked for Anne. It was then discovered that Miss Yeo had not been seen at all since early that morning, when she had come to Hyacinth's room, merely nodded and gone out again. It appeared that she had left the house at nine o'clock in her golf-cap and mackintosh, taking the key and a parcel. This had surprised no-one, as it was thought that she had gone to get some little thing for Hyacinth before dressing. She had not been seen since.

Well, it was no use searching! Everyone knew her odd ways. It was evident that she had chosen not to be present. Hyacinth had to go without saying good-bye to her, but she scribbled a note full of affectionate reproaches. She was sorry, but it could not be helped. She was disappointed, but she would see her when she came back.

After all, at such a moment, she really couldn't worry about Anne.

And so, pursued by rice and rejoicings—and ridicule from the little boys in the street by the awning—the newly-married couple drove to the station, ' en route,' as the papers said, with delightful vagueness, ' for the Continent.'

What did they usually talk about when alone?

Cecil wondered.

The only thing he felt clearly, vividly, and definitely was a furious resentment against Lord Selsey.

' Do you love me, Cecil? Will you aways love me? Are you happy?'

Ashamed of his strange, horrible mood of black jealousy, Cecil turned to his wife.

CHAPTER XXV

Accounts

'H o w about your play, Bruce? Aren't you going to work at it this evening?'

'Why no; not just at present. I'm not in the mood. You don't understand, Edith. The Artist must work when the inspiration seizes him.'

'Of course, I know all that, Bruce; but it's six months since you had the inspiration.'

'Ah, but it isn't that only; but the trend of public taste is so bad —it gets worse and worse. Good heavens, I can't write down to the level of the vulgar public!'

'But can you write at all?'

'Certainly; certainly I can; but I need encouragement. My kind of talent, Edith, is like a sort of flower—are you listening?—a flower that needs the watering and tending, and that sort of thing, of appreciation. Appreciation! that's what I need—that's all I ask for. Besides, I'm a business man, and unless I have a proper contract with one of the Managers—a regular arrangement and agreement about my work being produced at a certain time—and, mind you, with a cast that *I* select—I just shan't do it at all.'

'I see. Have you taken any steps?'

'Of course I've taken steps—at least I've taken stalls at most of the theatres, as you know. There isn't a play going on at this moment that isn't full of faults—faults of the most blatant kind— mistakes that I myself would never have made. To begin with, for instance, take Shakespeare.'

'Shakespeare?'

'Yes. A play like *The Merchant of Venice*, for example. My dear girl, it's only the glamour of the name, believe me! It's a wretched play, improbable, badly constructed, full of padding — good gracious! do you suppose that if *I* had written that play and sent it to Tree, that he would have put it up?'

' I can't suppose it, Bruce.'

' It isn't sense, Edith; it isn't true to life. Why, who ever heard of a case being conducted in any Court of Law as that is? Do you suppose all kinds of people are allowed to stand up and talk just when they like, and say just what they choose—in blank verse, too? Do you think now, if someone brought an action against me and you wanted me to win it, that you and Bennett could calmly walk off to the Law Courts disguised as a barrister and his clerk, and that you could get me off? Do you suppose, even, that you would be let in? People don't walk in calmly saying that they're barristers and do exactly what they please, and talk any nonsense that comes into their head.

'I know that; but this is poetry, and years and years ago, in Elizabeth's time.'

' Oh, good gracious, Edith, that's no excuse! It isn't sense. Then take a play like *The Merry Widow*. What about that? Do you suppose that if I liked I couldn't do something better than that? Look here, Edith, tell me, what's the point? Why are you so anxious that I should write this play?'

He looked at her narrowly, in his suspicious way.

' First of all, because I think it would amuse you.'

' Amuse me, indeed!'

' And then, far more, because—Bruce, do you remember assuring me that you were going to make £5,000 a year at least?'

' Well, so I shall, so I shall. You must give a fellow time. Rome wasn't built in a day.'

' I know it wasn't, and if it had been it would be no help to me. Will you look at the bills?'

' Oh, confound it!'

' Bruce dear, if you're not going to work at your play tonight, won't you just glance at the accounts?'

' You know perfectly well, Edith, if there's one thing I hate more than another it's glancing at accounts. Besides, what good is it? What earthly use is it?'

' Of course it would be use if you would kindly explain how I'm going to pay them?'

' Why, of course, we'll pay them—gradually.'

' But they're getting bigger gradually.'

' Dear me, Edith, didn't we a year or two ago make a Budget?

Didn't we write down exactly how much every single item of our expenditure would be?'

' Yes; I know we did; but—'

' Well, good heavens, what more do you want?'

' Lots more. You made frightful mistakes in the Budget, Bruce; at any rate, it was extraordinarily under-estimated.'

' Why, I remember I left a margin for unexpected calls.'

' I know you left a margin, but you left out coals and clothes altogether.'

' Oh, did I?'

' And the margin went in a week, the first week of your holiday. You never counted holidays in the Budget.'

' Oh! I—I—well, I suppose it escaped my recollection.'

' Never mind that. It can't be helped now. You see, Bruce, we simply haven't enough for our expenses.'

' Oh, then what's the use of looking at the accounts?'

' Why, to see where we are. What we've done, and so on. What do you usually do when you receive a bill?'

' I put it in the fire. I don't believe in keeping heaps of useless papers; it's so disorderly. And so I destroy them.'

' That's all very well, but you know you really oughtn't to be in debt. It worries me. All I want you to do,' she continued, ' is just to go through the things with me to see how much we owe, how much we can pay, and how we can manage; and just be a little careful for the next few months.'

' Oh, if that's all you want—well, perhaps you're right, and we'll do it, some time or other; but not tonight.'

' Why not? You have nothing to do!'

' Perhaps not; but I can't be rushed. Of course, I know it's rather hard for you, old girl, being married to a poor man; but you know you *would* do it, and you mustn't reproach me with it now.'

She laughed.

' We're not a bit too hard up to have a very pleasant time, if only you weren't so—,' then she stopped.

' Go on; say it!' he exclaimed. ' You want to make out I'm extravagant, that's it! I *have* large ideas, I own it; it's difficult for me to be petty about trifles.'

' But, Bruce, I wasn't complaining at all of your large ideas. You hardly ever give me a farthing, and expect me to do marvels on next to nothing. Of course, I know you're not petty about some things.' She stopped again.

'All right then; I'll give up smoking and golfing, and all the little things that make life tolerable to a hard-working man.'

'Not at all, dear. Of course not. There's really only one luxury —if you won't think me unkind—that I think, perhaps, you might try to have less of.'

'What is that?'

'Well, dear, couldn't you manage not to be ill quite so often? You see, almost whenever you're bored you have a consultation. The doctors always say you're quite all right; but it does rather—well, run up, and you can't get much fun out of it. Now, don't be angry with me.'

'But, good God, Edith! If I didn't take it in time, you might be left a young widow, alone in the world, with Archie. Penny-wise and pound-foolish to neglect the health of the breadwinner! Do you reproach me because the doctor said I wasn't dangerously ill at the time?'

'Of course not; I'm only too thankful.'

'I'm sure you are really, dear. Now yesterday I felt very odd, very peculiar indeed.'

'Oh, what was it?'

'An indescribable sensation. At first it was a kind of heaviness in my feet, and a light sensation in my head, and a curious kind of emptiness—nervous exhaustion, I suppose.'

'It was just before lunch, no doubt. I daresay it went off. When I have little headache or don't feel quite up to the mark, I don't send for the doctor; I take no notice of it, and it goes away.'

'But you, my dear—you're as strong as a horse. That reminds me, will you fetch me my tonic?'

When she came back, he said—

'Look here, Edith, I'll tell you what you shall do, if you like. You're awfully good, dear, really, to worry about the bills and things, though it's a great nuisance, but I should suggest that you just run through them with my mother. You know how good-natured she is. She'll be flattered at your consulting her, and she'll be able to advise you if you *have* gone too far and got into a little debt. She knows perfectly well it's not the sort of thing *I* can stand. And, of course, if she were to offer to help a little, well! she's my mother; I wouldn't hurt her feelings by refusing for anything in the world, and the mater's awfully fond of you.'

'But, Bruce, I'd much rather—'

'Oh, stop, Edith. I'm sorry to have to say it, but you're becoming shockingly fussy. I never thought you would have grown into a fidgety, worrying person. How bright you used to seem in the old days! And of course the whole thing about the accounts, and so on, *must* have arisen through your want of management. But I won't reproach you, for I believe you mean well. . . . I've got one of my headaches coming on; I hope to goodness I'm not going to have an attack.'

He looked in the glass. ' I'm rather an odd colour, don't you think so?'

'No; I don't think so. It's the pink-shaded light.'

He sighed.

' Ah, suppose you had married a chap like Reeve—rolling in gold ! Are he and Hyacinth happy, do you think?'

'I think they seem very happy.'

'We're lunching there on Sunday, aren't we? Don't forget to order me a buttonhole the day before, Edith.'

' I'll remember.'

She looked at her engagement-book.

' It's not next Sunday, Bruce. Next Sunday we're lunching with your people. You'll be sure to come, won't you?'

' Oh, ah, yes ! If I'm well enough.'

CHAPTER XXVI

Confidences

'I KNOW who you are. You're the pretty lady. Mother won't be long. Shall I get you my bear?'

Hyacinth had come to see Edith, and was waiting for her in the little drawing-room of the flat. The neat white room with its miniature overmantel, pink walls, and brass fire-irons like toys, resembled more than ever an elaborate doll's house. The frail white chairs seemed too slender to be sat on. Could one ever write at that diminutive white writing-desk? The flat might have been made, and furnished by Waring, for midgets. Everything was still in fair and dainty repair, except that the ceiling, which was painted in imitation of a blue sky, was beginning to look cloudy. Hyacinth sat on a tiny blue sofa from where she could see her face in the glass. She was even prettier than before her marriage, now three months ago, but when in repose there was a slightly anxious look in her sweet, initiated eyes. She had neither the air of prosaic disillusion nor that of triumphant superiority that one sees in some young brides. She seemed intensely interested in life, but a little less reposeful than formerly.

'Why, Archie! What a big boy you've grown!'

'Shall I bring you my bear?'

'Oh, no; never mind the bear. Stay and talk to me.'

'Yes; but I'd better bring the bear. Mother would want me to amuse you.'

He ran out and returned with his beloved animal, and put it on her lap.

'Father calls him mangy, but he isn't, really. I'm going to cut its hair to make it ·grow thicker. I can say all the alphabet and lots of poetry. Shall I say my piece? No; I know what I'll do, I'll get you my cards, with E for ephalunt and X for swordfish on, and see if you can guess the animals.'

'That would be fun. I wonder if I shall guess?'

'You mustn't read the names on them, because that wouldn't be fair. You may only look at the pictures. Oh, won't you have tea? Do have tea.'

'I think I'll wait for your mother.'

'Oh, no; have tea now, quick. Then I can take some of your sugar.'

Hyacinth agreed; but scarcely had this point been settled when Edith returned and sent him off.

'Edith,' Hyacinth said, 'do you know I am rather worried about two things? I won't tell you the worst just yet.'

'It's sure to be all your fancy,' said Edith affectionately.

'Well, it isn't my fancy about Anne. Is it not the most extraordinary thing? Since the day of my wedding she's never been seen or heard of. She walked straight out into the street, and London seems to have swallowed her up. She took nothing with her but a large paper parcel, and left all her luggage, and even her dress that I made her get for the wedding was laid out on the bed. What can have become of her? Of course, I know she has plenty of money, and she could easily have bought an entirely new outfit, and gone away —to America or somewhere, under another name without telling anyone. We've inquired of her father, and he knows nothing about her. It really is a mysterious disappearance.'

'I don't feel as if anything had happened to her,' Edith said, after a pause. 'She's odd, and I fancy she hated your marrying, and didn't want to see you again. She'll get over it and come back. Surely if there had been an accident, we should have heard by now. Do you miss her, Hyacinth?'

'Of course I do, in a way. But everything's so different now. It isn't so much my missing her, if I only knew she was all right. There's something so sad about disappearing like that.'

'Well, everything has been done that can be done. It's not the slightest use worrying. I should try and forget about it, if I were you. What's the other trouble?'

Hyacinth hesitated.

'Well, you know how perfect Cecil is to me, and yet there's one thing I don't like. The Selseys have come back, and have asked us there, and Cecil won't go. Isn't it extraordinary? Can he be afraid of meeting her again?'

'Really, Hyacinth, you are fanciful! What now, now that

she's his aunt—practically? Can you really still be jealous?'

'Horribly,' said Hyacinth frankly. 'If she married his uncle a hundred times it wouldn't alter the fact that she's the only woman he's ever been madly in love with.'

'Why, he adores you, Hyacinth!'

'I am sure he does, in a way, but only as a wife!'

'Well, good heavens! What else do you want? You're too happy; too lucky; you're inventing things, searching for troubles. Why make yourself wretched about imaginary anxieties?'

'Suppose, dear, that though he's devoted to me, we suit each other perfectly, and so on, yet at the back of his brain there's always a little niche, a little ideal for that other woman just because she never cared for him? I believe there will always be—always.'

'Well, suppose there is; what on earth does it matter? What difference does it make? Why be jealous of a shadow?'

'It's just because it's such a shadow that it's so intangible—so unconquerable. If she had ever returned his affection he might have got tired of her, they might have quarrelled, he might have seen through her—realised her age and all that, and it would have been over—exploded! Instead of this, he became fascinated by her, she refused him; and then, to make it ever so much worse for me, Lord Selsey, whom he's so fond of and thinks such a lot of, goes and puts her upon a pedestal, constantly in sight, yet completely out of reach.'

'You are unreasonable, Hyacinth! Would you prefer a rival of flesh and blood. Don't be so fanciful, dear. It's too foolish. You've got your wish; enjoy it. I consider that you haven't a trouble in the world.'

'Dear Edith,' said Hyacinth, 'have you troubles?'

'Why, of course I have—small ones. Bruce has taken to having a different illness every day. His latest is that he *imagines* he's a *malade imaginaire!*'

'Good gracious, how complicated! What makes him think that?'

'Because he's been going to specialists for everything he could think of, and they all say he's specially well. Still, it's better than if he were really ill, I suppose. Only he's very tormenting, and hardly ever works, and lately he's taken to making jealous scenes.'

'Oh, that must be rather fun. Who is he jealous of?'

'Why, he thinks he's jealous of his friend Raggett—the most

impossible, harmless creature in the world; and the funny thing is whenever Bruce is jealous of anyone he keeps on inviting them—won't leave them alone. If I go out when Raggett appears, he says it's because I'm so deep; and if I stay he finds fault with everything I do. What do you advise me to do, Hyacinth?'

'Why, give him something more genuine to worry about—flirt with a real person. That would do Bruce good, and be a change for you.'

'I would—but I haven't got time! What chance is there for flirting when I have to be always contriving and economising, and every scrap of leisure I must be there or thereabouts in case Bruce has heart disease or some other illness suddenly? When you are living with a strong young man who thinks he's dangerously ill, flirting is not so easy as it sounds. When he isn't here I'm only too glad to rest by playing with Archie.'

'I see. What do you think could cure Bruce of his imaginary maladies?'

'Oh, not having to work, coming into some money. You see, it fills up the time which he can't afford to spend on amusements.'

Edith laughed.

'It's a bore for you. . . .'

'Oh, I don't mind much; but you see we all have our little troubles.'

'Then, how did you say I ought to behave about the Selseys?'

'Don't behave at all. Be perfectly natural, ignore it. By acting as if things were just as you liked, they often become so.'

There was a ring on the telephone.

Edith went into the next room to answer it, and came back to say—

'Bruce has just rung up. He wants to know if Raggett's here. He says he'll be home in half an hour. He doesn't feel up to the mark, and can't stay at the office.'

'Poor little Edith!'

'And don't for goodness sake bother yourself about Cecil. As if there was any man in the world who hadn't liked somebody some time or other!'

Hyacinth laughed, kissed her, and went away.

CHAPTER XXVII

Miss Wrenner

ONE day Bruce came into the flat much more briskly than usual. There was a certain subdued satisfaction in his air that Edith was glad to see. He sat down, lit a cigarette, and said—

'Edith, you know how strongly I disapprove of the modern fashion of husbands and wives each going their own way—don't you?'

'Where are you thinking of going, dear?'

'Who said I was thinking of going anywhere?'

'No-one. But it's obvious, or you wouldn't have begun like that.'

'Why? What did you think I was going to say next?'

'Of course, you were going to say, after that sentence about " *you know how strongly I disapprove,*" etc., something like, " *But, of course, there are exceptions to every rule, and in this particular instance I really think that I had better,*" and so on. Weren't you?'

'Odd. Very odd you should get it into your head that I should have any idea of leaving you. Is that why you're looking so cheerful—laughing so much?'

'Am I laughing? I thought I was only smiling.'

'I don't think it's a kind thing to smile at the idea of my going away. However, I'm sorry to disappoint you'—Bruce spoke rather bitterly—' very sorry indeed, for I see what a blow it will be to you. But, as a matter of fact, I had not intention *whatever* of leaving you at all, except, perhaps, for a few hours at a time. However, of course, if you wish it very much I might arrange to make it longer. Or even to remain away altogether, if you prefer it.'

'Oh, Bruce, don't talk such nonsense! You know I wish nothing of the kind. What's this about a few hours at a time?'

'Naturally,' Bruce said, getting up and looking in the glass; ' naturally, when one has an invitation like this—oh, I admit it's a compliment—I quite admit that—one doesn't want to decline it at once without thinking it over. Think how absurd I should appear

to a man like that, writing to say that my wife can't possibly spare
me for a couple of hours two or three times a week!'

'A man like what? Who is this mysterious man who wants you
for two or three hours two or three times a week?'

'My dear, it can't be done without it; and though, of course, it
is rather a nuisance, I daresay in a way it won't be bad fun. You
shall help me, dear, and I'm sure I shall be able to arrange for you
to see the performance. Yes! you've guessed it; I thought you would.
I've been asked to play in some amateur theatricals that are being
got up by Mitchell of the F O in aid of the ' Society for the Suppres-
sion of Numismatics ', or something—I can't think why he chose
me, of all people!'

'I wonder.'

'I don't see anything to wonder about. Perhaps he thought I'd do
it well. Possibly he supposed I had talent. He may have observed, in
the course of our acquaintance, that I was threatened with intelligence! Or again, of course, they want for theatricals a fellow of
decent appearance.'

'Ah, yes; of course they do.'

'It would be very absurd for the heroine of the play to be madly
in love with a chap who turned up looking like, God knows what!
Not that I mean for a moment to imply that I'm particularly good-
looking, Edith—I'm not such a fool as that. But—well, naturally,
it's always an advantage in playing the part of a *jeune premier* not
to be quite bald and to go in decently at the waist, and to— Fancy,
Miss Wrenner didn't know I was a married man!'

'Miss Wrenner! Who's Miss Wrenner?'

'Why she— Don't you know who Miss Wrenner is?'

'No.'

'Oh, Miss Wrenner's that girl who—a friend of the Mitchells;
you know.'

'I *don't* know. Miss Wrenner is quite new to me. So are the
Mitchells. What is she like?'

'*Like!*' exclaimed Bruce. ' You ask me what she's *like!* Why, she
isn't *like* anything. She's just Miss Wrenner—the well-known Miss
Wrenner, who's so celebrated as an amateur actress. Why, she was
going to play last Christmas at Raynham, only after all the performance never came off.'

'Is Miss Wrenner pretty?'

' Pretty? How do you mean?'

' What colour is her hair?'

' Well, I—I—I didn't notice, particularly.'

' Is she dark or fair? You must know, Bruce!'

' Well, I should say she was a little darker than you—not a great deal. But I'm not quite certain. Just fancy her not thinking I was married!'

' Did you tell her?'

' Tell her! Of course I didn't tell her. Do you suppose a girl like Miss Wrenner's got nothing to do but to listen to my autobiography? Do you imagine she collects marriage certificates? Do you think she makes a hobby of the census?'

' Oh! then you didn't tell her?'

' Yes, I did. Why should I palm myself off as a gay bachelor when I'm nothing of the sort?'

' When did you tell her, Bruce?'

' Why, I haven't told her yet—at least, not personally. What happened really was this: Mitchell said to me, " Miss Wrenner will be surprised to hear you're a married man," or something like that.'

' Where did all this happen?'

' At the office. Where else do I ever see Mitchell?'

' Then does Miss Wrenner come to the office?'

Bruce stared at her in silent pity.

' *Miss Wrenner! At the office!* Why you must be wool-gathering! Women are not allowed at the F O. Surely you know that, dear?'

' Well, then, where *did* you meet Miss Wrenner?'

' Miss Wrenner? Why do you ask?'

' Simply because I want to know.'

' Oh! Good heavens! What does it matter where I met Miss Wrenner?'

' You're right, Bruce; it doesn't really matter a bit. I suppose you've forgotten.'

' No; I haven't forgotten. I suppose I shall meet Miss Wrenner at the first rehearsal next week—at the Mitchells.'

' Was it there you met her before?'

' How could it be? I have never been to the Mitchells.'

' As a matter of fact, you've never seen Miss Wrenner?'

' Did I say I had? I didn't mean to. What I intended to convey was, not that I had seen Miss Wrenner, but that *Mitchell* said Miss Wrenner would be surprised to hear I was married.'

' Funny he should say that—very curious it should occur to him to picture Miss Wrenner's astonishment at the marriage of a man she didn't know, and had never seen.'

' No—no—no; that wasn't it, dear; you've got the whole thing wrong—you've got hold of the wrong end of the stick. He—Mitchell, you know—mentioned to me the names of the people who were going to be asked to act, and among them, Miss Wrenner's name cropped up—I think he said Miss Wrenner was going to be asked to play the heroine if they could get her—no—I'm wrong, it was that *she* had asked to play the heroine, and that they meant to get out of it if they could. So, *then*, I said, wouldn't she be surprised at having to play the principal part with a married man.'

' I see. *You* said it, not Mitchell. Then are you playing the hero?'

' Good gracious! no—of course not. Is it likely that Mitchell, who's mad on acting and is getting up the whole thing himself, is jolly well going to let me play the principal part? Is it human nature? Of course it isn't. You can't expect it. I never said Mitchell was not human—did I?'

' What *is* your part, dear?'

' They're going to send it to me tomorrow—typewritten. It's not a long part, and not very important, apparently; but Mitchell says there's a lot to be got out of it by a good actor; sometimes one of these comparatively small parts will make the hit of the evening.'

' What sort of part is it?'

' Oh, no particular *sort*. I don't come on until the second act. As I told you, one of the chief points is to have a good appearance— look a gentleman; that sort of thing.'

' Well?'

' I come on in the second act, dressed as a mandarin.'

' A mandarin! Then you play the part of a Chinaman?'

' No, I don't. It's at the ball. In the second act, there's a ball on the stage—for the hero's coming of age—and I have to be a mandarin.'

' Is the ball given at the Chinese Embassy?'

' No; at the hero's country house. Didn't I tell you—it's a fancy ball!'

' Oh, I see! Then I shouldn't have thought it would have

mattered so very much about whether you're good-looking or not. And Miss Wrenner—how will she be dressed at the fancy ball?'

' Miss Wrenner? Oh! Didn't I tell you—Miss Wrenner isn't going to act—they've got someone else instead.'

CHAPTER XXVIII

———

Anne Returns

I T was about six o'clock, and Hyacinth was sitting in her boudoir alone. It was a lovely room and she herself looked lovely, but, for a bride of four months, a little discontented. She was wondering why she was not happier. What was this unreasonable misery, this constant care, this anxious jealousy that seemed to poison her very existence? It was as intangible as a shadow, but it was always there. Hyacinth constantly felt that there was something in Cecil that escaped her, something that she missed. And yet he was kind, affectionate, even devoted.

Sometimes when they spent evenings at home together, which were calm and peaceful and should have been happy, the girl would know, with the second-sight of love, that he was thinking about Eugenia. And this phantom, of which she never spoke to him and could not have borne him to know of, tormented her indescribably. It seemed like a spell that she knew not how to break. It was only a thought, yet how much it made her suffer! Giving way for the moment to the useless and futile bitterness of her jealousy, she had leant her head on the cushion of the little sofa where she sat, when, with a sudden sensation that she was no longer alone, she raised it again and looked up.

Standing near the door she saw a tall, thin figure with a rather wooden face and no expression—a queer figure, oddly dressed in a mackintosh and a golf-cap.

'Why do you burn so much electric light?' Anne said dryly, in a reproachful voice, as she turned a button on the wall.

Hyacinth sprang up with a cry of surprise.

Anne hardly looked at her and walked round the room.

'Sit down. I want to look at your new room. Silk walls and Dresden china. I suppose this is what is called gilded luxury. Do you ever see that the servants dust it, or do they do as they like?'

'Anne! How can you? Do you know how anxious we've been

about you? Do you know we weren't sure you were not dead?'

'Weren't you? I wasn't very sure myself at one time. I see you took the chances, though, and didn't go into mourning for me. That was sensible.'

'Anne, will you have the ordinary decency to tell me where you've been, after frightening me out of my life?'

'Oh, it wouldn't interest you. I went to several places. I just went away, because at the last minute I felt I couldn't stand the wedding. Besides, you had a honeymoon. I didn't see why I shouldn't. And mine was much jollier—freer, because I was alone. Cheaper, too, thank goodness!'

'What an extraordinary creature you are, Anne! Not caring whether you heard from me, or of me, for four months, and then coolly walking in like this.'

'It was the only way to walk in. I really had meant never to see you again, Hyacinth. You didn't want me. I was only in the way. I was no longer needed, now you've got that young man you were always worrying about. What's his name? Reeve. But I missed you too much. I was too bored without you. I made up my mind to take a back seat, if only I could see you sometimes. I had to come and have news of you. Well, and how do you like him now you've got him? Hardly worth all that bother—was he?'

'I'll tell you, Anne. You are the very person I want. I need you immensely. You're the only creature in the world that could be the slightest help to me.'

'Oh, so there is a crumpled rose-leaf! I told you he was exactly like any other young man.'

'Oh, but he isn't, Anne. Tell me first about you. Where are you —where are you staying?'

'That's my business. I'm staying with some delightful friends. You wouldn't know them—wouldn't want to either.'

'Nonsense! You used to say you had no friends except mine. You must come and stay here. Cecil would be delighted to see you.'

'I daresay—but I'm not coming. I may be a fool, but I'm not stupid enough for that. I should hate it, besides! No; but I'll look in and see you from time to time, and give you a word of advice. You doing housekeeping, indeed!' She laughed as she looked round. 'Who engaged your servants?'

'Why, I did.'

'I suppose you were too sweet and polite to ask for their characters, for fear of hurting their feelings? I suppose you gave them twice as much as they asked? This is the sort of house servants like. Do you allow followers?'

'How should I know? No; I suppose not. Of course, I let them see their friends when they like. Why shouldn't they? They let me see mine.'

'Yes! that's jolly of them—awfully kind. Of course you wouldn't know. And I suppose the young man, Cecil, or whatever you call him, is just as ignorant as you are, and thinks you do it beautifully?'

'My dear Anne, I assure you—'

'I know what you are going to say. You order the dinner. That's nothing; so can anyone. There's nothing clever in ordering! What are you making yourself miserable about? What's the matter?'

'Tell me first where you're staying and what you're doing. I insist on being told at once.'

'I'm staying with charming people. I tell you. At a boarding-house in Bloomsbury. I'm a great favourite there; no—now I come to think of it—I'm hated. But they don't want me to leave them.'

'Now, Anne, why live like that? Even if you wouldn't stay with us, it's ridiculous of you to live in this wretched, uncomfortable way.'

'Not at all. It isn't wretched, and I thoroughly enjoy it. I pay hardly anything, because I help with the housekeeping. Of course it isn't so much fun as it used to be with you. It's a little sordid; it isn't very pretty, but it's interesting. It's not old-fashioned; there's no wax fruit, nor round table in the middle of the room. It's only about twenty-five years out of date. There are Japanese fans and bead curtains. They think the bead curtains—instead of folding-doors—quite smart and Oriental—rather wicked. Oh, and we have musical evenings on Sundays; sometimes we play dumb crambo. Now, tell me about the little rift within the lute.'

'I always told you every little thing, Anne—didn't I?'

Anne turned away her head.

'Who arranges your flowers?'

'I do.'

'Oh, you *do* do something! They look all right, but I did it much better. Oh—by the way—you mustn't think these are the only clothes I've got. I have a very smart tailor-made coat and skirt which I bought at a sale at a little shop in Brixton. I went to Brixton for the season. There's nothing like the suburbs for real style—I mean real, thoroughly English style. And the funny part is that the suburban English dresses all come from Vienna. Isn't it queer?'

' All right, come to see me next time in your Brixton-Viennese costume, and we'll have a long talk. I think you're pleased I've got a little trouble. Aren't you?'

' Oh, no—I don't want you to have trouble. But I should like you to own *he* isn't so wonderful, after all.'

' But I don't own that—not in the least. The thing is, you see '— she waited a minute—' I believe I'm still jealous of Mrs Raymond.'

' But she isn't Mrs Raymond any more. You surely don't imagine that he flirts with his aunt?'

' Of course not—how absurd you are! That's a ridiculous way to put it. No—he won't even see her.'

' Is that what you complain of?'

' His avoiding her shows he still thinks of her. It's a bad sign— isn't it? What I feel is, that he still puts her on a pedestal.'

' Well, that's all right. Let her stay there. Now, Hyacinth, when people know what they want—really *want* something acutely and definitely—and don't get it, I can pity them. They're frustrated— scored off by fate, as it were; and even if it's good for them, I'm sorry. But when they *have* got what they wanted, and then find fault and are not satisfied, I can't give them any sympathy at all. Who was it said there is no tragedy like not getting your wish— except getting it? You wanted Cecil Reeve. You've got him. How would you have felt if the other woman had got him instead?'

' You're right, Anne—I suppose. And yet—do you think he'll ever quite forget her?'

' Do you think, if you really tried hard, you could manage to find out what your grievance is, Hyacinth?'

' Yes.'

' Well, then, try; and when you've found it, just keep it. Don't part with it. A sentimental grievance is a resource—it's a consolation for all the prosaic miseries of life. Now I must go, or I shall be late for high tea.'

CHAPTER XXIX

The Ingratitude of Mitchell

S I N C E Bruce had had the amateur-theatrical trouble, he had forgotten to have any other illness. But he spent many, many half-hours walking up and down in front of the glass rehearsing his part —which consisted of the words, ' *Ah, Miss Vavasour, how charming you look—a true Queen of Night! May a humble mandarin petition for a dance?*' He tried this in many different tones; sometimes serious and romantic, sometimes humorous, but in every case he was much pleased with his reading of the part and counted on a brilliant success.

One evening he had come home looking perturbed, and said he thought he had caught a chill. Eucalyptus, quinine, sal-volatile, and clinical thermometers were lavishly applied, and after dinner he said he was better, but did not feel sufficiently up to the mark to go through his part with Edith as usual, and was rather silent during the rest of the evening.

When he came down to breakfast the next morning, Edith said—

' Do you know Anne's come back?'

' Who's Anne?'

' Anne. Hyacinth's companion. Miss Yeo, I mean.'

' Come back from where?'

' Don't you remember about her going away—about her mysterious disappearance?'

' I seem to remember now. I suppose I had more important things to think about.'

' Well, at any rate, she *has* come back—I've just had a letter— Hyacinth wants me to go out with her this afternoon and hear all about it. At four. I can, of course; it's the day you rehearse, isn't it?'

Bruce waited a minute, then said—

' Curious thing, you *can't* get our cook to make a hot omelette! And we've tried her again and again.'

' It *was* a hot omelette, Bruce—very hot—about three-quarters of an hour ago. Shall I order another?'

' No—oh, no—pray don't—not for me. I haven't the time. I've got to work. You have rather a way, Edith, of keeping me talking. You seem to think I've nothing else to do, and it's serious that I should be punctual at the office. By the way—I shouldn't go out with Hyacinth today, if I were you—I'd rather you didn't.'

' Why not, Bruce?'

' Well, I may want you.'

' Then aren't you going to the Mitchells'?'

' The Mitchells'? No—I am certainly *not* going to the Mitchells' —under the present circumstances.'

He threw down a piece of toast, got up, and stood with his back to the fire.

' How you can expect me to go to the Mitchells' again after their conduct is more than I can understand! Have you no pride, Edith?'

Edith looked bewildered.

' Has anything happened? What have the Mitchells done?' she asked.

' What have they done!' Bruce almost shouted. He then went and shut the door carefully and came back.

' Done! How do you think I've been treated by these Mitchells— by my friend Mitchell—after slaving night and day at their infernal theatricals? I *have* slaved, haven't I, Edith? Worked hard at my part?'

' Indeed you have, dear.'

' Well, you know the last rehearsal? I had got on particularly well. I told you so, didn't I? I played the little part with a certain amount of spirit, I think. I certainly threw a good deal of feeling and suppressed emotion, and also a tinge of humorous irony into my speech to Miss Vavasour. Of course, I know quite well it doesn't seem of any very great importance, but a lot hinges on that speech, and it isn't everyone who could make the very most of it, as I really believe I did. Well, I happened to be pointing out to Mitchell, yesterday at the office, how much I had done for his play, and how much time and so forth I'd given up towards making the thing a success, then, what do you think he turned round and said? Oh, he is a brute!'

' I can't think!'

' He said, " Oh, by the way, Ottley, old chap, I was going to tell
you there's been a change in the scheme. We've altered our plans
a little, and I really don't think we shall need to trouble you after
all. The fact is, I've decided to cut out the fancy ball altogether."
And then people talk of gratitude!'

' Oh, dear, Bruce, that does seem a pity!'

' Seems a pity? Is that all you've got to say! It's an outrage—a
slight on *me*. It isn't treating me with proper deference. But it isn't
that I care personally, except for the principle of the thing. For
my own sake I'm only too pleased—delighted, relieved. It's for *their*
sake I'm so sorry. The whole thing is bound to be a failure now—
not a chance of anything else. The fancy ball in the second act and
my little scene with Miss Vavasour, especially, was the point of the
play. As Mitchell said at first, when he was asking me to play the
part, it would have been *the* attraction.'

' But why is he taking out the fancy ball?'

' He says they can't get enough people. Says they won't make
fools of themselves and buy fancy dresses just to make one in a
crowd and not be noticed—not even recognised. Says the large fancy
ball for the coming of age of the hero in his ancestral halls would
have consisted of one mandarin, one Queen of the Night, and a
chap in a powdered wig. He thinks it wouldn't have been worth it.'

' Well, I am sorry! Still, couldn't you say your part just the same
in an ordinary dress?'

' What! " *Ah, Miss Vavasour, how charming you look—a true
Queen of Night!*" Why, do you remember the lines, Edith? Don't
you recollect how they refer to our costumes? How could I say them
if we weren't in fancy dress?'

' Still, if the whole plot hinges on your scene—'

' Well! all I know is, out it goes—and out I go. The second act
will be an utter frost now. They're making a terrible mistake, mind
you. But that's Mitchell's business, not mine. It's no kind of depriva-
tion to *me*—you know that. What possible gratification can it be
for a man like me—a man of the world—to paint my face and
put on a ridiculous dress and make a general ass of myself, just to
help Mitchell's rotten performance to go off all right!'

' I don't know. I daresay it would have amused you. I'm sorry,
anyhow.'

' I'm sorry enough, too—sorry for them. But if you really want to know the root of the matter, I shrewdly suspect it's really jealousy! Yes, jealousy! It's very odd, when people get keen on this sort of thing, how vain they begin to get! Perfectly childish! Yes, he didn't want me to make a hit. Old Mitchell didn't want to be cut out! Natural enough, in a way, when one comes to think it over; but a bit thick when one remembers the hours I've worked for that man—isn't it?'

'What did you say to him, Bruce, when he first told you?'

'Say? Oh, nothing. I took it very coolly—as a man of the world. I merely said, " Well, upon my word, Mitchell, this is pretty rough," or something of that sort. I didn't show I was hurt or offended in any way. I said, of course, it was like his beastly ingratitude—or words to that effect.'

'Oh! Was he angry?'

'Yes. He was very angry—furious.'

'Then you've had a quarrel with Mitchell?'

'Not a quarrel, Edith, because I wouldn't quarrel. I merely rubbed in his ingratitude, and he didn't like it. He said, " Well, let's hope if you're no longer wasting your valuable life on my theatricals you'll now be able to arrive at the office in fairly decent time," or something nasty like that. Disgusting—wasn't it?'

Edith looked at the clock.

'Too bad,' she said. ' Well, you must tell me all about it—a long account of the whole thing—this afternoon. I won't go out. I'll be at home when you come—to hear all about it. And now—'

'But that wasn't nearly all,' continued Bruce, without moving; 'you'd hardly believe it, but Mitchell actually said that he didn't think I had the smallest talent for the stage! He said I made much too much of my part—over-acted—exaggerated! When I made a point of keeping my rendering of the little scene *particularly* restrained! The fact is, Mitchell's a conceited ass. He knows no more of acting than that chair, and he thinks he knows everything.'

'It's fortunate you hadn't ordered your costume.'

'Yes, indeed. As I told him, the whole thing might have cost me a tremendous lot—far more than I could afford—put me to tremendous expense; and all for nothing! But he said no doubt the costumier would take it back. Take it back, indeed! And that if he wouldn't I could send the costume to him—Mitchell—*and* the bill —it would be sure to come in useful some time or other—the costume, I mean. As though I'd dream of letting him pay for it! I told him at once there could be no question of such a thing.'

'Well, there won't, as you haven't ordered it.'

'Now, Edith, let me beg you not to argue. Isn't it bad enough that I'm slighted by my so-called friends, and treated with the basest ingratitude, without being argued with and nagged at in my own home?'

'I didn't know I was arguing. I beg your pardon. You mustn't worry about this, dear. After all, I suppose if they found at the rehearsals that they didn't really *need* a mandarin—I mean, that the fancy-ball scene wasn't necessary—perhaps from their point of view they were right to cut it out. Don't have a lasting feud with Mitchell—isn't he rather an important friend for you—at the office?'

'Edith, Mitchell shall never set foot under my roof—never darken these doors again!'

'I wonder why, when people are angry, they talk about their roofs and doors? If you were pleased with Mitchell again, you wouldn't *ask* him to set foot under your roof—nor to darken the door. You'd ask him to come and see us. Anyhow, he won't feel it so very much—because he'll not notice it. He's never been here yet.'

'I know; but Mrs Mitchell was going to call. You will be out to her now, remember.'

'I can safely promise, I think, never to receive her, Bruce.'

'Good heavens!' cried Bruce, looking at the clock. 'Do you know what the time is? I told you so! I knew it! You've made me late at the office!'

CHAPTER XXX

Mitchell Behaves Decently

FOR the last few days Bruce had been greatly depressed, his temper more variable than ever, and he had managed to collect a quite extraordinary number of entirely new imaginary illnesses. He was very capricious about them and never carried one completely through, but abandoned it almost as soon as he had proved to Edith that he really had the symptoms. Until she was convinced he never gave it up; but the moment she appeared suitably anxious about one disease he adopted another. She had no doubt that he would continue to ring the changes on varieties of ill-health until he had to some extent recovered from the black ingratitude, as he considered it, of Mitchell, in (what *he* called) hounding him out of the amateur theatricals, and not letting him play the part of one line at which he had slaved night and day.

One evening he came home in quite a different mood, bright and cheerful. He played with Archie, and looked in the glass a good deal; both of which signs Edith recognised as hopeful.

'How is your temperature tonight, do you think?' she asked tentatively.

'Oh, *I* don't know. I can't worry about that. A rather gratifying thing has happened today, in fact, *very* gratifying.' He smiled.

'Really? You must tell me about it.'

'However badly a chap behaves—still, when he's really sorry—I mean to say when he climbs down and begs your pardon, positively crawls at your feet, you can't hold out, Edith!'

'Of course not. Then did Mitchell—'

'And when you have known a fellow a good many years, and he has always been fairly decent to you except in the one instance—and when he is in a real difficulty— Oh, hang it! One is glad to do what one can.'

'Do I gather that there has been a touching scene between you and Mitchell at the office?'

137

He glanced at her suspiciously. 'May I ask if you are laughing?'

'Oh, no, no! I was smiling with pleasure, hoping you had made it up.'

'Well, yes, it may be weak of me, but I couldn't see the poor fellow's scheme absolutely *ruined* without lending a helping hand. I have got my share of proper pride, as you know, Edith, but, after all, one has a heart.'

'What did he do?'

'Do!' exclaimed Bruce triumphantly. 'Do! Only apologised— only begged me to act with them again—only said that the piece was nothing without me, that's all! So I forgave him, and he was jolly grateful, I can tell you.'

'Fancy! Is it the same part?'

'Of course not. Didn't I tell you that the fancy ball in the second act has been cut out, so of course they don't want a mandarin. No; but Frank Luscombe has given up his part—chucked it, and they have asked me to take it.'

'Is it as long as the other one?'

'Longer! I appear twice. Mind you, in a way it's not such an important part as the other would have been; but the play wouldn't hold together without it, and, as Mitchell said, Frank Luscombe is such a conceited chap he thought himself too grand to play a footman. He didn't have the proper artistic feeling for the whole effect; it appears that he was grumbling all the time and at last gave it up. Then it occurred to Mitchell that perhaps I would help him out, and I said I would. It *is* a bit of a triumph, isn't it, Edith?'

'A great triumph. Then you will be going back to the rehearsals again?'

'Of course I shall; they begin tomorrow. Mitchell thinks that I shall make the hit of the evening. Some of these comparatively un-important parts, when they are really well played, are more effective than the chief characters. Mitchell says he saw before, by the re-hearsals, what a tremendous lot of talent I had. But it isn't merely talent, as he said; what they all noticed was my Personal Magnetism —and I expect that's it. Fancy a man like Mitchell coming cringing to me, after all that has passed between us! Mind you, it's a distinct score, Edith!'

'It is, indeed. If you have not got your part with you, you won't want to work at it tonight. I wonder, as you seem better, whether you would feel up to listening while I tell you something about the accounts?'

'There you are! How like a woman! The very moment I am a bit cheered up and hopeful and feeling a little stronger, you begin worrying me again.'

'Dear Bruce, I wasn't going to worry you. I don't want you to do anything—anything at all but listen, and it really will take hardly any time at all. You remember you said you weren't strong enough to go through them, and suggested I should show them to your mother? Well, I went today, and I only want to tell you what happened.'

'Awfully good of you. What did she say?'

'She didn't say much, and she thought she could arrange it, but not without speaking to your father.'

'Oh, I say, really? Well, that's all right then. The girl who plays Miss Vavasour is quite as good as any professional actress, you know; in fact, she would have made a fortune on the stage. She's a Miss Flummerfelt. Her father was German by birth. If she weren't a little bit inclined to be fat, she would be wonderfully handsome. I shall have a little scene with her in the third act, at least, not really a scene exactly, but I have to announce her. I open the door and say, "Miss Vavasour!" and then she rushes up to Lady Jenkins, who is sitting on the sofa, and tells her the bracelet has been found, and I shut the door. But there's a great deal, you know, in the tone in which I announce her. I have to do it in an apparently supercilious but really admiring tone, to show that all the servants think Miss Vavasour had taken the bracelet, but that *I* am certain it isn't true. Frank Luscombe, it seems, used to say the words without any expression at all, just "Miss Vavasour!" like that, in an unmeaning sort of way.'

'I see. Your father was at home at the time, so your mother most kindly said she would go in to him at once, and try to get it settled, just to spare you the suspense of waiting for a letter about it. Isn't it sweet and considerate of her?'

'Awfully. In the second act, Lady Jenkins says to me, "Parker, has an emerald snake bracelet with a ruby head been found in any of the rooms?" and I have to say, "I will inquire, my lady." And then I move about the room, putting things in order. She says, "That will do, Parker; you can go."'

' You seem to make yourself rather a nuisance, then; but do listen, Bruce. I waited, feeling most frightfully uncomfortable, and I am afraid there was a fearful row—I felt so sorry for your mother, but you know the way she has of going straight to the point. She really wasn't long, though it *seemed* long. She came back and said—'

' Of course there's one thing Mitchell asked me to do, but I was obliged to refuse. I can't shave off my moustache.'

' Heavens! You aren't going to play the part of a powdered footman with a moustache?'

' Yes, I shall; Mitchell doesn't know it yet, but I mean to. I can carry it off. I can carry off anything.'

' Well, your mother came back and said that your father had given an ultimatum.'

' Is that all he's given?'

' He will put the thing straight on one condition—it seems it is quite an easy condition; he's going to write and tell it you. Your mother says you must agree at once, not argue, and then everything will be all right.'

' Oh, I am glad. It's all through you, Edith. Thanks, awfully. It's really very good of you. You should have seen how pleased Mitchell was when I said I'd do this for him. Simply delighted. Oh, and Mrs Mitchell is going to call on you. I'll find out which day.'

' I suppose I am to be at home to her now? You told me before not to receive her, you know.'

' Well, no; if you could manage it without being rude, I would rather she only left a card. The Mansions look all right from outside, and they are in a decent neighbourhood and all that, but the flat is so *very* small. I hardly like her to see it.'

' Really, Bruce, you are absurd. Does Mitchell suppose that you live in a palace?'

' Not a *palace*, exactly; but I expect I have given him an impression that it is—well—all right.'

' Well, so it is. If you think the flat unworthy to be seen by Mrs Mitchell, why be on visiting terms with her at all? I don't want to be.'

' But, Edith, you can't refuse the advances of a woman like that, the wife of such a friend of mine as Mitchell. He's a most valuable friend—a splendid fellow—a thoroughly good sort. You've no idea how upset he was about our little quarrel the other day. He said he couldn't sleep at night thinking about it; and his wife, too, was fretting dreadfully, making herself quite ill. But now, of course, it is all right.'

'I am not so sure that it is all right; perhaps you will quarrel again on the moustache question.'

'Oh, no, we shan't! There can't be any more choppings and changings. After telling the whole company that we buried the hatchet and that I am going to take Luscombe's part, he wouldn't care to disappoint them all again. They are very keen, too, on pleasing Miss Flummerfelt, and it seems Mitchell thought she would be particularly glad I was going to act with her instead of Luscombe, because, as I say, Luscombe put so little meaning into the words. It never would have got over the footlights. Old Mitchell will be too pleased to get me back to worry about a trifle like that.'

'Well, that's all right. But do you mind writing to your mother tonight, just a line to thank her for being so kind? It was awfully nice of her, you know—she stuck up for you like anything, and put all the little extravagances on to your ill-health; and, you see, she has spared you having a scene with your father—he is just going to write you a nice note.'

'Yes, I understand, you told me before; but I have got to write a letter tonight, a rather important one. I'll write to the mater tomorrow.'

'Oh, Bruce!'

'My dear girl, business first, pleasure after. To write to one's mother is a pleasure. I wonder what the blessed ultimatum is. Look here, Edith, don't take any engagements for the next two or three weeks, will you? I shall want you every evening for rehearsing. I mean to make a good piece of work of this. I think I shall rather surprise Miss Flummerfelt and Mitchell.'

'Very well; but still I think you might write to your mother. Who is the very important business letter to?'

'Why, it's to Clarkson.'

CHAPTER XXXI

Jane's Sister

'I HAVE made up my mind, Charles, never to go and see Hyacinth again!'

'Indeed! What's the matter? What has happened?'

Sir Charles looked up rather wearily from his book and took off his gold-rimmed spectacles.

'Why should I wear myself out giving advice that is never followed?' indignantly said the lady.

'Why, indeed?'

Lady Cannon looked more than ever like a part of her own furniture, being tightly upholstered in velvet and buttons, with a touch of gold round the neck. She was distinctly put out. Her husband glanced at her and then at the door, as she poured out tea with an ominous air.

'You know how gratified I was, how thankful to see no more of that odious Miss Yeo. I always disapproved of her. I felt she had a bad influence—at any rate not a good one—in the household. I was simply delighted to hear that Hyacinth never saw her now. Well, today I called in to give Hyacinth a suggestion about her under-housemaid—I knew she wanted a new one; and Jane has a sister out of a situation who, I felt certain, would be the very person for her; when, who do I find sitting chatting with Hyacinth, and taking the lead in the conversation in the same odious way she always did, but Miss Yeo!'

'Oh, she has come back, has she? Well, I'm glad she's all right. Poor old Anne! How is she looking?'

'Looking!' almost screamed Lady Cannon. 'As if it mattered how she looked! What did she ever look like? She looked the same as ever. Although it's a lovely day, she had on a mackintosh and a golf-cap and dogskin riding-gloves. She was dressed for a country walk in the rain, but hardly suitable for a visit to Hyacinth. However, that is not the point. The point is her extraordinary impertinence and disrespect to *me*. I naturally took scarcely any notice of her presence beyond a slight bow. I made no reference whatever to her sudden disappearance, which, though exceedingly ill-bred and abrupt, I personally happened to be very glad of. I merely said what I had come to say to Hyacinth: that Jane's sister was looking for a situation, and that Hyacinth's was the very one to suit her. Instead of allowing Hyacinth to speak, what does Miss Yeo do but most impertinently snap me up by saying—what do you suppose she asked me, Charles?'

'How on earth could I possibly guess?'

'She asked me, in a hectoring tone, mind, what I knew about Jane's sister! Daring to ask me a thing like that!'

'What did you say?'

'I answered, in a very proper and dignified way, of course, that I personally knew nothing whatever about her, but that I was always glad to get a good place for a relative of any domestic of mine; so Miss Yeo answered that she thought her sister—I mean Jane—having been with me five years was a circumstance not in her favour at all, quite the contrary, and she would strongly advise Hyacinth not to take Jane's sister on so flimsy recommendation. I was thunderstruck. But this is not all. Before I left Miss Yeo dared to invite me to go to see her and her friends, and even went so far as to say she could get me an invitation to a musical party they are giving in a boarding-house in Bloomsbury! She says they have charming musical evenings every Sunday, and sometimes play dumb crambo! It was really almost pathetic. To ask *me* to play dumb crambo! The woman can have no sense of humour!'

'I'm not so sure of that,' murmured Sir Charles.

'I merely replied that I had a great deal to do, and could make no engagements at present. I did not like to hurt her feelings by pointing out the glaring incongruity of her suggestion, but really I *was* astonished; and when I said this about the engagements, she answered, "Oh well, never mind; no doubt we shall often meet here," almost as if she guessed my strong aversion to seeing her at Hyacinth's house. Then she went away; and I took the opportunity to advise Hyacinth against encouraging her. Hyacinth seemed extremely vexed and did not take my suggestion at all well. So now, if I know I am to run the risk of meeting that person there and, as I say, am to give advice to no purpose, I prefer to keep away altogether.'

'Did you ask Hyacinth how it was Miss Yeo turned up again?'

'I did; and she answered that Anne could not live without her!
Did you ever hear of anything so ridiculous in your life?'

'One can understand it,' said Sir Charles.

'I can't. What use can she possibly be to Hyacinth?'

'It isn't only a question of use, I suppose. They've been great
friends for years, but as far as that goes, there's not the slightest
doubt Anne could be of great use if she chose. Hyacinth isn't
practical, and has never learnt to be, and Anne is.'

'Then you approve?' said Lady Cannon in a low voice of anger;
'you defend my being insulted, contradicted, and—and—asked to
play dumb crambo by such a person as Miss Yeo!'

'Oh, no, my dear; of course I don't. But I daresay she didn't mean
to be rude; she was always rather eccentric, and she can be very
tactful when she likes. She never was in the slightest degree in the
way when she was Hyacinth's companion and actually lived with
her, so I don't see how she possibly can be now by going to see her
occasionally. Really, I rather like Anne Yeo.'

'Oh, you do,' said his wife furiously; 'then I regret to say we
differ very radically. It is *most* unnecessary that you should like her
at all.'

'No doubt it is unnecessary, but how can it possibly hurt you?
When I say I like her, I mean that I have a friendly sort of feeling
for her. I think she's a very good sort, that's all.'

'Then perhaps if you were Cecil Reeve you would like her to live
in the house altogether?'

'Oh, I don't go so far as that,' said Sir Charles.

'What I *can't* get over,' continued Lady Cannon, who could never
forgive the slightest opposition, and was intensely annoyed and
surprised at her husband for once being of a different opinion, 'what
I *can't* forgive is her astonishing interference on the question of
Jane's sister! When I know that it is the very situation to suit the
girl! Now, in future, whatever difficulty Hyacinth may be in, I
shall never come forward again with *my* help and experience. I wash
my hands of it. It was bad enough before; Hyacinth forgot every
single thing I told her, but she never contradicted me and seemed
grateful for my advice. But now—now that she has that creature
to make her believe that my opinions are not worth considering, of
course it is all over. I am sorry for Hyacinth, very sorry. By this, by

her own folly, she loses a chance that very few young married women have—a chance of getting an under-housemaid, whose sister has been with me for five years! I have no doubt whatever in my own mind that it would have been arranged today, and that I should have brought the good news back to Jane, if it hadn't been for that unpleasant and unnecessary Miss Yeo. Poor thing! It is very hard on her.'

'What extraordinary creatures women are!' said Sir Charles. 'May I ask whom you are pitying now, Anne or Hyacinth?'

'Neither,' said Lady Cannon, with dignity as she left the room. 'I was pitying Jane's sister.'

CHAPTER XXXII

The Drive

FROM time to time invitations had been received from the Selseys, all of which Cecil had asked Hyacinth to refuse on various pretexts. As she was convinced that he intended never to see Lady Selsey again if he could possibly help it, she made no objection, and did not even remark to him that it would look odd.

One afternoon Cecil was in St James's Street when he remembered that there was an exhibition at Carfax's. He strolled in, and was for the moment quite taken by surprise at the evident gaiety of the crowd. It seemed so incongruous to hear laughter at a private view, where it is now usual to behave with the embarrassed and respectful gloom appropriate to a visit of condolence (with the corpse in the next room).

Then he remembered that it was an exhibition of Max Beerbohm's caricatures, and that people's spirits were naturally raised at the sight of the cruel distortions, ridiculous situations, and fantastic misrepresentations of their friends and acquaintances on the walls.

Cecil was smiling to himself at a charming picture of the Archbishop of Canterbury, when someone touched him on the shoulder.

He turned round. It was Lord Selsey with his wife. He looked suave and debonair as ever, with his touch of attenuated Georgian dandyism. She had not changed, nor had her long brown eyes lost their sly and fascinating twinkle. Evidently Lord Selsey had not been able—if indeed he had tried—to persuade her to take much trouble about her appearance, but he had somehow succeeded in making her carelessness seem picturesque. The long, rather vague cloak that she wore might pass—at any rate, in a picture-gallery—as artistic, and the flat hat with its long brown feather suggested a Rembrandt, and must have been chosen for her against her will, no doubt by her husband. She really looked particularly plain this afternoon, but at the first glance Cecil admired her as much as ever.

'It's most fortunate we've met you. I have to go on somewhere, and you must drive Eugenia home. You must have a lot to talk about,' Lord Selsey said.

Cecil began to make an excuse.

'Oh, you can't refuse! Are you afraid of me? Don't you want to have a talk with your aunt?' said Eugenia.

He had no choice, and ten minutes later found himself driving in a hansom with his old love.

'Well, tell me, Cecil, aren't you happy? Weren't we quite right?'

'Of course,' said he.

'What an absurd boy you are. It's nice to see you again. I feel just like a mother to you. When am I going to see Hyacinth? Why won't you let me be friends with her? I fell in love with her at first sight. I suppose she worships you, eh? And you take it as a matter of course, and give yourself airs. Oh, I know you! I like Ted very much. He's a wonderful man. He knows everything. He's— what's the word—volatile? No, versatile. He's a walking encyclopædia of knowledge. He can write Persian poetry as soon as look at you, and everything he hasn't learnt he knows by instinct. He has the disposition of an angel and the voice of a gazelle. No, wait a minute; do I mean gazelles? Gazelles don't sing, do they? I must mean nightingales. He sings and plays really beautifully. Why didn't you tell me what a rare creature your uncle is? He has the artistic temperament, as they call it—without any of the nasty temper and horrid unpunctuality that goes with it. I really do admire Ted, Cecil. I think he's perfect.'

'That is most satisfactory,' said Cecil.

She burst out laughing.

'Oh, Cecil, you haven't changed a bit! But marvellous and angelic as Ted is, it's a sort of relief in a way to meet an ordinary man. *You* don't know all about everything, do you? If I asked you the most difficult question about art or science or history or metaphysics, or even dress, you wouldn't be able to answer it, would you? Do you always keep your temper? Is your judgement thoroughly sound? Can you talk modern Greek, and Arabian? I think not. You're full of faults, and delightfully ignorant and commonplace. And it's jolly to see you again.'

'Eugenia, you're the same as ever. Don't go home yet. Let's go for a drive.'

'But oughtn't you to go back to your wife? I daresay she's counting the minutes. Nothing could ever grow prosaic to her, not even being married to you.'

'She's gone out somewhere, with Anne Yeo, I think. Do, Eugenia; I shall never ask you again. Just for once, like old times. I couldn't stand the idea of going to see you at Selsey House; it depressed and irritated me. This is different.'

'All right,' said Eugenia. 'Then make the most of it. I shan't do it again.'

'Where shall we drive?'

'I've always wondered what happened at the very end of the Cromwell Road. Let's drive there, and then you can leave me at home. That will be quite a long way. It's rather a mad idea, Cecil, but it's fun. Isn't it just like Ted to ask you to take me home? You see what a darling, clever creature he is. He guessed—he knew we should be a little excited at meeting again. He wanted to get it over by leaving us quite free to talk.'

'I must say I shouldn't have done that in his place,' said Cecil.

'Oh, you! You might have had some cause of jealousy. He never could. But don't think I shall allow any more freaks like this. In a way I'm rather pleased you haven't forgotten me, Cecil.'

'Who could ever forget you? Who could ever get tired of you?'

'You could; and you would have by now, if I had been foolish enough to marry you.'

She seemed to Cecil, as ever, a delightful medley of impulses, whims, and fancies. For him there was always some magic about her; in her pale radiance he still found the old dazzling, unaccountable charm. . . .

'Hyacinth, do let us score off Lady Cannon, and get the housemaid without her help.'

'Why, I have, Anne, I advertised all by myself. Several came to see me yesterday.'

'Well, what did you do about it?'

'Nothing particular. Oh yes; I did. I wrote down the address of one or two. Emma Sinfield, Maude Frick, Annie Crutcher, and Mary Garstin. Which shall I have, Anne—which name do you like best?'

'Emma Sinfield, I think, or if she doesn't do, I rather fancy Garstin. Where does Emma live?'

'In the Cromwell Road. We ought to go and ask for her character today.'

'You go, then, and I'll go with you. You won't know what to ask. I'll do it for you.'

'All right. We may as well drive there as anywhere.'

Anne declared the character quite satisfactory, for Emma Sinfield's late employer, although displaying the most acute conscientiousness, could find no fault with her except a vaulting ambition and wild desire to better herself, which is not unknown in other walks of life, and they were driving away in the motor when they came face to face with Cecil and Eugenia in a hansom. He was talking with so much animation that he did not see them. She was looking straight before her.

Hyacinth turned pale as death and seized Anne's hand. Anne said nothing.

CHAPTER XXXIII

The Quarrel

'So that's why he wouldn't take me to see her! He's been meeting her in secret. My instinct was right, but I didn't think he would do that now. Oh, to think he's been deceiving me!'

'But you mustn't be in such a hurry to judge.' protested Anne; 'it may be just some accidental thing. Hyacinth, do take my advice. Don't say anything about it to him, and see if he mentions it. If he doesn't, then you'll have some reason for suspecting him, and we'll see what can be done.'

'He won't mention it—I know he won't. What accident could make them meet in a hansom in the Cromwell Road? It's too cruel! And I thought she was good. I didn't know she'd be so wicked as this. Why, they've only been married a few months. He never loved me; I told you so, Anne. He ought not to have married me. He only did it out of pique. He never cared for anyone but that woman.'

'Is it hopeless to ask you to listen to reason? So far you have no proof of anything of the kind. Certainly not that he cares for her now.'

'Didn't I see his face? I don't think he's ever looked like that at me.'

If Anne had had a momentary feeling of triumph, of that resignation to the troubles of other people that we are all apt to feel when the trouble is caused by one of whom we are jealous, the unworthy sentiment could not last at the sight of her friend's grief.

'This is serious, Hyacinth. And everything depends on your being clever now. I don't believe that she can possibly mean any harm. She never did. Why on earth should she now? And if you remember, she didn't look a bit interested. There must be some simple explanation.'

'And if there isn't?'

'Then a strong line must be taken. He must be got away from her.'

'To think of having to say that! And he says he loves me! On our honeymoon I began to believe it. Since we have been home I told you I had vague fears, but nothing like this. It's an outrage.'

'It isn't necessarily an outrage for your husband to drive his aunt in a hansom.'

'Don't make fun of me, Anne, when you know she was formerly—'

'But she wasn't, my dear. That's just the point. I'm perfectly sure, I *really* believe, that she never regarded him in that way at all. She looks on him as a boy, and quite an ordinary boy.'

'Ah, but he isn't ordinary!'

'What ever you do, Hyacinth, don't meet him by making a scene. At present he associates you with nothing but gentleness, affection, and pleasure. That is your power over him. It's a power that grows. Don't let him have any painful recollections of you.'

'But the other woman, according to you, never gave him pleasure and gentleness and all that—yet you see he turns to her.'

'That's a different thing. She didn't love him.'

There was a pause.

'And if I find he doesn't mention the meeting, deceives me about it, don't you even advise me to charge him with it then?'

'It is what I should advise, if I wanted you to have a frightful quarrel—perhaps a complete rupture. If you found out he had deceived you, what would you really do?'

Hyacinth stood up.

'I should—no, I couldn't live without him!'

She broke down.

'I give you two minutes by the clock to cry,' said Anne dryly, 'not a second more. If you spoil your eyes and give yourself a frightful headache, what thanks do you suppose you'll get?'

Hyacinth dried her eyes.

'Nothing he says, nothing he tells me, even if he's perfectly open about the drive this afternoon, will ever convince me that he's not in love with her, and that's the awful thing.'

'Even if that were true, it's not incurable. You're his wife. A thousand times prettier—and twenty years younger! The longer he lives with you the more fond he'll grow of you. You are his life—and a very charming life—not exactly a dull duty. She is merely—at the worst—a whim.'

'Horrid creature! I believe she's a witch,' Hyacinth cried.

'Don't let us talk it over any more. Just as if your own instinct won't tell you what to do far better than I ever could! Besides, you understand men; you know how to deal with them by nature—I never could. I see through them too well. I merely wanted to warn you—being myself a cool looker-on—to be prudent, not to say or do anything irrevocable. If you find you can't help making a scene, well, make one. It can't do much harm. It's only that making oneself unpleasant is apt to destroy one's influence. Naturally, people won't stand being bullied and interfered with if they can help it. It isn't human nature.'

'No; and it isn't human nature to share the person one loves with anyone else. That I could never do. I shall show him that.'

'The question doesn't arise. I feel certain you're making a mountain out of a molehill, dear. Well—cheer up!'

Anne took her departure.

As Cecil came in, looking, Hyacinth thought, particularly and irritatingly handsome, she felt a fresh attack of acute jealousy. And yet, in spite of her anger, her first sensation was a sort of relenting—a wish to let him off, not to entrap him into deceiving her by pretending not to know, not to act a part, but to throw herself into his arms, violently abusing Eugenia, forgiving him, and imploring him vaguely to take her away.

She did not, however, give way to this wild impulse, but behaved precisely as usual; and he, also, showed no difference. He told her about the pictures, and said she must come and see them with him, but he said nothing whatever of having seen Lady Selsey. He *was* deceiving her, then! How heartless, treacherous, faithless—and horribly handsome and attractive he was! She was wondering how much longer she could keep her anger to herself, when by the last post she received a note. It was from the Selseys, asking her and Cecil to dine with them on an evening near at hand.

Her hand trembled as she passed the letter to Cecil.

'Am I to refuse?' she asked.

He answered carelessly—

'Oh, no! I suppose we may as well accept.'

The words 'Have you seen her yet?' were on her lips, but she dared not say them. She was afraid he would tell her the truth.

' Have you any objection?' he asked.

She didn't answer, but walked to the door and then turned round and said—

' None whatever—to *your* going. You can go where you please, and do as you like. But I shall certainly not go with you!'

' Hyacinth!'

' You've been deceiving me, Cecil. Don't speak—please don't—because you would lie to me, and I couldn't bear it. I saw you driving with that woman today. I quite understand that you're beginning to think it would be better I should go to her house. No doubt you arranged it with her. But I'm not going to make it so convenient for you as all that!'

' My dear child, stop, listen!—let me explain. We met accidentally at the picture-gallery, and her husband himself asked me to drive her home. I couldn't get out of it.'

' Oh! He asked you to drive her home! You went a long way round, Cecil. The Cromwell Road is scarcely on the way to Regent's Park from St James's Street. Anyhow, you need not have done it. I have felt for some time that you don't really care for me, and I'm not going to play the part of the deceived and ridiculous wife, nor to live an existence of continual wrangling. I'm disappointed, and I must accept the disappointment.'

' My dearest girl, what do you mean?'

' Let us separate!' she answered. ' I will go abroad somewhere with Anne, and you can stay here and go on with your intrigue. I doubt if it will make you very happy in the end—it is too base, under the circumstances. At any rate, you're perfectly free.'

' You are absolutely wrong, Hyacinth. Terribly wrong—utterly mistaken! I swear to you that today is the first time I've seen her since she married. She wants to know you better—to be your friend. That is why she asked us again. She's devoted to her husband. It was a mere chance, our drive today—there's nothing in it. But still, though I'm absolutely innocent, if you *wish* to leave me, I shall not stand in your way. You want to go abroad with Anne Yeo, do you? Upon my word, I believe you prefer her to me!'

' You are grotesque, Cecil. But, at least, I can believe what she says. I know she would not be treacherous to me.'

' I suppose it was she who put this pretty fancy in your head—this nonsense about my imaginary flirtation with—Lady Selsey?'

'Was it Anne who made you drive with Lady Selsey, and not tell me about it? No, I can't believe you—I wish I could. This is all I've seen, so it's all you acknowledge. For a long time I've known that it was she who was between us. You have always cared for her. I suppose you always will. Well, I am not going to fight with her.'

She threw the note on the table.

'You can answer it! Say you'll go, but that I am going away. I shall probably go tomorrow.'

The door closed behind her. Cecil was left alone.

'By Jove!' he said to himself; and then more slowly, 'By—Jove!'

He lighted a cigarette and immediately threw it away. He rang the bell, and when the servant came, said he didn't want anything. He went into the dining-room, poured out some brandy-and-soda. He looked at it and left it untouched. Then, suddenly, he went upstairs. There was an expression on his face of mingled anxiety, slight amusement, and surprise. He went to her room. The door was locked.

'Hyacinth,' he said in a low voice, 'Hyacinth, darling, do open the door. . . . I want to speak to you. Do answer. You are quite mistaken, you know. . . . You know I don't care for anyone but you, dear. It's too absurd. Open the door!'

'Please go away, Cecil.'

'But, I say, I *insist* on your opening the door! I *will* come in; you're treating me shamefully, and I won't stand it. Do you hear?'

She came close to the door and said in a low, distinct voice—

'I don't wish to see you, and you must please leave me alone. I'm busy.'

'Busy! Good Lord! What are you doing?'

'I'm packing,' she answered.

He waited a second, and then went downstairs again and sat down in the arm-chair.

'By Jove!' he exclaimed again. 'By—Jove!'

His thoughts were more eloquent. But a baffled Englishman is rarely very articulate.

CHAPTER XXXIV

——

Anne and Eugenia

'IF you please, my lady, there's someone called to see you.'

Eugenia looked up in surprise. She was in the library, occupied in cataloguing Lord Selsey's books.

'It's a—well—it's not exactly a young person, my lady. She says she's sure you will see her. The name is Miss Yeo.'

'Miss Yeo?' Eugenia looked puzzled. 'Show her in at once.'

Anne came in, coolly.

'I'm afraid you hardly remember me, Lady Selsey,' she said. 'We met last summer. I was Miss Verney's companion.'

Eugenia held out her hand cordially.

'Of course, I remember you very well. Why, it was here we met! At that musical party! Do sit down, Miss Yeo. Won't you take off your mackintosh?'

'No, thanks. I must apologise for intruding. The fact is I've come about something important. It's about Mrs Reeve.'

'Mrs Reeve?' Eugenia leant eagerly forward. 'Do, do tell me! Anything about her interests me so much.'

'You'll think me very impertinent, Lady Selsey. But I can't help it. I'll come straight to the point.'

'Do, please.'

'Mrs Reeve has had a terrible quarrel with her husband. She would have left him this morning, but that I persuaded her to wait. I came to tell you because I felt sure you would be sorry. It's about you, Lady Selsey.'

'About me!'

'Yes. She saw you driving with her husband, and he didn't mention it. She's jealous of you. Of course he explained it, but she doesn't believe him. I thought he probably would not say anything about it to you. I know, of course, it's a sort of misunderstanding. But I thought perhaps you could do something about it to make it all right.'

155

' I *am* grieved,' said Eugenia, clasping her hands. ' You know Cecil was an old friend of mine, don't you? I met him again after many months, and in a foolish impulse we went for a drive. That is all, of course. Miss Yeo, I'm sure you're her true friend. This quarrel must be made up. What can I do? What do you advise?'

' Even if this particular quarrel is patched up, she would always be suspicious and jealous of you. It makes her miserable.'

' Poor darling, how ridiculous! I'm sure I'd be only too pleased never to see the silly boy again.'

' I quite understand all that, but, you see, she's very proud. That sort of rupture—all being connected as you are—would be noticeable to other people, and she's very sensitive—she couldn't stand it.'

Eugenia thought a moment.

' Suppose we went away somewhere for a year? That would give her time to forget this nonsense. My husband has been trying to persuade me to go to the Ionian Islands with him—yachting. He'll be only too pleased if I say I will. I'm a wretched sailor, but if it would do any good—'

' It would be perfect. It would all come right.'

' Then I'll do it. I had asked them to dinner for next week. I haven't had an answer yet. I'll telegraph, putting them off, and explaining why.'

' That would be splendid,' said Anne.

' Then it's settled,' answered Eugenia briefly.

Anne got up.

' Of course it must be understood that you know nothing about it—I mean about the quarrel,' she said.

' Of course not. Not a soul, not my husband, nor Cecil, nor his wife shall ever know a word about your visit, Miss Yeo.'

' That is very kind of you, Lady Selsey. I—well, you know I'm devoted to Hyacinth. At first I was almost selfishly glad about this. I could have got her back. We could have gone away together. But I can't see her miserable. She has such a mania for Cecil Reeve! Isn't it extraordinary?'

' Most extraordinary,' replied Eugenia emphatically.

' And since she's got him, she may as well be happy with him,' Anne added.

' Of course. And she will. This misunderstanding won't do any harm in the long run,' said Eugenia. ' If he had any real fear of losing her, it would do him a great deal of good. He's devoted to her really, more than either of them knows.'

'I daresay,' said Anne dryly. 'It's sure to be fixed up soon, and then I'm going away too.'

'You are! Why, Miss Yeo?'

'Oh, I don't know. I feel I'm not in the picture. I hate the sight of turtle-doves. If I've been able to do her a good turn in this little trouble, it will be a great consolation where I'm going.'

'I'm afraid you're not happy, Miss Yeo?' said Eugenia impulsively.

'I don't know that I am, particularly. But does it matter? We can't all be happy.'

'I'm sorry. I want everyone to be happy.'

'I suppose it's always a mistake to make an idol of anyone,' said Anne. 'I'm afraid Hyacinth thinks that is what her husband has done about you.'

'*That* would indeed be inexcusable!'

'She thought that the hopelessness of it had made him idealise you, and even that worried her; but when she saw you together, and it seemed—well, concrete treachery—she was furious.'

'It will bring them nearer than they have ever been before,' assured Eugenia.

'Good-bye,' said Anne. 'I'll write to you—once—and tell you what has happened.'

'Do, and be quick; I shall be busy buying yachting dresses. By the way, you might take the telegram.'

Anne waited while she wrote—

'Frightfully sorry, dinner next week unavoidably postponed as unexpectedly leaving town for season. Writing. Eugenia Selsey.'

'I will write to her when I've arranged it with my husband.'

Anne took the telegram.

CHAPTER XXXV

'That Woman'

B Y the end of their drive Eugenia had quite come to the conclusion that Cecil was as foolish as ever, and that she would not be alone with him again. At first it had amused her to see him once more, but when she saw the infatuation revive, she was bored and sorry—and particularly sorry she had given him the opportunity of expressing it. She had told him, definitely, that she would not see him again except with Hyacinth. He had declared it was merely the excitement of having met her, and implored forgiveness, undertaking in future to regard her as a friend merely.

This reconciliation—for they had had quite a quarrel in the cab coming back—and the solemn compact and promise on Cecil's part to ignore the old terms, had led to the invitation that Hyacinth regarded as an insult added to injury.

Cecil's conscience, then, as he sat by the fire that night pricked him not at all, for had he not made the best of resolutions? Indeed, privately, he rather plumed himself on his honourable conduct, forgetting perhaps that it was inspired more by Eugenia's attitude than by his own inclination.

Probably he hardly realised that, had Eugenia used her influence differently, there was hardly anything he would not have done. To him facts were everything—and he believed he had meant no harm.

He was still, he knew, to a great extent under the charm of his old friend. Still, that did not seem to have anything to do with his love for Hyacinth. He did not believe her threat of leaving him, but the mere picture of such a thing gave him great pain. He thought that if he had not been exactly in love with her when they married he was now; and could not at all imagine himself living without her. What, then, did he really want? He did not formulate it.

Au fond, he was more flattered than annoyed at the position

Hyacinth took up. He was amused, positively impressed, at her spirit. Had she not been so excessively pretty, it would have made him more angry and more anxious to rebel at the idea of her dictation. Perhaps his happiness with Hyacinth had gone almost too smoothly. He had become quite spoilt by her exquisite responsiveness, too much accustomed to the delightful homage of her being so much in love with him, to her charm in every way. He didn't at all fancy the idea of the smallest amount of this tribute being diminished. Suppose he offered never to see Eugenia again? After all, he had avoided her until today. He could continue to do so. But he had just arranged with her that they should all be friends. It would seem ridiculous. Besides, he *wanted* to see her!

Oh! what an infernal nuisance the whole thing was! It was such an awkward situation. As the thought developed, gradually, that he really would have to choose, there could be no sort of doubt that he would choose Hyacinth. . . . Yes, his fancy for Eugenia was the shadow, a will-o'-the-wisp; Hyacinth was the reality—a very lovely and loving reality. Hers was the insidious charm that grows rather than dazzles, the attraction that increases with time. He could not imagine, however long they might be married, her becoming ever a comrade merely. Mentally and physically, she held him far more since their marriage than before; he had found in her a thousand delightful qualities of which he had never dreamed.

Then that mad, capricious creature, Eugenia, meeting him, must make him take her for a drive and spoil it all! He began to get rather angry with her. Certainly since this row about her, he felt he liked her less. Why couldn't she stick to Uncle Ted—as she thought him so marvellous—and leave *him* alone?

With this unjust and inconsistent movement of irritation, he again attempted speaking to Hyacinth through the door, assuring her that if she would only open it, he would convince her. But as he received no answer, he was too proud to say any more, and retired sulkily to his own room.

To his great surprise, he fell asleep almost immediately.

The next morning he went out without seeing Hyacinth, but left a message that he would be in at one, and wished to speak to her. He thought this would give her time to recover, or even perhaps to speak to Anne. At heart he did not believe Anne would give her any but sensible advice, though he now began to feel a little jealous of her influence.

When he came back he found Hyacinth in the boudoir. She looked pale, but particularly pretty, with a little air of tragic composure.

'May I ask if you still think seriously of leaving me?' he asked sarcastically.

'I haven't settled anything yet.'

'Why is that? Won't Anne go with you?'

She avoided answering, but said, ' I've been thinking things over, Cecil, and assuming that what you told me yesterday was true—that you met *that woman* for the first time again yesterday—I will not— go away. We will remain outwardly as we have been. But as long as I believe, as I do, that you are in love with her, I intend to be merely a friend to you.'

'A friend? What utter nonsense! I refuse to consent to anything so absurd. I won't stand it!'

'I shall not,' continued Hyacinth, taking no notice, ' interfere with your freedom at all. I don't ask you not to see her. You can go there when you like. I couldn't bear the idea that I was putting a restraint on your liberty, so that even if you offered—which you haven't—to give up seeing her at all—I wouldn't accept such a *sacrifice!*'

Cecil laughed impatiently.

'Considering I've avoided her till yesterday—'

'Ah, you admit it! That shows—that proves you care for her.'

'Don't you own yourself you were probably wrong—that you misunderstood about the drive?' he asked.

'I assume that I can believe your word—that is why I'm not leaving you. Do you accept my terms?'

His eyes flashed; he walked towards her violently, overturning a little table.

'No, I don't,' he said, ' and I never shall! It's infernal, unjust, ridiculous. You are my wife!'

She seemed not offended at his violence, but she said—

'Think it over till tomorrow. You understand that unless you agree to our each going our own way I shall not remain here.'

He came a step nearer. At this moment the door opened and the servant announced lunch.

Cecil, without saying another word, went out of the house. The door banged loudly.

At the sound Hyacinth burst into tears. 'Oh, why am I so miserable?' she sobbed.

CHAPTER XXXVI

Raggett's Sense of Humour

'E D I T H ,' said Bruce, ' I'm rather worried about Raggett.'

' Are you? Why?'

' Well, the last time I met him, he came up and asked me if I knew the difference between a sardine and a hedgehog. Of course I said no, thinking it was some riddle, but he only answered, " Then you *must* be a fool!" '

Edith smiled.

' Is that all?'

' No, it is *not* all. It will give you a shock, what I'm going to tell you now. At the office—at the *office*, mind—I received a letter from Raggett, written on a crumpet.'

' On a what?'

' On a crumpet. The letter was gummed on; the thing had a stamp, and was properly addressed to me, and it came through the post. The note itself was quite rational, but the postscript—what do you suppose the postscript said?'

' I can't think.'

' It said, " P s—Please excuse my writing to you on a crumpet, as I haven't a muffin!" '

Edith laughed.

' It's all very well to laugh, but it's a very sad thing. The poor chap is going off his head. I don't know what to do about it.'

' He isn't really, Bruce. I know what it is. I can explain the whole thing. Last time I saw him—he called the day you were rehearsing —he said he had given up being a Legitimist, and was going to try, if possible, to develop a sense of humour. He thinks for one thing it will please *me*. I'm sure he hopes you will tell me the story about the crumpet, and that I shall admire him for it.'

' Do you seriously mean that he's trying to be funny on your account?'

' That's the idea.'

'But what have you to do with his career? What is it to you? I
mean, what is it to him—whether you like people to be funny or
serious?'

'Nothing, really.'

'You admit openly, Edith, that you know he has such a liking
for you that he is becoming a clown in the hope that you will think
him witty?'

'That is it. He's afraid he's a bore—too dull. He wants to amuse
me. That's all.'

'What right has he to wish anything of the kind? Have you not
got me, if you wish to be amused? If I thought that you were right
—but, mind you, I don't; all women have their little vanities, and
I believe it's a delusion of yours about Raggett—I think he's simply
been getting a little queer in the head lately. However, if I did
think it, I should consider it an outrage. To write me a letter on a
crumpet, as a *joke!* Joke, indeed! Men have been called out for less,
Edith.'

Bruce thought a little while, then he said—

'I'll take no notice of it this time. But if I have any more nonsense from Raggett, I shall ask for an explanation. I shall say to
him, "My wife tells me that your tone, which I consider greatly
wanting in deference to me, is meant as homage to her! What do
you mean?" I shall say to Raggett, just like this, "What the—"'

Edith already regretted her candour. 'No, no; you mustn't bully
poor Raggett. Perhaps I was wrong. I daresay he wanted to amuse
us both.'

'That is more likely,' said Bruce, relenting. 'But he's going the
wrong way to work if he wishes to retain my good opinion of him.
And so I shall tell him if he gives me any more of this sort of
thing.'

'Instead of bothering about Raggett, I do wish you would answer
your father's letter, Bruce.'

'Good gracious; surely I need not answer it at once!'

'I think you should.'

'Well, what does he say?'

Bruce had such a dislike to plain facts that he never, if he could
avoid it, would read a letter to himself containing any business
details.

Edith took out the letter.

'Why I've told you already, but you wouldn't listen. On condition that you are not late at the office or absent from it except on holidays, for any reason, either pleasure or illness, for the next two years, your father will pay the debt and help you to start fresh.'

'But how can I be sure I shan't be ill? A man in my delicate state.'

'Oh, assume that you won't. Try not to be—promise to be well. Surely it's worth it?'

'Very well, perhaps it is. What a curious, eccentric man the governor is! No other man would make such extraordinary conditions. Look here, you can write for me, Edith dear, and say I accept the arrangement, and I'm awfully obliged and grateful and all that. You'll know how to put it. It's a great nuisance though, for I was thinking of giving up the whole of tomorrow to rehearsing—and chucking the office. And now I can't. It's very awkward.'

'Well, I'll write for you, though you certainly ought to do it yourself, but I shall say you are going to see them, and you will—next Sunday, won't you?'

'Sunday would be rather an awkward day. I've made a sort of vague engagement. However, if you insist, very well.'

'I can't quite understand,' said Edith, after a pause, 'how it is that the rehearsals take so long now. Yesterday you said you had to begin at eleven and it wasn't over till half-past four. And yet you have only two or three words to say in the second act and to announce someone in the first.'

'Ah, you don't understand, my dear. One has to be there the whole time so as to get into the spirit of the thing. Rehearsals sometimes take half the night; especially when you're getting to the end. You just stop for a minute or two for a little food, and then start again. Yesterday, for instance, it was just like that.'

'Where did you lunch?'

'Oh, I and one or two of the other men looked in at the Carlton.'

'It can't have taken a minute or two. It's a good distance from Victoria Street.'

'I know, but we went in the Mitchells' motor. It took no time. And then we rushed back, and went on rehearsing. *How* we work!'

'And what were you going to do tomorrow?'

He hesitated. 'Oh, tomorrow? Well, now, after this promise to the governor, I shan't be able to get there till half-past four. I should have liked to get there by twelve. And it's very awkward indeed, because Miss Flummerfelt asked me to take her out to lunch, and I half promised. In fact, I could hardly get out of it.'

' She asked you to take her alone?'

' Oh, in a thing like this you all become such pals and comrades; you don't stop to think about chaperones and things. Besides, of course, I meant to ask you to join us.'

' Very sweet of you.'

' There's the post,' remarked Bruce.

He went out into the little hall. Edith went with him.

' Who is your letter from?' asked Edith, as they went back.

Bruce blushed a little.

' It *looks* something like Miss Flummerfelt's handwriting.'

' Oh, do show me the letter!' said Edith, as he seemed about, having read it, to put it in the fire. He was obliged to allow her to take it, and she read:—

' DEAR MR OTTLEY,

' It's very kind of you to ask me to lunch tomorrow, but I can't possibly manage it. I'm engaged tomorrow, besides which I never go out anywhere without my mother.

' Yours sincerely,

' ELSA FLUMMERFELT.'

Edith smiled. ' That's fortunate,' she said. ' After all, you won't have the awkwardness of putting her off. What a good thing.'

' I assure you, Edith,' said Bruce, looking very uncomfortable, ' that I had forgotten which way it was. But, of course, I felt I ought —as a matter of decent civility to Mitchell, don't you know—to ask her once. I suppose now that you won't like me going to the rehearsals any more?'

' Oh, no! not at all,' said Edith serenely. ' I see, on the contrary, that there is nothing at all to be alarmed at. What a nice girl Miss Flummerfelt must be! I like her handwriting.'

' I see nothing particularly nice about her.'

' But she's wonderfully handsome, isn't she?'

' Why no; she has a clumsy figure, drab hair, and a colourless complexion. Not at all the type that I admire.'

' You told me the other day that she was an ideal blonde. But, of course, that,' said Edith, ' was before she refused to lunch with you!'

CHAPTER XXXVII

———

Sir Charles

E A R L Y that afternoon Hyacinth was sitting in the library in the depths of depression when Sir Charles Cannon was announced. She had forgotten to say she was not at home, or she would not have received him; but it was now too late.

He came in, and affecting not to see there was anything the matter, he said—

' I've come for some consolation, Hyacinth.'

' Consolation? Is Aunt Janet in a bad temper? I saw her pass yesterday in a green bonnet. I was afraid there was something wrong.'

' Is that so? This is interesting. Can you actually tell the shade of her temper from the shade of her clothes?'

' Yes. Can't you?'

' I don't know that I ever thought of it.'

' When Auntie is amiable she wears crimson or violet. When she's cross she always introduces green or brown into the scheme. You watch her and you'll find I'm right.'

' I have observed,' said Sir Charles slowly, ' that when we're going out somewhere that she isn't very keen about she always wears a good deal of shiny jet, and when we're at home alone and something has happened to vex her I seem to remember that she puts on a certain shaded silk dress that I particularly hate—because you never know where you are with it, sometimes it's brown and sometimes it's yellow. It depends on the light, and anyhow it's hideous; it's very stiff, and rustles.'

' I know. Shot taffeta! Oh, that's a *very* bad sign. Has she worn it lately?'

' Yes, she has, a good deal.'

' What's been the matter?'

' Oh, she has—may I smoke? Thanks—some mysterious grievance against you. She's simply furious. It seems it has something to do with somebody called Jane's sister.'

'Oh! Tell me about it.'

'Well, it appears Jane's sister wants to come and be your house-maid, and you won't let her, and she's very disappointed. You've no idea how badly you've behaved to Jane's sister.'

'Fancy! How horrid of me! Tell me some more.'

'And it's all through Miss Yeo. In fact, Anne's enmity to Jane's sister is quite extraordinary—unheard of. By some deep and malicious plot it seems she prevented you yielding to your better nature —or something—and there it is. Oh, Hyacinth, I wish she hadn't! It makes your aunt so nasty to me. Yes, *I* get the worst of it, I can tell you.'

'Poor Charles! I am sorry. If I'd known that you were going to suffer for it, I should have insisted on engaging her. Is it too late now? I believe we've got another housemaid, but can't she come too?'

'I fear it is too late. And when Janet has got accustomed to a grievance she doesn't like having it taken away either. No, nothing can be done. And I *am* having a time of it! However, it's a great comfort to see you. You're never worried are you?'

'Never worried! Why, Charles, if you only knew—of course I've *been* divinely happy, but just now I'm in real trouble.'

He looked at her.

'But I can't bear anyone to know it.'

'Then don't tell me,' he said.

'Oh, I must tell you! Besides, very likely you'll hear it soon.' Then she added, 'It's not impossible that Cecil and I may separate.'

'My dear child!'

'I believe he likes someone else better.'

'This is nonsense, Hyacinth. A mere lovers' quarrel. Of course, you must make it up at once. He's devoted to you. Who could help it?'

She broke down.

'Oh, Charles, I'm so unhappy.'

Sir Charles felt furious indignation at the idea that any man could cause those tears to flow. He put his arm round her as if she had been a child.

'My dear Hyacinth, don't be foolish. This is not serious; it can't be.' He had known her intimately since she was ten and had never seen her cry before.

The old tenderness surged up in his heart.

'Can I do anything, dear?'

'No, no, Charles. I should *die* if he knew I had told you!'

'Surely it must be your imagination.'

'I think he deceives me, and I know he prefers that horrid woman.'

'Don't cry, Hyacinth.'

She cried more, with her face buried in a cushion.

He kissed the top of her head pityingly, as if in absence of mind. He remembered it was the first time for eight years. Then he got up and looked out of the window.

'Cecil can't be such a blackguard. He's a very good fellow. Who is this new friend that you're making yourself miserable about?'

'It isn't a new friend; it's Lady Selsey.'

Sir Charles stared in amazement.

'Eugenia! Why she's the best creature in the world—utterly incapable of—I'm perfectly certain she cares for nobody in the world but Selsey. Besides, to regard her as a rival of yours at all is grotesque, child.'

'Ah, yes; you say that because you regard me almost as your daughter, and you think I'm pretty and younger, and so on. But that's not everything. There are no standards, no rules in these things. And even if there were, the point is not what she is, but what he thinks her. He thinks her wonderful.'

'Well, what has happened?'

'Never mind the details. I know his *feelings*—and that is everything.'

'You've had a quarrel, I suppose, and he's gone out of the house in a temper. Is that it?'

'I told him that I should leave him and go away somewhere with Anne.'

'Anne wouldn't go, of course.'

'You're right. She wouldn't when I asked her this morning, or I should be on my way to Paris by now.'

'If he treated you really badly,' said Sir Charles, 'she would have gone. It must be that she knows there's nothing in it.'

'I've offered to remain, on condition that we are merely friends. And he won't hear of it.'

'No wonder,' said Sir Charles. 'Now Hyacinth you know you've always been a spoilt child and had everything on earth you wanted. You must remember in life sometimes little things won't go right.'

'Anything might have gone wrong—anything in the world, and I would have borne it and not cared—but *that!*'

'I would do anything to see you happy again,' he said. 'You know that.'

She looked up. There is a tone in the accents of genuine love that nothing can simulate. She was touched.

'Look here, Hyacinth, promise me to do nothing without letting me know.'

'I promise, Charles.'

'And I assure you that everything will come right. I know—I've had a little experience of the world. Won't you trust my judgement?'

'I'll try. You are a comfort, Charles.'

'And to think that I came to you for consolation!' he said. 'Well, Hyacinth, I shall bury this—forget all about it. Next time I see you you'll be beaming again. It's a passing cloud. Now, what do you think *I've* got to do? I've got to go home and fetch Janet to go to a meeting of the Dante Society at Broadwater House.'

'Good gracious! What on earth does Aunt Janet know about Dante?'

'Nothing, indeed. I believe she thinks he wrote a poem called "Petrarch and Laura." But someone told her it's the right thing to do; and when Janet thinks anything is the right thing—!' He took his hat and stick. 'Try and forgive Cecil. I'm sure he adores you. We all do.'

'Thanks, Charles. And I do hope Aunt Janet won't be wearing her green bonnet this afternoon.'

'Thank you, dear, I trust not. Good-bye.'

CHAPTER XXXVIII

Rehearsing

'How did you get on at the rehearsal today?' Edith asked.

Bruce was looking rather depressed.

'Not very well. You can't think how much jealousy there is in these things! When you rehearse with people day after day you begin to find out what their real characters are. And Mitchell always had a very nasty temper. Of course, *he* says it's quick and soon over. He thinks that's the best kind to have. I think he's rather proud of it. The fact is he has it so often that it's as bad as if it were slow and *not* soon over. First of all, you know, there was a kind of scene about whether or not I should shave for the part of the footman. *He* said I ought. *I* declared I wouldn't ruin my appearance just for the sake of a miserable little part like that; in fact, I might say for a few minutes in a couple of hours during one evening in my life! At last we compromised. I'm to wear a kind of thing invented by Clarkson, or somebody like that, which gums down the moustache, so that you don't notice it.'

'But you don't notice it, anyhow, much.'

'What do you mean by that?'

'I don't mean anything. But I never heard of anybody noticing it. No-one has ever made any remark to me about it.'

'They wouldn't take the liberty. It can't have passed *unnoticed*, because, if it had, why should Mitchell ask me to shave?'

'There is something in that, I must admit,' she answered.

'Well, I consented to this suggestion of Mitchell's, though I don't like it at all, and I daresay it will spoil my appearance altogether. It was about something else we had a bit of a tiff this afternoon. We were going through the whole play, and one or two people were to be allowed to see us. Mitchell said he expected a certain manager, who is a pal of his, to criticise us—give us some hints, and so on. I saw a man who hadn't been there before, and I spotted him at once. He looked like a celebrity. Without waiting for an introduction, I went up and asked him what he thought of our performance. He said it seemed all right. Then I asked him if he considered my reading of my part what he would have done himself, and he laughed and said, "Yes, very much the same." We were criticising the other actors and having a long talk—at least *I* was having a long talk,—*he* didn't say much—when he suddenly said, "I'm afraid you must excuse me," and went away. Then Mitchell came up to me and said, "How on earth is it you had so much to say to that chap?" I said (still believing he was the manager) that he was an old acquaintance of mine, at least, I had known him a long time— on and off—and that he seemed very pleased to see me again. Mitchell said, "Oh, you met him before today, did you?" I answered, "Yes, rather," and I said, "He was very friendly, I must say. He's very pleased with my performance. I shouldn't be sur- prised if he sends me a box for his First Night. If he does you must come, you and Mrs Mitchell." As a matter of fact, I *had* hinted that I should like a box for the First Night at the Haymarket, and he had laughed good-naturedly, and said, "Oh, yes." So it was really no wonder that I regarded that as a promise. Well, when I told him that, Mitchell said, "He offered you a box, did he? Very nice of him. You know who he is, don't you? He's a man who has come to see about the electric lighting for the footlights. *I've* never seen him before." Now, you know, Edith, it was a most infernal shame of Mitchell to let me make the mistake with his eyes open. Here was I talking about acting and plays, deferentially consulting him, asking for artistic hints and boxes from an electrical engineer! Oh, it's too bad, it really is.'

'So you quarrelled with Mitchell again?'

'We had a few words.'

'Then the manager was not there?'

'No; he'd promised, but didn't turn up. I told Mitchell what I thought of him in very plain terms. I went so far even as to threaten to throw up my part, and he said, "Well, all right, if you don't like it you can give it up at any time," I said, "Who else could you get at the last minute to play a footman's part?" and he said, "Our footman!"'

'That would be realism, wouldn't it?'

'I was awfully hurt, but it was settled I was to stick to it. Then there are other things. That horrid Miss Flummerfelt—how I do dislike that girl—had been silly enough to go boasting to Mrs Mitchell of my invitation to lunch the other day.'

' Boasting!' said Edith.

' Yes, it was a shame, because of course I only asked her simply and solely as a way of returning some of the Mitchells' hospitality—'

' Then why did you mind their knowing?' Edith inquired.

' I *didn't* mind their knowing. How stupid you are, Edith. But I objected strongly to the tone in which Miss Flummerfelt had evidently spoken of it—to the light in which she had represented the whole thing. Mrs Mitchell came up to me in her soft purring way— what a horrid little woman she is!'

' Why, you told me she was so sweet and charming!'

' I didn't know her so well then. She came up to me and said, " Oh, Mr Ottley, will you think it rude of me if I suggest that you don't ask dear Elsa out to lunch any more? She said it's so awkward always refusing, but she's not allowed to go out like that without her mother. In fact, though her father is German by birth, she's been brought up quite in the French style. And though, of course, we know you meant no harm, she's positively shocked. You really mustn't flirt with her, Mr Ottley. She doesn't like it. In fact, she asked me to speak to you about it." There was a nice position for me, Edith! Isn't Miss Flummerfelt a treacherous little beast?'

' I thought you said she was so enormously tall. A regal-looking creature was what you called her the first time you met her. Anyhow, you must have been trying to flirt with her, Bruce. I think it rather serves you right. Well, what happened?'

' I said that I was very much astonished at Miss Flummerfelt's misunderstanding me so completely. I even said that some girls have a way of taking everything as if it was meant—in that sort of way, and that I had only asked her to lunch to meet my wife. But, of course, I promised not to do it again. And now it will be rather awful at the rehearsals, because Mrs Mitchell, of course, told her back, and Miss Flummerfelt and I don't speak.'

' Well, after all, it doesn't matter so very much. You only have to announce her. It's with the woman who plays Lady Jenkins you have your longer scene, isn't it? What is she like?'

' Mrs Abbot, do you mean? Oh, I don't think much of her. She's acted before and thinks herself quite as good as a professional, and frightfully smart. She's the most absurd snob you ever saw. She had

the cheek to criticise me and say that I don't move about the room
naturally, like a real footman. I told her, rather ironically, that I was
afraid I'd never been one. So she answered, " Still, you might have
seen one." Oh, I have a good deal to go through, one way and
another!'

' You'll be glad when it's over, won't you?'

' Very glad. The strain's telling on my health. But I've been better
on the whole, I think, don't you?'

' Yes, indeed. You know you have to be,' Edith said.

' Of course—I know. Try not to make me late again tomorrow.'

CHAPTER XXXIX

The Solution

A s Sir Charles was walking back from the Reeves' house, he met Anne Yeo in Piccadilly. She had just taken the telegram from Eugenia. He greeted her warmly and asked her to walk a little way with him, to which she agreed, silently giving him credit for so heroically concealing his consciousness of her odd appearance. She herself was well aware that in her mackintosh, driving-gloves, and eternal golf-cap she presented a sufficiently singular effect, and that there were not many people in London at three o'clock on a sunny afternoon who would care to be found dead with her.

' I've just seen Hyacinth,' he said.

' Then you know about the trouble?'

' What trouble?'

' As if she could help telling you! However, it's going to be all right.'

' Do you think so?'

' I'm certain.'

' I never thought him good enough for her,' Sir Charles said.

' Who is?' she asked.

' Has he really been—philandering?'

' Probably. Don't all men?'

' You're as great a cynic as ever, I see,' he laughingly said.

' And you're as noble as ever. But I won't tax your chivalry too far. Good-bye,' and she abruptly left him.

She was on her way to Cook's. She had suddenly decided to emigrate.

Sir Charles wondered why Anne was so sure, but her words had comforted him. He believed her. He not only thought that she must be right, but he instinctively felt certain that she had taken some steps in the matter which would result in success. Some people liked Anne, many detested her, but she inspired in both friends and enemies a species of trust.

At half-past seven that evening Cecil turned the key in the door and went into the house. It was the first time he had ever come home with a feeling of uneasiness and dread; a sensation at once of fear and of boredom. Until now he had always known that he would receive a delighted welcome, all sweetness and affection. He had always had the delicious incense of worshipping admiration swung before him in the perfumed atmosphere of love and peace. Had he held all this too cheaply? Had he accepted the devotion a little pontifically and condescendingly? Had he been behaving like a pompous ass? He had really enjoyed his wife's homage the more because he had liked to think that he still yearned for the impossible, that he had been deprived by Fate of his ideal, that absence and distance had only raised higher in his thoughts the one romantic passion of his life. What a fool he had been! All he felt at this moment about Eugenia was impatient annoyance. There is a great deal of the schoolboy in an Englishman of thirty. Cecil just now regarded her simply as the person who had got him into a row. Why had she taken him for that imprudent drive?

As he went into the little boudoir it happened that Hyacinth was turning her back to him. It was usually a part of their ritual that she came to meet him. So this seemed to him an evil omen.

She stood looking out of the window, very tall, very slender, her brown hair piled in its dense mass on her small head. When she turned round he saw she held a telegram in her hand.

'What is the meaning of this?' she said, as she held it out to him.

He took it from her and sat down to read it, feeling as he did so unpleasantly heavy, stupid, and stolid in contrast to the flash of her blue eyes and the pale tragedy in her face. It was the first time he had ever felt her inferior. As a rule the person found out in a betrayal of love holds, all the same, the superior position of the two. It is the betrayed one who is humiliated.

'What does it mean?' he said. 'Why it means that they have to put us off. They are evidently going away. What it means is fairly obvious.'

'Ah, *why* have they put us off? You have been to see her! You must have arranged this. Yes, you have given me away to her, Cecil; you have let her know I was jealous! It is worse than anything else! I shall never forgive you for this.'

He gave her back the telegram with an air of dazed resignation.

'My dear girl, I give you my solemn word of honour that I know nothing whatever about it.'

'Really? Well, it is very strange. It is most extraordinary! She says she is writing. I suppose we shall hear.'

'Are we going to have dinner?'

'You agree to what I suggested this morning, Cecil?'

'No, I don't.'

'Very well, then; I shan't dine with you.'

'Oh, confound it! I don't want to go out again.'

'Pray don't. I shall dine in my room,' and she walked to the door. As she left the room she turned round and said—

'Oh, to think how that creature must be enjoying it!' and went upstairs.

'If she isn't enjoying it any more than I am, she isn't having much of a time,' said Cecil aloud to himself. He then dined in solemn silence, Hyacinth (with a headache) being served in her own room.

When dinner was over he was glancing through the paper, wondering how he should spend the evening, when a note arrived by a messenger. He saw it was for Hyacinth, and in Eugenia's handwriting.

A few minutes later she came down, holding it in her hand.

'Cecil, she has written to me. She says they're going for a long yachting cruise, that they won't be back in their house for a year.'

'Well, have you any objection?'

'Have you?' she asked, looking at him narrowly.

'No, I'm only too glad!'

'Did you ask her to do this?'

'Don't be idiotic. How could I ask her? I've neither seen nor communicated with her.'

'Then how do you account for it, Cecil?'

'I don't account for it. Why should I? It isn't the first time Uncle Ted's gone yachting. Though he hasn't done it for some years. He was always saying he wanted to go to Crete, Samos, and the Ionian Islands. He used to talk a good deal about wanting to see the Leucadian Rock.'

'What's that?' She spoke suspiciously.

'A place that some woman threw herself into the sea from.'

'Lately, do you mean?'

'Oh, no—some time ago. Anyhow, he wanted to see it. I'm sure *I* don't know why. But that was his idea.'

'Well, she *says* they're going to Greece, so perhaps you're right. And are you really, really not sorry that she's going?'

'Not at all, if I'm going to have a little peace now.'

'Oh, Cecil,' she implored, 'have I been unfair to you?'

'Horribly unfair.'

'I'm very, very sorry. I see I was wrong. Oh, how could I be so horrid?'

'You *were* down on me! Why, you wanted to go away! You did make me pretty miserable.'

'Oh, poor boy! Then you don't care a bit for that woman, really?'

'Do you mean Eugenia? Not a straw!'

'And, oh, Cecil, if I'm *never* so horrid and bad-tempered again, will you forgive me?'

'Well, I'll try,' said Cecil.

Tenterhooks

TO ROBERT ROSS

CHAPTER I

A Verbal Invitation

BECAUSE Edith had not been feeling very well, that seemed no reason why she should be the centre of interest; and Bruce, with that jealousy of the privileges of the invalid and in that curious spirit of rivalry which his wife had so often observed, had started, with enterprise, an indisposition of his own, as if to divert public attention. While he was at Carlsbad he heard the news. Then he received a letter from Edith, speaking with deference and solicitude of Bruce's rheumatism, entreating him to do the cure thoroughly, and suggesting that they should call the little girl Matilda, after a rich and sainted—though still living—aunt of Edith's. It might be an advantage to the child's future (in every sense) to have a god-mother so wealthy and so religious. It appeared from the detailed description that the new daughter had, as a matter of course (and at two days old), long golden hair, far below her waist, sweeping lashes and pencilled brows, a rosebud mouth, an intellectual fore-head, chiselled features and a tall, elegant figure. She was a magni-ficent, regal-looking creature and was a superb beauty of the classic type, and yet with it she was dainty and winsome. She had great talent for music. This, it appeared, was shown by the breadth be-tween the eyes and the timbre of her voice.

Overwhelmed with joy at the advent of such a paragon, and horrified at Edith's choice of a name, Bruce had replied at once by wire, impulsively:

'*Certainly not Matilda I would rather she were called Aspasia.*'

Edith read this expression of feeling on a colourless telegraph form, and as she was, at Knightsbridge, unable to hear the ironical tone of the message she took it literally.

She criticised the name, but was easily persuaded by her mother-in-law to make no objection. The elder Mrs Ottley pointed out that it might have been very much worse.

'But it's not a pretty name,' objected Edith. ' If it wasn't to be

Matilda, I should rather have called her something out of Maeter-
linck—Ygraine, or Ysolyn—something like that.'

'Yes, dear, Mygraine's a nice name, too,' said Mrs Ottley, in her
humouring way, ' and so is Vaselyn. But what does it really matter?
I shouldn't hold out on a point like this. One gets used to a name.
Let the poor child be called Asparagus if he wishes it, and let him
feel he has got his own way.'

So the young girl was named Aspasia Matilda Ottley. It was
characteristic of Edith that she kept to her own point, though not
aggressively. When Bruce returned after his after-cure, it was too
late to do anything but pretend he had meant it seriously.

Archie called his sister Dilly.

Archie had been rather hurt at the—as it seemed to him—unnecessary excitement about Dilly. Not that he was jealous in any
way. It was rather that he was afraid it would spoil her to be made
so much of at her age; make her, perhaps, egotistical and vain. But
it was not Archie's way to show these fears openly. He did not weep
loudly or throw things about as many boys might have done. His
methods were more roundabout, more subtle. He gave hints and
suggestions of his views that should have been understood by the
intelligent. He said one morning with some indirectness:

'I had such a lovely dream last night, Mother.'

'Did you, pet? How sweet of you. What was it?'

'Oh, nothing much. It was all right. Very nice. It was a lovely
dream. I dreamt I was in heaven.'

'Really! How delightful. Who was there?'

This is always a woman's first question.

'Oh, you were there, of course. And father. Nurse, too. It was a
lovely dream. Such a nice place.'

'Was Dilly there?'

'Dilly? Er—no—no—she wasn't. She was in the night nursery,
with Satan.'

Sometimes Edith thought that her daughter's names were decidedly
a failure—Aspasia by mistake, Matilda through obstinacy, and Dilly
by accident. However the child herself was a success. She was four
years old when the incident occurred about the Mitchells. The whole
of this story turns eventually on the Mitchells.

The Ottleys lived in a concise white flat at Knightsbridge. Bruce's father had some time ago left him a good income on certain conditions; one was that he was not to leave the Foreign Office before he was fifty.

One afternoon Edith was talking to the telephone in a voice of agonised entreaty that would have melted the hardest of hearts, but did not seem to have much effect on the Exchange, which, evidently, was not responsive to pathos that day.

'Oh! Exchange, *why* are you ringing off? *Please* try again. . . . Do I want any number? Yes, I do want any number, of course, or why should I ring up? . . . I want 6375 Gerrard.'

Here Archie interposed.

'Mother, can I have your long buttonhook?'

'No, Archie, you can't just now, dear. . . . Go away Archie. . . . Yes, I said 6375 Gerrard. Only 6375 Gerrard! . . . Are you there? Oh, *don't* keep on asking me if I've got them! . . . No, they *haven't* answered. . . . Are you 6375? . . . Oh—wrong number—sorry. . . . 6375 Gerrard? Only six—are you there? . . . Not 6375 Gerrard? . . . Are you anyone else? . . . Oh, is it you, Vincy? . . . I want to tell you—'

'Mother, can I have your long buttonhook?'

Here Bruce came in. Edith rang off. Archie disappeared.

'It's really rather wonderful, Edith, what that Sandow exerciser has done for me! You laughed at me at first, but I've improved marvellously.'

Bruce was walking about doing very mild gymnastics, and occasionally hitting himself on the left arm with the right fist. 'Look at my muscle—look at it—and all in such a short time!'

'Wonderful!' said Edith.

'The reason I know what an extraordinary effect these few days have had on me is something I have just done which I couldn't have done before. Of course I'm naturally a very powerful man, and only need a little—'

'What have you done?'

'Why—you know that great ridiculous old wooden chest that your awful Aunt Matilda sent you for your birthday—absurd present I call it—mere lumber.'

'Yes?'

'When it came I could barely push it from one side of the room

to the other. Now I've lifted it from your room to the box-room.
Quite easily. Pretty good, isn't it?'

'Yes, of course it's very good for you to do all these exercises; no
doubt it's capital. . . . Er—you know I've had all the things taken
out of the chest since you tried it before, don't you?'

'Things—what things? I didn't know there was anything in it.'

'Only a silver tea-service, and a couple of salvers,' said Edith, in
a low voice. . . .

. . . He calmed down fairly soon and said: 'Edith, I have some news
for you. You know the Mitchells?'

'Do I know the *Mitchells*? Mitchell, your hero in your office, that
you're always being offended with—at *least* I know the Mitchells
by *name*. I ought to.'

'Well, what do you think they've done? They've asked us to
dinner.'

'Have they? Fancy!'

'Yes, and what I thought was so particularly jolly of him was
that it was a verbal invitation. Mitchell said to me, just like this,
"Ottley, old chap, are you doing anything on Sunday evening?"'

Here Archie came to the door and said, 'Mother, can I have your
long buttonhook?'

Edith shook her head and frowned.

'"Ottley, old chap,"' continued Bruce, '"are you and your
wife doing anything on Sunday? If not, I do wish you would waive
ceremony and come and dine with us. Would Mrs Ottley excuse a
verbal invitation, do you think?" I said, "Well, Mitchell, as a
matter of fact I don't believe we have got anything on. Yes, old boy,
we shall be delighted." I accepted, you see. I accepted straight out.
When you're treated in a friendly way, I always say why be un-
friendly? And Mrs Mitchell is a charming little woman—I'm sure
you'd like her. It seems she's been dying to know you.'

'Fancy! I wonder she's still alive, then, because you and Mitchell
have known each other for eight years, and I've never met her
yet.'

'Well, you will now. Let bygones be bygones. They live in
Hamilton Place.'

'Oh yes. . . . Park Lane?'

'I told you he was doing very well, and his wife has private means.'

'Mother,' Archie began again, like a litany, 'can I have your long buttonhook? I know where it is.'

'No, Archie, certainly not; you can't fasten laced boots with a buttonhook. . . . Well, that will be fun, Bruce.'

'I believe they're going to have games after dinner,' said Bruce. 'All very jolly—musical crambo—that sort of thing. . . . What shall you wear, Edith?'

'Mother, do let me have your long buttonhook. I want it. It isn't for my boots.'

'*Certainly* not. What a nuisance you are! Do go away. . . . I think I shall wear my salmon-coloured dress with the sort of mayonnaise-coloured sash. . . . (No, you're not to have it, Archie).'

'But, Mother, I've got it. . . . I can soon mend it, Mother.'

On Sunday evening Bruce's high spirits seemed to flag; he had one of his sudden reactions. He looked at everything on its dark side.

'What on earth's that thing in your hair, Edith?'

'It's a bandeau.'

'I don't like it. Your hair looks very nice without it. What on *earth* did you get it for?'

'For about six-and-eleven, I think.'

'Don't be trivial, Edith. We shall be late. Ah! It really does seem rather a pity, the very first time one dines with people like the Mitchells.'

'We sha'n't be late, Bruce. It's eight o'clock, and eight o'clock I suppose means—well, eight. Sure you've got the number right?'

'Really. Edith! . . . My memory is unerring, dear. I never make a mistake. Haven't you ever noticed it?'

'A—oh yes—I think I have.'

'Well, it's 168 Hamilton Place. Look sharp, dear.'

On their way in the taxi he gave her a good many instructions and advised her to be perfectly at her ease and *absolutely natural*; there was nothing to make one otherwise, in either Mr or Mrs Mitchell. Also, he said, it didn't matter a bit what she wore, as long as she had put on her *best* dress. It seemed a pity she had not got a new one, but this couldn't be helped, as there was now no time. Edith agreed that she knew of no really suitable place where she could buy a new evening dress at eight-thirty on Sunday evening. And, anyhow, he said, she looked quite nice, really very smart; besides, Mrs Mitchell was not the sort of person who would think any the less of a pretty woman for being a little dowdy and out of fashion.

When they drove up to what house agents call in their emotional way a superb, desirable, magnificent town mansion, they saw that a large dinner-party was evidently going on. A hall porter and four powdered footmen were in evidence.

' By Jove!' said Bruce, as he got out, ' I'd no idea old Mitchell did himself so well as this.' . . . The butler had never heard of the Mitchells. The house belonged to Lord Rosenberg.

' Confound it!' said Bruce, as he flung himself into the taxi. ' Well! I've made a mistake for once in my life. I admit it. Of course, it's really Hamilton Gardens. Sorry. Yet somehow I'm rather glad Mitchell doesn't live in that house.'

' You are perfectly right,' said Edith: ' the bankruptcy of an old friend and colleague could be no satisfaction to any man.'

Hamilton Gardens was a gloomy little place, like a tenement building out of Marylebone Road. Bruce, in trying to ring the bell, unfortunately turned out all the electric light in the house, and was standing alone in despair in the dark when, fortunately the porter, who had been out to post a letter, ran back, and turned up the light again. . . . ' I shouldn't have thought they could play musical crambo here,' he called out to Edith while he was waiting. ' And now isn't it odd? I have a funny kind of feeling that the right address is Hamilton House.'

' I suppose you're perfectly certain they don't live at a private idiot asylum?' Edith suggested doubtfully.

On inquiry it appeared the Mitchells did not live at Hamilton Gardens. An idea occurred to Edith, and she asked for a directory.

The Winthrop Mitchells lived at Hamilton Terrace, St John's Wood.

' At last!' said Bruce. ' Now we shall be too disgracefully late for the first time. But be perfectly at your ease, dear. Promise me that. Go in quite naturally.'

' How else can I go in?'

' I mean as if nothing had happened.'

' I think we'd better tell them what *has* happened,' said Edith;

' it will make them laugh. I hope they will have begun their dinner.'

' Surely they will have finished it.'

' Perhaps we may find them at their games !'

' Now, now, don't be bitter, Edith dear—never be bitter—life has its ups and downs. . . . Well ! I'm rather glad, after all, that Mitchell doesn't live in that horrid little hole.'

' I'm sure you are,' said Edith; ' it could be no possible satisfaction to you to know that a friend and colleague of yours is either distressingly hard up or painfully penurious.'

They arrived at the house, but there were no lights, and no sign of life. The Mitchells lived here all right, but they were out. The parlourmaid explained. The dinner-party had been Saturday, the night before. . . .

' Strange,' said Bruce, as he got in again. ' I had a curious presentiment that something was going wrong about this dinner at the Mitchells'.'

' What dinner at the Mitchells'? There doesn't seem to be any.'

' Do you know,' Bruce continued his train of thought, ' I felt certain somehow that it would be a failure. Wasn't it odd? I often think I'm a pessimist, and yet look how well I'm taking it. I'm more like a fatalist—sometimes I hardly know what I am.'

' I could tell you what you are,' said Edith, ' but I won't, because now you must take me to the Carlton. We shall get there before it's closed.'

CHAPTER II

Opera Glasses

WHETHER to behave with some coolness to Mitchell, and be stand-offish, as though it had been all his fault, or to be lavishly apologetic, was the question. Bruce could not make up his mind which attitude to take. In a way, it was all the Mitchells' fault. They oughtn't to have given him a verbal invitation. It was rude, Bohemian, wanting in good form; it showed an absolute and complete ignorance of the most ordinary and elementary usages of society. It was wanting in common courtesy; really, when one came to think about it, it was an insult. On the other hand, technically, Bruce was in the wrong. Having accepted he ought to have turned up on the right night. It may have served them right (as he said), but the fact of going on the wrong night being a lesson to them seemed a little obscure. Edith found it difficult to see the point.

Then he had a more brilliant idea; to go into the office as cheerily as ever, and say to Mitchell pleasantly, ' We're looking forward to next Saturday, old chap,' pretending to have believed from the first that the invitation had been for the Saturday week; and that the dinner was still to come. . . .

This, Edith said, would have been excellent, provided that the parlourmaid hadn't told them that she and Bruce had arrived about a quarter to ten on Sunday evening and asked if the Mitchells had begun dinner. The chances against the servant having kept this curious incident to herself were almost too great.

After long argument and great indecision the matter was settled by a cordial letter from Mrs Mitchell, asking them to dinner on the following Thursday, and saying she feared there had been some mistake. So that was all right.

Bruce was in good spirits again; he was pleased too, because he was going to the theatre that evening with Edith and Vincy, to see a play that he thought wouldn't be very good. He had almost beforehand settled what he thought of it, and practically what he intended to say.

But when he came in that evening he was overheard to have a strenuous and increasingly violent argument with Archie in the hall.

Edith opened the door and wanted to know what the row was about.

' Will you tell me, Edith, where your son learns such language? He keeps on worrying me to take him to the Zoological Gardens to see the—well—you'll hear what he says. The child's a perfect nuisance. Who put it into his head to want to go and see this animal? I was obliged to speak quite firmly to him about it.'

Edith was not alarmed that Bruce had been severe. She thought it much more likely that Archie had spoken very firmly to him. He was always strict with his father, and when he was good Bruce found fault with him. As soon as he grew really tiresome his father became abjectly apologetic.

Archie was called and came in, dragging his feet, and pouting, in tears that he was making a strenuous effort to encourage.

' You must be firm with him,' continued Bruce. ' Hang it! Good heavens! Am I master in my own house or am I not?'

There was no reply to this rhetorical question.

He turned to Archie and said in a gentle, conciliating voice :

' Archie, old chap, tell your mother what it is you want to see. Don't cry, dear.'

' Want to see the damned chameleon,' said Archie, with his hands in his eyes. ' Want father to take me to the Zoo.'

' You can't go to the Zoo this time of the evening. What do you mean?'

' I want to see the damned chameleon.'

' You hear!' exclaimed Bruce to Edith.

' Who taught you this language?'

' Miss Townsend taught it me.'

' There! It's dreadful, Edith; he's becoming a reckless liar. Fancy her dreaming of teaching him such things! If she did, of course she must be mad, and you must send her away at once. But I'm quite sure she didn't.'

' Come, Archie, you know Miss Townsend never taught you to say that. What have you got into your head?'

' Well, she didn't exactly teach me to say it—she didn't give me

lessons in it—but she says it herself. She said the damned chameleon
was lovely; and I want to see it. She didn't say I ought to see it.
But I want to. I've been wanting to ever since. She said it at lunch
today, and I do want to. Lots of other boys go to the Zoo, and why
shouldn't I? I want to see it so much.'

'Edith, I must speak to Miss Townsend about this very seriously.
In the first place, people have got no right to talk about queer
animals to the boy at all—we all know what he is—and in such
language! I should have thought a girl like Miss Townsend, who
has passed examinations in Germany, and so forth, would have had
more sense of her responsibility—more tact. It shows a dreadful
want of—I hardly know what to think of it—the daughter of a
clergyman, too!'

'It's all right, Bruce,' Edith laughed. 'Miss Townsend told me
she had been to see the *Dame aux Camélias* some time ago. She was
enthusiastic about it. Archie dear, I'll take you to the Zoological
Gardens and we'll see lots of other animals. And don't use that
expression.'

'What! Can't I see the da—'

'Mr Vincy,' announced the servant.

'I must go and dress,' said Bruce.

Vincy Wenham Vincy was always called by everyone simply Vincy.
Applied to him it seemed like a pet name. He had arrived at the
right moment, as he always did. He was very devoted to both Edith
and Bruce, and he was a confidant of both. He sometimes said to
Edith that he felt he was just what was wanted in the little home;
an intimate stranger coming in occasionally with a fresh atmosphere
was often of great value (as, for instance, now) in calming or
averting storms.

Had anyone asked Vincy exactly what he was he would probably
have said he was an Observer, and really he did very little else,
though after he left Oxford he had taken to writing a little, and
painting less. He was very fair, the fairest person one could imagine
over five years old. He had pale silky hair, a minute fair moustache,
very good features, a single eyeglass, and the appearance, always,
of having been very recently taken out of a bandbox.

But when people fancied from this look of his that he was an
empty-headed fop they soon found themselves immensely mistaken.

He was thirty-eight, but looked a gilded youth of twenty; and *was* sufficiently gilded (as he said), not perhaps exactly to be comfortable, but to enable him to get about comfortably, and see those who were.

He had a number of relatives in high places, who bored him, and were always trying to get him married. He had taken up various occupations and travelled a good deal. But his greatest pleasure was the study of people. There was nothing cold in his observation, nothing of the cynical analyst. He was impulsive, though very quiet, immensely and ardently sympathetic and almost too impressionable and enthusiastic. It was not surprising that he was immensely popular generally, as well as specially; he was so interested in everyone except himself.

No-one was ever a greater general favourite. There seemed to be no type of person on whom he jarred. People who disagreed on every other subject agreed in liking Vincy.

But he did not care in the least for acquaintances, and spent much ingenuity in trying to avoid them; he only liked intimate friends, and of all he had perhaps the Ottleys were his greatest favourites.

His affection for them dated from a summer they had spent in the same hotel in France. He had become extraordinarily interested in them. He delighted in Bruce, but had with Edith, of course, more mutual understanding and intellectual sympathy, and though they met constantly, his friendship with her had never been misunderstood. Frivolous friends of his who did not know her might amuse themselves by being humorous and flippant about Vincy's little Ottleys, but no-one who had ever seen them together could possibly make a mistake. They were an example of the absurdity of a tradition—' the world's ' proneness to calumny. Such friendships, when genuine, are never misconstrued. Perhaps society is more often taken in the other way. But as a matter of fact the truth on this subject, as on most others, is always known in time. No-one had ever even tried to explain away the intimacy, though Bruce had all the air of being unable to do without Vincy's society sometimes cynically attributed to husbands in a different position.

Vincy was pleased with the story of the Mitchells that Edith told him, and she was glad to hear that he knew the Mitchells and had been to the house.

' How like you to know everyone. What did they do?'

' The night I was there they played games,' said Vincy. He spoke in a soft, even voice. ' It was just a little—well—perhaps just a *tiny* bit ghastly, I thought; but don't tell Bruce. That evening I thought the people weren't quite young enough, and when they played " Oranges and Lemons, and the Bells of St Clements," and so on— their bones seemed to—well, sort of rattle, if you know what I mean. But still perhaps it was only my fancy. Mitchell has such very high spirits, you see, and is determined to make everything go. He won't have conventional parties, and insists on plenty of verve; so, of course, one's forced to have it.' He sighed. ' They haven't any children, and they make a kind of hobby of entertaining in an unconventional way.'

' It sounds rather fun. Perhaps you will be asked next Thursday. Try.'

' I'll try. I'll call, and remind her of me. I daresay she'll ask me. She's very good-natured. She believes in spiritualism, too.'

' I wonder who'll be there?'

' Anyone might be there, or anyone else. As they say of marriage, it's a lottery. They might have roulette, or a spiritual séance, or Kubelik, or fancy dress heads.'

' Fancy dress heads!'

' Yes. Or a cotillion, or just bridge. You never know. The house is rather like a country house, and they behave accordingly. Even hide-and-seek, I believe, sometimes. And Mitchell adores unpractical jokes, too.'

' *I* see. It's rather exciting that I'm going to the Mitchells at last.'

' Yes, perhaps it will be the turning-point of your life,' said Vincy. ' Ah! here's Bruce.'

' I don't think much of that opera glass your mother gave you,' Bruce remarked to his wife, soon after the curtain rose.

' It's the fashion,' said Edith. ' It's jade—the latest thing.'

' I don't care if it is the fashion. It's no use. Here, try it, Vincy.'

He handed it to Vincy, who gave Bruce a quick look, and then tried it.

' Rather quaint and pretty, I think. I like the effect,' he said, handing it back to Bruce.

' It may be quaint and pretty, and it may be the latest thing, and it may be jade,' said Bruce rather sarcastically, ' but I'm not a slave to fashion. I never was. And I don't see any use whatever in an opera glass that makes everything look smaller instead of larger, and at a greater distance instead of nearer. I call it rot. I always say what I think. And you can tell your mother what I said if you like.'

' You're looking through it the wrong side, dear,' said Edith.

CHAPTER III

The Golden Quoribus

EDITH had been very pretty at twenty, but at twenty-eight her prettiness had immensely increased; she had really become a beauty of a particularly troubling type. She had long, deep blue eyes, clearly-cut features, hair of that soft, fine light brown just tinged with red called by the French châtain clair; and a flower-like complexion. She was slim, but not angular, and had a reposeful grace and a decided attraction for both men and women. They generally tried to express this fascination by discovering resemblances in her to various well-known pictures of celebrated artists. She had been compared to almost every type of all the great painters: Botticelli, Sir Peter Lely, Gainsborough, Burne-Jones. Some people said she was like a Sargent, others called her a post-impressionist type; there was no end to the old and new masters of whom she seemed to remind people; and she certainly had the rather insidious charm of somehow recalling the past while suggesting something undiscovered in the future. There was a good deal that was enigmatic about her. It was natural, not assumed as a pose of mysteriousness. She was not all on the surface: not obvious. One wondered. Was she capable of any depth of feeling? Was she always just sweet and tactful and clever, or could there be another side to her character? Had she (for instance) a temperament? This question was considered one of interest,—so Edith had a great many admirers. Some were new and fickle, others were old and faithful. She had never yet shown more than a conversational interest in any of them, but always seemed to be laughing with a soft mockery at her own success.

Edith was not a vain woman, not even much interested in dress, though she had a quick eye and a sure impressionistic gift for it. She was always an immense favourite with women, who felt subconsciously grateful to her for her wonderful forbearance. To have the power and not to use it! To be so pretty, yet never *to take*

194

anyone away!—not even coldly display her conquests. But this liking she did not, as a rule, return in any decided fashion. She had dreadfully little to say to the average woman, except to a few intimate friends, and frankly preferred the society of the average man, although she had not as yet developed a taste for coquetry, for which she had, however, many natural gifts. She was much taken up by Bruce, by Archie and Dilly, and was fond of losing herself in ideas and in books, and in various artistic movements and fads in which her interest was cultivated and perhaps inspired by Vincy. Vincy was her greatest friend and confidant. He was really a great safety-valve, and she told him nearly every thought.

Still, Archie was, so far, her greatest interest. He was a particularly pretty boy, and she was justified in thinking him rather unusual. At this period he spent a considerable amount of his leisure time not only in longing to see real animals, but in inventing and drawing pictures of non-existent ones — horrible creatures, or quaint creatures, for which he found the strangest names. He told Dilly about them, but Dilly was not his audience—she was rather his confidante and literary adviser; or even sometimes his collaborator. His public consisted principally of his mother. It was a convention that Edith should be frightened, shocked and horrified at the creatures of his imagination, while Dilly privately revelled in their success. Miss Townsend, the governess, was rather coldly ignored in this matter. She had a way of speaking of the animals with a smile, as a nice occupation to keep the children quiet. She did not understand.

' Please, Madam, would you kindly go into the nursery; Master Archie wishes you to come and hear about the golden—something he's just made up like,' said Dilly's nurse with an expression of resignation.

Edith jumped up at once.

' Oh dear! Tell Master Archie I'm coming.'

She ran into the nursery and found Archie and Dilly both looking rather excited; Archie, fairly self-controlled, with a paper in his hand on which was a rough sketch which he would not let her see, and hid behind him.

'Mother,' Archie began in a low, solemn voice, rather slowly, 'the golden quoribus is the most horrible animal, the most awful-*looking* animal, you ever heard of in *your* life!'

'Oh-h-h! How awful!' said Edith, beginning to shiver. 'Wait a moment—let me sit down quietly and hear about it.'

She sat down by the fire and clasped her hands, looking at him with a terrified expression which was part of the ritual.

Dilly giggled, and put her thumb in her mouth, watching the effect with widely opened eyes.

'Much more awful than the gazeka, of course, I suppose?' Edith said rather rashly.

'Much,' said Dilly.

'(Be quiet, Dilly!) Mother!' he was reproachful, 'what do you mean? The gazeka? Why—the gazeka's nothing at all—it's a rotten little animal. It doesn't count. Besides, it isn't real—it never was real. Gazeka, indeed!'

'Oh, I beg your pardon,' said Edith repentantly; 'do go on.'

'No . . . the golden quoribus is far-ar-r-r-r more frightening even than the jilbery. Do you remember how awful *that* was? And much larger.'

'What! Worse than the jilbery! Oh, good gracious! How dreadful! What's it like?'

'First of all—it's as long as from here to Brighton,' said Archie.

'A little longer,' said Dilly.

'(Shut up, miss!) As long. It's called the golden quoribus because it's bright gold, except the bumps; and the bumps are green.'

'Bright green,' said Dilly.

'(Oh, will you hold your tongue, Dilly?) Green.'

'How terrible! . . . And what shape is it?'

'All pointed and sharp, and three-cornered.'

'Does it breathe fire?' asked Edith.

Archie smiled contemptuously.

'Breathe fire! Oh, Mother! Do you think it's a silly dragon in a fairy story? Of course it doesn't. How can it breathe fire?'

'Sorry,' said Edith apologetically. 'Go on.'

'*But,* the peculiar thing about it, besides that it lives entirely on muffins and mutton and the frightening part, I'm coming to now.' He became emphatic, and spoke slowly. 'The golden quoribus has more claws than any . . . other . . . animal . . . in the whole world!'

'Oh-h-h,' she shuddered.

'Yes,' said Archie solemnly. 'It has large claws coming out of its head.'

'Its head! Good gracious!'

'It has claws here and claws there; claws coming out of the eyes; and claws coming out of the ears; and claws coming out of its shoulders; and claws coming out of the forehead!'

Edith shivered with fright and held up her hands in front of her eyes to ward off the picture.

'And claws coming out of the mouth,' said Archie, coming a step nearer to her and raising his voice.

Edith jumped.

'And claws coming out of the hands, and claws coming out of the feet!'

'Yes,' said Dilly, wildly and recklessly and jumping up and down, 'and claws on the ceiling, and claws on the floor, and claws all over the world!'

With one violent slap she was sent sprawling.

Shrieks, sobs and tears filled the quiet nursery.

'I know,' said Archie, when he had been persuaded to apologise, 'of course I know a gentleman oughtn't to hit a lady, not even—I mean, especially not if she's his little sister. But oh, Mother, *ought* a lady to interrupt a story?'

When Edith told Vincy he entirely took Archie's side.

Suppose Sargent were painting a beautiful picture, and one of his pupils, snatching the paint-brush from him, insisted on finishing it, and spoiling it—how would *he* like it? Imagine a poet who had just written a great poem, and been interrupted in reciting it by someone who quickly finished it off all wrong! The author might be forgiven under such circumstances if in his irritation he took a strong line. In Vincy's opinion it served Dilly jolly well right. Young? Of course she was young, but four (he said) was not a day too soon to begin to learn to respect the work of the artist. Edith owned that Archie was not easily exasperated, and was as a rule very patient with the child. Bruce took an entirely different view. He was quite gloomy about it and feared that Archie showed every sign of growing up to be an Apache.

CHAPTER IV

The Mitchells

THE Mitchells were, as Vincy had said, extremely hospitable; they had a perfect mania for receiving; they practically lived for it, and the big house at Hampstead, with its large garden covered in, and a sort of studio built out, was scarcely ever without guests. When they didn't have some sort of party they invariably went out.

Mitchell's great joy was to make his parties different from others by some childish fantasy or other. He especially delighted in a surprise. He often took the trouble (for instance) to have a telegram sent to every one of his guests during the course of the evening. Each of these wires contained some personal chaff or practical joke. At other times he would give everyone little presents, concealed in some way. Christmas didn't come once a year to the Mitchells; it seemed never to go away. One was always surprised not to find a Christmas tree and crackers. These entertainments, always splendidly done materially, and curiously erratic socially, were sometimes extremely amusing; at others, of course, a frost; it was rather a toss-up.

And the guests were, without exception, the most extraordinary mixture in London. They included delightful people, absurd people, average people; people who were smart and people who were dowdy, some who were respectable and nothing else, some who were deplorable, others beautiful, and many merely dull. There was never the slightest attempt at any sort of harmonising, or of suitability; there was a great deal of kindness to the hard-up, and a wild and extravagant delight in any novelty. In fact, the Mitchells were everything except exclusive, and as they were not guided by any sort of rule, they really lived, in St John's Wood, superior to suburban or indeed any other restrictions. They would ask the same guests to dinner time after time, six or seven times in succession. They would invite cordially a person of no attraction whatsoever whom they had only just met, and they would behave with casual coolness to desirable acquaintances or favourite friends whom they had known all their lives. However, there was no doubt that their parties had got the name for being funny, and that was quite enough. London people in every set are so desperate for something out of the ordinary way, for variety and oddness, that the Mitchells were frequently asked for invitations by most distinguished persons who hoped, in their blasé fatigue, to meet something new and queer.

For the real Londoner is a good deal of a child, and loves Punch and Judy shows, and conjuring tricks (symbolically speaking)—and is also often dreaming of the chance of meeting some spring novelty, in the way of romance. Although the Mitchells were proud of these successes they were as free from snobbishness as almost anyone could be. On the whole Mrs Mitchell had a slight weakness for celebrities, while Mr Mitchell preferred pretty women, or people who romped. It was merely from carelessness that the Ottleys had never been asked before.

When Edith and Bruce found themselves in the large square country-house-looking hall, with its oak beams and early English fireplace, about twenty people had arrived, and as many more were expected. A lively chatter had already begun; for each woman had been offered on her arrival a basket from which she had to choose a brightly coloured ribbon. These ribbons matched the rosettes presented in an equally haphazard way to every man. As Vincy observed, it gave one the rather ghastly impression that there was going to be a cotillion at once, on sight, before dinner; which was a little frightening. In reality it was merely so that the partners for the meal should be chosen by chance. Mitchell thought this more fun than arranging guests; but there was an element of gambling about it that made wary people nervous. Everyone present would have cheated had it been possible. But it was not.

Mrs Mitchell was a tiny brown-eyed creature, who looked absurdly young; she was kind, sprightly, and rather like a grouse. Mitchell was a jovial-looking man, with a high forehead, almost too much ease of manner, and a twinkling eye.

The chief guests tonight consisted of Lord Rye, a middle-aged suffraget, who was known for his habit of barking before he spoke and for his wonderful ear for music—he could play all Richard, Oscar and Johann Strauss's compositions by ear on the piano, and never mixed them up; Aylmer Ross, the handsome barrister; Myra Mooney, who had been on the stage; and an intelligent foreigner from the embassy, with a decoration, a goat-like beard, and an Armenian accent. Mrs Mitchell said he was the minister from some place with a name like Ruritania. She had a vague memory. There was also a Mr Cricker, a very young man of whom it was said that he could dance like Nijinsky, but never would; and the rest were chiefly Foreign Office clerks (like Mitchell and Bruce), more barristers and their wives, a soldier or two, some undergraduates, a lady photographer, a few pretty girls, and vague people. There were to be forty guests for dinner and a few more in the evening.

Almost immediately on her arrival Edith noticed a tall, clean-shaven man, with smooth fair hair, observant blue eyes, and a rather humorous expression, and she instantly decided that she would try to will him to take her to dinner. (Rather a superfluous effort of magnetism, since it must have been settled already by fate and the ribbons.) It was obvious from one quick glance that he shared the wish. To their absurdly great mutual disappointment (a lot of ground was covered very quickly at the Mitchells), their ribbons didn't match, and she was taken to dinner by Captain Willis, who looked dull. Fortune, however, favoured her. On her other side she found the man who looked amusing. He was introduced to her across the table by Mrs Mitchell, with *empressement*, as Mr Aylmer Ross.

Edith felt happy tonight; her spirits were raised by what she felt to be an atmosphere *tiède*, as the French say; full of indulgence, sympathetic, relaxing, in which either cleverness or stupidity could float equally at its ease. The puerility of the silly little arrangements to amuse removed all sense of ceremony. The note is always struck by the hostess, and she was everything that was amiable, without effort or affectation.

No-one was ever afraid of her.

Bruce's neighbour at dinner was the delicate, battered-looking actress, in a Royal fringe and a tight bodice with short sleeves, who had once been a celebrity, though no-one remembered for what. Miss Myra Mooney, formerly a beauty, had known her days of success. She had been the supreme performer of ladylike parts. She

had been known as the very quintessence of refinement. It was
assumed when she first came out that a duke would go to the devil
for her in her youth, and that in her late maturity she would tour
the provinces with *The Three Musketeers*. Neither of these prophecies had, however, been fulfilled. She still occasionally took small
middle-aged titled parts in repertoire matinees. She was unable to
help referring constantly to the hit she made in *Peril* at Manchester
in 1887; nor could she ever resist speaking of the young man who
sent her red carnations every day of his blighted existence for fifteen
years; a pure romance, indeed, for, as she owned, he never even
wished to be introduced to her. She still called him poor boy,
oblivious of the fact that he was now sixty-eight, and, according
to the illustrated papers, spent his entire time in giving away a
numberless succession of daughters in brilliant marriage at St
George's, Hanover Square.

In this way Miss Mooney lived a good deal in the past, but she
was not unaware of the present, and was always particularly nice to
people generally regarded as bores. So she was never without plenty
of invitations. Mitchell had had formerly a slight *tendre* for her, and
in his good nature pretended to think she had not altered a bit. She
was still refined *comme cela ne se fait plus*; it was practically no
longer possible to find such a perfect lady, even on the stage. As she
also had all the easy good nature of the artist, and made herself
extremely agreeable, Bruce was delighted with her, and evidently
thought he had drawn a prize.

'I wondered,' Aylmer Ross said, 'whether this could possibly
happen. First I half hoped it might; then I gave it up in despair.'

'So did I,' said Edith; 'and yet I generally know. I've a touch of
second sight, I think—at dinner-parties.'

'Oh, well, I have second sight too—any amount; only it's always
wrong. However! . . .'

'Aren't the Mitchells dears?' said Edith.

'Oh, quite. Do you know them well?'

'Very well, indeed. But I've never seen them before.'

'Ah, I see. Well, now we've found our way here—broken the ice
and that sort of thing—we must often come and dine with them,
mustn't we, Mrs Ottley? Can't we come again next week?'

'Very sweet of you to ask us, I'm sure.'

'Not at all; very jolly of us to turn up. The boot is on the other

leg, or whatever the phrase is. By the way, I'm sure you know
everything, Mrs Ottley, tell me, did people ever wear only one
boot at a time, do you think, or how did this expression originate?'

'I wonder.'

Something in his suave manner of taking everything for granted
seemed to make them know each other almost too quickly, and gave
her an odd sort of self-consciousness. She turned to Captain Willis
on her other side.

'I say,' he said querulously, 'isn't this a bit off? We've got the
same coloured ribbons and you haven't said a word to me yet!
Rather rot, isn't it, what?'

'Oh, haven't I? I will now.'

Captain Willis lowered his voice to a confidential tone and said:

'Do you know, what I always say is—live and let live and let it
go at that; what?'

'That's a dark saying,' said Edith.

'Have a burnt almond,' said Captain Willis inconsequently, as
though it would help her to understand. 'Yes, Mrs Ottley, that's
what I always say. . . . But people won't, you know—they won't—
and there it is.' He seemed resigned. 'Good chap, Mitchell, isn't he?
Musical chairs, I believe—that's what we're to play this evening;
or bridge, whichever we like. I shall go in for bridge. I'm not
musical.'

'And which shall you do?' asked Aylmer of Edith. He had
evidently been listening.

'Neither.'

'We'll talk then, shall we? I can't play bridge either. . . . Mrs
Ottley—which is your husband? I didn't notice when you came in.'

'Over there, opposite; the left-hand corner.'

'Good-looking chap with the light moustache—next to Myra
Mooney?'

'That's it,' she said. 'He seems to be enjoying himself. I'm glad
he's got Miss Mooney. He's lucky.'

'He is indeed,' said Aylmer.

'She's a wonderful-looking woman—like an old photograph, or
someone in a book,' said Edith.

'Do you care for books?'

'Oh, yes, rather. I've just been discovering Bourget. Fancy, I
didn't know about him! I've just read *Mensonges* for the first time.'

H*

'Oh yes. Rather a pompous chap, isn't he? But you could do worse than read *Mensonges* for the first time.'

'I *have* done worse. I've been reading Rudyard Kipling for the last time.'

'Really! Don't you like him? Why?'

'I feel all the time, somehow, as if he were calling me by my Christian name without an introduction, or as if he wanted me to exchange hats with him,' she said. 'He's so fearfully familiar with his readers.'

'But you think he keeps at a respectful distance from his characters? However—why worry about books at all, Mrs Ottley? Flowers, lilies of the field, and so forth, don't toil or spin; why should they belong to libraries? I don't think you ever ought to read— except perhaps sometimes a little poetry, or romance. . . . You see, that is what you are, rather, isn't it?'

'Don't you care for books?' she answered, ignoring the compliment. 'I should have thought you loved them, and knew everything about them. I'm not sure that I know.'

'You know quite enough, believe me,' he answered earnestly. 'Oh, don't be cultured—don't talk about Lloyd George! Don't take an intelligent interest in the subjects of the day!'

'All right; I'll try not.'

She turned with a laugh to Captain Willis, who seemed very depressed.

'I say, you know,' he said complainingly, 'this is all very well. It's all very well no doubt. But I only ask one thing—just one. Is this cricket? I merely ask, you know. Just that—is it cricket; what?'

'It isn't meant to be. What's the matter?'   •

'Why, I'm simply fed up and broken-hearted, you know. Hardly two words have I had with you tonight, Mrs Ottley. . . . I suppose that chap's awfully amusing, what? I'm not amusing. . . . I know that.'

'Oh, don't say that. Indeed you are.' she consoled him.

'Am I though?'

'Well, you amuse *me*!'

'Right!' He laughed cheerily. He always filled up pauses with a laugh.

CHAPTER V

The Surprise

CERTAINLY Mrs Mitchell on one side and Captain Willis on the other had suffered neglect. But they seemed to become hardened to it towards the end of dinner . . .

'I have a boy, too,' Aylmer remarked irrelevantly, 'rather a nice chap. Just ten.'

Though only by the merest, slightest movement of an eyelash Edith could not avoid showing her surprise. No one ever had less the air of a married man. Also, she was quite ridiculously disappointed. One can't say why, but one doesn't talk to a married man quite in the same way or so frankly as to a bachelor—if one is a married woman. She did not ask about his wife, but said:

'Fancy! Boys are rather nice things to have about, aren't they?'

She was looking round the table, trying to divine which was Mrs Aylmer Ross. No, she wasn't there. Edith felt sure of it. It was an unaccountable satisfaction.

'Yes; he's all right. And now give me a detailed description of *your* children.'

'I can't. I never could talk about them.'

'I see . . . I should like to see them . . . I saw you speak to Vincy. Dear little fellow, isn't he?'

'He's a great friend of mine.'

'I'm tremendously devoted to him, too. He's what used to be called an exquisite. And he *is* exquisite; he has an exquisite mind. But, of course, you know what a good sort he is.'

'Rather.'

'He seems rather to look at life than to act in it, doesn't he?' continued Aylmer. 'He's a brilliant sort of spectator. Vincy thinks that all the world's a stage, but *he's* always in the front row of the stalls. I never could be like that . . . I always want to be right in the thick of it, on in every scene, and always performing!'

' To an audience?' said Edith.

He smiled and went on.

' What's so jolly about him is that though he's so quiet, yet he's genial; not chilly and reserved. He's frank, I mean—and confiding. Without ever saying much. He expresses himself in his own way.'

' That's quite true.'

' And, after all, it's really only expression that makes things real. " If you don't talk about a thing, it has never happened." '

' But it doesn't always follow that a thing has happened because you do talk about it,' said Edith. ' Ah, Mrs Mitchell's going!'

She floated away.

He remained in a rather ecstatic state of absence of mind.

Mrs Mitchell gladly told Edith all about Aylmer Ross, how clever he was, how nice, how devoted to his little boy. He had married very young, it seemed, and had lost his wife two years after. This was ten years ago, and according to Mrs Mitchell he had never looked at another woman since. Women love to simplify in this sentimental way.

' However,' she said consolingly, ' he's still quite young, under forty, and he's sure to fall in love and marry again.'

' No doubt,' said Edith, wishing the first wife had remained alive. She disliked the non-existent second one.

Nearly all the men had now joined the ladies in the studio, with the exception of Bruce and of Aylmer Ross. Mrs Mitchell had taken an immense fancy to Edith and showed it by telling her all about a wonderful little tailor who made coats and skirts better than Lucile for next to nothing, and by introducing to her Lord Rye and the embassy man, and Mr Cricker. Edith was sitting in a becoming corner under a shaded light from which she could watch the door, when Vincy came up to talk to her.

' You seemed to get on rather well at dinner,' he said.

' Yes; isn't Captain Willis a dear?'

' Oh, simply sweet. So bright and clever. I was sure you'd like him, Edith.'

Captain Willis here came up and said, a shade more jovially than he had spoken at dinner, with his laugh:

' Well, you know, Mrs Ottley, what I always say is—live and let live and let it go at that; what? But they never *do*, you know! They won't—and there it is!'

Edith now did a thing she had never done in her life before and which was entirely unlike her. She tried her utmost to retain the group round her, and to hold their attention. For a reason of which she was hardly conscious, she wanted Aylmer Ross to see her surrounded. The minister from the place with a name like Ruritania was so immensely bowled over that he was already murmuring in a low voice (almost a hiss, as they say in melodrama): '*Vous êtes chez vous, quand? Dites un mot, un mot seulement, et je me précipiterai à vos pieds,*' while at the same time, in her other ear, Lord Rye was explaining (to her pretended intense interest) how he could play the whole of *Elektra, The Chocolate Soldier* and *Night-birds* by ear without a single mistake. ('Perfectly sound!' grumbled Captain Willis, 'but why do it?') Vincy was listening, enjoying himself. Bruce came in at last, evidently engaged in an absorbed and intimate conversation with Aylmer Ross. They seemed so much interested in their talk that they went to the other end of the room and sat down there together. Aylmer gave her one glance only.

Edith was unreasonably annoyed. What on earth could he and Bruce find to talk about? At length, growing tired of her position, she got up, and walked across the room to look at a picture on the wall, turning her graceful back to the room.

Bruce had now at last left his companion, but still Aylmer Ross did not go and speak to her, though he was sitting alone.

Musical chairs began in the studio. Someone was playing 'Baby, look-a-here,' stopping suddenly in the middle to shouts of laughter and shrieks from the romping players. In the drawing-room some of the people were playing bridge. How dull the rest of the evening was! Just before the party practically broke up, Edith had an opportunity of saying as she passed Aylmer:

'I thought we were going to have a talk instead of playing games?'

'I saw you were occupied,' he answered ceremoniously. 'I didn't like—to interrupt.'

She laughed. 'Is this a jealous scene, Mr Ross?'

'I wonder,' he said, smiling, 'and if so, whose. Well, I hope to see you again soon.'

'*What* a success your charming wife has had tonight,' said Mrs
Mitchell to Bruce, as they took leave. " Everyone is quite wild about
her. How pretty she is! You *must* be proud of her.'

They were nearly the last. Mr Cricker, who had firmly refused
the whole evening, in spite of abject entreaties, to dance like
Nijinsky, suddenly relented when everyone had forgotten all about
it, and was leaping alone in the studio, while Lord Rye, always a
great lingerer, was playing Richard Strauss to himself on the baby
Grand, and smoking a huge cigar.

' Edith,' said Bruce solemnly, as they drove away, ' I've made a
friend tonight. There was one really charming man there—he took
an immense fancy to me.'

' Oh—who was that?'

' Who was that?' he mimicked her, but quite good-naturedly.
' How stupid women are in some things! Why, Aylmer Ross, the
chap who sat next to you at dinner! I suppose you didn't appreciate
him. Very clever, very interesting. He was anxious to know several
things which I was glad to be in a position to tell him. Yes—an
awfully good sort. I asked him to dine at my club one day, to go
on with our conversation.'

' Oh, did you?'

' Yes. Why shouldn't I? However, it seems from what he said that
he thinks the Carlton's nicer for a talk, so I'm going to ask him
there instead. You can come too, dear. He won't mind; it won't
prevent our talking.'

' Oh, are we going to give a dinner at the Carlton?'

' I wish you wouldn't oppose me, Edith. Once in a way! Of course
I shall. Our flat's too small to give a decent dinner. He's one of
the nicest chaps I've ever met.'

' Well, do you want me to write tomorrow morning then, dear?'

' Er—no—I have asked him already.'

' Oh, really—which day?'

' Well, I *suggested* next Thursday—but he thought tomorrow
would be better; he's engaged for every other day. Now don't go and
say you're engaged tomorrow. If you are, you'll have to chuck it!'

' Oh no; I'm not engaged.'

Mentally rearranging her evening dress, Edith drove home
thoughtfully. She was attracted and did not know why, and for the
first time hoped she had made an impression. It had been a long

evening, and her headache, she said, necessitated solitude and darkness at once.

'All right. I've got a much worse headache—gout, I think, but never mind about me. Don't be anxious, dear! I say, that Miss Mooney is a very charming woman. She took rather a fancy to me, Edith. Er—you might ask her to dinner too, if you like, to make a fourth!'

'But—really! Ought we to snatch all the Mitchells' friends the first time, Bruce?'

'Why, of course, it's only courteous. It's all right. One must return their hospitality.'

CHAPTER VI

The Visit

THE following afternoon Edith was standing by the piano in her condensed white drawing-room, trying over a song, which she was accompanying with one hand, when to her surprise the maid announced 'Mr Aylmer Ross.' It was a warm day, and though there was a fire the windows were open, letting in the scent of the mauve and pink hyacinths in the little window-boxes. She thought as she came forward to meet him that he seemed entirely different from last night. Her first impression was that he was too big for the room, her second that he was very handsome, and also a little agitated.

'I really hardly know how to apologise, Mrs Ottley. I oughtn't to have turned up in this cool way. But your husband has kindly asked me to dine with you tonight, and I wasn't sure of the time. I thought I'd come and ask you.' He waited a minute. 'Of course, if I hadn't been so fortunate as to find you in. I should just have left a note.' He looked round the room.

Obviously it was quite unnecessary for him to have called; he could have sent the note that he had brought with him. She was flattered. She thought that she liked his voice and the flash of his white teeth when he smiled.

'Oh, I'm glad I'm at home,' she said, in a gentle way that put him at his ease, and yet at an immense distance. 'I felt in the mood to stop at home and play the piano today. I'm delighted to see you.' They sat down by the fire. 'It's at eight tonight. Shall we have tea?'

'Oh no, thanks; isn't it too early? I sha'n't keep you a moment. Thanks very much. . . . You were playing something when I came in. I wish you'd play it to me over again.'

Nine women out of ten would have refused, saying they knew nothing of music, or that they were out of practice, or that they never played except for their own amusement, or something of the kind; especially if they took no pride whatever in that accomplishment. But Edith went back to the piano at once, and went on trying over the song that she didn't know, without making any excuse for the faltering notes.

'That's charming,' he said. 'Thanks. Tosti, of course.'

She came back to the fireplace. 'Of course. We had great fun last night, didn't we?'

'Oh, *I* enjoyed myself immensely; part of the time at least.'

'But after dinner you were rather horrid, Mr Ross. You wouldn't come and talk to me, would you?'

'Wouldn't I? I was afraid. Tell me, do I seem many years older since last night?' he asked.

'I don't see any difference. Why?'

'Because I've lived months—almost years—since I saw you last. Time doesn't go by hours, does it? . . . What a charming little room this is. It suits you. There's hardly anything in it, but everything is right.'

'I don't like to have many things in a room,' said Edith, holding out her delicate hands to the fire. 'It makes me nervous. I have gradually accustomed Bruce to my idea by removing one thing at a time—photographs, pictures, horrid old wedding presents, all the little things people have. They suggest too many different trains of thought. They worry me. He's getting used to it now. He says, soon there'll be nothing left but a couple of chairs and a bookcase!'

'And how right! I've had rather the same idea in my house, but I couldn't keep it up. It's different for a man alone; things seem to accumulate; especially pictures. I know such a lot of artists. I'm very unfortunate in that respect. . . . I really feel I oughtn't to have turned up like this, Mrs Ottley.'

'Why not?'

'You're very kind. . . . Excuse my country manners, but how nice your husband is. He was very kind to me.'

'He liked *you* very much, too.'

'He seems charming,' he repeated, then said with a change of tone and with his occasional impulsive brusqueness, 'I wonder—does he ever jar on you in any way?'

'Oh no. Never. He couldn't. He amuses me,' Edith replied softly.

'Oh, does he? . . . If I had the opportunity I wonder if I should *amuse* you,' he spoke thoughtfully.

'No; I don't think you would at all,' said Edith, looking him straight in the face.

'That's quite fair,' he laughed, and seemed rather pleased. 'You mean I should bore you to death! Do forgive me, Mrs Ottley. Let's go on with our talk of last night. . . . I feel it's rather like the Palace of Truth here; I don't know why. There must be something in the atmosphere—I seem to find it difficult not to think aloud—Vincy, now—do you see much of Vincy?'

'Oh yes; he comes here most days, or we talk on the telephone.'

'I see; he's your confidant, and you're his. Dear Vincy. By the way, he asked me last night to go to a tea-party at his flat next week. He was going to ask one or two other kindred spirits—as I think they're called. To see something—some collection. Including you, of course?'

'I shall certainly go,' said Edith, 'whether he asks me or not.'

Aylmer seemed to be trying to leave. He nearly got up once or twice and sat down again.

'Well, I shall see you tonight,' he said. 'At eight.'

'Yes.'

'What shall you wear, Mrs Ottley?'

'Oh, I thought, perhaps, my mauve chiffon? What do you advise?' she smiled.

'Not what you wore last night?'

'Oh no.'

'It was very jolly. I liked it. Er—red, wasn't it?'

'Oh *no*! It was pink!' she answered.

Then there was an extraordinary pause, in which neither of them seemed able to think of anything to say. There was a curious sort of vibration in the air.

'Isn't it getting quite springy?' said Edith, as she glanced at the window. 'It's one of those sort of warm days that seem to have got mixed up by mistake with the winter.'

'Very,' was his reply, which was not very relevant.

Another pause was beginning.

'Mr Vincy,' announced the servant.

He was received with enthusiasm, and Aylmer Ross now recovered his ease and soon went away.

'Edith!' said Vincy, in a reproving tone. '*Really!* How *very* soon!'

'He came to know what time we dine. He was just passing.'

'Oh, yes. He would want to know. He lives in Jermyn Street. I suppose Knightsbridge is on his way to there.'

'From where?' she asked.

'From here,' said Vincy.

'What happened after we left?' said Edith. 'I saw the Cricker man beginning to dance with hardly anyone looking at him.'

'Isn't his imitation of Nijinsky wonderful?' asked Vincy.

'Simply marvellous! I thought he was imitating George Grossmith. Do you know, I love the Mitchells, Vincy. It's really great fun there. Fancy, Bruce seems so delighted with Aylmer Ross and Miss Mooney that he insisted on their both dining with us tonight.'

'He seemed rather carried away, I thought. There's a fascination about Aylmer. There are so many things he's not,' said Vincy.

'Tell me some of them.'

'Well, for one thing, he's not fatuous, though he's so good-looking. He's not a lady-killing sort of person or anything else tedious.'

She was delighted at this especially.

'If he took a fancy to a person—well, it might be rather serious, if you take my meaning,' said Vincy.

'How sweet of him! So unusual. Do you like Myra Mooney?'

'Me? Oh, rather; I'm devoted to her. She's a delightful type. Get her on to the subject of the red carnations. She's splendid about them. . . . She received them every day at breakfast-time for fifteen years. Another jolly thing about Aylmer is that he has none of that awful old-fashioned modernness, thank goodness!'

'Ah, I noticed that.'

'I suppose he wasn't brilliant today. He was too thrilled. But, do be just a teeny bit careful, Edith dear, because when he is at all he's very much so. Do you see?'

'What a lot you seem to think of one little visit, Vincy! After all, it was only one.'

'There hasn't been time yet for many more, has there, Edith dear? He could hardly call twice the same day, on the first day, too. . . . Yes, I come over quite queer and you might have knocked me down with a feather, in a manner of speaking, when I clapped eyes on him setting here.'

Edith liked Vincy to talk in his favourite Cockney strain. It contrasted pleasantly with his soft, even voice and *raffiné* appearance.

'Here's Bruce,' she said.

Bruce came in carrying an enormous basket of gilded straw. It was filled with white heather, violets, lilies, jonquils, gardenias and mimosa. The handle was trimmed with mauve ribbon.

'Oh, Bruce! How angelic of you!'

'Don't be in such a hurry, dear. These are not from me. They arrived just at the same time that I did. Brought by a commissionaire. There was hardly room for it in the lift.'

Edith looked quickly at the card. It bore the name of the minister of the place with a name like Ruritania.

'What cheek!' exclaimed Bruce, who was really flattered. 'What infernal impertinence. Upon my word I've more than half a mind to go and tell him what I think of him—straight from the shoulder. *What's* the address?'

'Grosvenor Square.'

'Well, I don't care. I shall go straight to the embassy,' said Bruce. 'No, I sha'n't. I'll send them back and write him a line—tell him that Englishwomen are not in the habit of accepting presents from undesirable aliens. . . . I consider it a great liberty. Aren't I right, Vincy?'

'Quite. But perhaps he means no harm, Bruce. I daresay it's the custom in the place with the funny name. You see, you never know, in a place like that.'

'Then you don't think I ought to take it up?'

'I don't want them. It's a very oppressive basket,' Edith said.

'How like you, Edith! I thought you were fond of flowers.'

'So I am, but I like one at a time. This is too miscellaneous and crowded.'

'Some women are never satisfied. It's very rude and ungrateful to the poor old man, who meant to be nice, no doubt, and to show his respect for Englishwomen. I think you ought to write and thank him,' said Bruce. 'And let me see the letter before it goes.'

CHAPTER VII

—

Coup de Foudre

W H E N Aylmer Ross got back to the little brown house in Jermyn Street he went to his library, and took from a certain drawer an ivory miniature framed in black. He looked at it for some time. It had a sweet, old-fashioned face, with a very high forehead, blue eyes, and dark hair arranged in two festoons of plaits, turned up at the sides. It represented his mother in the early sixties, and he thought it was like Edith. He had a great devotion and cult for the memory of his mother. When he was charmed with a woman he always imagined her to be like his mother.

He had never thought this about his wife. People had said how extraordinarily Aylmer must have been in love to have married that uninteresting girl, no-one in particular, not pretty and a little second-rate. As a matter of fact the marriage had happened entirely by accident. It had occurred through a misunderstanding during a game of consequences in a country house. She was terribly literal. Having taken some joke of his seriously, she had sent him a touchingly coy letter, saying she was overwhelmed at his offer (feeling she was hardly worthy to be his wife) and must think it over. He did not like to hurt her feelings by explaining, and when she relented and accepted him he couldn't bear to tell her the truth. He was absurdly tender-hearted, and he thought that, after all, it didn't matter so very much. The little house left him by his mother needed a mistress; he would probably marry somebody or other, anyhow; and she seemed such a harmless little thing. It would please her so much! When the hurried marriage had come to a pathetic end by her early death everyone was tragic about it except Aylmer. All his friends declared he was heart-broken and lonely and would never marry again. He had indeed been shocked and grieved at her death, but only for her—not at being left alone. That part was a relief. The poor little late Mrs Aylmer Ross had turned out a terrible

215

mistake. She had said the wrong thing from morning till night, and, combining a prim, refined manner with a vulgar point of view, had been in every way dreadfully impossible. He had really been patience and unselfishness itself to her, but he had suffered. The fact was, he had never even liked her. That was the reason he had not married again.

But he was devoted to his boy in a quiet way. He was the sort of man who is adored by children, animals, servants and women. Tall, strong and handsome, with intelligence beyond the average, yet with nothing alarming about him, good-humoured about trifles, jealous in matters of love—perhaps that is, after all, the type women really like best. It is sheer nonsense to say that women enjoy being tyrannised over. No doubt there are some who would rather be bullied than ignored. But the hectoring man is, with few exceptions, secretly detested. In so far as one can generalise (always a dangerous thing to do) it may be said that women like best a kind, clever man who can be always trusted; and occasionally (if necessary) deceived.

Aylmer hardly ever got angry except in an argument about ideas. Yet his feelings were violent; he was impulsive, and under his suave and easy-going manner emotional. He was certainly good-looking, but had he not been he would have pleased all the same. He seemed to radiate warmth, life, a certain careless good-humour. To be near him was like warming one's hands at a warm fire. Superficially susceptible and inclined to be experimental he had not the instinct of the collector and was devoid of fatuousness. But he could have had more genuine successes than all the Don Juans and Romeos and Fausts who ever climbed rope ladders. Besides his physical attraction he inspired a feeling of reliance. Women felt safe with him; he would never treat anyone badly. He inspired that kind of trust enormously in men also, and his house was constantly filled with people asking his advice and begging him to do things—sometimes not very easy ones. He was always being left guardian to young persons who would never require one, and said himself he had become almost a professional trustee.

As Aylmer was generous and very extravagant in a way of his own (though he cared nothing for show), he really worked hard at the bar to add to his already large income. He always wanted a great deal of money. He required ease, margin and elbow-room. He had no special hobbies, but he needed luxury in general of a kind, and especially the luxury of getting things in a hurry, his theory being that everything comes to the man who won't wait. He was not above detesting little material hardships. He was not the sort of man, for instance, even in his youngest days, who would go by omnibus to the gallery to the opera, to hear a favourite singer or a special performance; not that he had the faintest tinge of snobbishness, but simply because such trifling drawbacks irritated him, and spoilt his pleasure.

Impressionistic as he was in life, on the other hand, curiously, Aylmer's real taste in art and decoration was Pre-Raphaelite; delicate, detailed and meticulous almost to preciousness. He often had delightful things in his house, but never for long. He had no pleasure in property; valuable possessions worried him, and after any amount of trouble to get some object of art he would often give it away the next week. For he really liked money only for freedom and ease. The general look of the house was, consequently, distinguished, sincere and extremely comfortable. It was neither hackneyed nor bizarre, and, while it contained some interesting things, had no superfluities.

Aylmer had been spoilt as a boy and was still wilful and a little impatient. For instance he could never wait even for a boy-messenger, but always sent his notes by taxi to wait for an answer. And now he wanted something in a hurry, and was very much afraid he would never get it.

Aylmer was, as I have said, often a little susceptible. This time he felt completely bowled over. He had only seen her twice. That made no difference.

The truth was—it sounds romantic, but is really scientific, all romance being, perhaps, based on science—that Edith's appearance corresponded in every particular with an ideal that had grown up with him. Whether he had seen some picture as a child that had left a vague and lasting impression, or whatever the reason was, the moment he saw her he felt, with a curious mental sensation, as of something that fell into its place with a click ('Ça y est!'), that she realised some half-forgotten dream. In fact, it was a rare and genuine case of *coup de foudre*. Had she been a girl he would have proposed to her the next day, and they might quite possibly have married in a month, and lived happily ever after. These things occasionally happen. But she was married already.

Had she been a fool, or a bore, a silly little idiot or a fisher of men, a social sham who prattled of duchesses or a strenuous feminine politician who babbled of votes; a Christian Scientist bent on converting, an adventuress without adventures (the worst kind), a mind-healer or a body-snatcher, a hockey-player or even a lady novelist, it would have been exactly the same; whatever she had been, mentally or morally, he would undoubtedly have fallen in love with her physically, at first sight. But it was very much worse than that. He found her delightful, and clever; he was certain she was an angel. She was married to Ottley. Ottley was all right. . . . Rather an ass . . . rather ridiculous; apparently in every way but one.

So absurdly hard hit was Aylmer that it seemed to him as if to see her again as soon as possible was already the sole object in his life. Did she like him? Intuitively he felt that during his little visit his intense feeling had radiated, and not displeased—perhaps a little impressed—her. He could easily, he knew, form a friendship with them; arrange to see her often. He was going to meet her tonight, through his own arrangement. He would get them to come and dine with him soon—no, the next day.

What was the good?

Well, where was the harm?

Aylmer had about the same code of morals as the best of his numerous friends in Bohemia, in clubland and in social London. He was no more scrupulous on most subjects than the ordinary man of his own class. Still, *he had been married himself.* That made an immense difference, for he was positively capable of seeing (and with sympathy) from the husband's point of view. Even now, indifferent as he had been to his own wife, and after ten years, it would have caused him pain and fury had he found out that she had ever tried to play him false. Of course, cases varied. He knew that if Edith had been free his one thought would have been to marry her. Had she been different, and differently placed, he would have blindly tried for anything he could get, in any possible way. But, as she was? . . . He felt convinced he could never succeed in making her care for him; there was not the slightest chance of it. And, supposing even that he could? And here came in the delicacy and scruple of the man who had been married himself. He thought he

wouldn't even wish to spoil, by the vulgarity of compromising, or
by the shadow of a secret, the serenity of her face, the gay prettiness
of that life. No, he wouldn't if he could. And yet how exciting it
would be to rouse her from that cool composure. She was rather
enigmatic. But he thought she could be roused. And she was so
clever. How well she would carry it off! How she would never bore
a man! And he suddenly imagined a day with her in the country.
. . . Then he thought that his imagination was flying on far too fast.
He decided not to be a hopeless fool, but just to go ahead, and talk
to her, and get to know her; not to think too much about her. She
needn't even know how he felt. To idolise her from a distance would
be quite delightful enough. When a passion is not realised, he
thought, it fades away, or becomes ideal worship—Dante—Petrarch
—that sort of thing! It could never fade away in this case, he was
sure. How pretty she was, how lovely her mouth was when she
smiled! She had no prejudices, apparently; no affectations; how she
played and sang that song again when he asked her! With what a
delightful sense of humour she had dealt with him, and also with
Bruce, at the Mitchells. Ottley must be a little difficult sometimes.
She had read and thought; she had the same tastes as he. He wondered if she would have liked that thing in *The Academy*, on
Gardens, that he had just read. He began looking for it. He thought
he would send it to her, asking her opinion; then he would get an
answer, and see her handwriting. You don't know a woman until
you have had a letter from her.

But no—what a fool he would look! Besides he was going to see
her tonight. It was about time to get ready. . . . Knowing subconsciously that he had made some slight favourable impression—at
any rate that he hadn't repelled or bored her—he dressed with all
the anxiety, joy and thrills of excitement of a boy of twenty; and no
boy of twenty can ever feel these things as keenly or half as elaborately as a man nearly twice that age, since all the added experiences,
disillusions, practice, knowledge and life of the additional years help
to form a part of the same emotion, making it infinitely deeper,
and all the stronger because so much more *averti* and conscious of
itself.

He seemed so nervous while dressing that Soames, the valet, to
whom he was a hero, ventured respectfully to hope there was
nothing wrong.

' No. I'm all right,' said Aylmer. ' I'm never ill. I think, Soames, I shall probably die of middle age.'

He went out laughing, leaving the valet smiling coldly out of politeness.

Soames never understood any kind of jest. He took himself and everyone else seriously. But he already knew perfectly well that his master had fallen in love last night, and he disapproved very strongly. He thought all that sort of thing ought to be put a stop to.

CHAPTER VIII

Archie's Essay

'MRS OTTLEY,' said Miss Townsend, 'do you mind looking at this essay of Archie's? I really don't know what to think of it. I think it shows talent, except the spelling. But it's *very* naughty of him to have written what is at the end.'

Edith took the paper and read:

'TRAYS OF CHARACTER

trays of character will always show threw how ever much you may polish it up trays of character will always show threw the grane of the wood.

A burd will keep on singing because he wants to and they can't help doing what it wants this is instinkt. and it is the same with trays of charicter. having thus shown my theory that trays of carocter will always show threw in spite of all trubble and in any circemstances whatever I will conclude Archibald Bruce Ottley please t.o.'

On the other side of the paper was written very neatly, still in Archie's writing:

'3 LINDEN MANSIONS,
CADOGAN SQUARE,
KNIGHTSBRIDGE.
Second Floor

1. Mr Bruce Ottley (F O)
2. Mrs Bruce Ottley
3. Master Archibald Bruce Ottley
4. Little *beast*
5. Mary Johnson housemaid
6. Miss Thrupp Cook
7. Marie maid

8. Dorothy Margaret Miss Townsend governess
9. Ellen Maud Parrot nurse.'

'Do you see?' said Miss Townsend. 'It's his way of slyly calling poor Dilly a beast, because he's angry with her. Isn't it a shame? What shall I do?'

Both of them laughed and enjoyed it.

'Archie, what is the meaning of this? Why did you make this census of your home?' Edith asked him gently.

'Why, I didn't make senses of my home; I just wrote down who lived here.'

Edith looked at him reproachfully.

'Well, I didn't call Dilly a beast. I haven't broken Miss Townsend's rules. She made a new rule I wasn't to call her a beast before breakfast—'

'What, you're allowed to call her these awful names after breakfast?'

'No. She made a rule before breakfast I wasn't to call Dilly a beast, and I haven't. How did you know it meant her anyway? It might have meant somebody else.'

'That's prevaricating; it's mean—not like you, Archie.'

'Well, I never called her a beast. No-one can say I did. And besides, anybody would have called her a beast after how she went on.'

'What are you angry with the child for?'

'Oh, she bothers so. The moment I imitate the man with the German accent she begins to cry. She says she doesn't like me to do it. She says she can't bear me to. Then she goes and tells Miss Townsend I slapped her, and Miss Townsend blames me.'

'Then you shouldn't have slapped her; it was horrid of you; you ought to remember she's a little girl and weaker than you.'

'I did remember . .'

'Oh, Archie!'

'Well, I'll make it up if she begs my pardon; not unless she does I sha'n't,' said Archie magnanimously.

'I shall certainly not allow her to do anything of the kind.'

At this moment Dilly came in, with her finger in her tiny mouth, and went up to Archie, drawling with a pout, and in a whining voice:

' I didn't *mean* to.'

Archie beamed at once.

' That's all right, Dilly,' he said forgivingly.

Then he turned to his mother.

' Mother, have you got that paper?'

' Yes, I have indeed!'

' Well, cross out—*that*, and put in Aspasia Matilda Ottley. Sorry, Dilly!' He kissed her, and they ran off together hand in hand; looking like cherubs, and laughing musically.

CHAPTER IX

Aylmer

A t the Carlton Aylmer had easily persuaded Bruce and Edith to dine with him next day, although they were engaged to the elder Mrs Ottley already. He said he expected two or three friends, and he convinced them they must come too. It is only in London that people meet for the first time at a friend's house, and then, if they take to each other, practically live together for weeks after. No matter what social engagements they may happen to have, these are all thrown aside for the new friend. London people, with all their correctness, are really more unconventional than any other people in the world. For instance, in Paris such a thing could never happen in any kind of *monde*, unless, perhaps, it were among artists and Bohemians; and even then it would be their great object to prove to one another that they were not wanting in distractions and were very much in demand; the lady, especially, would make the man wait for an opportunity of seeing her again, from calculation, to make herself seem of more value. Such second-rate solicitudes would never even occur to Edith. But she had a scruple about throwing over old Mrs Ottley.

'Won't your mother be disappointed?' Edith asked.

'My dear Edith, you can safely leave that to me. Of course she'll be disappointed, but you can go round and see her, and speak to her nicely and tell her that after all we can't come because we've got another engagement.'

'And am I to tell her it's a subsequent one? Otherwise she'll wonder we didn't mention it before.'

'Don't be in a hurry, dear. Don't rush things; remember . . . she's my mother. Perhaps to you, Edith, it seems a rather old-fashioned idea, and I daresay you think it's rot, but to me there's something very sacred about the idea of a mother.' He lit a cigarette and looked in the glass.

'Yes, dear. Then, don't you think we really ought to have kept our promise to dine with her? She'll probably be looking forward to it. I daresay she's asked one or two people she thinks we like, to meet us.'

'Circumstances alter cases, Edith. If it comes to that, Aylmer Ross has got two or three people coming to dine with him whom he thinks we might like. He said so himself. That's why he's asked us.'

'Yes, but he can't have asked them on purpose, Bruce, because, you see, we didn't know him on Thursday.'

'Well, why should he have asked them on purpose? *How* you argue! *How* you go on! It really seems to me you're getting absurdly exacting and touchy, Edith dear. I believe all those flowers from the embassy have positively turned your head. *Why* should he have asked them on purpose You admit yourself that we didn't even know the man last Thursday, and yet you expect—' Bruce stopped. He had got into a slight tangle.

Edith looked away. She had not quite mastered the art of the inward smile.

'Far better, in my opinion,' continued Bruce, walking up and down the room.—'Now, don't interrupt me in your impulsive way, but hear me out—it would be far more kind and sensible in every way for you to sit right down at that little writing-table, take out your stylographic pen and write and tell my mother that I have a bad attack of influenza. . . . Yes; one should always be considerate to one's parents. I suppose it really is the way I was brought up that makes me feel this so keenly,' he explained.

Edith sat down to the writing-table. 'How bad is your influenza?'

'Oh, not very bad; because it would worry her: a slight attack.—Stop! Not so very slight—we must let her think it's the ordinary kind, and then she'll think it's catching and she won't come here for a few days, and that will avoid our going into the matter in detail, which would be better.'

'If she thinks it's catching, dear, she'll want Archie and Dilly, and Miss Townsend and Nurse to go and stay with her in South Kensington, and that will be quite an affair.'

'Right as usual; very thoughtful of you; you're a clever little woman sometimes, Edith. Wait!'—he put up his hand with a gesture frequent with him, like a policeman stopping the traffic at

Hyde Park Corner. ' Wait!—leave out the influenza altogether, and just say I've caught a slight chill.'

' Yes. Then she'll come over at once, and you'll have to go to bed.'

' My dear Edith,' said Bruce, ' you're over-anxious; I shall do nothing of the kind. There's no need that I should be laid up for this. It's not serious.'

He was beginning to believe in his own illness, as usual.

' Air! (I want to go round to the club)—tonic treatment!—that's the thing!—that's often the very best thing for a chill—this sort of chill. . . . Ah, that will do very nicely. Very neatly written. . . . Good-bye, dear.'

As soon as Bruce had gone out Edith rang up the elder Mrs Ottley on the telephone, and relieved her anxiety in advance. They were great friends; the sense of humour possessed by her mother-in-law took the sting out of the relationship.

The dinner at Aylmer's house was a great success. Bruce enjoyed himelf enormously, for he liked nothing better in the world than to give his opinion. And Aylmer was specially anxious for his view as to the authenticity of a little Old Master he had acquired, and took notes, also, of a word of advice with regard to electric lighting, admitting he was not a very practical man, and Bruce evidently was.

Edith was interested and pleased to go to the house of her new friend and to reconstruct the scene as it must have been when Mrs Aylmer Ross had been there.

Freddy, the boy, was at school, but there was a portrait of him. Evidently he resembled his father. The sketch represented him with the same broad forehead, smooth, dense light hair, pale blue eyes under eyebrows with a slight frown in them, and the charming mouth rather fully curved, expressing an amiable and pleasure-loving nature. The boy was good-looking, but not, Edith thought, as handsome as Aylmer.

The only other woman present was Lady Everard, a plump, talk-ative, middle-aged woman in black; the smiling widow of Lord Everard, and well known for her lavish musical hospitality and her vague and indiscriminate good nature. She bristled with aigrettes and sparkled with diamonds and determination. She was marvellously garrulous about nothing in particular. She was a woman who never stopped talking for a single moment, but in a way that resembled leaking rather than laying down the law. Tepidly, indifferently and rather amusingly she prattled on without ceasing, on every subject under the sun, and was socially a valuable help because where she was there was never an awkward pause—or any other kind.

Vincy was there and young Cricker, whose occasional depressed silences were alternated with what he called a certain amount of sparkling chaff.

Lady Everard told Edith that she felt quite like a sort of mother to Aylmer.

' Don't you think it's sad, Mrs Ottley,' she said, when they were alone, ' to think that the dear fellow has no wife to look after this dear little house? It always seems to me such a pity, but still, I always say, at any rate Aylmer's married once, and that's more than most of them do nowadays. It's simply horse's work to get them to do it at all. Sometimes I think it's perfectly disgraceful. And yet I can't help seeing how sensible it is of them too; you know, when you think of it, what with one thing and another, what does a man of the present day need a wife for? What with the flats, where everything on earth is done for them, and the kindness of friends—just think how bachelors are spoilt by their married friends!—and their clubs, and the frightful expense of everything, it seems to me, as a general rule, that the average man must be madly unselfish or a perfect idiot to marry at all—that's what it seems to me—don't you? When you think of all the responsibilities they take upon themselves!—and I'm sure there are not many modern wives who expect to do anything on earth but have their bills and bridge debts paid, and their perpetual young men asked to dinner, and one thing and another. Of course, though, there are some exceptions.' She smiled amiably. ' Aylmer tells me you have two children; very sweet of you, I'm sure. What darling pets they must be! Angels!— Angels! Oh, I'm so fond of children! But, particularly—isn't it funny?—when they're not there, because I can't stand their noise. Now my little grandchildren—my daughter Eva's been married ten years—Lady Lindley, you know—hers are perfect pets and heavenly angels, but I can't stand them for more than a few minutes at a time. I have nerves, so much so, do you know (partly because I go in a

good deal for music and intellect and so on), so much so, that I very
nearly had a rest cure at the end of last season, and I should have
had, probably, but that new young French singer came over with a
letter of introduction to me, and of course I couldn't desert him,
but had to do my very best. Ever heard him sing? Yes, you would,
of course. Oh, how wonderful it is!'

Edith waited in vain for a pause to say she didn't know the name
of the singer. Lady Everard went on, leaning comfortably back in
Aylmer's arm-chair.

'Willie Cricker dances very prettily, too; he came to one of my
evenings and had quite a success. Only an amateur, of course; but
rather nice. However, like all amateurs he wants to perform only
when people would rather he didn't, and when they want him to he
won't; he refuses. That's the amateur all over. The professional
comes up to the scratch when wanted and stops when the performance is not required. It's all the difference in the world, isn't it,
Mrs Ottley? Still, he's a nice boy. Are you fond of music?'

'Very. Really fond of it; but I'm only a listener.'

Lady Everard seemed delighted and brightened up.

'Oh, you don't sing or play?—you must come to one of my
Musical Evenings. We have all the stars in the season at times—
dear Melba and Caruso—and darling Bemberk and dear Debussy!
Oh! don't laugh at my enthusiasm, my dear; but I'm quite music-
mad—and then, of course, we have any amount of amateurs, and all
the new young professionals that are coming on. In my opinion
Paul La France, that's the young man I was telling you about, will
be one of the very very best—quite at the top of the tree, and I'm
determined he shall. But of course, he needs care and encouragement. I think of his giving a *Conférence*, in which he'll lecture on
his own singing. I shall be on the platform to make a sort of intro-
ductory speech and Monti, of course, will accompany. He is the only
accompanist that counts. But then I suppose he's been accompanying somebody or other ever since he was a little boy, so it's second
nature to him. And you must come, and bring your husband. Does
he go with you to places? Very nice of him. Nowadays if husbands
and wives don't occasionally go to the same parties they have hardly
any opportunity of meeting at all; that's what I always say. But
then, of course, *you're* still almost on your honeymoon, aren't you?
Charming!'

In the dining-room Cricker was confiding in Aylmer, while Vincy and Bruce discussed the Old Master.

'Awful, you know,' Cricker said, in a low voice—'this girl's mania for me! I get wires and telephones all day long; she hardly gives me time to shave. And she's jolly pretty, so I don't like to chuck it; in fact, I daren't. But her one cry is "Cold; cold; cold!" She says I'm as cold as a stone. What do you thing of that?'

'You may be a stone, and a rolling one at that,' said Aylmer, 'but there are other pebbles on the beach, I daresay.'

'I bet not one of them as stony as I am!' cried Cricker.

Cricker came a little nearer, lowering his voice again.

'It's a very peculiar case,' he said proudly.

'Of course; it always is.'

'You see, she's frightfully pretty, on the stage, and married! One of the most awkward positions a person can be in. Mind you, I'm sorry for her. I thought of consulting you about something if you'll give me a minute or two, old chap.'

He took out a letter-case.

'I don't mean I'll show you this—oh no, I can't show it—it isn't compromising.'

'Of course not. No-one really likes to show a really lukewarm love letter. Besides, it would hardly be—'

Cricker put the case back.

'My dear chap! I wasn't going to show it to you—I shouldn't dream of such a thing—to anybody; but I was just going to read you out a sentence from which you can form an opinion of my predicament. It's no good mincing matters, old boy, the woman is crazy mad about me—there you've got it straight—in a nutshell.— Crazy!'

'She certainly can't be very sane,' returned Aylmer.

Before the end of the evening Aylmer had arranged to take the Ottleys to see a play that was having a run. After this he dropped in to tea to discuss it and Bruce kept him to dinner.

Day after day went on, and they saw him continually. He had never shown by word or manner any more of his sentiment than on the second occasion when they had met, but Edith was growing thoroughly accustomed to this new interest, and it certainly gave a zest to her existence, for she knew, as women do know, or at any rate she believed, that she had an attraction for him, which he didn't

intend to give away. The situation was pleasant and, notwithstanding Vincy's slight anxiety, she persisted in seeing nothing in it to
fear in any way. Aylmer didn't even flirt.

One day, at Vincy's rooms, she thought he seemed different.

Vincy, with all his gentle manner, had in art an extraordinary
taste for brutality and violence, and his rooms were covered with
pictures by Futurists and Cubists, wild studies by wild men from
Tahiti and a curious collection of savage ornaments and weapons.

'I don't quite see Vincy handling that double-edged Chinese
sword, do you?' said Aylmer, laughing.

'No, nor do I; but I do like to look at it,' Vincy said.

They went into the little dining-room, which was curiously
furnished with a green marble dining-table, narrow, as in the
pictures of the Last Supper, at which the guests could sit on one
side only, to be waited on from the other. On it as decoration (it
was laid for two, side by side) were some curious straw mats, a few
laurel leaves, a little marble statuette of Pan, and three Tangerine
oranges.

'Oh, Vincy, do tell me—what are you going to eat tonight?'
Edith exclaimed. 'Unless you're with other people I can never
imagine you sitting down to a proper meal.'

'Eat? Oh, a nice orange, I think,' said he. 'Sometimes when I'm
alone I just have a nice egg and a glass of water, I do myself very
well. Don't worry about me, Edith.'

When they were alone for a moment Aylmer looked out of the
window. It was rather high up, and they looked down on the
hustling crowds of people pushing along through the warm air in
Victoria Street.

'It's getting decent weather,' he said.

'Yes, quite warm.'

They always suddenly talked commonplaces when they were first
left alone.

'I may be going away pretty soon,' he said.

'Going away! Oh, where?'

'I'm not quite sure yet.'

There was a pause.

'Well, you'll come to tea tomorrow, won't you?' said Edith.

'Yes, indeed, thank you—thank you so much. I shall look forward
to it. At five?' He spoke formally.

'At four,' said Edith.

'I shall be lunching not very far from you tomorrow.'

'At a quarter to four,' said Edith.

'I wonder who this other place is laid for,' said Aylmer, looking at the table.

'How indiscreet of you! So do I. One must find out.'

'How? By asking?'

'Good heavens, no!' cried Edith. 'What an extraordinary idea!'

CHAPTER X

Shopping Chez Soi

E D I T H was expecting Aylmer to call that afternoon before he went away. She was surprised to find how perturbed she was at the idea of his going away. He had become almost a part of their daily existence, and seeing him was certainly quite the most amusing and exciting experience she had ever had. And now it was coming to an end. Some obscure clairvoyance told her that his leaving and telling her of it in this vague way had some reference to her; but perhaps (she thought) she was wrong; perhaps it was simply that, after the pleasant intercourse and semi-intimacy of the last few weeks, he was going to something that interested him more? He was a widower; and still a young man. Perhaps he was in love with someone. This idea was far from agreeable, although except the first and second time they met he had never said a word that could be described even as flirtation. He showed admiration for her, and pleasure in her society, but he rarely saw her alone. The few visits and *tête-à-têtes* had always begun by conventional commonplace phrases and embarrassment, and had ended in a delightful sympathy, in animated conversation, in a flowing confidence and gaiety, and in long discussions on books, and art, and principally people. That was all. In fact he had become, in two or three weeks, in a sense *l'ami de la maison*; they went everywhere with him and met nearly every day, and Bruce appeared to adore him. It was entirely different from her long and really intimate friendship with Vincy. Vincy was her confidant, her friend. She could tell *him* everything, and she did, and he confided in her and told her all except one side of his life, of which she was aware, but to which she never referred. This was his secret romance with a certain girl artist of whom he never spoke, although Edith knew that some day he would tell her about that also.

But with Aylmer there was, and would always be, less real freedom and impersonal frankness, because there was so much more selfconsciousness; in fact because there was an unacknowledged but very strong mutual physical attraction. Edith had, however, felt until now merely the agreeable excitement of knowing that a man she liked, and in whom she was immensely interested, was growing apparently devoted to her, while *she* had always believed that she would know how to deal with the case in such a way that it could never lead to anything more—that is to say, to more than *she* wished.

And now, he was going away. Why? And where? However, the first thing to consider was that she would see him today. The result of this consideration was the obvious one. She must do some shopping.

Edith was remarkably feminine in every attribute, in manner, in movement and in appearance; indeed, for a woman of the present day unusually and refreshingly feminine. Yet she had certain mental characteristics which were entirely unlike most women. One was her extreme aversion for shops, and indeed for going into any concrete little details. It has been said that her feeling for dress was sure and unerring. But it was entirely that of the artist; it was impressionistic. Edith was very clever, indeed, most ingenious, in managing practical affairs, as long as she was the director, the general of the campaign. But she did not like carrying out in detail her plans. She liked to be the architect, not the workman.

For example, the small household affairs in the flat went on wheels; everything was almost always perfect. But Edith did not rattle her housekeeping keys, or count the coals, nor did she even go through accounts, or into the kitchen every day. The secret was simple. She had a good cook and housekeeper, who managed all these important but tedious details admirably, under her suggestions. In order to do this Edith had to practise a little fraud on Bruce, a justifiable and quite unselfish one. She gave the cook and housekeeper a quarter of her dress allowance, in addition to the wages Bruce considered sufficient; because Bruce believed that they could not afford more than a certain amount for a cook, while he admitted that Edith, who had a few hundred pounds a year of her own, might need to spend this on dress. Very little of it went on dress, although Edith was not very economical. But she had a plan of her own; she knew that to be dressed in a very ordinary style (that is to say, simple, conventional, *comme il faut*) suited her, by throwing her unusual beauty into relief. Occasionally a touch of individuality was added, when she wanted to have a special effect. But she never entered a shop; very rarely interviewed a milliner. It was always done for her. She was easy to dress, being tall, slim and remarkably pretty. She thought that most women make a great mistake in allowing dress to be the master instead of the servant of their good looks; many women were, she considered, entirely crushed and made insignificant by the beauty of their clothes. The important thing was to have a distinguished appearance, and this cannot, of course, easily be obtained without expensive elegance. But Edith was twenty-eight, and looked younger, so she could dress simply.

This morning Edith had telephoned to her friend, Miss Bennett, an old schoolfellow who had nothing to do, and adored commissions. Edith, sitting by the fire or at the 'phone, gave her orders, which were always decisive, short and yet meticulous. Miss Bennett was a little late this morning, and Edith had been getting quite anxious to see her. When she at last arrived—she was a nondescript-looking girl, with a small hat squashed on her head, a serge coat and skirt, black gloves and shoes with spats—Edith greeted her rather reproachfully with:

' You're late, Grace.'

' Sorry,' said Grace.

The name suited her singularly badly. She was plain, but had a pleasant face, a pink complexion, small bright eyes, protruding teeth and a scenario for a figure, merely a collection of bones on which a dress could be hung. She was devoted to Edith, and to a few other friends of both sexes, of whom she made idols. She was hard, abrupt, enthusiastic, ignorant and humorous.

' Sorry, but I had to do a lot of—'

' All right,' interrupted Edith. ' You couldn't help it. Listen to what I want you to do.'

' Go ahead,' said Miss Bennett, taking out a note-book and pencil.

Edith spoke in her low, soft, impressive voice, rather slowly.

' Go anywhere you like and bring me back two or three perfectly simple tea-gowns—you know the sort of shape, rather like evening cloaks—straight lines—none of the new draperies and curves—in red, blue and black.'

' On appro.?' asked Miss Bennett.

'On anything you like, but made of Liberty satin, with a dull surface.'

'There's no such thing.' Grace Bennett laughed. 'You mean charmeuse, or crepe-de-chine, perhaps?'

'Call it what you like, only get it. You must bring them back in a taxi.'

'Extravagant girl!'

'They're not to cost more than—oh! not much,' added Edith, 'at the most.'

'Economical woman! Why not have a really good tea-gown while you're about it?'

'These *will* be good. I want to have a hard outline like a Fergusson.'

'Oh, really? What's that?'

'Never mind. And suppose you can't get the shape, Grace.'

'Yes?'

'Bring some evening cloaks—the kimonoish kind—I could wear one over a lace blouse; it would look exactly the same.'

'Edith, what curious ideas you have! But you're right enough. Anything else?' said Miss Bennett, standing up, ready to go. 'I like shopping for you. You know what you want.'

'Buy me an azalea, not a large one, and a bit of some dull material of the same colour to drape round it.'

'How extraordinary it is the way you hate anything shiny!' exclaimed Miss Bennett, making a note.

'I know; I only like *mat* effects. Oh, and in case I choose a light-coloured gown, get me just one very large black velvet orchid, too.'

'Right. That all?'

Edith looked at her shoes; they were perfect, tiny, pointed and made of black suède. She decided they would do.

'Yes, that's all, dear.'

'And might I kindly ask,' said Miss Bennett, getting up, 'any particular reason for all this? Are you going to have the flu, or a party, or what?'

'No,' said Edith, who was always frank when it was possible. 'I'm expecting a visitor who's never seen me in anything but a coat and skirt, or in evening dress.'

'Oh! He wants a change, does he?'

I*

'Don't be vulgar, Grace. Thanks awfully, dear. You're really kind.'

They both laughed, and Edith gently pushed her friend out of the room. Then she sat down on a sofa, put up her feet, and began to read *Rhythm* to divert her thoughts. Vincy had brought it to convert her to Post-Impressionism.

When Archie and Dilly were out, and Edith, who always got up rather early, was alone, she often passed her morning hours in reading, dreaming, playing the piano, or even in thinking. She was one of the few women who really can think, and enjoy it. This morning she soon put down the mad clever little prophetic Oxford journal. Considering she was usually the most reposeful woman in London, she was rather restless today. She glanced round the little room; there was nothing in it to distract or irritate, or even to suggest a train of thought; except perhaps the books; everything was calming and soothing, with a touch of gaiety in the lightness of the wall decorations. An azalea, certainly, would be a good note. The carpet, and almost everything in the room, was green, except the small white enamelled piano. Today she felt that she wanted to use all her influence to get Aylmer to confide in her more. Perhaps he was slipping away from her—she would have been only a little incident in his existence—while *she* certainly wished it to go on. Seeing this, perhaps it oughtn't to go on. She wondered if he would laugh or be serious today . . . whether . . .

★

Miss Bennett had come up in the lift with a heap of cardboard boxes, and the azalea. A taxi was waiting at the door.

Edith opened the boxes, cutting the string with scissors. She put four gowns out on the sofa. Grace explained that two were cloaks, two were gowns—all she could get.

'That's the one,' said Edith, taking out one of a deep blue colour, like an Italian sky on a coloured picture post-card. It had a collar of the same deep blue, spotted with white—a birdseye effect. Taking off her coat Edith slipped the gown over her dress, and went to her room (followed closely by Miss Bennett) to see herself in the long mirror.

'Perfect!' said Edith. 'Only I must cut off those buttons. I hate buttons.'

'How are you going to fasten it, then, dear?'

'With hooks and eyes. Marie can sew them on.'

The deep blue with the white spots had a vivid and charming effect, and suited her blonde colouring; she saw she was very pretty in it, and was pleased.

'Aren't you going to try the others on, dear?' asked Grace.

'No; what's the good? This one will do.'

'Right. Then I'll take them back.'

'You're sweet. Won't you come back to lunch?'

'I'll come back to lunch tomorrow,' said Miss Bennett, 'and you can tell me about your tea-party. Oh, and here's a little bit of stuff for the plant. I suppose you'll put the azalea into the large pewter vase?'

'Yes, and I'll tie this round its neck.'

'Sorry it's cotton,' said Miss Bennett. 'I couldn't get any silk the right colour.'

'Oh, I like cotton, if only it's not called sateen! Good-bye, darling. You're delightfully quick!'

'Yes, I don't waste time,' said Miss Bennett. 'Mother says, too, that I'm the best shopper in the world.' She turned round to add, 'I'm dying to know why you want to look so pretty. Who is it?'

With a quiet smile, Edith dismissed her.

CHAPTER XI

—

P.P.C.

'I t always seems to me so unlike you,' Aylmer said (he had arrived punctually at twenty minutes to four)—' your extreme fondness for newspapers. You're quite celebrated as a collector of Last Editions, aren't you?'

' I know it's very unliterary of me, but I enjoy reading newspapers better than reading anything else in the world. After all, it's contemporary history, that's my defence. But I suppose it is because I'm so intensely interested in life.'

' Tell me exactly, what papers do you really read?'

She laughed. ' Four morning papers—never mind their names—four evening papers; five Sunday papers: *The Academy, The Saturday Review, The Bookman, The World, The English Review.*'

' Well, I think it's wicked of you to encourage all this frivolity. And what price *The Queen, Home Notes,* or *The Tatler?*'

' Oh, we have those too—for Bruce.'

' And does Archie show any of this morbid desire for journalism?'

' Oh yes. He takes in *Chums* and *Little Folks.*'

' And I see you're reading *Rhythm.* That's Vincy's fault, of course.'

' Perhaps it is.'

' How do you find time for all this culture?'

' I read quickly, and what I have to do I do rather quickly.'

' Is that why you never seem in a hurry? I think you're the only leisured-looking woman I know in London.'

' I do think I've solved the problem of labour-saving; I've reduced it to a science.'

' How?'

' By not working, I suppose.'

' You're wonderful. And that blue. . . .'

' Do you really think so?'

He was beginning to get carried away. He stood up and looked out of the window. The pink and white hyacinths were strongly scented in the warm air. He turned round.

She said demurely: 'It will be nice weather for you to go away now, won't it?'

'I don't think so.' He spoke impulsively. 'I shall hate it; I shall be miserable.'

'Really!' in a tone of great surprise.

'You're dying to ask me something,' he said.

'Which am I dying to ask you: *where* you're going, or *why* you're going?' She gave her most vivid smile. He sat down with a sigh. People still sigh, sometimes, even nowadays.

'I don't know where I'm going; but I'll tell you why. . . . I'm seeing too much of you.'

She was silent.

'You see, Mrs Ottley, seeing a great deal of you is very entrancing, but it's dangerous.'

'In what way?'

'Well—your society—you see one gets to feel one can't do without it, do you see?'

'But why should you do without it?'

He looked at her. 'You mean there's no reason why we shouldn't keep on going to plays with Bruce, dining with Bruce, being always with Bruce?' (Bruce and Aylmer had become so intimate that they called each other by their Christian names.) 'Don't you see, it makes one sometimes feel one wants more and more of you—of your society I mean. One could talk better alone.'

'But you can come and see me sometimes, can't you?'

'Yes; that's the worst of all,' he answered, with emphasis.

'Oh.'

Aylmer spoke decidedly: 'I'm not a man who could ever be a tame cat. And also I'm not, I hope, a man who—who would dare to think, or even wish, to spoil—to—'

'And is that really why you're going?' she asked gently.

'You're forcing me to answer you.'

'And shall you soon forget all about it?'

He changed his position and sat next to her on the sofa.

'And so you won't miss me a bit,' he said caressingly. 'You wouldn't care if you never saw me again, would you?'

'Yes, I should care. Why, you know we're awfully good friends; I like you immensely.'

'As much as Vincy?'

'Oh! So differently.'

'I'm glad of that, at any rate!'

There was an embarrassed pause.

'So this is really the last time I'm to see you for ages, Mrs Ottley?'

'But aren't we all going to the theatre tomorrow? With you, I mean? Bruce said so.'

'Oh yes. I mean the last time alone. Yes, I've got a box for *The Moonshine Girl*. Bruce said you'd come. Lady Everard and Vincy will be there.'

'That will be fun—I love that sort of show. It takes one right away from life instead of struggling to imitate it badly like most plays.'

'It's always delightful to hear what you say. And anything I see with *you* I enjoy, and believe to be better than it is,' said Aylmer. 'You know you cast a glamour over anything. But the next day I'm going away for three months at least.'

'A long time.'

'Is it? Will it seem long to you?'

'Why, of course. We shall—I shall miss you very much. I told you so.'

'Really?' he insisted.

'Really,' she smiled.

They looked at each other.

Edith felt less mistress of the situation than she had expected. She was faced with a choice; she felt it; she knew it. She didn't want him to go. Still, perhaps. . . . There was a vibration in the air. Suddenly a sharp ring was heard.

Overpowered by a sudden impulse, Aylmer seized her impetuously by the shoulders, kissed her roughly and at random before she could stop him, and said incoherently: 'Edith! Good-bye. I love you, Edith,' and then stood up by the mantelpiece.

'Mr Vincy,' announced the servant.

CHAPTER XII

'The Moonshine Girl'

THE next evening Bruce and Edith were going to the Society Theatre with Aylmer. It was their last meeting before he was to go away. Edith half expected that he would put it off, but there was no change made in the plans, and they met in the box as arranged.

Aylmer had expected during the whole day to hear that she had managed to postpone the party. At one moment he was frightened and rather horrified when he thought of what he had done. At another he was delighted and enchanted about it, and told himself that it was absolutely justified. After all, he couldn't do more than go away if he found he was too fond of her. No hero of romance could be expected to do more than that, and he wasn't a hero of romance; he didn't pretend to be. But he *was* a good fellow—and though Bruce's absurdities irritated him a great deal he had a feeling of delicacy towards him, and a scrupulousness that is not to be found every day. At other moments Aylmer swore to himself, cursing his impulsiveness, fearing she now would really not ever think of him as he wished, but as a hustling sort of brute. But no—he didn't care. He had come at last to close quarters with her. He had kissed the pretty little mouth that he had so often watched with longing. He admitted to himself that he had really wished to pose a little in her eyes: to be the noble hero in the third act who goes away from temptation. But who does not wish for the *beau rôle* before one's idol?

★

This meeting at the play tonight was the sort of anti-climax that is almost invariable in a London romance. How he looked forward to it! For after Vincy came in only a few banalities had been said. He was to see her now for the last time—the first time since he had given himself away to her. Probably it was only her usual kindness

241

to others that prevented her getting out of the evening plans, he thought. Or—did she want to see him once more?

At dinner before the play Edith was very bright, and particularly pretty. Bruce, too, was in good spirits.

' It's rather sickening,' he remarked, ' Aylmer going away like this; we shall miss him horribly, sha'n't we? And then, where's the sense, Edith, in a chap leaving London where he's been the whole of the awful winter, just as it begins to be pleasant here? Pass the salt; don't spill it—that's unlucky. Not that I believe in any superstitious rot. I can see the charm of the quaint old ideas about black cats and so forth, but I don't for one moment attach any importance to them, nor to the number thirteen, nor any of that sort of bosh. Indeed as a matter of fact, I walked round a ladder only today rather than go under it. But that's simply because I don't go in for trying to be especially original.'

' No, dear. I think you're quite right.'

' And oddly enough—as I was trying to tell you just now, only you didn't seem to be listening—a black cat ran across my path only this afternoon.' He smiled, gratified at the recollection.

' How do you mean, your path? I didn't know you had one—or that there were any paths about here.'

' How literal women are! I mean *I* nearly ran over it in a taxi. When I say I nearly ran over it, I mean that a black cat on the same side of the taxi (if you must have details) ran away as the taxi drove on. . . . Yes, Aylmer is a thoroughly good chap, and he and I have enormous sympathy. I don't know any man in the world with whom I have more intellectual sympathy than Aylmer Ross. Do you remember how I pointed him out to you at once at the Mitchells'? And sometimes when I think how you used to sneer at the Mitchells —oh, you did, you know, dear, before you knew them—and I remember all the trouble I had to get you to go there, I wonder—I simply wonder! Don't you see, through going there, as I advised, we've made one of the nicest friends we ever had.'

' Really, Bruce, you didn't have *any* trouble to get me to go to the Mitchells; you're forgetting. The trouble was I couldn't go there very well until I was asked. The very first time we were asked (if you recollect), we flew!'

' Flew? Why, we went on the wrong night. That doesn't look as if I was very keen about it! However, I'm not blaming you, dear. It wasn't your fault. Mind you,' continued Bruce, 'I consider the Society Theatre pure frivolity. But one thing I'll say, a bad show there is better than a good show anywhere else. There's always jolly music, pretty dresses, pretty girls—you don't mind my saying so, dear, do you?'

'No, indeed. I think so myself.'

'Of course, the first row of the chorus is not what it was when I was a bachelor,' continued Bruce, frowning thoughtfully. 'Either they're not so good-looking, or I don't admire them so much, or they don't admire *me* as much, or they're a different class, or—or—something!' he laughed.

'You're pleased to be facetious,' remarked Edith.

'My dear girl, you know perfectly well I think there's no-one else in the world like you. Wherever I go I always say there's no-one to touch my wife. No-one!'

Edith got up. 'Very sweet of you.'

'But,' continued Bruce, 'because I think you pretty, it doesn't follow that I think everybody else is hideous. I tell you that straight from the shoulder, and I must say this for you, dear, I've never seen any sign of jealousy on your part.'

'I'd show it soon enough if I felt it—if I thought I'd any cause,' said Edith; 'but I didn't think I had.'

Bruce gave a rather fatuous smile. 'Oh, go and get ready, my dear,' he answered. 'Don't let's talk nonsense. Who's going to be there tonight, do you know?'

'Oh, only Lady Everard and Vincy.'

'Lady Everard is a nice woman. You're going to that musical thing of hers, I suppose?'

'Yes, I suppose so.'

'It's in the afternoon, and it's not very easy for me to get away in the afternoon, but to please you, I'll take you—see? I loathe music (except musical comedies), and I think if ever there was a set of appalling rotters—I feel inclined to knock them off the music-stool the way they go on at Lady Everard's—at the same time, some of them are very cultured and intelligent chaps, and *she's* a very charming woman. One can't get in a word edgeways, but *when* one does—well, she listens, and laughs at one's jokes, and that sort of thing. I think I'm rather glad you're not musical, Edith, it takes a woman away from her husband.'

'Not musical! Oh dear! I thought I was,' said Edith.

'Oh, anyhow, not when I'm here, so it doesn't matter. Besides, your being appreciative and that sort of thing is very nice. Look what a social success you've had at the Everards', for instance, through listening and understanding these things; it is not an accomplishment to throw away. No, Edith dear, I should tell you, if you would only listen to me, to keep up your music, but you won't and there's an end of it. . . . That *soufflé* was really very good. Cook's improving. For a plain little cook like that, with such small wages, and no kitchenmaid, she does quite well.'

'Oh yes, she's not bad,' said Edith. She knew that if Bruce had been aware the cook's remuneration was adequate he would not have enjoyed his dinner.

★

They were in the box in the pretty theatre. Lady Everard, very smart in black, sparkling with diamonds, was already there with Aylmer. Vincy had not arrived.

The house was crammed to the ceiling. Gay, electrical music of exhilarating futility was being played by the orchestra. The scene consisted of model cottages; a chorus of pretty girls in striped cotton were singing. The heroine came on; she was well known for her smile, which had become public property on picture post-cards and the Obosh bottles. She was dressed as a work-girl also, but in striped silk with a real lace apron and a few diamonds. Then the hero arrived. He wore a red shirt, brown boots, and had a tenor voice. He explained an interesting little bit of the plot, which included an eccentric will and other novelties. The humorous dandy of the play was greeted with shouts of joy by the chorus and equal enthusiasm by the audience. He agreed to change places with the hero, who wished to give up one hundred and forty thousand pounds a year to marry the heroine.

'Very disinterested,' murmured Lady Everard. 'Very nice of him, I'm sure. It isn't many people that would do a thing like that. A nice voice, too. Of course, this is not what *I* call good music, but it's very bright in its way, and the words—I always think these words are so clever. So witty. Listen to them—do listen to them, dear Mrs Ottley.'

They listened to the beautiful words sung, of which the refrain ran as follows:—

> ' *The Author told the Actor,*
>   *(The Actor had a fit).*
> *The Box Office man told the Programme-girl,*
>   *The Theatre all was in quite a whirl.*
> *The call-boy told the Chorus.*
>   *(Whatever could it be?)*
> *The super asked the Manager,*
>   *What did the Censor see?*'

' Charming,' murmured Lady Everard; ' brilliant—I know his father so well.'

' Whose father—the censor's?'

' Oh, the father of the composer—a very charming man. When he was young he used to come to my parties—my Wednesdays. I used to have Wednesdays then. I don't have Wednesdays now. I think it better to telephone at the last minute any particular day for my afternoons because, after all, you never know when the artists one wants are disengaged, does one? You're coming on Wednesday to hear Paul La France sing, dear Mrs Ottley?'

Edith smiled and nodded assent, trying to stop the incessant trickle of Lady Everard's leaking conversation. She loved theatres, and she enjoyed hearing every word, which was impossible while there was more dialogue in the box than on the stage; also, Aylmer was sitting behind her.

The comic lady now came on; there were shrieks of laughter at her unnecessary and irrelevant green boots and crinoline and Cockney accent. She proposed to marry the hero, who ran away from her. There was more chorus; and the curtain fell.

In the interval Vincy arrived. He and Bruce went into the little salon behind the box. Lady Everard joined them there. Edith and Aylmer looked round the house. The audience at the Society Theatre is a special one; as at the plays in which the favourite actor-managers and *jeunes premiers* perform there are always far more women than men, at this theatre there are always far more men than women.

The stage box opposite our friends was filled with a party of about ten men.

'It looks like a jury,' said Edith. 'Perhaps it is.'

'Probably a board of directors,' said Aylmer.

The first two rows of the stalls were principally occupied by middle-aged and rather elderly gentlemen. Many had grey moustaches and a military bearing. Others were inclined to be stout, with brilliant exuberant manners and very dark hair that simply wouldn't lie flat. There were a great many parties made up like those of our friends—of somebody in love with somebody, surrounded by chaperons. These were the social people, and also there were a certain number of young men with pretty women who were too fashionably dressed, too much made up, and who were looking forward too much to supper. These ladies seemed inclined to crab the play, and to find unimportant little faults with the unimportant actresses. There were many Americans—who took it seriously; and altogether one could see it was an immense success; in other words everyone had paid for their seats. . . .

The play was over; Aylmer had not had a word with Edith. He was going away the next day, and he asked them all to supper. Of course he drove Edith, and Lady Everard took the other two in her motor. . . .

'You're an angel if you've forgiven me,' he said, as they went out.

CHAPTER XIII

The Supper-party

'Have you forgiven me?' he asked anxiously, as soon as they were in the dark shelter of the cab.

'Yes, oh yes. Please don't let's talk about it any more. . . . What time do you start tomorrow?'

'You think I ought to go then?'

'You say so.'

'But you'd rather I remained here; rather we should go on as we are—wouldn't you?'

'Well, you know I should never have dreamt of suggesting you should go away. I like you to be here.'

'At any cost to me? No, Edith; I can't stand it. And since I've told you it's harder. Your knowing makes it harder.'

'I should have thought that if you liked anyone so *very* much, you would want to see them all the time, as much as possible, always —even with other people . . . anything rather than not see them— be away altogether. At least, that's how I should feel.'

'No doubt you would; that's a woman's view. And besides, you see, you don't care!'

'The more I cared, the less I should go away, I think.'

'But, haven't I tried? And I can't bear it. You don't know how cruel you are with your sweetness, Edith. . . . Oh, put yourself in my place! How do you suppose I feel when I've been with you like this, near you, looking at you, delighting in you the whole evening —and then, after supper, you go away with Bruce? *You've* had a very pleasant evening, no doubt; it's all right for you to feel you've got me, as you know you have—and with no fear, no danger. Yes, *you* enjoy it!'

'Oh, Aylmer!'

He saw in the half-darkness that her eyes looked reproachful.

'I didn't mean it. I'm sorry—I'm alway being sorry.' His bitter tone changed to gentleness. 'I want to speak to you now, Edith. We haven't much time. Don't take away your hand a minute. . . . I always told you, didn't I, that the atmosphere round you is so clear that I feel with you I'm in the Palace of Truth? You're so *real*. You're the only woman I ever met who really cared for truth. You're not afraid of it; and you're as straight and honourable as a man! I don't mean you can't diplomatise if you choose, of course, and better than anyone; but it isn't your nature to deceive yourself, nor anyone else. I recognise that in you. I love it. And that's why I can't pretend or act with you; I must be frank.'

'Please, do be frank.'

'I love you. I'm madly in love with you. I adore you.'

Aylmer stopped, deeply moved at the sound of his own words. Few people realise the effect such words have on the speaker. Saying them to her was a great joy, and an indulgence, but it increased painfully his passionate feeling, making it more accentuated and acute. To let himself go verbally was a wild, bitter pleasure. It hurt him, and he enjoyed it.

'And I'd do anything in the world to get you. And I'd do anything in the world for you, too. And if you cared for me I'd go away all the same. At least, I believe I should. . . . We shall be there in a minute.

'Listen, dear. I want you, occasionally, to write to me; there's no earthly reason why you shouldn't. I'll let you know my address. It will prevent my being too miserable, or rushing back. And will you do something else for me?'

'Anything.'

'Angel! Well, when you write, call me Aylmer. You never have yet, in a letter. Treat me just like a friend—as you treat Vincy. Tell me what you're doing, where you're going, who you see; about Archie and Dilly; about your new dresses and hats; what you're reading—any little thing, so that I'm still in touch with you.'

'Yes, I will; I shall like to. And don't be depressed, Aylmer. Do enjoy your journey; write to me, too.'

'Yes, I'm going to write to you, but only in an official way, only for Bruce. And, listen. Take care of yourself. You're too unselfish. Do what you want sometimes, not what other people want all the time. Don't read too much by electric light and try your eyes. And don't go out in these thin shoes in damp weather—promise!'

She laughed a little—touched.

'Be a great deal with the children. I like to think of you with them. And I hope you won't be always going out,' he continued, in a tone of unconscious command, which she enjoyed. . . . 'Please don't be continually at Lady Everard's, or at the Mitchells', or anywhere. I hate you to be admired—how I hate it!'

'Fancy! And I was always brought up to believe people are proud of what's called the " success " of the people that they—like.'

'Don't you believe it, Edith! That's all bosh—vanity and nonsense. At any rate, I know I'm not. In fact, as I can't have you myself, I would really like you to be shut up. Very happy, very well, with everything in the world you like, even thinking of me a little, but absolutely shut up! And if you did go out, for a breath of air, I should like no-one to see you. I'd like you to cover up your head—wear a thick veil—and a thick loose dress!'

'You're very Oriental!' she laughed.

'I'm not a bit Oriental; I'm human. It's selfish, I suppose, you think? Well, let me tell you, if you care to know, that it's *love*, and nothing else, Edith. . . . Now, is there anything in the world I can do for you while I'm away? It would be kind to ask me. Remember I sha'n't see you for three months. I may come back in September. Can't I send you something—do *something* that you'd like? I count on you to ask me at any time if there's anything in the world I could do for you, no matter what!'

No woman could help being really pleased at such whole-hearted devotion and such Bluebeard-like views—especially when they were not going to be carried out. Edith was thrilled by the passionate emotion she felt near her. How cold it would be when he had gone! He *was* nice, handsome, clever—a darling!

'Don't forget me, Aylmer. I don't want you to forget me. Later on we'll have a real friendship.'

'*Friendship!* Don't use that word. It's so false—such humbug—for *me* at any rate. To say I could care for you as a friend is simply blasphemy! How can it be possible for *me*? But I'll try. Thanks for *any*thing! You're an angel—I'll try.'

'And it's horribly inconsistent, and no doubt very wicked of me, but, do you know, I should be rather pained if I heard you had fallen in love with someone else.'

'Ah, that would be impossible!' he cried. 'Never—never! It's the real thing; there never was anyone like you, there never will be.

Let me look at you once more. . . . Oh, Edith! And now—here we are.'

Edith took away her hand.

'Your scarf's coming off, you'll catch cold,' said Aylmer, and as he was trying, rather awkwardly, to put the piece of blue chiffon round her head he drew the dear head to him and kissed her harshly. She could not protest; it was too final; besides, they were arriving; the cab stopped. Vincy came to the door.

'Welcome to Normanhurst!' cried Vincy, with unnecessary facetiousness, giving them a slightly anxious glance. He thought Edith had more colour than usual. Aylmer was pale.

The supper was an absolute and complete failure; the guests displayed the forced gaiety and real depression, and constrained absent-mindedness, of genuine and hopeless boredom. Except for Lady Everard's ceaseless flow of empty prattle the pauses would have been too obvious. Edith, for whom it was a dreary anti-climax, was rather silent. Aylmer talked more, and a little more loudly, than usual, and looked worn. Bruce, whom champagne quickly saddened, became vaguely reminiscent and communicative about old, dead, forgotten grievances of the past, while Vincy, who was a little shocked at what he saw (and he always saw everything), did his very best, just saving the entertainment from being a too disastrous frost.

'Well! Good luck!' said Aylmer, lifting his glass with sham conviviality. 'I start tomorrow morning by the Orient Express.'

'Hooray!' whispered Vincy primly.

'Doesn't it sound romantic and exciting?' Edith said. 'The two words together are so delightfully adventurous. Orient—the languid East, and yet express—quickness, speed. It's a fascinating blend of ideas.'

'Whether it's adventurous or not isn't the question, my dear girl; I only wish we were going too,' said Bruce, with a sigh; 'but, I never can get away from my wretched work, to have any fun, like you lucky chaps, with no responsibilities or troubles! I suppose perhaps we may take the children to Westgate for Whitsuntide, and that's about all. Not that there isn't quite a good hotel there, and of course it's all right for me, because I shall play golf all day and run up to town when I want to. Still, it's very different from one of these jolly long journeys that you gay bachelors can indulge in.'

'But I'm not a gay bachelor. My boy is coming to join me in the summer holidays, wherever I am,' said Aylmer.

'Ah, but that's not the point. I should like to go with you now— at once. Don't you wish we were both going, Edith? Why aren't we going with him tomorrow?'

'Surely June's just the nice time in London, Bruce,' said Vincy, in his demure voice.

'Won't it be terribly hot?' said Lady Everard vaguely. She always thought every place must be terribly hot. ' Venice? Are you going to Venice? Delightful! The Viennese are so charming, and the Austrian officers— Oh, you're going to Sicily first? Far too hot. Paul La France—the young singer, you know—told me that when he was in Sicily his voice completely altered; the heat quite affected the *velouté* of his voice, as the French call it—and what a voice it is at its best! It's not the *highest* tenor, of course, but the medium is so wonderfully soft and well developed. I don't say for a moment that he will ever be a Caruso, but as far as he goes—and he goes pretty far, mind—it's really wonderful. You're coming on Wednesday, aren't you, dear Mrs Ottley? Ah!' . . . She stopped and held up her small beaded fan, ' what's that the band's playing? I know it so well; everyone knows it; it's either *Pagliacci* or *Bohème*, or something. No, isn't it really? What is it? All the old Italian operas are coming in again, by the way, you know, my dear . . . *Rigoletto, Lucia, Traviata*—the *bel canto*—that sort of thing; there's nothing like it for showing off the voice. Wagner's practically gone out (at least what *I* call out), and I always said Debussy wouldn't last. Paul La France still clings to Brahms—Brahms suits his voice better than anyone else. He always falls back on Brahms, and dear de Lara; and Tosti; of course, Tosti. I remember . . ."

Aylmer and his guests had reached the stage of being apparently all lost in their own thoughts, and the conversation had been practically reduced to a disjointed monologue on music by Lady Everard, when the lights began to be lowered, and the party broke up.

'I'm coming to see you *so* soon,' said Vincy.

CHAPTER XIV

The Letter

I T was about a fortnight later.

Edith and Bruce, from different directions, arrived at the same moment at their door, and went up together in the lift. On the little hall-table was a letter addressed to Edith. She took it up rather quickly, and went into the drawing-room. Bruce followed her.

'That a letter, Edith?'

'What do you suppose it is, Bruce?'

'What *could* I have supposed it was, Edith? A plum pudding?' He laughed very much.

'You are very humorous today, Bruce.'

She sat down with her hat, veil and gloves on, holding the letter. She did not go to her room, because that would leave her no further retreat. Bruce sat down exactly opposite to her, with his coat and gloves on. He slowly drew off one glove, folded it carefully, and put it down. Then he said amiably, a little huskily:

'Letter from a friend?'

'I beg your pardon? What did you say, dear?'

He raised his voice unnecessarily:

'I said A LETTER FROM A FRIEND!'

She started. 'Oh yes! I heard this time.'

'Edith, I know of an excellent aurist in Bond Street. I wish you'd go and see him. I'll give you the address.'

'I know of a very good elocutionist in Oxford Street. I think I would go and have some lessons, if I were you, Bruce; the summer classes are just beginning. They teach you to speak so clearly, to get your voice over the footlights, as it were. I think all men require to study oratory and elocution. It comes in so useful!'

Bruce lowered his voice almost to a whisper.

'Are you playing the fool with me?'

She nodded amiably in the manner of a person perfectly deaf, but who is pretending to hear.

'Yes, dear; yes, quite right.'

'What do you mean by "quite right"?' He unfastened his coat and threw it open, glaring at her a little.

'Who—me? *I* don't know.'

'Who is that letter from, Edith?' he said breezily, in a tone of sudden careless and cheery interest.

'I haven't read it yet, Bruce,' she answered, in the same tone, brightly.

'Oh. Why don't you read it?'

'Oh! I shall presently.'

'When?'

'When I've opened it.'

He took off his other glove, folded it with the first one, made them into a ball, and threw it across the room against the window, while his colour deepened.

'Oh, do you want to have a game? Shall I send for Archie?'

'Edith, why don't you take off your hat?'

'I can't think. Why don't you take off your coat?'

'I haven't time. Show me that letter.'

'What letter?'

'Don't prevaricate with me.' Bruce had now definitely lost his temper. 'I can stand anything except prevarication. Anything in the world, but prevarication, I can endure, with patience. But *not* that! As if you didn't know perfectly well there's only one letter I want to see.'

'Really?'

'Who's your letter from?'

'How should I know?'

Edith got up and went towards the door. Bruce was beforehand with her and barred the way, standing with his arms outstretched and his back to the door.

'Edith, I'm pained and surprised at your conduct!'

'Conduct!' she exclaimed.

'Don't echo my words! I will *not* be echoed, do you hear? . . . Behaviour, then, if you prefer the word. . . . Why don't you wish me to see that letter?'

Edith quickly looked at the letter. Until this moment she had had an unreasonable and nervous terror that Aylmer might have forgotten his intention of writing what he called officially, and might have written her what she now inwardly termed a lot of nonsense. But she now saw she had made a mistake: it was not his handwriting nor his postmark. She became firmer.

'Look here Bruce,' she said, in a decided voice, quietly. 'We have been married eight years, and I consider you ought to trust me sufficiently to allow me to open my own letters.'

'Oh, you do, do you? What next? What next! I suppose the next thing you'll wish is to be a suffragette.'

'The question,' said Edith, in the most cool, high, irritating voice she could command, 'really, of votes for women hardly enters into our argument here. As a matter of fact, I take no interest in any kind of politics, and, I may be entirely wrong, but if I were compelled to take sides on the subject, I should be an anti-suffragist.'

'Oh, you would, would you? That's as well to know! That's interesting. Give me that letter.'

'Do you think you have the right to speak to me like that?'

'Edith,' he said rather pathetically, trying to control himself. 'I beg you, I *implore* you to let me see the letter! Hang it all! You know perfectly well, old girl, how fond I am of you. I may worry you a bit sometimes, but you know my heart's all right.'

'Of course, Bruce; I'm not finding fault with you. I only want to read my own letter, that's all.'

'But if I let you out of this room without having shown it me, then if there's something you don't want me to see, you'll tear it up or chuck it in the fire.'

Edith was quite impressed at this flash of prophetic insight. She admitted to herself he was right.

'It's entirely a matter of principle,' she said after another reassuring look at the envelope. 'It's only a matter of principle, dear, I'm twenty-eight years old, we've been married eight years; you leave the housekeeping, the whole ordering of the children's education, and heaps of other quite important things, entirely to me; in fact, you lead almost the life of a schoolboy, without any of the tiresome part, and with freedom, going to school in the day and amusing yourself in the evening, while everything disagreeable and important is thought of and seen to for you. You only have the children with you when they amuse you. *I* have all the responsibility; I have to be patient, thoughtful—in fact, you leave things to me more than most men do to their wives, Bruce. You won't be bothered even to look at an account—to do a thing. But I'm not complaining.'

'Oh, you're not! It sounded a little like it.'

'But it isn't. I don't *mind* all this responsibility, but I ought, at least, to be allowed to read my letters.'

'Well, darling, you shall, as a rule. Look here, old girl, you shall. I promise you, faithfully, dear. Oh, Edith, you're looking awfully pretty; I like that hat. Look here, I promise you, dear, I'll *never* ask you again, never as long as I live. But I've a fancy to read this particular letter. Why not just gratify it? It's a very harmless whim.' His tone suddenly changed. 'What do you suppose there's *in* the damned letter? Something you're jolly well anxious I shouldn't see.'

She made a step forward. He rushed at her, snatched the letter out of her hand, and went to the window with it.

She went into her own room, shut the door, and threw herself on the bed, her whole frame shaking with suppressed laughter.

Bruce, alone, with trembling fingers tore open the envelope. Never in his life had he been opposed by Edith before in this way.

He read these words in stereotyped writing:

'*Van will call on receipt of post-card. The Lavender Laundry hopes that you will give them a trial, as their terms are extremely mod—*'

Bruce rushed to the door and called out:

'Edith! Sorry! Edie, I say, I'm sorry. Come back.'

There was no answer.

He pushed the letter under the door of her room, and said through the keyhole:

'Edith, look here, I'm just going for a little walk. I'll be back to dinner. Don't be angry.'

Bruce brought her home a large bunch of Parma violets. But neither of them ever referred to the question again, and for some time there was a little less of the refrain of 'Am I master in my own house, or am I not?'

The next morning, when a long letter came from Aylmer, from Spain, Edith read it at breakfast and Bruce didn't ask a single question. However, she left it on his plate, as if by mistake. He might just as well read it.

CHAPTER XV

Mavis Argles

VINCY had the reputation of spending his fortune with elaborate yet careful lavishness, buying nothing that he did not enjoy, and giving away everything he did not want. At the same time his friends occasionally wondered on what he *did* spend both his time and his money. He was immensely popular, quite sought after socially; but he declined half his invitations and lived a rather quiet existence in the small flat, with its Oriental decorations and violent post-impressions and fierce Chinese weapons, high up in Victoria Street. Vincy really concealed under an amiable and gentle exterior the kindest heart of any man in London. There was ' more in him than met the eye,' as people say, and, frank and confidential as he was to his really intimate friends, at least one side of his life was lived in shadow. It was his secret romance with a certain young girl artist, whom he saw rarely, for sufficient reasons. He was not devoted to her in the way that he was to Edith, for whom he had the whole-hearted enthusiasm of a loyal friend, and the idolising worship of a fanatic admirer. It was perhaps Vincy's nature, a little, to sacrifice himself for anyone he was fond of. He spent a great deal of time thinking out means of helping materially the young art-student, and always he succeeded in this object by his elaborate and tactful care. For he knew she was very, very poor, and that her pride was of an old-fashioned order—she never said she was hard up, as every modern person does, whether rich or poor, but he knew that she really lacked what he considered very nearly—if not quite—the necessities of life.

Vincy's feeling for her was a curious one. He had known her since she was sixteen (she was now twenty-four). Yet he did not trust her, and she troubled him. He had met her at a studio at a time when he had thought of studying art seriously. Sometimes, something about her worried and wearied him, yet he couldn't do without her for long. The fact that he knew he was of great help to her fascinated him; he often thought that if she had been rich and he poor he would never wish to see her again. Certainly it was the touch of pathos in her life that held him; also, of course, she was pretty, with a pale thin face, deep blue eyes, and rich dark red frizzy hair that was always coming down—the untidy hair of the art-student.

He was very much afraid of compromising her, and *she* was very much afraid of the elderly aunt with whom she lived. She had no parents, which made her more pathetic, but no more free. He could not go and see her, with any satisfaction to either of them, at *her* home, though he did so occasionally. This was why she first went to see him at his flat. But these visits, as they were both placed, could, of course, happen rarely.

Mavis Argles—this was the girl's extraordinary name—had a curious fascination for him. He was rather fond of her, yet the greatest wish he had in the world was to break it off. When with her he felt himself to be at once a criminal and a benefactor, a sinner and a saint. Theoretically, theatrically, and perhaps conventionally, his relations with her constituted him the villain of the piece. Yet he behaved to her more like Don Quixote than Don Juan. . . .

One afternoon about four o'clock—he was expecting her—Vincy had arranged an elaborate tea on his little green marble dining-table. Everything was there that she liked. She was particularly attached to scones; he also had cream-cakes, sandwiches, sweets, chocolate and strawberries. As he heard the well-known slightly creaking step, his heart began to beat loudly—quick beats. He changed colour, smiled, and nervously went to the door.

'Here you are, Mavis!' He calmed her and himself by this banal welcome.

He made a movement to help her off with her coat, but she stopped him, and he didn't insist, guessing that she supposed her blouse to be unfit for publication.

She sat down on the sofa, and leaned back, looking at him with her pretty, weary, dreary, young, blue eyes.

'It seems such a long time since I saw you,' said Vincy. 'You're tired; I wish I had a lift.'

'I am tired,' she spoke in rather a hoarse voice always. 'And I ought not to stop long.'

'Oh, stay a *minute* longer, won't you?' he asked.

'Well, I like that! I've only just this moment arrived!'

'Oh, Mavis, don't say that! Have some tea.'

He waited on her till she looked brighter.

'How is Aunt Jessie?'

'Aunt Jessie's been rather ill.'

'Still that nasty pain?' asked Vincy.

She stared at him, then laughed.

'As if you remember anything about it.'

'Oh, Mavis! I do remember it. I remember what was the matter with her quite well.'

'I bet you don't. What was it?' she asked, with childish eagerness.

'It was that wind round the heart that she gets sometimes. She told me about it. Nothing seems to shift it, either.'

Mavis laughed—hoarse, childlike laughter that brought tears to her eyes.

'It's a shame to make fun of Aunt Jessie; she's a very, very good sort.'

'Oh, good gracious, Mavis, if it comes to sorts, I'm sure she's quite at the top of the tree. But don't let's bother about her now.'

'What *do* you want to bother about?'

'Couldn't you come out and dine with me, Mavis? It would be a change'—he was going to say 'for you', but altered it—'for me.'

'Oh no, Vincy; you can't take me out to dinner. I don't look up to the mark.' She looked in a glass. 'My hat—it's a very good hat—it cost more than you'd think—but it shows signs of wear.'

'Oh, that reminds me,' began Vincy. 'What *do* you think happened the other day? A cousin of mine who was up in London a little while bought a hat—it didn't suit her, and she insisted on giving it to *me*! She didn't know what to do to get rid of it! I'd given her something or other, for her birthday, and *she* declared she would give this to *me* for *my* birthday, and so—I've got it on my hands.'

'What a very queer thing! It doesn't sound true.'

'No; does it? Do have some more tea, Mavis darling.'

'No, thanks; I'll have another cake.'

'May I smoke?'

She laughed. 'Asking *me*! You do what you like in your own house.'

'It's yours,' he answered, 'when you're here. And when you're not, even more,' he added as an afterthought.

He struck a match; she laughed and said: 'I don't believe I understand you a bit.'

'Oh—I went to the play last night,' said Vincy. 'Oh, Mavis, it was such a wearing play.'

'All about nothing, I suppose? They always are, now.'

'Oh no. It was all about everything. The people were so clever; it was something cruel how clever they were. One man did lay down the law! Oh, didn't he though! I don't hold with being bullied and lectured from the stage, do you, Mavis? It seems so unfair when you can't answer back.'

'Was it Bernard Shaw?' she asked.

'No; it wasn't; not this time; it was someone else. Oh, I do feel sometimes when I'm sitting in my stall, so good and quiet, holding my programme nicely and sitting up straight to the table, as it were, and then a fellow lets me have it, tells me where I'm wrong and all that; I should like to stand up and give a back answer, wouldn't you?'

'No; I'd like to see you do it! Er—what colour is that hat that your cousin gave you?'

'Oh, colour?' he said thoughtfully, smoking. 'Let me see—what colour was it? It doesn't seem to me that it was any particular colour. It was a very curious colour. Sort of mole-colour. Or was it cerise? Or violet? . . . You wouldn't like to see it, would you?'

'Why, yes, I'd like to see it; I wouldn't try it on of course.'

He opened the box.

'Why, what a jolly hat!' she exclaimed. 'You may not know it, but that would just suit me; it would go with my dress, too.'

'Fancy.'

She took off her own hat, and touched up her hair with her fingers, and tried on the other. Under it her eyes brightened in front of the glass; her colour rose; she changed as one looked at her—she was sixteen again—the child he had first met at the Art School.

'Don't you think it suits me?' she said, turning round.

'Yes, I think you look very charming in it. Shall I put it back?' There was a pause.

'I sha'n't know what on earth to do with it,' he said discontentedly. 'It's so silly having a hat about in a place like this. Of course you wouldn't dare to keep it, I suppose? It does suit you all right, you know; it would be awfully kind of you.'

'What a funny person you are, Vincy. I *should* like to keep it. What could I tell Aunt Jessie?'

'Ah, well, you see, that's where it is! I suppose it wouldn't do for you to tell her the truth.'

'What do you mean by the truth?'

'I mean what I told you—how my cousin, Cissie Cavanack,' he smiled a little as he invented this name, 'came up to town, chose the wrong hat, didn't know what to do with it—and, you know!'

'I could tell her all that, of course.'

'All right,' said Vincy, putting the other hat—the old one—in the box. 'Where shall we dine?'

'Oh, Vincy, I think you're very sweet to me, but how late dare I get back to Ravenscourt Park?'

'Why not miss the eight-five train?—then you'll catch the quarter to ten and get back at about eleven.'

'Which would you *rather* I did?'

'Well, need you ask?'

'I don't know, Vincy. I have a curious feeling sometimes. I believe you're rather glad when I've gone—relieved!'

'Well, my dear,' he answered, 'look how you worry all the time! If you'd only have what I call a quiet set-down and a chat, without being always on the fidget, always looking either at the glass or at the clock, one might *not* have that feeling.'

Her colour rose, and tears came to her eyes. 'Oh, then you *are* glad when I'm gone!' She pouted. 'You don't care for me a bit, Vincy,' she said, in a plaintive voice.

He sat down next to her on the little striped sofa, and took her hand.

'Oh, give over, Mavis, do give over! I wish you wouldn't carry on like that; you do carry on, Mavis dear, don't you? Some days you go on something cruel, you do really. Reely, I mean. Now, cheer up and be jolly. Give a kiss to the pretty gentleman, and look at all these pretty good-conduct stripes on the sofa! There! That's better.'

'Don't speak as if I were a baby!'

'Do you mind telling me what we're quarrelling about, my dear? I only ask for information.'

'Oh, we're *not*. You're awfully sweet. You know I love you, Vincy.'

'I thought, perhaps, it was really all right.'

'Sometimes I feel miserable and jealous.'

He smiled. 'Ah! What are you jealous of, Mavis?'

'Oh, everything—everyone—all the people you meet.'

'Is that all? Well, you're the only person I ever meet—by appointment, at any rate.'

'Well—the Ottleys!'

His eye instinctively travelled to a photograph of Edith, all tulle and roses; a rather fascinating portrait.

'What about *her*?' asked Mavis. 'What price Mrs Ottley?'

'Really, Mavis!—What price? No price. Nothing about her; she's just a great friend of mine. I think I told you that before. . . . What a frightfully bright light there is in the room,' Vincy said. He got up and drew the blind down. He came back to her.

'Your hair's coming down,' he remarked.

'I'm sorry,' she said. 'But at the back it generally is.'

'Don't move—let me do it.'

Pretending to arrange it, he took all the hairpins out, and the cloud of dark red hair fell down on her shoulders.

'I like your hair, Mavis.'

'It seems too awful I should have been with you such a long time this afternoon,' she exclaimed.

'It *isn't* long.'

'And sometimes it seems so dreadful to think I can't be with you always.'

'Yes, doesn't it? Mavis dear, will you do up your hair and come out to dinner?'

'Vincy dear, I think I'd better not, because of Aunt Jessie.'

'Oh, very well; all right. Then you will another time?'

'Oh, you don't want me to stay?'

'Yes, I do; do stay.'

'No, next time—next Tuesday.'

'Very well, very well.'

He took a dark red carnation out of one of the vases and pinned it on to her coat.

' The next time I see you,' she said, ' I want to have a long, *long* talk.'

' Oh yes; we must, mustn't we?'

He took her downstairs, put her into a cab. It was half-past six.

He felt something false, worrying, unreliable and incalculable in Mavis. She didn't seem real. . . . He wished she were fortunate and happy; but he wished even more that he were never going to see her again. And still! . . .

He walked a little way, then got into a taxi and drove to see Edith. When he was in this peculiar condition of mind—the odd mixture of self-reproach, satisfaction, amusement and boredom that he felt now —he always went to see Edith, throwing himself into the little affairs of her life as if he had nothing else on his mind. He was a little anxious about Edith. It seemed to him that since Aylmer had been away she had altered a little.

CHAPTER XVI

More of the Mitchells

E D I T H had become an immense favourite with the Mitchells. They hardly ever had any entertainment without her. Her success with their friends delighted Mrs Mitchell, who was not capable of commonplace feminine jealousy, and who regarded Edith as a find of her own. She often reproached Winthrop, her husband, for having known Bruce eight years without discovering his charming wife.

One evening they had a particularly gay party. Immediately after dinner Mitchell had insisted on dressing up, and was solemnly announced in his own house as Prince Gonoff, a Russian noble. He had a mania for disguising himself. He had once travelled five hundred miles under the name of Prince Gotoffski, in a fur coat, a foreign accent, a false moustache and a special saloon carriage. Indeed, only his wife knew all the secrets of Mitchell's wild early career of unpractical jokes, to some of which he still clung. When he was younger he had carried it pretty far. She encouraged him, yet at the same time she acted as ballast, and was always explaining his jokes; sometimes she was in danger of explaining him entirely away. She loved to tell of his earlier exploits. How often, when younger, he had collected money for charities (particularly for the Deaf and Dumb Cats' League, in which he took special interest), by painting halves of salmon and ships on fire on the cold grey pavement! Armed with an accordion, and masked to the eyes, he had appeared at Eastbourne, and also at the Henley Regatta, as a Mysterious Musician. At the regatta he had been warned off the course, to his great pride and joy. Mrs Mitchell assured Edith that his bath-chair race with a few choice spirits was still talked of at St Leonard's (bath-chairmen, of course, are put in the chairs, and you pull them along). Mr Mitchell was beaten by a short head, but that, Mrs Mitchell declared, was really most unfair, because he was so handicapped—his man was much stouter than any of the others—and the race, by rights, should have been run again.

When he was at Oxford he had been well known for concealing
under a slightly rowdy exterior the highest spirits of any of the
undergraduates. He was looked upon as the most fascinating of
farceurs. It seems that he had distinguished himself there less for
writing Greek verse, though he was good at it, than for the wonderful variety of fireworks that he persistently used to let off under
the dean's window. It was this fancy of his that led, first, to his
popularity, and afterwards to the unfortunate episode of his being
sent down; soon after which he had married privately, chiefly in
order to send his parents an announcement of his wedding in *The
Morning Post*, as a surprise.

Some people had come in after dinner—for there was going to be
a little *sauterie intime*, as Mrs Mitchell called it, speaking in an
accent of her own, so appalling that, as Vincy observed, it made
it sound quite improper. Edith watched, intensely amused, as she
saw that there were really one or two people present who, never
having seen Mitchell before, naturally did not recognise him now,
so that the disguise was considered a triumph. There was something
truly agreeable in the deference he was showing to a peculiarly
yellow lady in red, adorned with ugly real lace, and beautiful false hair. She was obviously delighted with the Russian
prince.

'Winthrop is a wonderful man!' said Mrs Mitchell to Edith, as
she watched her husband proudly. 'Who would dream he was
clean-shaven! Look at that moustache! Look at the wonderful way
his coat doesn't fit; he's got just that Russian touch with his clothes;
I don't know how he's done it, I'm sure. How I wish dear Aylmer
Ross was here; he *would* appreciate it so much.'

'Yes, I wish he were,' said Edith.

'I can't think what he went away for. I suppose he heard the
East a-calling, and all that sort of thing. The old wandering craving
you read of came over him again, I suppose. Well, let's hope he'll
meet some charming girl and bring her back as his bride. Where is
he now, do you know, Mrs Ottley?'

'In Armenia, I fancy,' said Edith.

'Oh, well, we don't want him to bring home an Armenian, do we?
What colour are they? Blue, or brown, or what? I hope no-one

will tell Lady Hartland that is my husband. She'll expect to see Winthrop tonight; she never met him, you know; but he really ought to be introduced to her. I think I shall tell him to go and undress, when they've had a little dancing and she's been down to supper.'

Lady Hartland was the yellow lady in red, who thought she was flirting with a fascinating Slav.

'She's a sort of celebrity,' continued Mrs Mitchell. 'She was an American once, and she married Sir Charles Hartland for her money. I hate these interested marriages, don't you?—especially when they're international. Sir Charles isn't here; he's such a sweet boy. He's a friend of Mr Cricker; it's through Mr Cricker I know them, really. Lady Everard has taken *such* a fancy to young Cricker; she won't leave him alone. After all he's *my* friend, and as he's not musical I don't see that she has any special right to him; but he's there every Wednesday now, and does his dances on their Sunday evenings too. He's got a new one—lovely, quite lovely—an imitation of Lydia Kyasht as a water-nymph. I wanted him to do it here tonight, but Lady Everard has taken him to the opera. Now, won't you dance? Your husband promised he would. You both look so young!'

Edith refused to dance. She sat in a corner with Vincy and watched the dancers.

By special permission, as it was so *intime*, the Turkey Trot was allowed. Bruce wanted to attempt it with Myra Mooney, but she was horrified, and insisted on dancing the 1880 *trois-temps* to a jerky American two-step.

'Edith,' said Vincy; 'I think you're quieter than you used to be. Sometimes you seem rather absent-minded.'

'Am I? I'm sorry; there's nothing so tedious to other people. Why do you think I'm more serious?'

'I think you miss Aylmer.'

'Yes, I do. He gave a sort of meaning to everything. He's always interesting. And there's something about him—I don't know what it is. Oh, don't be frightened, Vincy, I'm not going to use the word personality. Isn't that one of the words that ought to be forbidden altogether? In all novels and newspapers that poor, tired word is always cropping up.'

'Yes, that and magnetism, and temperament, and technique. Let's cut out technique altogether. Don't let there be any, that's the best way; then no-one can say anything about it. I'm fed up with it. Aren't you?'

'Oh, I don't agree with you at all. I think there ought to be any amount of technique, and personality, and magnetism, and temperament. I don't mind *how* much technique there is, as long as nobody talks about it. But neither of these expressions is quite so bad as that dreadful thing you always find in American books, and that lots of people have caught up—especially palmists and manicures—mentality.'

'Yes, mentality's *very* depressing,' said Vincy. 'I could get along nicely without it, I think. . . . I had a long letter from Aylmer today. He seemed unhappy.'

'I had a few lines yesterday,' said Edith. 'He said he was having a very good time. What did he say to you?'

'Oh, he wrote frankly to *me*.'

'Bored, is he?'

'Miserable; enamoured of sorrow; got the hump; frightfully off colour; wants to come back to London. He misses the Mitchells. I suppose it's the Mitchells.'

Edith smiled and looked pleased. 'He asked me not to come here much.'

'Ah! But he wouldn't want you to go anywhere. That is so like Aylmer. He's not jealous, of course. How could he be? It's only a little exclusiveness. . . . And how delightfully rare that is, Edith dear. I admire him for it. Most people now seem to treasure anything they value in proportion to the extent that it's followed about and surrounded by the vulgar public. I sympathise with that feeling of wishing to keep—anything of that sort—to oneself.'

'You are more secretive than jealous, yourself. But I have very much the same feeling,' Edith said. 'Many women I know think the ideal of happiness is to be in love with a great man, or to be the wife of a great public success; to share his triumph! They forget you share the man as well!'

'I suppose the idea is that, after the publicity and the acclamation and the fame and the public glory and the shouting, you take the person home, and feel he is only yours, really.'

'But, can a famous person be only yours? No. I shouldn't like it.

It isn't that I don't *like* cleverness and brilliance, but I don't care for the public glory.'

'I see; you don't mind how great a genius he is, as long as he isn't appreciated,' replied Vincy. 'Well, then, in heaven's name let us stick to our obscurities!'

CHAPTER XVII

The Agonies of Aylmer

I N the fresh cheerfulness of the early morning, after sleep, with the hot June sun shining in at the window, Aylmer used to think he was better. He would read his letters and papers, dress slowly, look out of the window at the crowds on the pavement—he had come back to Paris—feel the infectious cheeriness and sense of adventure of the city; then he would say to himself that his trip had been successful. He *was* better. When he went out his heart began to sink a little already, but he fought it off; there would be a glimpse of an English face flashing past in a carriage—he thought of Edith, but he put it aside. Then came lunch. For some reason, immediately after lunch his malady—for, of course, such love *is* a malady—incongruously attacked him in an acute form. 'Why after lunch?' he asked himself. Could it be that only when he was absolutely rested, before he had had any sort of fatigue, that the deceptive improvement would show itself? He felt a wondering humiliation at his own narrow grief.

However, this was the hour that it recurred; he didn't know why. He had tried all sorts of physical cures—for there is no disguising the fact that such suffering is physical, and so why should the cure not be, also? He had tried wine, no wine, exercise, distraction, everything—and especially a constant change of scene. This last was the worst of all. He felt so exiled in Sicily, and in Spain—so terribly far away—it was unbearable. He was happier directly he got to Paris, because he seemed more in touch with England and her. Yes; the pain *had* begun again. . . .

Aylmer went and sat alone outside the café. It was not his nature to dwell on his own sensations. He would diagnose them quickly and acutely, and then throw them aside. He was quickly bored with himself; he was no egotist. But today, he thought, he *would* analyse his state, to see what could be done.

Six weeks! He had not seen her for six weeks. The longing was no better. The pain seemed to begin at his throat, pressing down gradually on the chest. It was that feeling of oppression, he supposed, that makes one sigh; as though there were a weight on the heart. And certain little memories made it acute; sudden flashing vivid recollection of that last drive was like a sharp jagged tear. Had they ever been on nearer terms, and had she treated him badly, it would not have caused this slow and insidious suffering. He was a man of spirit; he was proud and energetic; he would have thrown it off. If he could have been angry with her, or despised her, he could have cured himself in time. Instead of that, all the recollections were of an almost sickening sweetness; particularly that kiss on the day he went to see her. And the other, the *second*, was also the last; so it had a greater bitterness.

> *' Rapture sharper than a sword,*
> *Joy like a sudden spear.'*

These words, casually read somewhere, came back to him whenever he remembered her!

Aylmer had read, heard of these obsessions, but never believed in them. It was folly, madness!

He stood up, tossing his head as though to throw it off.

He went to fetch some friends, went with them to see pictures, to have tea, and to drive in the Bois, accepting also an invitation to dine with a man—a nice boy—a fellow who had been at Oxford with him, and was at the embassy here, a young attaché.

He was quite nice: a little dull, and a little too fond of talking about his chief.

Aylmer got home at about half-past six to dress for dinner. Then the torture began again. It was always worse towards evening—an agony of longing, regret, fury, vague jealousy and desire.

He stood and looked out of the window again at the crowd, hurrying along now to their pleasures or their happy homes. So many people in the world, like stars in the sky—why want the one star only? Why cry for the moon?

He had no photograph of her, but he still thought she was like his mother's miniature, and often looked at it. He wished he wasn't going to dine with that young man tonight. Aylmer was the most genial and sociable of men; he usually disliked being alone; yet just now being with people bored him; it seemed an interruption. He was going through a crisis.

Yes; he could not stand anyone this evening. He rang the bell and sent a *petit bleu* to say he was prevented from dining with his friend. What a relief when he had sent this—now he could think of her alone in peace. . . .

She had never asked him to go away. It was his own idea. He had come away to get over it. Well, he hadn't got over it. He was worse. But it wasn't because he didn't see her; no, he didn't deceive himself. The more he saw of her the worse he would be. Not one man in a thousand was capable of feeling so intensely and deeply as Aylmer felt, and never in his life before had he felt anything like it. And now it came on again with the ebb and flow of passion, like an illness. Why was he so miserable—why would nothing else *do*? He suddenly remembered with a smile that when he was five years old he had adored a certain nurse, and for some reason or other his mother sent her away. He had cried and cried for her to come back. He remembered even now how people had said: ' Oh, the child will soon forget.' But he wore out their patience; he cried himself to sleep every night. And his perseverance had at last been rewarded. After six weeks the nurse came back. His mother sent for her in despair at the boy's misery. How well he remembered that evening and her plain brown face, with the twinkling eyes. How he kissed his mother, and thanked her! The nurse stayed till he went to school and then he soon forgot all about her. Perhaps it was in his nature at rare intervals to want one particular person so terribly, to pine and die for someone!

That was a recollection of babyhood, and yet he remembered even now that obstinate, aching longing. . . . He suddenly felt angry, furious. What was Edith doing now? Saying good-night to Archie and Dilly? They certainly did look, as she had said, heavenly angels in their night attire (he had been privileged to see them). Then she was dressing for dinner and going out with Bruce. Good heavens! what noble action had Bruce ever done for *him* that he should go away? Why make such a sacrifice— for Bruce?

Perhaps, sometimes, she really missed him a little. They had had great fun together; she looked upon him as a friend; not only that, but he knew that he amused her, that she liked him, thought him clever, and—admired him even.

But that was all. Yet she *could* have cared for him. He knew that. And not only in one way, but in every way. They could have been comrades interested in the same things; they had the same sense of humour, much the same point of view. She would have made him, probably, self-restrained and patient as she was, in certain things. But, in others, wouldn't he have fired her with his own ideas and feelings, and violent passions and enthusiasms!

She was to be always with Bruce! That was to be her life!— Bruce, who was almost indescribable because he was neither bad, nor stupid, nor bad-looking. He had only one fault. ' *Il n'a qu'un défaut—il est impossible,*' said Aylmer aloud to himself.

He took up a book—of course one of *her* books, something she had lent him.

Now it was time to go out again—to dinner. He couldn't; it was too much effort. Tonight he would give way, and suffer grief and desire and longing like a physical pain. He hadn't heard from her lately. Suppose she should be ill? Suppose she was forgetting him entirely? Soon they would be going away to some summer place with the children. He stamped his foot like an angry child as he imagined her in her thin summer clothes. How people would admire her! How young she would look! Why couldn't he find some fault with her?—imagine her cold, priggish, dull, too cautious. But he could only think of her as lovely, as beyond expression attractive, drawing him like a magnet, as marvellously kind, gentle, graceful, and clever. He was obliged to use the stupid word clever, as there was no other. He suddenly remembered her teeth when she smiled, and a certain slight wave in her thick hair that was a natural one. It is really barely decent to write about poor Aylmer as he is alone, suffering, thinking himself unwatched. He suddenly threw himself on his bed and gave way to a crisis of despair.

About an hour later, when the pain had somehow become stupefied, he lit a cigarette, ashamed of his emotion even to himself, and rang. The servant brought him a letter—the English post.

He had thought so much of her, felt her so deeply the last few days that he fancied it must somehow have reached her. He read:

'MY DEAR AYLMER,

'I'm glad you are in Paris; it seems nearer home. Last night I went to the Mitchells' and Mr Mitchell disguised himself as a Russian Count. Nobody worried about it, and then he went and undisguised himself again. But Lady Hartland worried about it, and as she didn't know the Mitchells before, when he was introduced to her properly she begged him to give her the address of that charming Russian. And Vincy was there, and darling Vincy told me you'd written him a letter saying you weren't so very happy. And oh, Aylmer, I don't see the point of your waiting till September to come back. Why don't you come *now*?

'We're going away for Archie's holidays. Come back and see us and take Freddie with us somewhere in England. You told me to ask you when I wanted you—ask you anything I wanted. Well, I want to see you. I miss you too much. You arrived in Paris last night. Let me know when you can come. I want you.

EDITH.'

The bell was rung violently. Orders were given, arrangements made, packing was done. Aylmer was suddenly quite well, quite happy.

In a few hours he was in the midnight express due to arrive in London at six in the morning—happy beyond expression.

By ten o'clock in the morning he would hear her voice on the telephone.

He met a poor man just outside the hotel selling matches, in rags. Aylmer gave him three hundred francs. He pretended to himself that he didn't want any more French money. He felt he wanted someone else to be happy too.

CHAPTER XVIII

A Contretemps

EDITH did not know, herself, what had induced her to write that letter to Paris. Some gradual obscure influence, in an impulsive moment of weakness, a conventional dread of Paris for one's idol. Then, what Vincy told her had convinced her Aylmer was unhappy. She thought that surely there might be some compromise; that matters could be adjusted. Couldn't they go on seeing each other just as friends? Surely both would be happier than separated? For, yes— there was no doubt she missed him, and longed to see him. Is there any woman in the world on whom a sincere declaration from a charming, interesting person doesn't make an impression, and par- ticularly if that person goes away practically the next day, leaving a blank? Edith had a high opinion of her own strength of will. When she appeared weak it was on some subject about which she was in- different. She took a great pride in her own self-poise; her self- control, which was neither coldness nor density. She had made up her mind to bear always with the little irritations Bruce caused her; to guide him in the right direction; keep her influence with him in order to be able to arrange everything about the children just as *she* wished. The children were a deep and intense preoccupation. To say she adored them is insufficient. Archie she regarded almost as her greatest friend, Dilly as a pet; for both she had the strongest feeling that a mother could have. And yet the fact remained that they did not nearly fill her life. With Edith's intellect and tempera- ment they could only fill a part.

Bending down to a lower stature of intelligence all day long would make one's head ache; standing on tiptoe and stretching up would do the same; one needs a contemporary and a comrade.

Perhaps till Edith met Aylmer she had not quite realised what such real comradeship might mean, coupled with another feeling—not the intellectual sympathy she had for Vincy, but something quite

different. When she recollected their last drive her heart beat
quickly, and the little memories of the few weeks of their friendship gave her unwonted moments of sentiment. Above all, it was
a real, solid happiness—an uplifting pleasure, to believe he was
utterly devoted to her. And so, in a moment of depression, a feeling
of the sense of the futility of her life, she had, perhaps a little
wantonly, written to ask him to come back. It is human to play with
what one loves.

She thought she had a soft, tender admiration for him, that he had
a charm for her; that she admired him. But she had not the slightest
idea that on her side there was anything that could disturb her in
any way. And so that his sentiment, which she had found to be
rather infectious, should never carry her away, she meant only to
see him now and then; to meet again and be friends.

As soon as she had written the letter and sent it she felt
again a cheerful excitement. She felt sure he would come in a
day or two.

Aylmer arrived, as I have said, eight hours after he received the
letter. His first intention was to ring her up, or to speak to Bruce on
the telephone. But it so happened that it was engaged. This decided
him to have a short rest, and then go and surprise her with a visit.
He thought he would have lunch at one (he knew she always
lunched with the children at this hour), and would call on her unexpectedly at two, before she would have time to go out. They might
have a long talk; he would give her the books and things he had
bought for her, and he would have the pleasure of surprising her
and seeing on her face that first look that no-one can disguise, the
look of real welcome.

Merely to be back in the same town made him nearly wild with
joy. How jolly London looked at the beginning of July! So gay, so
full of life. And then he read a letter in a writing he didn't know;
it was from Mavis Argles, the friend of Vincy—the young art-
student: Vincy had given her his address some time ago—asking
him for some special privilege which he possessed, to see some of
the Chinese pictures in the British Museum. He was to oblige her
with a letter to the museum. She would call for it. Vincy was away.
and evidently she had by accident chosen the day of Aylmer's

return without knowing anything of his absence. She had never seen him in her life.

Aylmer was wandering about the half-dismantled house *désœuvré*, with nothing to do, restlessly counting the minutes till two in the afternoon. He remembered the very little that Vincy had told him of Mavis; how proud she was and how hard up. He saw her through the window. She looked pale and rather shabby. He told the servant to show her in.

' I've just this moment got your letter, Miss Argles. But, of course, I'm only too delighted.'

' Thank you. Mr Vincy said you'd give me the letter.'

The girl sat down. stiffly on the edge of a chair. Vincy had said she was pretty. Aylmer could not see it. But he felt brimming over with sympathy and kindness for her—for everyone, in fact.

She wore a thin light grey cotton dress, and a small grey hat; her hair looked rich, red, and fluffy as ever; her face white and rather thin. She looked about seventeen. When she smiled she was pretty; she had a Rossetti mouth; that must have been what Vincy admired. Aylmer had no idea that Vincy did more than admire her very mildly.

' Won't you let me take you there?' suggested Aylmer suddenly. He had nothing on earth to do, and thought it would fill up the time. ' Yes! I'll drive you there and show you the pictures. And then, wouldn't you come and have lunch? I've got an appointment at two.'

She firmly declined lunch, but consented that he should drive her, and they went.

Aylmer talked with the eagerness produced by his restless excitement and she listened with interest, somewhat fascinated, as people always were, with his warmth and vitality.

As they were driving along Oxford Street Edith, walking with Archie, saw them clearly. She had been taking him on some mission of clothes. (For the children only she went into shops.) He was talking with such animation that he did not see her, to a pale young girl with bright red hair. Edith knew the girl by sight, knew perfectly well that she was Vincy's friend—there was a photograph of her at his rooms. Aylmer did not see her. After a start she kept it to herself. She walked a few steps, then got into a cab. She felt ill.

So Aylmer had never got her letter? He had been in London without telling her. He had forgotten her. Perhaps he was deceiving her? And he was making love obviously to that sickening, irritating red-haired fool (so Edith thought of her), Vincy's silly, affected art-student.

When Edith went home she had a bad quarter of an hour. She never even asked herself what right she had to mind so much; she only knew it hurt. A messenger boy at once, of course.

'DEAR MR ROSS,

I saw you this morning. I wrote you a line to Paris, not knowing you had returned. When you get the note forwarded, will you do me the little favour to tear it up unopened? I'm sure you will do this to please me.

' We are going away in a day or two, but I don't know where. Please don't trouble to come and see me.

' Good-bye.

'EDITH OTTLEY.'

Aylmer left Miss Argles at the British Museum. When he went back, he found this letter.

CHAPTER XIX

An Extraordinary Afternoon

AYLMER guessed at once she had seen him driving. Being a man of sense, and not an impossible hero in a feuilleton, instead of going away again and leaving the misunderstanding to ripen, he went to the telephone, endeavoured to get on, and to explain, in few words, what had obviously happened. To follow the explanation by an immediate visit was his plan. Though, of course, slightly irritated that she had seen him under circumstances conveying a false impression, on the other hand he was delighted at the pique her letter showed, especially coming immediately after the almost tender letter in Paris.

He rang and rang (and used language), and after much difficulty getting an answer he asked, '*Why he could not get on,*' a pathetic question asked plaintively by many people (not only on the telephone).

'The line is out of order.'

In about twenty minutes he was at her door. The lift seemed to him preternaturally slow.

'Mrs Ottley?'

'Mrs Ottley is not at home, sir.'

At his blank expression the servant, who knew him, and of course liked him, as they always did, offered the further information that Mrs Ottley had gone out for the whole afternoon.

'Are the children at home, or out with Miss Townsend?'

'The children are out, sir, but not with Miss Townsend. They are spending the day with their grandmother.'

'Oh! Do you happen to know if Mr and Mrs Ottley will be at home to dinner?'

'I've heard nothing to the contrary, sir.'

'May I come in and write a note?'

He went into the little drawing-room. It was intensely associated with her. He felt a little *ému*. . . . There was the writing-table, there the bookcase, the few chairs, the grey walls; some pale roses fading in a pewter vase. . . . The restfulness of the surroundings filled him, and feeling happier he wrote on the grey notepaper:

'DEAR MRS OTTLEY,

I arrived early this morning. I started, in fact, from Paris immediately after receiving a few lines you very kindly sent me there. I'm so disappointed not to see you. Unless I hear to the contrary—and even if I do, I think!—I propose to come round this evening about nine, and tell you and Bruce all about my travels.

'Excuse my country manners in thus inviting myself. But I know you will say no if you don't want me. And in that case I shall have to come another time, very soon, instead, as I really must see you and show you something I've got for Archie. Yours always—'

He paused, and then added:

'Sincerely,
'AYLMER ROSS'

He went to his club, there to try and pass the time until the evening. He meant to go in the evening, even if she put him off again; and, if they were out, to wait until they returned, pretending he had not heard from her again.

He was no better. He had been away six weeks and was rather more in love than ever. He would only see her—she *did* want to see him before they all separated for the summer! He could not think further than of the immediate future; he would see her; they could make plans afterwards. Of course, her letter was simply pique! She had given herself away—twice—once in the angry letter, also in the previous one to Paris. Where was she now? What did it mean? Why did she go out for the whole afternoon? Where was she?

★

After Edith had written and sent her letter to Aylmer in the morning, Mrs Ottley the elder came to fetch the children to dine, and Edith told Miss Townsend to go for the afternoon. She was glad she would be absolutely alone.

'Aren't you very well, dear Mrs Ottley?' asked this young lady, in her sweet, sympathetic way.

Edith was fond of her, and, by implication only, occasionally confided in her on other subjects than the children. Today, however, Edith answered that she was *very* well *indeed*, but was going to see about things before they went away. ' I don't know how we shall manage without you for the holidays, Miss Townsend. I think you had better come with us for the first fortnight, if you don't mind much.'

Miss Townsend said she would do whatever Edith liked. She could easily arrange to go with them at once. This was a relief, for just at this moment Edith felt as if even the children would be a burden.

Sweet, gentle Miss Townsend went away. She was dressed rather like herself, Edith observed; she imitated Edith. She had the soft, graceful manner and sweet voice of her employer. She was slim and had a pretty figure, but was entirely without Edith's charm or beauty. Vaguely Edith wondered if she would ever have a love affair, ever marry. She hoped so, but (selfishly) not till Archie went to Eton.

Then she found herself looking at her lonely lunch; she tried to eat, gave it up, asked for a cup of tea.

At last, she could bear the flat no longer. It was a glorious day, very hot, Edith felt peculiar. She thought that if she spent all the afternoon out and alone, it would comfort her, and she would think it out. Trees and sky and sun had always a soothing effect on her. She went out, walked a little, felt worried by the crowd of shoppers swarming to Sloane Street and the Brompton Road, got into a taxi and drove to the gate of Kensington Gardens, opposite Kensington Gore. Here she soon found a seat. At this time of the day the gardens were rather unoccupied, and in the burning July afternoon she felt almost as if in the country. She took off her gloves—a gesture habitual with her whenever possible. She looked utterly restful. She had nothing in her hands, for she never carried either a parasol or a bag, nor even in winter a muff or in the evening a fan. All these little accessories seemed unnecessary to her. She liked to simplify. She hated fuss, anything worrying, agitating.

... And now she felt deeply miserable, perturbed and agitated. What a punishment for giving way to that half-coquettish, half self-indulgent impulse that had made her write to Paris! She had begged him to come back; while, really, he was here, and had not even let her know. She had never liked what she had heard of Mavis Argles, but had vaguely pitied her, wondering what Vincy saw in her, and wishing to believe the best. *Now*, she assumed the worst! As soon as Vincy had gone out of town—he was staying in Surrey with some of his relatives—*she*, the minx, began flirting or carrying on with Aylmer. How far had it gone? she wondered jealously. She did not believe Aylmer's love-making to be harmless. He was so easily carried away. His feelings were impulsive. Yet it was only a very short time since Vincy had told her of Aylmer's miserable letter. Edith was not interested in herself, and seldom thought much of her own feelings, but she hated self-deception; and now she faced facts. She adored Aylmer! It had been purely jealousy that made her write to Paris so touchingly, asking him to come back—vague fears that, if he were so depressed in Spain, perhaps he might try by amusements to forget her in Paris. He had once said to her that, of all places, he thought Paris the least attractive for a romance, because it was all so obvious, so prepared, so professional. He liked the unexpected, the veiled and somewhat more hypocritical atmosphere, and in the fogs of London, he had said, were more romantic mysteries than in any other city. Still, she had feared. And besides she longed to see him. So she had unbent and thought herself soon after somewhat reckless; it was a little wanton and unfair to bring him back. But she was not a saint; she was a woman; and sometimes Bruce was trying. . . .

Edith belonged to the superior class of human being whom jealousy chills and cures, and does not stimulate to further efforts. It was not in her to go in for competition. The moment she believed someone else took her place she relaxed her hold. This is the finer temperament, but it suffers most.

She would not try to take Aylmer away. Let him remain with his red-haired Miss Argles! He might even marry her. He deserved it.

She meant to tell Vincy, of course. Poor Vincy, *he* didn't know of the treachery.

Now she must devote herself to the children, and be good and kind to Bruce. At least, Bruce was *true* to her in his way.

He had been in love when they married, but Edith shrewdly suspected he was not capable of very much more than a weak rather fatuous sentiment for any woman. And anyone but herself would have lost him many years ago, would very likely have given him up. But she had kept it all together, had really helped him, and was touched when she remembered that jealous scene he made about the letter. The letter she wouldn't at first let him see. Poor Bruce! Well, they were linked together. There were Archie, the angel, and Dilly, the pet. . . . She was twenty-eight and Aylmer forty. He ought not to hold so strong a position in her mind. But he did. Yes, she was in love with him in a way—it was a mania, an obsession. But she would now soon wrestle with it and conquer it. The great charm had been his exclusive devotion—but also his appearance, his figure, his voice. He looked sunburnt and handsome. He was laughing as he talked to the miserable creature (so Edith called her in her own mind).

Then Edith had a reaction. She would cure herself today! No more flirtation, no more *amitié amoureuse*. They were going away. The children, darlings, how they loved her! And Bruce. She was reminding herself she must be gentle, good, to Bruce. He had at least never deceived her!

She got up and walked on and on. It was about five o'clock now. As she walked, she thought how fortunate she was in Miss Townsend; what a nice girl she was, what a good friend to her and the children. She had a sort of intuition that made her always have the right word, the right manner. She had seemed a little odd lately, but she was quite pleased to come with them to the country. What made her think of Miss Townsend? Some way off was a girl, with her back to Edith, walking with a man. Her figure was like Miss Townsend's, and she wore a dress like the one copied from Edith's. Edith walked more quickly, it was the retired part of the gardens on the way towards the Bayswater Road. The two figures turned down a flowery path. . . . It was Miss Townsend! She had turned her face. Edith was surprised, was interested, and walked on a few steps. She had not seen the man clearly. Then they both sat down on a seat. He took her hand. She left it in his. There was something familiar in his figure and clothes, and Edith saw his face.

Yes, it was Bruce.

Edith turned round and went home.

CHAPTER XX

―

Journeys End

So that was how Bruce behaved to her!

The deceit of both of them hurt her immensely. But she pulled herself together. It was a case for action. She felt a bitter, amused contempt, but she felt it half-urgent *not* to do anything that would lead to a life of miserable bickering and mutual harm.

It must be stopped. And without making Bruce hate her.

She wrote the second note of this strange day and sent it by a messenger.

Giving no reason of any kind, she told the governess that she had decided the children's holidays should begin from that day, and that she was unexpectedly going away with them almost immediately, and she added that she would not require Miss Townsend any more. She enclosed a cheque, and said she would send on some books and small possessions that Miss Townsend had kept there.

This was sent by a messenger to Miss Townsend's home near Westbourne Grove. She would find it on her return from her walk!

And now Edith read Aylmer's note—it was so real, so sincere, she began to disbelieve her eyes this morning.

It gave her more courage; she wanted to be absolutely calm, and looking her very best, for Bruce's entrance.

He came in with his key. He avoided her eye a little—looked rather sheepish, she thought. It was about seven.

'Hallo! Aren't the children in yet? Far too late for them to be out.'

'Nurse fetched Dilly. She has gone to bed. Archie is coming presently; mother will send him all right.'

'How are you, Edith, old girl?'

'I'm quite well, Bruce.'

'I have a sort of idea, as you know,' he said, growing more at ease, 'that we shall rather miss—a—Miss Townsend, when we first go away. What do you think of taking her for part of the time?'

'Dinner's ready,' announced Edith, and they dined. Towards the end of dinner he was about to make the suggestion again, when Edith said in clear, calm but decided tones:

'Bruce, I am not going to take Miss Townsend away with us. She is not coming any more.'

'Not— Why? What the devil's the idea of this new scheme? What's the matter with Miss Townsend?'

'Bruce,' answered Edith, 'I prefer not to go into the question, and later you will be glad I did not. I've decided that Miss Townsend is not to come any more at all. I've written to tell her so. I'll look after the children with nurse until we come back. . . . It's all settled.'

Bruce was silent.

'Well upon my word!' he exclaimed, looking at her uneasily. 'Have it your own way, of course—but upon my word! Why?'

'Do you really want me to tell you exactly why? I would so much prefer not.'

'Oh, all right, Edith dear; after all—hang it all—you're the children's mother—it's for you to settle. . . . No, I don't want to know anything. Have it as you wish.'

'Then we won't discuss it again. Shall we?'

'All right.'

He was looking really rather shamefaced, and she thought she saw a gleam of remorse and also of relief in his eye. She went into the other room. She had not shown him Aylmer's letter.

After ten minutes he came in and said: 'Look here, Edith. Make what arrangements you like. *I* never want to see—Miss Townsend again.'

She looked a question.

'And I never shall.'

She was really pleased at this, and held out her hand. Bruce had tears in his eyes as he took it.

'Edith, old girl, I think I'll go round to the club for an hour or two.'

'Do. And look here, Bruce, leave it to me to tell the children. They'll forget after the holidays. Archie must not be upset.'

'Whatever you do, Edith, will be— What I mean to say is that— Well, good night; I sha'n't be long.'

Edith was really delighted, she felt she had won, and she *did* want that horrid little Townsend to be scored off! Wasn't it natural? She wanted to hear no more about it.

There was a ring. It was nine o'clock. It was Aylmer's voice.

CHAPTER XXI

The Great Exception

T H E absurdly simple explanation, made almost in dumb show, by action rather than in dialogue, was soon given. He was surprised, simply enchanted, at the entire frankness of her recognition; she acknowledged openly that it mattered to her tremendously whether or not he was on intimate terms or flirting with little Miss Argles, or with little Miss anybody. He was not even to look at any woman except herself, that was arranged between them now and understood. They were side by side, with hands clasped as a matter of course, things taken for granted that he formerly never dreamt of. The signs of emotion in her face he attributed of course to the morning's contretemps, knowing nothing of the other trouble.

' It's heavenly being here again. You're prettier than ever, Edith; sweeter than ever. What a time I had away. It got worse and worse.'

' Dear Aylmer!'

' You're far too good and kind to me. But I *have* suffered— awfully.'

' So have I, since this morning. I felt—'

' What did you feel? Tell me!'

' Must I?'

' Yes!'

' I felt, when I saw you with her, as if I hadn't got a friend in the world. I felt quite alone. I felt as if the ground were going to open and swallow me up. I relied on you so much, far more than I knew! I was struck dumb, and rooted to the spot, and knocked all of a heap, in a manner of speaking, as Vincy would say,' Edith went on, laughing. ' But now, you've cured me thoroughly; you're such a *real* person.'

' Angel!'

She still left her hand in his. Her eyes were very bright, the result of few but salt tears, the corners of her mouth were lifted by a

286

happy smile, not the tantalising, half-mocking smile he used to see. She was changed, and was, he thought, more lovable—prettier; today's emotion had shaken her out of herself. The reaction of this evening gave a brilliancy to her eyes, happy curves to her lips, and the slight disarrangement of her hair, not quite silky-smooth tonight, gave her a more irresponsible look. She seemed more careless—younger.

'Where's Bruce?' Aylmer asked suddenly.

'He's gone to the club. He'll be back rather soon, I should think.'

'I won't wait. I would rather not meet him this evening. When shall I see you again?'

'Oh, I don't know. I don't think I want to make any plans now.'

'As you wish. I say, do you really think Vincy can care for that girl?'

'I believe he has had a very long friendship of some kind with her. He's never told me actually, but I've felt it,' Edith said.

'Is he in love with her? Can he be?'

'In a way—in one of his peculiar ways.'

'She's in love with him, I suppose,' said Aylmer. 'It was only because she thought it would please him that she wanted to see those things at the museum. I think she's a little anxious. I found her a wild, irritating, unaccountable, empty creature. I believe she wants him to marry her.'

'I hope he won't, unless he *really* wants to,' said Edith. 'It would be a mistake for Vincy to sacrifice himself as much as that.'

'I hope indeed he won't,' exclaimed Aylmer. 'And I think it's out of the question. Miss Argles is only an incident, surely. She looks the slightest of episodes.'

'It's a very long episode. It might end, though—if she insists and he won't.'

'Oh, bother, never mind them!' Aylmer replied, with boyish impatience. 'Let me look at *you* again. Do you care for me a little bit, Edith?'

'Yes; I do.' '

'Well, what's going to be done about it?' he asked, with happy triviality.

'Don't talk nonsense,' she replied. 'We're just going to see each other sometimes.'

'I'll be satisfied with anything!' cried Aylmer, 'after what I've suffered not seeing you at all. We'll have a new game. You shall *make* the rules and I'll keep them.'

'Naturally.'

'About the summer?'

'Oh, no plans tonight. I must think.' She looked thoughtful.

'Tell me, how's Archie?' he said.

'Archie's all right—delightful. Dilly, too. But I'm rather bothered.'

'Why should you bother? What's it about? Tell me at once.'

She paused a moment. 'Miss Townsend won't be able to come back any more,' she said steadily.

'Really? What a pity. I suppose the fool of a girl's engaged, or something.'

'She won't come back any more,' answered Edith.

'Will you have to get a new Miss Townsend?'

'I thought of being their governess myself—during the holidays, anyhow.'

'But that will leave you hardly any time—no leisure.'

'Leisure for what?'

'For anything—for me, for instance,' said Aylmer boldly. He was full of the courage and audacity caused by the immense relief of seeing her again and finding her so responsive.

There is, of course, no joy so great as the cessation of pain; in fact all joy, active or passive, *is* the cessation of some pain, since it must be the satisfaction of a longing, even perhaps an unconscious longing. A desire is a sort of pain, even with hope, without it is despair. When, for example, one takes artistic pleasure in looking at something beautiful, that is a cessation of the pain of having been deprived of it until then, since what one enjoys one must have longed for even without knowing it.

'Look here,' said Aylmer suddenly. 'I don't believe I can do without you.'

'You said *I* was to make the rules.'

'Make them then; go on.'

'Well, we'll be intimate friends, and meet as often as we can. Once a week you may say you care for me, and I'll say the same. That's all. If you find you don't like it—can't stand it, as you say— then you'll have to go away again.'

'I agree to it all, to every word. You'll see if I don't stick to it absolutely.'

'Thank you, dear Aylmer.'

He paused.

'Then I mustn't kiss you?'

'No. Never again.'

'All right. Never again after tonight. Tonight is the great exception,' said Aylmer.

She made a tardy and futile protest. Then she said:

'Now, Aylmer, you must go.' She sighed. 'I have a lot of worries.'

'I never heard you say that before. Let me take them and demolish them for you. Can't you give them to me?'

'No; I shall give nothing more to you. Good-bye. . . .

'Remember, there are to be no more exceptions,' said Edith.

'I promise.'

She sat quietly alone for half-an-hour, waiting for Bruce.

She now felt sorry for Bruce, utterly and completely indifferent about 'the Townsend case', as she already humorously called it to herself. But, she thought, she *must* be strong! She was not prepared to lose her dignity, nor to allow the children to be educated by a woman whose faith at least with them and in their home was unreliable; their surroundings must be crystal-clear. It would make a certain difference to them, she thought. How could it not? There were so many little ways in which she might spoil them or tease them, scamp things, or rush them, or be nicer to one of them, or less nice, if she had any sort of concealed relation with their father. And as she had been treated absolutely as a confidante by Edith, the girl had certainly shown herself treacherous, and rather too clearly capable of dissimulation. Edith thought this must have a bad effect on the children.

Edith was essentially a very feminine woman though she had a mental attitude rightly held to be more characteristic of men. Being so feminine, so enraged under her calm and ease, she was, of course, not completely consistent. She was still angry, and very scornful of Miss Townsend. She was hurt with her; she felt a friend had played her false—a friend, too, in the position of deepest trust, of grave responsibility. Miss Townsend knew perfectly well what the children were to Edith, and, for all she knew, there was no-one in Edith's life except Bruce; so that it was rather cruel. Edith intended to keep up her dignity so absolutely that Miss Townsend could never see her again, that she could never speak to Edith on the subject. She wished also, *very* much, that Bruce should never see her again, but didn't know how to encompass this. She must find a way.

On the other hand, after the first shock and disgust at seeing him, Edith's anger with Bruce himself had entirely passed. Had she not known, for years, that he was a little weak, a little fatuous? He was just as good a sort now as he had ever been, and as she was not blinded by the resentment and fury of the real jealousy of passion, Edith saw clearly, and knew that Bruce cared far more for *her* than for anybody else; that in so far as he could love anybody he loved her in his way. And she wanted to keep the whole thing together on account of Archie, and for Dilly's sake. She must be so kind, yet so strong that Bruce would be at once grateful for her forbearance and afraid to take advantage of it. Rather a difficult undertaking! . . .

And she had seen Aylmer again! There was nothing in it about Miss Argles. What happiness! She ought to have trusted him. He cared for her. He loved her. His sentiment was worth having. And she cared for him too; how much she didn't quite know. She admired him; he fascinated her, and she also felt a deep gratitude because he gave her just the sort of passionate worship that she must have always unconsciously craved for.

Certainly the two little events of today had drawn her nearer to him. She had been far less reserved that evening. She closed her eyes and smiled to herself. But this mustn't happen again.

With a strong effort of self-coercion she banished all delightful recollections as she heard Bruce come up in the lift.

He came in with a slightly shy, uncomfortable manner. Again, she felt sorry for him.

' Hallo!' he said.

He gave her a quick glance, a sort of cautious look which made her feel rather inclined to laugh. Then he said:

' I've just been down to the club. What have you been doing?'

' Aylmer's been here.'

'Didn't know he was in town.'

'He's only come for a few days.'

'I should like to see him,' said Bruce, looking brighter. 'Did he ask after me?'

'Yes.'

He looked at her again and said suspiciously:

'I suppose you didn't mention—'

'Mention what?'

'Edith!'

'Yes?'

He cleared his throat and then said with an effort of self-assertion that she thought at once ridiculous and touching:

'Look here, I don't wish to blame you in any way for what—er—arrangements you like to make in your own household. But—er—have you written to Miss Townsend?'

'Yes; she won't come back.'

'Er—but won't she ask why?'

'I hope not.'

'Why?' asked Bruce, with a tinge of defiance.

'Because then I should have to explain. And I don't like explaining.'

There was another pause. Bruce seemed to take a great interest in his nails, which he examined separately one at a time, and then all together, holding both hands in front of him.

'Did Archie enjoy his day?'

'Oh yes,' said Edith.

Bruce suddenly stood up, and a franker, more manly expression came into his face. He looked at her with a look of pain. Tears were not far from his eyes.

'Edith, you're a brick. You're too good for me.'

She looked down and away without answering.

'Look here, is there anything I can do to please you?'

'Yes, there is.'

'What? I'll do it, whatever it is, on my word of honour.'

'Well, it's a funny thing to ask you, but you know our late governess, Miss Townsend? I should like you to promise never to see her again, even by accident. If you meet her—by accident, I mean—I want you not to see her.'

Bruce held out both his hands.

'I swear I'd never recognise her even if I should meet her accidentally.'

'I know it's a very odd thing to ask,' continued Edith, 'just a fancy; why should I mind your not seeing Miss Townsend?'

He didn't answer.

'However, I *do* mind, and I'll be grateful.'

Edith thought one might be unfaithful without being disloyal, and she believed Bruce now. She was too sensible to ask him never to write a line, never to telephone, never to do anything else; besides, it was beneath her dignity to go into these details, and common-sense told her that one or the other must write or communicate if the thing was to be stopped. If Miss Townsend wrote to him to the club, he would have to answer. Bruce meant not to see her again, and that was enough.

'Then you're not cross, Edith—not depressed?'

She gave her sweetest smile. She looked brilliantly happy and particularly pretty.

'Edith!'

With a violent reaction of remorse, and a sort of tenderness, he tried to put his arm round her. She moved away.

'Don't you forgive me, Edith, for anything I've done that you don't like?'

'Yes, I *entirely* forgive you. The incident is closed.'

'Really forgive me?'

'Absolutely. And I've had a tiring day and I'm going to sleep. Good night.'

With a kind little nod she left him standing in the middle of the room with that air of stupid distinction that he generally assumed when in a lift with other people, and that came to his rescue at awkward moments—a dull, aloof, rather haughty expression. But it was no use to him now.

He had considerable difficulty in refraining from venting his temper on the poor, dumb furniture; in fact, he did give a kick to a pretty little writing-table. It made no sound, but its curved shoulder looked resentful.

'What a day!' said Bruce to himself.

He went to his room, pouting like Archie. But he knew he had got off cheaply.

CHAPTER XXII

Another Side of Bruce

E v e r since his earliest youth, Bruce had always had, at intervals, some vague, vain, half-hearted entanglement with a woman. The slightest interest, practically even common civility, shown him by anyone of the feminine sex between the ages of sixteen and sixty, flattered his vanity to such an extraordinary extent that he immediately thought these ladies were in love with him, and it didn't take much more for him to be in love with them. And yet he didn't really care for women. With regard to them his point of view was entirely that of vanity, and in fact he only liked both men or women who made up to him, or who gave him the impression that they did. Edith was really the only woman for whom his weak and flickering passion had lingered at all long; and in addition to that (the first glamour of which had faded) she had a real hold over him. He felt for her the most genuine fondness of which he was capable, besides trust and a certain admiration. A sort of respect underlay all his patronising good-nature or caprices with her. But still he had got into the habit of some feeble flirtation, a little affair, and at first he missed it very much. He didn't care a straw for Miss Townsend; he never had. He thought her plain and tedious; she bored him more than any woman he had ever met, and yet he had slipped into a silly sort of intrigue, beginning by a few words of pity or sympathy to her, and by the idea that she looked up to him in admiration. He was very much ashamed of it and of the circumstances; he was not proud of his conquest with her, as he generally was. He felt that on account of the children, and altogether, he had been playing it a bit low down.

He was not incapable, either, of appreciating Edith's attitude. She had never cross-questioned him, never asked him for a single detail, never laboured the subject, nor driven the point home, nor condescended even to try to find out how far things had really gone. She hadn't even told him how she knew; he was ashamed to ask

And, after that promise of forgiveness, she never referred to it; there was never the slightest innuendo, teasing, reproach. Yes, by Jove! Edith was wonderful! And so Bruce meant to play the game too.

For several days he asked the porter at the club if there were any letters, receiving the usual reply, 'None, sir.'

The third day he received the following note, and took it to read with enjoyment of the secrecy combined with a sort of self-important shame. Until now he hadn't communicated with her : —

'DEAR MR OTTLEY,
Of course you know I'm not returning to the children after the holidays, nor am I going with you to Westgate. I'm very unhappy, for I fear I have offended Mrs Ottley. She has always been very kind to me till now; but I shall let the matter rest. Under the circumstances I suppose I shall not see you any more. May I ask that you should not call or write. I and mother are going to spend the summer at Bexhill with some friends. Our address will be Sandringham, Seaview Road, Bexhill, if you like to write just one line to say good-bye. I fear I have been rather to blame in seeing you without Mrs Ottley's knowledge, but you know how one's feelings sometimes lead one to do what one knows one ought not to . . .'

'Sandringham, indeed! Some boarding house, I suppose,' said Bruce to himself. 'What a lot of " ones "! . . . Fine grammar for a governess.'

'. . . Wishing you every happiness (I *shall* miss the children!).
Yours sincerely,
MARGARE T TOWNSEND.

'*P.S.*—I shall never forget how happy I was with you and Mrs Ottley.'

Bruce's expression as he read the last line was rather funny.
'She's a silly little fool, and I sha'n't answer,' he reflected.

Re-reading the letter, he found it more unsatisfactory still, and destroyed it.

The thought of Miss Townsend bored him unutterably; and indeed he was incapable of caring for any woman (however feebly) for more than two or three weeks. He was particularly fickle, vague, and scrappy in his emotions. Edith was the only woman for whom even a little affection could last, and he would have long tired of her but for her exceptional character and the extraordinary trouble and tact she used with him. He didn't appreciate her fine shades, he was not in love with her, didn't value her as another man might have done. But he was always coming back to a certain steady, renewed feeling of tenderness for her.

With the curious blindness common to all married people (and indeed to any people who live together), clever Edith had been entirely taken in, in a certain sense; she had always felt (until the ' Townsend case ') half disdainfully but satisfactorily certain of Bruce's fidelity. She knew that he had little sham flirtations, but she had never imagined his going anywhere near an intrigue. She saw now that in that she had been duped, and that if he didn't do more it was not from loyalty to her. Still, she now felt convinced that it wouldn't occur again. She had treated him well; she had spared him in the matter. He was a little grateful, and she believed he would be straight now, though her opinion of him had rather gone down. Edith always felt that she must go to the very extreme of loyalty to anyone who was faithful to her; she valued fidelity so deeply, and now this feeling was naturally relaxed a little. She hadn't the slightest desire for revenge, but she felt she had a slightly freer hand. She didn't see why she should, for instance, deprive herself of the pleasure of seeing Aylmer; she had not told him anything about it.

That day at the club, Bruce in his depression had a chat with Goldthorpe, his golfing companion and sometime confidant. Over a cigarette and other refreshments, Bruce murmured how he had put an end to the little affair for the sake of his wife.

' Rather jolly little girl, she was.'

' Oh yes,' said Goldthorpe indifferently. He thought Edith very attractive, and would have liked to have the duty of consoling her.

' One of those girls that sort of *get round* you, and appeal to you—*you* know.'

' Oh yes.'

' Grey eyes—no, by Jove! I should call them hazel, with black lashes, no, not exactly black—brown. Nice, white teeth, slim figure —perhaps a bit too straight. Brownish hair with a tinge of gold in the sun.'

'Oh yes.'

'About twenty,' continued Bruce dreamily. He knew that Miss Townsend was thirty-two, but suspected Goldthorpe of admiring flappers, and so, with a subconscious desire to impress him, rearranged the lady's age.

'About twenty—if that. Rather long, thin hands—the hands of a lady. Well, it's all over now.'

'That's all right,' said Goldthorpe. He seemed to have had enough of this retrospective inventory. He looked at his watch and found he had an appointment.

Bruce, thinking he seemed jealous, smiled to himself.

For a few days after what had passed there was a happy reaction in the house. Everyone was almost unnaturally sweet and polite and unselfish about trifles to everybody else. Edith was devoting herself to the children, Bruce had less of her society than usual. She seemed to assume they were to be like brother and sister. He wouldn't at present raise the question; thinking she would soon get over such a rotten idea. Besides, a great many people had left town; and they were, themselves, in the rather unsettled state of intending to go away in a fortnight. Though happy at getting off so easily, Bruce was really missing the meetings and notes (rather than the girl).

Fortunately, Vincy now returned; he was looking sunburnt and happy. He had been having a good time. Yet he looked a little anxious occasionally, as if perplexed.

One day he told Edith that he had just had a rather serious quarrel with someone who was awfully cross, and carried on like anything and wouldn't give over.

'I guess who she is. What does she want you to do?'

'She wants me to do what all my relations are always bothering me to do,' said Vincy, 'only with a different person.'

'What, to marry?'

'Yes.'

'To marry her, I suppose? Shall you?'

'I'm afraid not,' he said. 'I don't think I quite can.'

'Don't you think it would be rather unkind to her?'

Neither of them had mentioned Miss Argles' name. The fact that Vincy referred to it at all showed her that he had recovered from his infatuation.

'But do you think I'm treating the poor girl badly?'

'Vincy, even if you adored her it would end unhappily. As you don't, you would both be miserable from the first day. Be firm. Be nice and kind to her and tell her straight out, and come and stay with us in the country.'

'Well, that was rather my idea. Oh, but, Edith, it's hard to hurt anyone.'

'You know I saw her driving with Aylmer that day, and I thought he liked her. I found I was wrong.'

'Yes. He doesn't. I wish I could get some nice person to—er—take her out. I mean, take her on.'

'What sort of person? She's pretty in her way. I daresay she'll attract someone.'

'What sort of person? Oh, I don't know. Some nice earl would please her, or one of those artist chaps you read of in the feuilletons —the sort of artist who, when he once gets a tiny little picture skied at the Academy, immediately has fortune, and titles and things, rolling in. A little picture called " Eventide " or " Cows by Moonlight ", or something of that sort, in those jolly stories means ten thousand pounds a year at once. Jolly, isn't it?'

'Yes, Vincy dear, but we're not living in a feuilleton. What's really going to be done? Will she be nasty?'

'No. But I'm afraid Aunt Jessie will abuse me something cruel.' He thought a little while. 'In fact she has.'

'What does she say?'

'She says I'm no gentleman. She said I had no business to lead the poor girl on, in a manner of speaking, and walk out with her, and pay her marked attention, and then not propose marriage like a gentleman.'

'Then you're rather unhappy just now, Vincy?'

'Well, I spoke to *her* frankly, and said I would like to go on being her friend, but I didn't mean to marry. And *she* said she'd never see me again unless I did.'

'And what else?'

'That's about all, thanks very much,' said Vincy.

Here Bruce came in.

'Edith,' he said, 'have you asked Aylmer to come and stay with us at Westgate?'

'Oh no. I think I'd rather not.'

' Why on earth not? How absurd of you. It's a bit selfish, dear, if you'll excuse my saying so. It's all very well for you: you've got the children and Vincy to amuse you (you're coming, aren't you, Vincy?). What price me? I must have someone else who can go for walks and play golf, a real pal, and so forth. I need exercise, and intellectual sympathy. Aylmer didn't say he had anywhere else to go.'

' He's going to take his boy, Freddie, away to some seaside place. He doesn't like staying with people.'

' All right, then. I shall go and ask him to come and stay at the hotel, for at least a fortnight. I shall go and ask him now. You're inconsistent, Edith. At one moment you seem to like the man, but as soon as I want to make a pleasant arrangement you're off it. So like a woman, isn't it, Vincy?' He laughed.

' Isn't it?' answered Vincy.

' Well, look here, I'm going right down to Jermyn Street purposely to tell him. I'll be back to dinner; do stop, Vincy.'

Bruce was even more anxious than he used to be always to have a third person present whenever possible.

He walked through the hot July streets with that feeling of flatness—of the want of a mild excitement apart from his own home. He saw Aylmer and persuaded him to come.

While he was there a rather pretty pale girl, with rough red hair, was announced. Aylmer introduced Miss Argles.

' I only came for a minute, to bring back those books, Mr Ross,' she said shyly. ' I can't stop.'

' Oh, thank you so much,' said Aylmer. ' Won't you have tea?'

' No, nothing. I *must* go at *once*. I only brought you in the books myself to show you they were safe.'

She gave a slightly coquettish glance at Aylmer, a half-observant glance at Bruce, sighed heavily and went away. She was dressed in green serge, with a turned-down collar of black lace. She wore black suède gloves, a gold bangle and a smart and pretty hat, the hat Vincy pretended had been given to *him* by Cissie Cavanack, his entirely imaginary cousin, and which he'd really bought for her in Bond Street.

' Well, I'll be off then. I'll tell Edith you'll write for rooms. Look sharp about it, because they soon go at the best hotels.'

'At any rate I'll bring Freddie down for a week,' said Aylmer, 'and then we'll see.'

'Who is that girl?' asked Bruce, as he left.

'She's a young artist, and I lent her some books of old prints she wanted. She's not a particular friend of mine—I don't care for her much.'

Bruce didn't hear the last words, for he was flying out of the door. Miss Argles was walking very slowly; he joined her.

'Pardon me,' he said, raising his hat. 'It's so very hot—am I going your way? Would you allow me to see you home?'

'Oh, you're very kind, I'm sure,' she said sadly. 'But I don't think—I live at Ravenscourt Park.'

Bruce thought there was plenty of time.

'Why how very curious! That's just where I was going,' said he boldly.

He put up his stick. Instead of a taxi a hansom drove up. Bruce hailed it.

'Always like to give these chaps a turn when I can,' he said. It would take longer.

'How kind-hearted you are,' murmured the girl. 'But I'd really rather not, thank you.'

'Then how shall you get back?'

'Walk to the Tube.'

'Oh no; it's far too hot. Let me drop you, as I'm going in your direction.'

He gave her a rather fixed look of admiration, and smiled. She gave a slight look back and got into the cab.

'What ripping red hair,' said Bruce to himself as he followed her.

★

Before the end of the drive, which for him was a sort of adventure, Mavis had promised to meet Bruce when she left her Art School next Tuesday at a certain tea-shop in Bond Street.

Bruce went home happy and in good spirits again. There was no earthly harm in being kind to a poor little girl like this. He might do a great deal of good. She seemed to admire him. She thought him so clever. Funny thing, there was no doubt he had the gift; women liked him, and there you are. Look at Miss Mooney at the

L*

Mitchells' the other day, why, she was ever so nice to him; went for him like one o'clock; but he gave her no encouragement. Edith was there. He wouldn't worry her, dear girl.

As he came towards home he smiled again. And Edith, dear Edith —she, too, must be frightfully keen on him, when one came to think about it, to forgive him so readily about Margaret Tow— Oh, confound Miss Townsend. This girl was a picture, a sort of Rossetti, and she had had such trouble lately—terrible trouble. The man she had been devoted to for years had suddenly thrown her over, heartlessly. . . . What a brute he must have been! She was going to tell him all about it on Tuesday. That man must have been a fiend! . . .

'Holloa, Vincy! So glad you're still here. Let's have dinner, Edie.'

CHAPTER XXIII

At Lady Everard's

LADY EVERARD was sitting in her favourite attitude at her writing-table, with her face turned to the door. She had once been photographed at her writing-table, with a curtain behind her, and her face turned to the door. The photograph had appeared in *The Queen*, *The Ladies' Field*, *The Sketch*, *The Tatler*, *The Bystander*, *Home Chat*, *Home Notes*, *The Woman at Home*, and *Our Stately Homes of England*. It was a favourite photograph of hers; she had taken a fancy to it, and therefore she always liked to be found in this position. The photo had been called: ' Lady Everard at work in her Music-Room.'

What she was supposed to be working at, heaven only knew; for she never wrote a line of anything, and even her social notes and invitation cards were always written by her secretary.

As soon as a visitor came in, she rose from the suspiciously clean writing-table, put down the dry pen on a spotless blotter, went and sat in a large brocaded arm-chair in front of some palms, within view of the piano, and began to talk. The music-room was large, splendid and elaborately decorated. There was a frieze all round, representing variously coloured and somewhat shapeless creatures playing what were supposed to be musical instruments. One, in a short blue skirt, was blowing at something; another in pink drapery (who squinted) was strumming on a lyre; other figures were in white, with their mouths open like young birds preparing to be fed by older birds. They represented Harmony in all its forms. There were other attempts at the classical in the decoration of the room; but Lady Everard herself had reduced this idea to bathos by huge quantities of signed photographs in silver frames, by large waste-paper baskets, lined with blue satin and trimmed with pink rosettes, by fans which were pockets, stuffed cats which were paperweights, oranges which were pincushions, and other debris from those charitable and social bazaars of which she was a constant patroness.

With her usual curious combination of weak volubility and decided laying-down of the law, she was preparing to hold forth to young La France (whom she expected), on the subject of Debussy, Edvina, Marcoux, the appalling singing of all his young friends, his own good looks, and other subjects of musical interest, when Mr Cricker was announced.

She greeted him with less eagerness, if less patronage, than her other protégé, but graciously offered him tea and permitted a cigarette.

Lady Everard went in for being at once *grande dame* and Bohemian. She was truly good-natured and kind, except to rivals in her own sphere, but when jealous she was rather redoubtable.

' I'm pleased to see you, my dear Willie,' she said; ' all the more because I hear Mrs Mitchell has taken Wednesdays now. Not *quite* a nice thing to do, I think; although, after all, I suppose we could hardly really clash. True, we *do* happen to know a few of the same people.' (By that Lady Everard meant she had snatched as many of Mrs Mitchell's friends away as she thought desirable.) ' But as a general rule I suppose we're not really in the same set. But perhaps you're going on there afterwards?'

That had been Mr Cricker's intention, but he denied it, with surprise and apparent pain at the suspicion.

She settled down more comfortably.

' Ah, well, Mrs Mitchell is an extremely nice, hospitable woman, and her parties are, I know, considered *quite* amusing, but I do think—I really do—that her husband carries his practical jokes and things a *little* too far. It isn't good form, it really isn't, to see a man of his age, with his face blacked, coming in after dinner with a banjo, calling himself the Musical White-eyed Kaffir, as he did the last time I was there. I find it *déplacé*—that's the word, *déplacé*. He seemed to think that we were all children at a juvenile party! I was saying so to Lord Rye only last night. Lord Rye likes it, I think, but he says Mr Mitchell's mad—that's what it is, a little mad. Last time Lord Rye was there everybody had a present given them hidden in their table napkins. There had been some mistake in the parcels, I believe, and Miss Mooney—you know, the actress, Myra Mooney—received a safety razor, and Lord Rye a vanity bag. Everybody screamed with laughter, but I must say it seemed to me rather silly. I wasn't there myself.'

'I was,' said Mr Cricker. 'I got a very pretty little feather fan.
I suppose the things really had been mixed up, and after all I was
very glad of the fan; I was able to give it to—' He stopped, sighed
and looked down on the floor.

'And is that affair still going on, Willie dear? It seems to me
such a pity. I *do* wish you would try and give it up.'

'I know, but she *won't*,' he said in a voice hoarse with anxiety.
'Dear Lady Everard, you're a woman of the world, and know
everything—'

She smiled. 'Not everything, Willie; a little of music, perhaps. I
know a good voice when I hear it. I have a certain *flair* for what's
going to be a success in that direction, and of course I've been
everywhere and seen everything. I've a certain natural knowledge
of life, too, and keep well up to date with everything that's going on.
I knew about the Hendon Divorce Case long before anyone else,
though it never came off after all, but that's not the point. But then
I'm so discreet; people tell me things. At any rate, I always *know*.'

Indeed, Lady Everard firmly believed herself to be a great
authority on most subjects, but especially on contemporary gossip.
This was a delusion. In reality she had that marvellous talent for
not knowing things, that gift for ignorance, and genius for inaccuracy so frequently seen in that cultured section of society of
which she was so popular and distinguished a member. It is a talent
that rarely fails to please, particularly in a case like her own. There
is always a certain satisfaction in knowing that a woman of position
and wealth, who plumes herself on her early knowledge and special
information, is absolutely and entirely devoid of the one and in-
correct in the other. A marked ignorance in a professionally well-
informed person has always something touching and appealing to
those who are able, if not willing, to set that person right. It was
taken for granted among her acquaintances, and probably was one
of the qualities that endeared her to them most, that dear Lady
Everard was generally positive and always wrong.

'Yes, I do know most things, perhaps,' she said complacently.
'And one thing I know is that this woman friend of yours is making
you perfectly miserable. You're longing to shake it off. Ah, I know
you! You've far more real happiness in going to the opera with me
than even in seeing her, and the more she pursues you the less you
like it. Am I not right?'

'Yes, I suppose so. But as a matter of fact, Lady Everard, if she didn't—well—what you might call make a dash for it, I shouldn't worry about her at all.'

'Men,' continued Lady Everard, not listening, 'only like coldness; coldness, reserve. The only way in the world to draw a man on is to be always out to him, or to go away, and never even let him hear your name mentioned.'

'I daresay there's a lot in that,' said Cricker, wondering why she did not try that plan with young La France.

'Women of the present day,' she continued, growing animated, 'make such a terrible, terrible mistake! What do they do when they like a young man? Oh, I know! They write to him at his club; they call at his rooms and leave messages; they telephone whenever they can. The more he doesn't answer their invitations the more they invite him. It's appalling! And what's the result? Men are becoming cooler and cooler—as a class, I mean. Of course, there are exceptions. But it's such a mistake of women to run after the few young men there are. There are such a tremendous lot of girls and married women nowadays, there are so many more of them.'

'Well, perhaps that's why they do it,' said Cricker rather stupidly. 'At any rate—oh, well, I know if my friend hadn't been so jolly nice to me at first and kept it up so—oh, well, you know what I mean—kept on keeping on, if I may use the expression, I should have drifted away from her ages ago. Because, you see, supposing I'm beginning to think about something else, or somebody else, she doesn't stand it; she won't stand it. And the awkward part is, you see, her being *on* the stage *and* married makes the whole thing about as awkward as a case of that sort can possibly be.'

'I would not ask you her name for the world,' said Lady Everard smoothly. 'Of course I know she's a beautiful young comedy actress, or is it tragedy? I wonder if I could guess her first name? Will you tell me if I guess right?' She looked arch.

'Oh, I say, I can't tell you who it is, Lady Everard; really not.'

'Only the first name? I don't *want* you to tell me; I'm discretion itself, I prefer not to know. The Christian name is not Margaretta, is it? Ah! no, I thought not. It's Irene Pettifer! There, I've guessed. The fact is, I always knew it, my dear boy. Your secret is safe with me. I'm the tomb! I—'

'Excuse me, Lady Everard,' said Cricker, with every sign of an-

noyance, ' it's no more Irene Pettifer than it's you yourself. Please
believe me. First of all I don't *know* Irene Pettifer; I've never even
seen her photograph—she's not young, not married, and an entirely
different sort of person.'

' What did I tell you? I knew it wasn't; I only said that to draw
you. However, have a little more tea, or some iced coffee, it's so
much more refreshing I always think. My dear Willie, I was only
chaffing you. I knew perfectly well it wasn't either of the people I
suggested. The point is, it seems to prey on your mind, and worry
you, and you won't break it off.'

' But how can I?'

' I will dictate you a letter,' she said. ' Far be it from me to interfere, and I don't pretend to know more about this sort of thing than
anybody else. At the same time, if you'll take it down just as I tell
it, and send it off, you'll find it will do admirably. Have you got a
pencil?'

As if dully hypnotised, he took out a pencil and notebook.

' It would be awfully kind of you, Lady Everard. It might give
me an idea anyway.'

' All right.'

She leant back and half closed her eyes, as if in thought; then
started up with one finger out.

' We must be quick, because I'm expecting someone presently,'
she said. ' But we've got time for this. Now begin. July 7th, 1912.
Have you got that?'

' Yes, I've got that.'

' Or, perhaps, just Thursday. Thursday looks more casual, more
full of feeling than the exact date. Got Thursday?'

' Yes, but it isn't Thursday, it's Friday.'

' All right, Friday, or any day you like. The day is not the point.
You can send it tomorrow, or any time you like. Wednesday. My
dearest Irene.'

' Her name's not Irene.'

' Oh no, I forgot. Take that out. Dear Margaretta. Circumstances
have occurred since I last had the pleasure of seeing you that make
it absolutely impossible that I could ever meet you again.'

' Oh, I say !'

' Go on. Ever see you or meet you again. You wish to be kind to
her, I suppose?'

' Oh yes.'

' Then say: Duty has to come between us, but God knows I wish you well.' Tears were beginning to come to Lady Everard's eyes, and she spoke with a break in her voice. ' I wish you well, Irene.'

' It's not Irene.'

' I wish you well, Margaretta. Some day in the far distant future you'll think of me, and be thankful for what I have done. It's for your good and my own happiness that we part now, and for ever. Adieu, and may God bless you. How do you sign yourself?'

' Oh, Willie.'

' Very well then, be more serious this time: Always your faithful friend, William Stacey Cricker.'

He glanced over the note, his face falling more and more, while Lady Everard looked more and more satisfied.

' Copy that out, word for word, the moment you go back, and send it off,' she said, ' and all the worst of your troubles will be over.'

' I should think the worst is yet to come,' said he ruefully.

' But you promise to do it, Willie? Oh, promise me?'

' Oh yes rather,' said he half-heartedly.

' Word for word?'

' O Lord, yes. That's to say, unless anything—'

' Not a word, Willie; it will be your salvation. Come and see me soon, and tell me the result. Ah! here you are, cher maître!'

With a bright smile she welcomed Mr La France, who was now announced, gently dismissing Willie with a push of the left hand.

' Good heavens!' he said to himself, as he got into the cab, ' why, if I were to send a thing like that there would be murder and suicide! She'd show it to her husband, and he'd come round and knock me into a cocked hat for it. Dear Lady Everard—she's a dear, but she doesn't know anything about anything.'

He tore the pages out of his pocket-book, and called out to the cabman the address of the Mitchells.

' Ah, chère madame, que je suis fatigué!' exclaimed La France, as he threw himself back against the cushions.

His hair was long and smooth and fair, so fair that he had been spoken of by jealous singers as a peroxide blond. His eyes were greenish, and he had dark eyebrows and eyelashes. He was good-looking. His voice in speaking was harsh, but his manner soft and insidious. His talents were cosmopolitan; his tastes international; he had no duties, few pleasures and that entire want of leisure known only to those who have practically nothing whatever to do.

'Fatigued? That's what you always say,' said Lady Everard, laughing.

'But it is always true,' he said, with a strong French accent.

'You should take more exercise, Paul. Go out more in the air. You lead too secluded a life.'

'What exercises? I practise my voice every day, twenty minutes.'

'Ah, but I didn't mean that. I mean in the open air—sport—that sort of thing.'

'Ah, you wish I go horseback riding. Ver' nice, but not for me. I have never did it. I cannot begun now, Lady Everard. I spoil all the *velouté* of my voice. Have you seen again that pretty little lady I met here before? Delicious light brown hair, pretty blue eyes, a wonderful blue, a blue that seem to say to everyone something different.'

'What!' exclaimed Lady Everard. ' Are you referring to Mrs Ottley?' She calmed down again. 'Oh yes, she's charming, awfully sweet—devoted to her husband, you know—absolutely devoted to her husband; so rare and delightful nowadays in London.'

'Oh yes, ver' nice. Me, I am devoted to 'er husband too. I go to see him. He ask me.'

'What, without *me*?' exclaimed Lady Everard.

'I meet him the other night. He ask me to come round and sing him a song. I cannot ask if I may bring Lady Everard in my pocket.'

'Really, Paul, I don't think that quite a nice joke to make, I must say.' Then relenting she said: 'I know it's only your artistic fun.'

'So she ver' devoted to him? He have great confidence in her; he trust her quite; he sure she never have any flirt?'

'He has every confidence; he's certain, absolutely certain!' exclaimed Lady Everard.

'He wait till she come and tell him, I suppose. 'E is right.'

He continued in this strain for some time, constantly going back to his admiration for Edith, and then began (with a good deal of bitterness) on the subject of another young singer, whom he declared to be *un garcon charmant*, but no good. 'He could not sing for nuts.'

She heartily agreed, and they began to get on beautifully again, when she suddenly said to him:

'Is it true you were seen talking in the park to that girl Miss Turnbull, on Sunday?'

'If you say I was seen, I was. You could not know I talk to her unless I was seen. You could not know by wireless.'

'Don't talk nonsense, Paul,' she answered sharply. 'The point isn't that you were seen, but that you did it.'

'Who did it? Me? I didn't do anything.'

'I don't think it's fair to me, I must say; it hurt my feelings that you should meet Amy Turnbull in the park and talk to her.'

'But what could I say? It is ver' difficul. I walk through the park; she walk through it with another lady. She speak to me. She say: Ah, dear Mr La France, what pleasure to see you! I ask you, Lady Everard, could I, a foreigner, not even naturalised here, could I order her out of the park? Could I scream out to her: Go out, do not walk in ze Hyde Park! Lady Everard do not like you! I have no authority to say that. I am not responsible for the persons that walk in their own park in their own country. She might answer me to go to the devil! She might say to me: What, Lady Everard not like me, so I am not allowed in the park? What that got to do with it? In a case like this, chère madame, I have no legal power.'

She laughed forgivingly and said:

'Ah, well, one mustn't be *too* exacting!' and as she showed some signs of a desire to pat his hair he rose, sat down to the piano, greatly to her disappointment, and filled up the rest of the time by improvising (from memory). It was a little fatiguing, as she thought it her duty to keep up an expression of acute rapture during the whole of the performance, which lasted at least three-quarters of an hour.

CHAPTER XXIV

———

Miss Bennett

SINCE his return Aylmer saw everything through what he called a rose-coloured microscope—that is to say, every detail of his life, and everything connected with it, seemed to him perfect. He saw Edith as much as ever, and far less formally than before. She treated him with affectionate ease. She had admitted by her behaviour on the night he returned that she cared for him, and, for the moment, that was enough. A sort of general relaxation of formality, due to the waning of the season, and to people being too busy to bother, or already in thought away, seemed to give a greater freedom. Everyone seemed more natural, and more satisfied to follow their own inclinations and let other people follow theirs. London was getting stale and tired, and the last feverish flickers of the exhausted season alternated with a kind of languor in which nobody bothered much about anybody else's affairs. General interest was exhausted, and only a strong sense of self-preservation seemed to be left; people clung desperately to their last hopes. Edith was curiously peaceful and contented. She would have had scarcely any leisure but that her mother-in-law sometimes relieved her of the care of the children.

Being very anxious that they should not lose anything from Miss Townsend's absence, she gave them lessons every day.

One day, at the end of a history lesson, Archie said:

'Where's Miss Townsend?'

'She's at Bexhill.'

'Why is she at Bexhill?'

'Because she likes it.'

'Where's Bexhill?'

'In England.'

'Why isn't Miss Townsend?'

'What do you mean, Archie?'

'Well, why isn't she Miss Townsend any more?'

'She is.'

'But she's not our Miss Townsend any more. Why isn't she?'

'She's gone away.'

'Isn't she coming back?'

'No.'

Watching his mother's face he realised that she didn't regret this, so he said:

'Is Miss Townsend teaching anybody else?'

'I daresay she is, or she will, perhaps.'

'What are their names?'

'How should I know?'

'Do you think she'll teach anybody else called Archie?'

'It's possible.'

'I wonder if she'll ever be cross with the next boy she teaches.'

'Miss Townsend was very kind to you,' said Edith. 'But you need not think about her any more, because you will be going to school when you come back from the holidays.'

'That's what I told Dilly,' said Archie. 'But Dilly's not going to school. Dilly doesn't mind; she says she likes you better than Miss Townsend.'

'Very kind of her, I'm sure,' laughed Edith.

'You see you're not a real governess,' said Archie, putting his arm round her neck. 'You're not angry, are you, mother? Because you're not a real one it's more fun for us.'

'How do you mean, I'm not a real governess?'

'Well, I mean we're not *obliged* to do what you tell us!'

'Oh, aren't you? You've got to; you're to go now because I expect Miss Bennett.'

'Can't I see Miss Bennett?'

'Why do you want to see her?'

'I don't want to see her; but she always brings parcels. I like to see the parcels.'

'They are not for you; she brings parcels because I ask her to do shopping for me. It's very kind of her.'

She waited a minute, then he said:

'Mother, do let me be here when Miss Bennett brings the parcels. I'll be very useful. I can untie parcels with my teeth, like this. Look! I throw myself on the parcel just like a dog, and shake it and shake it, and then I untie it with my teeth. It would be awfully useful.'

She refused the kind offer.

Miss Bennett arrived as usual with the parcels, looking pleasantly business-like and important.

' I wonder if these things will do?' she said, as she put them out on the table.

' Oh, they're sure to do,' said Edith; ' they're perfect.'

' My dear, wait till you see them. I don't think I've completed all your list.' She took out a piece of paper.

' Where did you get everything?' Edith asked, without much interest.

' At Boots', principally. Then the novels—Arnold Bennett, Maxwell— Oh, and I've got you the poem: " What is it?" by Gilbert Frankau.'

' No, you mean, " One of us ",' corrected Edith.

' Then white serge for nurse to make Dilly's skirts—skirts a quarter of a yard long!—how sweet!—and heaps and heaps of muslin, you see, for her summer dresses. Won't she look an angel? Oh, and you told me to get some things to keep Archie quiet in the train.' She produced a drum, a trumpet, and a mechanical railway train. ' Will that do?'

' Beautifully.'

' And here's your travelling cloak from the other place.'

' It looks lovely,' said Edith.

' Aren't you going to try it on?'

' No; it's sure to be all right.'

' I never saw such a woman as you! Here are the hats. You've *got* to choose these.'

Here Edith showed more interest. She put them on, said all the colour must be taken out of them, white put in one, black velvet in the other. Otherwise they would do.

' Thanks, Grace; you're awfully kind and clever. Now do you know what you're going to do? You're going to the Academy with me and Aylmer. He's coming to fetch us.'

' Oh, really—what fun!'

At this moment he arrived. Edith introduced them.

' I've been having such a morning's shopping,' she said, ' I deserve a little treat afterwards, don't I?'

' What sort of shopping? I'll tell you what you ought to have—a great cricket match when the shopping season's over, between the Old Selfridgians, and the Old Harrodians,' he said, laughing.

They walked through acres of oil paintings and dozens of portraits of Chief Justices.

' I can't imagine anyone but Royalty enjoying these pictures,' said Edith.

' They don't go to see pictures; they go to view exhibits,' Aylmer answered.

Declaring they had ' Academy headache ' before they had been through the second room, they sat down and watched the people.

One sees people there that are to be seen nowhere else. An extraordinary large number of clergymen, a peculiar kind of provincial, and strange Londoners, almost impossible to place, in surprising clothes.

Then they gave it up, and Aylmer took them out to lunch at a club almost as huge and noisy and as miscellaneous as the Academy itself. However, they thoroughly enjoyed themselves.

Edith and Bruce were to take up their abode in their little country house at Westgate next day.

CHAPTER XXV

At Westgate

'I ' v e got to go up to town on special business,' said Bruce, one afternoon, after receiving a telegram which he had rather ostentatiously left about, hoping he would be questioned on the subject. It had, however, been persistently disregarded.

'Oh, have you?'

'Yes. Look at this wire.'

He read aloud:

'*Wish to see you at once if possible come up today M.*'

'Who *is* " M "?'

'Mitchell, of course. Who should it be?' He spoke aggressively, then softened down to explanation, 'Mitchell's in town a few days on business, too. I may be detained till Tuesday—or even Wednesday next.'

Bruce had been to town so often lately, his manner was so vague, he seemed at once so happy and so preoccupied, so excited, so pleased, so worried, and yet so unnaturally good-tempered, that Edith had begun to suspect he was seeing Miss Townsend again.

The suspicion hurt her, for he had given his word of honour, and had been nice to her ever since, and amiable (though rather absent and bored) with the children.

She walked down to the station with him, though he wished to go in the cab which took his box and suit-case, but he did not resist her wish. On the way he said, looking round as if he had only just arrived and had never seen it before:

'This is a very nice little place. It's just the right place for you and the children. If I were you, I should stay on here.'

It struck her he spoke in a very detached way, and some odd foreshadowing came to her.

'Why—aren't you coming back?' she asked jokingly.

'Me? *What* an idea! Yes, of course. But I've told you—this

business of mine—well, it'll take a little time to arrange. Still,
I expect to be back on Tuesday. Or quite on Wednesday—or
sooner.'

They walked on and had nearly reached the station.

'How funny you are, Bruce!'

'What do you mean? Are you angry with me for going up to see
about important business? Why, here you've got Aylmer and his boy
at the hotel, my mother and Vincy to stay with you. You've got
plenty of companions. I don't suppose you'll miss me much. You see
—a—this is a sort of business matter women don't understand.
Women are incapable of understanding it.'

'Of what nature is it?'

'How do you mean, nature? It's not of any particular *nature*.
Nature, indeed! How like a woman! It's just business.' He waited a
minute. 'Stockbroking; that's what it is. Yes, it's stockbroking. I
want to see a chap who's put me in to a good thing. A perfectly
safe thing. No gambling. But one has to see into it, you see.
Mitchell wants to see me at once, you see. Do you see? You saw
his wire, didn't you? I've explained, haven't I? Aren't you satisfied
with my explanation?'

'*You* appear to be—very. But I'm not asking you to tell me any
details about the business, whatever it may be.'

They arrived at the station, and Bruce gave her what she thought
a very queer look. It was a mixture of fear, daring, caution and a
sort of bravado. Anxiety was in it, as well as a pleased self-
consciousness.

'Tell me, frankly, something I'd like to know, Bruce.'

'Are you getting suspicious of me, Edith? That's not like you.
Mind you, it's a great mistake in a woman; women should always
trust. Mistrust sometimes drives a man to—to— Oh, anyhow, it's a
great mistake.'

'I only want you to tell me something, Bruce. I'll believe you
implicitly if you'll answer. . . . Do you ever see Miss Townsend
now?'

'Never, on my honour! I swear it.' He spoke with such genuine
good faith that she believed him at once.

'Thanks. I'm glad. And—have you never since—'

'Never seen her, never written to her, never communicated with
her since she left! Don't know where she is and don't care. Now you

do believe me?' he asked, with all the earnestness and energy of truth.

'Absolutely. Forgive me for asking.'

'Oh, that's all right.'

He was relieved, and smiled.

'All right, Bruce dear. I'm glad. It would have worried me.'

'Now go, Edith. Don't bother to wait till I get in. I'll write to you—I'll write to you soon.'

She still lingered, seeing something odd in his manner.

'Give my love to my mother,' he said, looking away. 'I say— Edith.'

'Yes, dear?'

'Oh, nothing.'

She waited on till the train started. His manner was alternately peevish and kind, but altogether odd. Her last glimpse was a rather pale smile from Bruce as he waved his hand and then turned to his paper. . . .

'Well, what *does* it matter so long as he *has* gone!' exclaimed Aylmer impatiently, when she expressed her wonder at Bruce's going. The tide was low, and they went for a long walk over the hard shining sand, followed by Archie picking up wonderful shells and slipping on the green seaweed. Everything seemed fresh, lovely. She herself was as fresh as the sea breeze, and Aylmer seemed to her as strong as the sea. (Privately, Edith thought him irresistible in country clothes.) Edith had everything here to make her happy, including Bruce's mother, who relieved her of the children when she wanted rest and in whose eyes she was perfection.

She saw restrained adoration in Aylmer's eyes, love and trust in the eyes of the children. She had all she wanted. And yet—something tugged at her heart, and worried her. She had a strange and melancholy presentiment.

But she threw it off. Probably there was nothing really wrong with Bruce; perhaps only one of those little imaginary romances that he liked to fabricate for himself; or, perhaps, it was really business? It was all right if Mr Mitchell knew about it. Yet she could not believe that ' M ' *was* Mitchell. Bruce had repeated it too often; and, why on earth should Mitchell suddenly take to sending Bruce fantastic telegrams and signing them, for no reason, with an initial? . . .

CHAPTER XXVI

Goggles

'WHAT divine heavenly pets and ducks of angels they are!' exclaimed Lady Everard rather distractedly. 'Angels! Divine! And so good, too! I never saw such darlings in my life. Look at them, Paul. Aren't they sweet?'

Lady Everard with her party (what Aylmer called her performing troupe) had driven over to Westgate, from where she was staying in the neighbourhood, to have tea with Edith. She had brought with her a sort of juvenile party, consisting of Mr Cricker, Captain Willis and, of course, Paul La France, the young singer. She never moved without him. She explained that two other women had been coming also, but they had deserted her at the last minute.

Paul La France had been trying for an hour and a half to make eyes through motor goggles, which, naturally, was not a success; so he seemed a little out of temper. Archie was staring at him as if fascinated. He went up and said:

'Voulez-vous lend me your goggles?'

'Mais certainement! Of course I will. Voilà mon petit.'

'The darling! How sweet and amusing of him! But they're only to be used in the motor, you know. Don't break them, darling, will you? Monsieur will want them again. Ah! how sweet he looks!' as he put them on, 'I never saw such a darling in the whole course of my life! Look at him, Mrs Ottley. Look at him, Paul!'

'Charmant. C'est délicieux,' grumbled La France.

'What a charming little lawn this is, going right down to the sea, too. Oh, Mr Ross, is that you? Isn't this a delightful little house? More tea? Yes, please. Mr La France doesn't take sugar, and—'

'You don't know what I am now,' said Archie, having fixed the goggles on his own fair head, to the delight of Dilly.

'Oh, I guess what you are! You're a motorist, aren't you, darling? That's it! It's extraordinary how well I always get on with children,

Mrs Ottley,' explained Lady Everard. 'I daresay it's through being used to my little grandchildren, Eva's two angels, you know, but I never see them because I can't stand their noise, and yet I simply adore them. Pets!'

'What am I?' asked Archie, in his persistent way, as he walked round the group on the lawn, in goggles, followed closely by Dilly, saying, 'Yes, what is he?' looking exactly like a live doll, with her golden hair and blue ribbons.

'You're a motorist, darling.'

'No, I'm not a silly motorist. Guess what I am?'

'It's so difficult to guess, such hot weather! Can you guess, Paul?'

'I sink he is a nuisance,' replied the Frenchman, laughing politely.

'No, that's wrong. You guess what I am.'

'Guess what he is,' echoed Dilly.

'O Lord! what does it matter? What I always say is—live and let live, and let it go at that,' said Captain Willis, with his loud laugh. 'What, Mrs Ottley? But they won't do it, you know—they won't—and there it is!'

'Guess what I am,' persisted Archie.

'Never mind what you are; do go and sit down, and take those things off,' said Edith.

'Not till you guess what I am.'

'Does Dilly know?'

'No, Dilly doesn't know. Guess what I am, grandmamma!'

'I give it up.'

'I thought you'd never guess. Well, I'm a blue-faced mandrill!' declared Archie, as he took the goggles off reluctantly and gave them back to La France, who put them under his chair.

'Yes, he's a two-faced mangle,' repeated Dilly.

He turned round on her sharply. 'Now, don't talk nonsense! You're a silly girl. I never said anything about being a two-faced mangle; I'm a blue-faced mandrill.'

'Well, I said so; a two-faced mangle.'

'Don't say anything at all if you can't say it right,' said Archie, raising his voice and losing his temper.

'Well, they's both the same.'

'No, they jolly well aren't.'

He drew her a little aside. 'A blue-faced mandrill, silly, is *real*; it's in my natural history book.'

'Sorry,' said Dilly apologetically.

'In my natural history book it is, a *real* thing. I'm a blue-faced mandrill. . . . Now say it after me.'

'You's a two-faced mangle.'

'Now you're doing it on purpose! If you weren't a little girl, Dilly—'

'I wasn't doing it on purpose.'

'Oh, get away before I hit you! You're a silly little fool.'

She slowly walked away, calling out: 'And you're a silly two-faced mangle,' in a very irritating tone. Archie made a tremendous effort to ignore her, then he ran after her saying:

'Will you shut up or will you not?'

Aylmer seized hold of him.

'What are you going to do, Archie?'

'Teach Dilly what I am. She says— Oh, she's *such* a fool!'

'No, Archie, leave her alone; she's only a baby. Come along, old boy. Give Mr Cricker a cup of tea; he hasn't had one yet.'

Archie was devoted to Aylmer. Following him, he handed the tea to Mr Cricker, saying pathetically:

'I'm a blue-faced mandrill, and she knew it. I told her so. Aren't girls fools? They do worry!'

'They *are* torments,' said Aylmer.

'I wish that Frenchman would give me his goggles to keep! He doesn't want them.'

'I'll give you a pair,' said Aylmer.

'Thanks,' said Cricker, 'I won't have any tea. I wish you'd come and have a little talk with me, Ross. Can I have a word with you alone?'

Aylmer good-naturedly went aside with him.

'It's worse than ever,' said Cricker, in low, mysterious tones. 'Since I've been staying with Lady Everard it's been wire, wire, wire —ring, ring, ring—and letters by every post! You see, I thought it was rather a good plan to get away for a bit, but I'm afraid I shall have to go back. Fancy, she's threatened suicide, and telling her husband, and confiding in Lady Everard! And giving up the stage, and oh, goodness knows what! There's no doubt the poor child is absolutely raving about me. No doubt whatever.'

Aylmer was as sympathetic as he knew how.

The party was just going off when La France found that the

goggles had disappeared. A search-party was organised; great ex-citement prevailed; but in the end they went away without the glasses.

When Dilly had just gone to sleep in her cot a frightening figure crept into her room and turned on the electric light.

'Oh, Archie! *What* is it! Who is it! Oh! . . . Oh!'

'Don't be frightened,' said Archie, in his deepest voice, obviously hoping she would be frightened. He was in pyjamas and goggles. 'Don't be frightened! *Now! Say what I am*. What am I?'

'A blue-faced mandrill,' she whined.

He took off the goggles and kissed her.

'Right! Good night, old girl!'

CHAPTER XXVII

The Elopement

T H E following Tuesday, Edith, Aylmer, Vincy and Mrs Ottley were sitting on the veranda after dinner. They had a charming little veranda which led on to a lawn, and from there straight down to the sea. It was their custom to sit there in the evening and talk. The elder Mrs Ottley enjoyed these evenings, and the most modern conversation never seemed to startle her. She would listen impassively, or with a smile, as if in silent approval, to the most monstrous of paradoxes or the most childish chaff.

Aylmer's attention and kind thought for her had absolutely won her heart. She consulted him about everything, and was only thoroughly satisfied when he was there. His strong, kind, decided voice, his good looks, his decision, and a sort of responsible impulsiveness, all appealed to her immensely. She looked up to him, in a kind of admiring maternal way; Edith often wondered, did she not see Aylmer's devotion? But, if she did, Mrs Ottley thought nothing of it. Her opinion of Edith was so high that she trusted her in any complications. . . .

' Isn't Bruce coming down tonight?' she asked Edith.

' I'm to have a wire.'

' Ah, here's the last post. Perhaps he's written instead.'

Vincy fetched the letters. There was one from Bruce.

Edith went into the drawing-room to read it; there was not sufficient light on the veranda. . . .

In growing amazement she read the following words: —

'DEAR EDITH,

' I hope what I am about to tell you will not worry you too much. At any rate I do hope you will not allow it to affect your health. It is inevitable, and you must make up your mind to it as soon as possible. I say this in no spirit of unkindness; far from it. It is hard to me to break the news to you, but it must be done.

' Mavis Argles and I are all in all to each other. We have made up our minds on account of certain *circumstances* to throw in our lot together, and we are starting for Australia today. When this reaches you, we shall have started. I enclose the address to write to me.

' In taking this step I have, I am sure, acted for the best. It may cause you great surprise and pain. I regret it, but we met and became very quickly devoted to one another. She cannot live without me. What I am doing is my duty. I now ask you, and believe you will grant my request, to make arrangements to *give me my freedom as soon as possible.* Mind you do this, Edith, for it is really my duty to give my name to Mavis, who, as I have said, is devoted to me heart and soul, and cannot live without me.

' I shall always have the greatest regard and respect for you, and *wish you well.*

' I am sorry also about my mother, but you must try and explain that it is for the best. You also will know exactly what to do, and how to bring up the children just as well without me as with.

' Hoping this sudden news will not affect your health in any way, and that you will try and stay on a good while at Westgate, as I am sure the air is doing you good, believe me, yours affectionately as always,

'BRUCE.

' *P.S.*—Mind you don't forget to divorce me as soon as you can for Mavis's sake. Vincy will give you all the advice you need. Don't think badly of me; I have meant well. Try and cheer up. I am sorry not to write more fully, but you can imagine how I was rushed to catch today's steamer.'

She sat alone gazing at the letter under the light. She was divided at first between a desire to laugh and cry. Bruce had actually eloped! His silly weakness had culminated, his vanity had been got hold of. Vincy's horrid little art-student had positively led him into running away, and leaving his wife and children.

Controlling herself, Edith went to the veranda and said to Mrs
Ottley that Bruce wasn't coming back for a day or two, that she had
neuralgia and was going to retire, but begged Aylmer not to go yet.
Of course at this he went at once.

The next morning Aylmer at his hotel received a little note asking
him to come round and see Edith, while the others were out.

It was there, in the cool, shady room, that Edith showed him the
letter.

' Good God!' he exclaimed, looking simply wild with joy. ' This
is too marvellous!—too heavenly! Do you realise it? Edith, don't
you see he wants you to make him free? You will be my wife—
that's settled—that's fixed up.'

He looked at her in delight almost too great for expression.

Edith knew she was going to have a hard task now. She was pale,
but looked completely composed. She said:

' You're wrong, Aylmer. I'm not going to set him free.'

' What?' he almost shouted. ' Are you mad? What! Stick to him
when he doesn't want you! Ruin the wretched girl's life!'

' That remains to be seen. I don't believe everything in the letter.
The children—'

' Edith!' he exclaimed. ' What—when he doesn't *want* the
children—when he deserts them?'

' He is their father.'

' Their father! Then, if you were married to a criminal who implored you to divorce him you wouldn't, because he was their
father!'

' Bruce is not a criminal. He is not bad. He is a fool. He has behaved idiotically, and I can never care for him in the way I used to,
but I mean to give him a chance. I'm not going to jump at his first
real folly to get rid of him. . . . Poor Bruce!'

She laughed.

Aylmer threw himself down in an arm-chair, staring at her.

' You amaze me,' he said. ' You amaze me. You're not human. Do
you adore this man, that you forgive him everything? You don't
even seem angry.'

' I don't adore him, that is why I'm not so very angry. I was
terribly hurt about Miss Townsend. My pride, my trust were hurt

but after that I can't ever feel that personal jealousy any more. What I have got to think of is what is best.'

'Edith, you don't care for me. I'd better go away.' He turned away; he had tears in his eyes.

'Oh, don't, Aylmer! You know I do!'

'Well, then, it's all right. Fate seems to have arranged this on purpose for us—don't you know, dear, how I'd be good to the children? How I'd do anything on this earth for them? Why, I'd reconcile Mrs Ottley to it in ten minutes; I'd do *anything*!' He started up.

'I'm not going to let Mrs Ottley know anything about it for the present.'

'You're not going to tell her?'

'No. I shall invent a story to account for his absence. No-one need know. But, of course, if, later—I mean if he persists—'

'Oh, Edith, don't be a fool! You're throwing away our happiness when you've got it in your hand.'

'There are some things that one *can't* do.' said Edith. 'It goes against the grain. I can't take advantage of his folly to make the path smoother—for myself. What will become of him when they quarrel! It's all nonsense. Bruce is only weak. He's a very good fellow, really. He has no spirit, and not much intellect; but with us to look after him,' she unconsciously said us, and could not help smiling at the absurdity of it, 'he will get along all right yet.'

'Edith, you're beyond me,' said Aylmer. 'I give up understanding you.'

She stood up again and looked out of the window.

'Let him have his silly holiday and his elopement and his trip! He thinks it will make a terrific sensation! And I hope she will be seasick. I'm sure she will; she's the sort of woman who would, and then—after—'

'And you'll take him back? You have no pride, Edith.'

She turned round. 'Take him back?—yes; officially. He has a right to live in his own house, with his own children. Why, ever since I found out about Miss Townsend . . . I'm sure I was nice to him, but only like a sister. Yes. I feel just like a sister to him now.'

'Oh, good God! I haven't patience with all this hair-splitting nonsense. Brotherly husbands who run away with other girls, and

M

beg you to divorce them; sisterly wives who forgive them and stick
to them against their will. . . .'

He suddenly stopped, and held out his hand.

'Forgive me, Edith. I believe whatever you say is right. Will you
forgive me?'

'You see, it's chiefly on account of the children. If it weren't for
them I *would* take advantage of this to be happy with you. At least
—no—I'm not sure that I would; not if I thought it would be
Bruce's ruin.'

'And you don't think I'd be good to the children?'

'Good? I know you would be an angel to them! But what's the
use? I tell you I can't do it.'

'I won't tease you, I won't worry you any more,' he said, in a
rather broken voice. 'At any rate, think what a terrible blow this is
to me. You show me the chance of heaven, then you voluntarily
dash it away. Don't you think you ought to consult someone? You
have asked no-one?'

'I have consulted *you*,' she said, with a slight smile.

'You take no notice of what I say.'

'As a matter of fact, I don't wish to consult anyone. I have made
my own decision. I have written my letter.'

She took it out of her bag. It was directed to Bruce, at the address
he had given her in Australia.

'I suppose you won't let me read it?' he said sadly.

'I think I'd rather not,' she said.

Terribly hurt, he turned to the door.

'No—no, you shall read it!' she exclaimed. 'But don't say anything, make no remark about it. You shall read it because I trust
you, because I really care for you.'

'Perhaps I oughtn't to,' he said. 'No, dear; keep it to yourself.'
His delicacy had revived and he was ashamed of his jealousy.

But now she insisted on showing it to him, and he read:

'DEAR BRUCE,

'I'm not going to make any appeal to your feelings with regard
to your mother and the children, because if you had thought even
of me a little this would not have happened. I'm very, very sorry
for it. I believe it happened from your weakness and foolishness,
or you could not have behaved with such irresponsibility, but I'm

trying to look at it quite calmly. I therefore propose to do nothing
at all for three months. If I acted on your suggestion you might
regret it ever after. If in three months you write to me again in
the same strain, still desiring to be free, I will think of it, though
I'm not sure that I should do it even then. But in case you change
your mind I propose to tell nobody, not even your mother. By the
time you get this letter, it will be six weeks since yours to me, and
you may look at things differently. Perhaps by then you will be
glad to hear that I have told your mother merely that you have
been ordered away for a change, and I shall say the same to anyone else who inquires for you. If you feel after this time still
responsible, and that you have a certain duty, still remember,
even *so*, you might be very unhappy together all your lives.
Excuse me, then, if I don't take you at your word.

' Another point occurs to me. In your hurry and excitement,
perhaps you forgot that your father's legacy depended on the
condition that you should not leave the Foreign Office before you
were fifty. That is about fourteen years from now. If you are
legally freed, and marry Miss Argles, you could hardly go back
there. I think it would be practically impossible under those
circumstances, while if you live in Australia you will have hardly
any means. I merely remind you of this, in case you had forgotten.

' I shall regard it all as an unfortunate aberration; and if you
regret it, and change your mind, you will be free at any time you
like to come back and nothing shall be ever said about it. But I'm
not begging you to do so. I may be wrong; perhaps she's the
woman to make you happy. Let me know within three months
how you feel about it. No-one will suffer except myself during
this time, as I shall keep it from your mother, and shall remain
here during this time. Perhaps you will be very angry with me
that I don't wish to take you at your word, Bruce. At first I
thought I would, but I'm doing what I think right, and one
cannot do more.

' I'm not going to reproach you, for if you don't feel the claims
of others on you, my words will make no difference.

' Think over what I say. Should you be unhappy and wish to
separate from her without knowing how, and if it becomes a
question of money, as so many things do, I would help you. I

did not remind you about your father's legacy to induce you to come back. If you really find happiness in the way you expect, we could arrange it. You see, I have thought of everything, in one night. But you *won't* be happy.

'EDITH OTTLEY.'

' Remember, whenever you like to come back, you will be welcomed, and nothing shall ever be said about it.'

Aylmer gave her back the letter. He was touched.

' You see,' she said eagerly, ' I haven't got a grain of jealousy. All that part is quite finished. That's the very reason why I can judge calmly.'

She fastened up the letter, and then said with a smile:

' And now, let's be happy the rest of the summer. Won't you?'

He answered that she was *impayable*—marvellous—that he would help her—devote himself to doing whatever she wished. On consideration he saw that there was still hope.

CHAPTER XXVIII

Bruce Returns

'NEVER, Edith!' exclaimed Vincy, fixing his eyeglass in his eye, and opening his mouth in astonishment. 'Never! Well, I'm gormed!'

A week had passed since the news of Bruce's elopement. The little group at Westgate didn't seem to have much been affected by it; and this was the less surprising as Aylmer and Edith had kept it to themselves. Mrs Ottley listened imperturbably to Edith's story, a somewhat incoherent concoction, but told with dash and decision, that Bruce had been ordered away for a sea-voyage for fear of a nervous breakdown. She cried a little, said nothing, kissed Edith more than usual, and took the children away for longer walks and drives. With a mother's flashlight of intuition she felt at once certain there was something wrong, but she didn't wish to probe the subject. Her confidence in Edith reached the point of superstition; she would never ask her questions. Edith had assured her that Bruce would come back all right, and that was enough. Personally, Mrs Ottley much preferred the society of Aylmer to that of her son. Aylmer was far more amusing, far more considerate to her, and to everybody else, and he didn't use his natural charm for those who amused him only, as the ordinary fascinating man does. Probably there was at the back of his attentions to Mrs Ottley a vague idea that he wanted to get her on his side—that she might be a useful ally; but he was always charming to elderly women, and inclined to be brusque with younger ones, excepting Edith; he remembered his own mother with so great a cult of devotion, and his late wife with such a depressed indifference.

Edith had asked Aylmer to try and forget what had happened— to make himself believe that Bruce had really only gone away medicinally. For the present, he did as she wished, but he was

longing to begin talking to her on the subject again, both
because it interested him passionately from the psychological
point of view, and far more, naturally, because he had hopes
of persuading her in time. She was not bound by letter;
she could change her mind. Bruce might and possibly would,
insist.

There was difficulty in keeping the secret from Vincy, who was
actually staying in the house, and whose wonderful nerves and
whimsical mind were so sensitive to every variation of his surroundings. He had the gift of reading people's minds. But it never annoyed
anyone; one felt he had no illusions; that he sympathised with
one's weaknesses and follies and, in a sense, enjoyed them, from a
literary point of view. Probably his friends forgave his clear vision
for the sake of his interest. Most people would far rather be seen
through than not be seen at all.

One day Vincy, alone on the beach with Edith, remarked that
he wondered what had happened to Mavis.

Edith told him that she had run away with a married man.

' Never, Edith! ' he exclaimed. ' Who would have thought it! It
seems almost too good to be true! '

' Don't say that, Vincy.'

' But how did you hear it? You know everything.'

' I heard it on good authority. I *know* it's true.'

' And to think I was passing the remark only the other day that I
thought I ought to look her up, in a manner of speaking, or write,
or something,' continued Vincy; ' and who *is* the poor dear man?
Do you know?'

He looked at her with a sudden vague suspicion of he knew not
what.

' Bruce was always inclined to be romantic, you know,' she said
steadily.

' Oh, give over! '

' Yes, that's it; I didn't want anyone to know about it. I'm so
afraid of making Mrs Ottley unhappy.'

' But you're not serious, Edith?'

' I suppose I'd better show you his letter. He tells me to ask your
advice.'

She gave it to him.

' There is only one word for what I feel about it,' Vincy said, as he gave it back. ' I'm gormed! Simply gormed! Gormed, Edith dear, is really the only word.'

' I'm not jealous,' said Edith. ' My last trouble with Bruce seems to have cured me of any feeling of the kind. But I have a sort of pity and affection for him still in a way—almost like a mother! I'm really afraid he will be miserable with her, and then he'll feel tied to her and be wretched all his life. So I'm giving him a chance.'

He looked at her with admiring sympathy.

' But what about other friends?'

' Well—oh, you know—'

' Edith, I'm awfully sorry; I wish I'd married her now, then she wouldn't have bothered about Bruce.'

' But you can't stand her, Vincy.'

' I know, Edith dear; but I'd marry any number of people to prevent anything tiresome for you. And Aylmer, of course—Edith, really, I think Aylmer ought to go away; I'm sure he ought. It is a mistake to let him stay here under these circumstances.'

' Why?' said Edith. ' I don't see that; if I were going to take Bruce at his word, then it would be different, of course.'

' It does seem a pity not to, in some ways; everything would be all nicely settled up, just like the fourth act of a play. And *then* I should be glad I hadn't married Mavis. . . . Oh, do let it be like the fourth act, Edith.'

' How can life be like a play? It's hopeless to attempt it,' she said rather sadly.

' Edith, do you think if Bruce knew—how much you liked Aylmer —he would have written that letter?'

' No. And I don't believe he would ever have gone away.'

' Still, I think you ought to send Aylmer away now.'

' Why?' she repeated. ' Nothing could be more intensely correct. Mrs Ottley's staying with me—why shouldn't I have the pleasure of seeing Aylmer because Bruce is having a heavenly time on board ship?'

' I suppose there's that point of view,' said Vincy, rather bewildered. ' I say, Edith!'

' About Bruce having a heavenly time on board ship—a—she always grumbles; she's always complaining. She's never, never satisfied. . . . She keeps on making scenes.'

' So does Bruce.'

' Yes. But I suppose if there's a certain predicament—then— Oh, Edith—are you unhappy?'

' No, not a bit now. I think I'm only really unhappy when I'm undecided. Once I've taken a line—no matter what it is—I can be happy again. I can adjust myself to my good fortune.'

Curiously, when Edith had once got over the pain and shock that the letter first gave her, she was positively happier now than she ever had been before. Bruce really must have been a more formidable bore than she had known, since his absence left such a delicious freedom. The certainty of having done the right, the wisest thing, was a support, a proud satisfaction.

During these summer days Aylmer was not so peacefully happy. His devotion was assiduous, silent, discreet, and sometimes his feelings were almost uncontrollable, but he hoped; and he consoled himself by the thought that some day he would really have his wish—anything might happen; the chances were all in his favour.

What an extraordinary woman she was—and how pretty—how subtle; how perfect their life might be together. . . .

He implored Vincy to use his influence.

' I can't see Edith in anything so crude as the—as—that court,' Vincy said.

' But Bruce begs her to do it. What could their life be together afterwards? It's simply a deliberate sacrifice.'

' There's every hope that Miss Argles will never let him go,' said Vincy. ' One has to be very firm to get away from her. Oh, ever so firm, and *obstinate*, you can't think! How many times a day she must be reproaching Bruce—that will be rather a change for him. However, anything may happen,' said Vincy soothingly. He still maintained, for he had a very strong sense of propriety in matters of form, that Aylmer ought to go away. But Edith would not agree.

So the children played and enjoyed themselves, and sometimes asked after their father, and Mrs Ottley, though a little anxious, enjoyed herself too, and Edith had never been so happy. She was having a holiday. She dismissed all trouble and lived in a sort of dream.

Towards the end of the summer, hearing no more from Bruce, Aylmer grew still more hopeful; he began to regard it as practically settled. The next letter in answer to Edith's would doubtless convince her, and he would then persuade her; it was, tacitly, he thought, almost agreed now; it was not spoken of between them, but he believed it was all right. . . .

Aylmer had come back to London in the early days of September and was wandering through his house thinking how he would have it done up and how he wouldn't leave it when they were married, when a telephone message summoned him to Knightsbridge.

He went, and found the elder Mrs Ottley just going away. He thought she looked at him rather strangely.

'I think Edith wants to speak to you,' she said, as she left the room. 'Dear Edith! Be nice to her.' And she fled.

Aylmer waited alone, looking round the room that he loved because he associated it with her.

It was one of the first cold damp days of the autumn, and there was a fire. Edith came in, in a dark dress, looking pale, and different, he thought. She had seemed the very spirit of summer only a day or two before.

A chill presentiment struck to his heart.

'You've had a letter? Go on; don't keep me in suspense.' He spoke with nervous impatience, and no self-restraint.

She sat down by him. She had no wish to create an effect, but she found it difficult to speak.

'Yes, I've had a letter,' she said quietly. 'They've quarrelled. They quarrelled on board. He hates her. He says he would rather die than remain with her. He's written me a rather nice letter. They quarrelled so frightfully that a young man on board interfered,' she said, smiling faintly. 'As soon as they arrived the young man married her. He's a commercial traveller. He's only twenty-five. . . . It seems he pitied her so much that he proposed to her on board, and she left Bruce. It wasn't true about the predicament. It was—a mistake. Bruce was grateful for my letter. He's glad I've not told anyone—not done anything. Now the children will never know. But I've told Mrs Ottley all about it. I thought I'd better, now it's over. She won't ask him questions. . . . Bruce is on his way home.'

'All right!' said Aylmer, getting up. 'Let him come. Forgive him again, that's right! Would you have done that for *me*?'

'No! Never! If you had once been unfaithful, and I knew it,
I'd never have forgiven you.'

'I quite believe it. But why?'

'Because I care for you too much. If you had been in Bruce's
position I should never have seen you again. With him it's different.
It's a feeling of—it's for him, not for me. I've felt no jealousy, no
passion, so I could judge calmly.'

'All right,' repeated Aylmer ironically; 'all right! Judge calmly!
Do the right thing. You know best.' He stopped a moment, and then
said, taking his hat: 'I understand now. I see clearly at last. You've
had the opportunity and you wouldn't take it; you don't care for me.
I'm going.'

He went to the door.

'Oh, come back, Aylmer! Don't go like that! You know I care for
you, but what could I do? I foresaw this. . . . You know, I can't feel
no responsibility about Bruce. I couldn't make my happiness out of
someone else's misery. He would have been miserable and, not only
that, it would have been his ruin. Bruce could never be safe, happy,
or all right, except here.'

'And you think he'll alter, now, be grateful and devoted, I suppose—appreciate you?'

'Do people alter?' she answered.

'I neither know nor care if he will, but you? *I* could have made
you happy. You won't let me. Oh, Edith, how could you torture me
like this all the summer?'

'I didn't mean to torture you. We enjoyed being together.'

'Yes. But it makes this so much harder.'

'It would be such a risk!' she answered.

'But is anything worth having unless you're ready to risk everything to get it?'

'I *would* risk everything, for myself. But not for others. . . . If you
feel you want to go away,' she said, 'let it be only for a little while.'

'A little while! I hope I shall *never* see you again! Do you think
I'm such a miserable fool—do you think I could endure the position
of a tame cat? You forget I'm a man! . . . No; I'll never see you
again now, not if it kills me!'

At these words, the first harsh ones she had ever heard from him,
her nerves gave way, and she burst into tears.

This made him irresolute, for his tender-heartedness almost

reached the point of weakness. He went up to her, as she lifted her head, and looked at her once more. Then he said:

'No, you've chosen. You *have* been cruel to me, and you're too good to him. But I suppose you must carry out your own nature, Edith. I've been the victim. That's all.'

'And won't you be friends?' she said.

'No. I won't and I can't.'

He waited one moment more.

'If you'll change your mind—you still can—we can still be happy. We can be everything to each other. . . . Give him up. Give him up.'

'I can't,' said Edith.

'Then, good-bye.'

CHAPTER XXIX

Intellectual Sympathy

' W H A T are you going to wear tonight, Edith?'

' Oh; anything!'

' Don't say anything. I don't wish you to wear anything. I'm anxious you should look your best, really nice, especially as we haven't been to the Mitchells' for so long. Wear your new blue dress.'

' Very well.'

Bruce got up and walked across the room and looked in the glass.

' Certainly, I'm a bit sunburnt,' he remarked thoughtfully. ' But it doesn't suit me badly, not really badly; does it?'

' Not at all.'

' Edith.'

' Yes?'

' If I've spoken about it once, I've spoken about it forty times. This ink-bottle is too full.'

' I'll see about it.'

' Don't let me have to speak about it again, will you? I wonder who will be at the Mitchells' tonight?'

' Oh, I suppose there'll be the new person—the woman with the dramatic contralto foghorn voice; and the usual people: Mr Cricker, Lady Everard, Miss Mooney—'

' Miss Mooney! I hope not! I can't stand that woman. I think she's absurd; she's a mass of affectation and prudishness. And—Edith!'

' Yes?'

' I don't want to interfere between mother and daughter—I know you're perfectly capable and thoroughly well suited to bringing up a girl, but I really do think you're encouraging Dilly in too great extravagance.'

' Oh! In what way?'

'I found her making a pinafore for her doll out of a lace flounce of real old Venetian lace. Dilly said she found it on the floor. " On the floor, indeed," I said to her. " You mustn't use real lace!" She said, "Why not? It's a real doll!" Lately Dilly's got a way of answering back that I don't like at all. Speak to her about it, will you, Edith?'

'Oh yes, of course I will.'

'I'm afraid my mother spoils them. However, Archie will be going to school soon. Of course it isn't for me to interfere. I have always made a point of letting you do exactly as you like about the children, haven't I, Edith? But I'm beginning to think, really, Dilly ought to have another gov—' He stopped, looking self-conscious.

'Oh, she's only five, quite a baby,' said Edith. 'I daresay I can manage her for the present. Leave it to me.'

Since his return, Edith had never once referred to Bruce's sea-voyage. Once or twice he had thanked her with real gratitude, and even remorse, for the line she had taken, but her one revenge had been to change the subject immediately. If Bruce wished to discuss the elopement that she had so laboriously concealed, he would have to go elsewhere.

A brilliantly coloured version, glittering with success and lurid with melodrama, had been given (greatly against the hearer's will) to Goldthorpe at the club. One of the most annoying things to Bruce was that he was perfectly convinced, when he was confessing the exact truth, that Goldthorpe didn't believe a word of it.

It was unfortunate, too, for Bruce, that he felt it incumbent on him to keep it from Vincy; and not to speak of the affair at all was a real sacrifice on Vincy's part, also. For they would both have enjoyed discussing it, while Goldthorpe, the only human being in whom Bruce ever really confided, was not only bored but incredulous. He considered Bruce not only tedious to the verge of imbecility, but unreliable beyond the pardonable point of inaccuracy. In fact, Bruce was his ideal of the most wearisome of liars and the most untruthful of bores; and here was poor Vincy dying to hear all about his old friend, Mavis (he never knew even whether she had mentioned his name), ready to revel, with his peculiar humour, in every detail of the strange romance, particularly to enjoy her sudden desertion of Bruce for an unmarried commercial traveller who had fallen in love with her on board.— And yet, it had to be withheld! Bruce felt it would be disloyal, and he had the decency to be ashamed to speak of his escapade to an intimate friend of his wife.

Bruce complained very much of the dullness of the early autumn in London without Aylmer. This sudden mania for long journeys on Aylmer's part was a most annoying hobby. He would never get such a pleasant friend as Aylmer again. Aylmer was his hero.

'Why do you think he's gone away?' he rather irritatingly persisted.

'I haven't the slightest idea.'

'Do you know, Edith, it has sometimes occurred to me that if— that, well—well, you know what I mean—if things had turned out differently, and you had done as I asked you—'

'Well?'

'Why, I have a sort of idea,' he looked away, ' that Aylmer might —well, might have proposed to *you*!'

'Oh! *What* an extraordinary idea!'

'But he never did show any sign whatever, I suppose of—well, of —being more interested in you than he ought to have been?'

'Good heavens, no!'

'Oh, of course, I know that—you're not his style. You liked him very much, didn't you, Edith? . . .'

'I like him very much now.'

'However, I doubt if you ever quite appreciated him. He's so full of ability; such an intellectual chap! Aylmer is more a man's man. *I* miss him, of course. He was a very great friend of mine. And he didn't ever at all, in the least—seem to—'

'Seem to what?'

'It would have been a very unfair advantage to take of my absence if he had,' continued Bruce.

'Oh!'

'But he was incapable of it, of course.'

'Of course.'

'He *never* showed any special interest, then, beyond—'

'Never.'

'I was right, I suppose, as usual. You never appreciated him; he was not the sort of man a woman *would* appreciate. . . . But he's a

great loss to me, Edith. I need a man who can understand—
intellectual sympathy—'

' Mr Vincy!' announced the servant.

Vincy had not lost his extraordinary gift for turning up at the
right moment. He was more welcome than ever now.

Love at Second Sight

TO TACITUS

CHAPTER I

An appalling crash, piercing shrieks, a loud, unequal quarrel on a staircase, the sharp bang of a door. . . .

Edith started up from her restful corner on the blue sofa by the fire, where she had been thinking about her guest, and rushed to the door.

'Archie—Archie! Come here directly! What's that noise?'

A boy of ten came calmly into the room.

'It wasn't me that made the noise,' he said, 'it was Madame Frabelle.'

His mother looked at him. He was a handsome, fair boy with clear grey eyes that looked you straight in the face without telling you anything at all, long eyelashes that softened, but gave a sly humour to his glance, a round face, a very large forehead, and smooth straw-coloured hair. Already at this early age he had the expressionless reserve of the public school where he was to be sent, with something of the suave superiority of the university for which he was intended. Edith thought he inherited both of these traits from her.

She gazed at him, wondering, as she had often wondered, at the impossibility of guessing, even vaguely, what was really going on behind that large brow. And he looked back observantly, but not expressively, at her. She was a slim, fair, pretty woman, with more vividness and character than usually goes with her type. Like the boy, she had long-lashed grey eyes, and *blond-cendre* hair: her mouth and chin were of the Burne-Jones order, and her charm, which was great but unintentional, and generally unconscious, appealed partly to the senses and partly to the intellect. She was essentially not one of those women who irritate all their own sex by their power (and still more by their fixed determination) to attract men; she was really and unusually indifferent to general admiration. Still, that she was not a cold woman, not incapable of passionate feeling, was obvious to any physiognomist; the fully curved lips showed her generous and pleasure-loving temperament, while the softly glancing, intelligent, smiling eyes spoke fastidiousness and discrimination. Her voice was low and soft, with a vibrating sound in it, and she laughed often and easily, being very ready to see and enjoy the amusing side of life. But observation and emotion alike were instinctively veiled by a quiet, reposeful manner, so that she made herself further popular by appearing retiring. Edith Ottley might so easily have been the centre of any group, and yet—she was not! Women were grateful to her, and in return admitted that she was pretty, unaffected and charming. Today she was dressed very simply in dark blue and might have passed for Archie's elder sister.

'It isn't anything. It wasn't my fault. It was her fault. Madame Frabelle said *she* would teach me to take away her mandolin and use it for a cricket bat. She needn't teach me; I know already.'

'Now, Archie, you know perfectly well you've no right to go into her room when she isn't there.'

'How can I go in when she is there? . . . She won't let me. Besides, I don't want to.'

'It isn't nice of you; you ought not to go into her room without her permission.'

'It isn't her room; it's your room. At least, it's the spare room.'

'Have you done any harm to the mandolin?'

He paused a little, as he often did before answering, as if in absence of mind, and then said, as though starting up from a reverie:

'Er—no. No harm.'

'Well, what have you done?'

'I can mend it,' he answered.

'Madame Frabelle has been very kind to you, Archie. I'm sorry you're not behaving nicely to a guest in your mother's house. It isn't the act of a gentleman.'

'Oh. Well, there are a great many things in her room, Mother; some of them are rather jolly.'

'Go and say you're sorry, Archie. And you mustn't do it again.'

'Will it be the act of a gentleman to say I'm sorry? It'll be the act of a story-teller, you know.'

'What! Aren't you sorry to have bothered her?'

'I'm sorry she found it out,' he said, as he turned to the door.

' These perpetual scenes and quarrels between my son and my guest are most painful to me,' Edith said, with assumed solemnity.

He looked grave. ' Well, she needn't have quarrelled.'

' But isn't she very kind to you?'

' Yes, she isn't bad sometimes. I like it when she tells me lies about what her husband used to do—I mean stories. She's not a bad sort. . . . Is she a homeless refugette, Mother?'

' Not exactly that. She's a widow, and she's staying with us, and we must be nice to her. Now, you won't forget again, will you?'

' Right. But I can mend it.'

' I think I'd better go up and see her,' said Edith.

Archie politely opened the door for his mother.

' I shouldn't, if I were you,' he said.

Edith slowly went back to the fire.

' Well, I'll leave her a little while, perhaps. Now do go and do something useful.'

' What, useful? Gracious! I haven't got much more of my holidays, Mother.'

' That's no reason why you should spend your time in worrying everybody, and smashing the musical instruments of guests that are under your roof.'

He looked up at the ceiling and smiled, as if pleased at this way of putting it.

' I suppose she's very glad to have a roof to her mouth—I mean to her head,' he hurriedly corrected. ' But, Mother, she isn't poor. She has an amber necklace. Besides, she gave Dilly sixpence the other day for not being frightened of a cow. If she can afford to give a little girl sixpence for every animal she says she isn't afraid of !' . . .

' That only proves she's kind. And I didn't say she was poor; that's not the point. We must be nice and considerate to anyone staying with us—don't you see?'

He became absent-minded again for a minute.

' Well, I shouldn't be surprised if she'll be able to use it again,' he said consolingly—' the mandolin, I mean. Besides, what's the good of it anyway? I say, Mother, are all foreigners bad-tempered?'

' Madame Frabelle is not a foreigner.'

' I never said she was. But her husband was. He used to get into frightful rages with her sometimes. She says he was a noble fellow.

She liked him awfully, but she says he never understood her. Do you suppose she talked English to him?'

'That's enough, Archie. Go and find something to do.'

As he went out he turned round again and said:

'Does father like her?'

'Why, yes, of course he does.'

'How funny!' said Archie. 'Well, I'll say I'm sorry . . . when I see her again.'

Edith kissed him, a proceeding that he bore heroically. He was kissable, but she seldom gave way to the temptation. Then she went back to the sofa. She wanted to go on thinking about that mystery, her guest.

CHAPTER II

MADAME FRABELLE had arrived about a fortnight ago, with a letter of introduction from Lady Conroy. Lady Conroy herself was a vague, amiable Irishwoman, with a very large family of children. She and Edith, who knew each other slightly before, had grown intimate when they met, the previous summer, at a French watering-place. The letter asked Edith, with urgent inconsequence, to be kind to Madame Frabelle, of whom Lady Conroy said nothing except that she was of good family—she had been a Miss Eglantine Pollard— and was the widow of a well-to-do French wine merchant.

She was described as a clever, interesting woman who wished to study English life in her native land. It did not surprise Lady Conroy in the least that an Englishwoman should wish to study English in England; but she was a woman who was never surprised at anything except the obvious and the inevitable.

Edith had not had the faintest idea of asking Madame Frabelle to stay at her very small house in Sloane Street, for which invitation, indeed, there seemed no possible need or occasion. Yet she found herself asking her visitor to stay for a few days until a house or a hotel should be found; and Bruce, who detested guests in the house, seconded the invitation with warmth and enthusiasm. As Bruce was a subconscious snob, he may have been slightly influenced by the letter from Lady Conroy, who was the wife of an unprominent Cabinet Minister and, in a casual way, rather *grande dame*, if not exactly smart. But this consideration could not weigh with Eidth, and its effect on Bruce must have long passed away. Madame Frabelle accepted the invitation as a matter of course, made use of it as a matter of convenience, and had remained ever since, showing no sign of leaving. Edith was deeply interested in her.

And Bruce was more genuinely impressed and unconsciously bored by Madame Frabelle than by any woman he had ever met. Yet she was not at all extraordinary. She was a tall woman of about fifty,

well bred without being distinguished, who could never have been
handsome but was graceful, dignified, and pleasing. She was neither
dark nor fair. She had a broad, good-natured face, and a pale, clear
complexion. She was inclined to be fat; not locally, in the manner
of a pincushion, but with the generally diffused plumpness described
in shops as stock size. She was not the sort of modern woman of
fifty, with a thin figure and a good deal of rouge, who looks young
from the back when dancing or walking, and talks volubly and confidentially of her young men. She had, of course, nothing of the
middle-aged woman of the past, who at her age would have been
definitely on the shelf, doing wool-work or collecting recipes there.
Nor did she resemble the strong-minded type in perpetual tailor-
made clothes, with short grey hair and eye-glasses, who belongs to
clubs and talks chiefly of the franchise. Madame Frabelle was soft,
womanly, amiable, yet extremely outspoken, very firm, and inclined
to lay down the law. She was certainly charming, as Bruce and
Edith agreed every day (even now, when they were beginning to
wonder when she was going away!). She had an extraordinary
amount of personal magnetism, since she convinced both the Ottleys,
as she had convinced Lady Conroy, that she was wonderfully clever:
in fact, that she knew everything.

A fortnight had passed, and Edith was beginning to grow doubtful. Was she so clever? Did she know everything? Did she know
anything at all? Long arguments, that grew quite heated and excited
at luncheon or dinner, about the origin of a word, the author of a
book, and various debatable questions of the kind, invariably ended,
after reference to a dictionary or an encyclopædia, in Madame
Frabelle proving herself, with an air of triumph, to be completely
and entirely wrong. She was as generally positive as she was fatally
mistaken. Yet so intense a belief had she in her intuition as well as
in her own inaccurate information that her hypnotised hosts were
growing daily more and more under her thumb. She took it for
granted that everyone would take her for granted—and everyone
did.

Was all this agreeable or otherwise? Edith thought it must be, or
how could they bear it at all? If it had not been extremely pleasant
it would have been simply impossible.

The fair, gentle, pretty Edith, who was more subtle than she
appeared on the surface, while apparently indolent, had a very active

brain. Madame Frabelle caused her to use it more than she had ever done before. Edith was intensely curious and until she understood her visitor she could not rest satisfied. She made her a psychological study.

For example, here was a curious little point. Madame Frabelle did not look young for her age, nor did she seem in the least inclined to wish to be admired, nor ever to have been a flirt. The word ' fast ', for example, would have been quite grotesque as associated with her, though she was by no means prudish as to subjects of conversation, nor prim in the middle-class way. Yet somehow it would not have seemed incongruous or surprising if one had found out that there was even now some romance in her life. But, doubtless, the most striking thing about her—and what made her popular—was her intense interest in other people. It went so far as to reach the very verge of being interference; but she was so pleasant that one could scarcely resent it either as curiosity or intrusion. Since she had stayed with the Ottleys, she appeared to think of no-one and nothing else in the world. One would think that no-one else existed for her. And, after all, such extreme interest is flattering. Bruce, Archie, Edith, even Dilly's nurse, all had, in her, an audience : interested, absorbed, enchanted. Who could help enjoying it?

Edith was still thinking about Madame Frabelle when a few minutes later, Bruce came in.

Bruce also was fair, besides being tall, good-looking and well built. Known by their friends for some reason as the little Ottleys, these two were a rather fine-looking pair, and (at a casual glance) admirably suited to one another. They appeared to be exactly like thousands of other English married couples of the upper middle class between thirty and forty; he looked as manly (through being sunburnt from knocking a little ball over the links) as if he habitually went tiger-shooting; but, though not without charm, he had much less distinction than his wife. Most people smiled when Bruce's name was mentioned, and it was usual for his intimates to clap him on the back and call him a silly ass, which proves he was not unpopular. On the other hand, Edith was described as a very pretty woman, or a nice little thing, and by the more discriminating, jolly clever when you know her, and don't you forget it.

When Bruce told his wife that no-one had ever regretted consult-

ing him on a difficult, secret, and delicate matter, Edith had said she
was quite sure they hadn't. Perhaps she thought no-one had ever
regretted consulting him on such a subject, simply because no-one
had ever tried.

'Oh, please don't move, Edith,' he said, in the tone which means,
'Oh, please do move.' 'I like to see you comfortable.'

There was something in his manner that made her feel apologetic,
and she changed her position with the feeling of guilt about nothing,
and a tinge of shame for something she hadn't done, easily produced by an air of self-sacrifice Bruce was apt to show at such
moments.

'Your hair's coming down, Edith,' he said kindly, to add to her
vague embarrassment.

As a matter of fact, a curl by the right ear was only about one-
tenth of an inch farther on the cheek than it was intended to be.
But, by this observation, he got the advantage of her by giving the
impression that she looked wild, unkempt, and ruffled, though she
was, in reality, exactly as trim and neat as always.

'Well—about the delicate matter you were going to talk over
with me, Bruce?'

'Oh yes. Oh, by the way,' he said, 'before we go into that, I
wonder if you could help me about something? You could do me a
really great service by helping me to find a certain book.'

'Why, of course, Bruce, with pleasure. What is the book?' asked
the amiable wife, looking alert.

Bruce looked at her with pity.

'What is the book? My dear Edith, don't you see I shouldn't have
come to you about it if I knew what the book was.'

'I beg your pardon, Bruce,' said Edith, now feeling thoroughly in
the wrong, and looking round the room. 'But if you can't give me
the name of the book I scarcely see how I can find it.'

'And if I knew its name I shouldn't want your assistance.'

It seemed a deadlock.

Going to the bookcase, Edith said:

'Can't you give me some idea of what it's like?'

'Certainly I can. I've seen it a hundred times in this very room;
in fact it's always here, except when it's wanted.'

Edith went down on her knees in front of the bookcase and cross-
questioned Bruce on the physiognomy of the volume. She asked

whether it was a novel, whether it was blue, whether it belonged to
the library, whether it was Stevenson, whether it was French, or if
it was suitable for the children.

To all of these questions he returned a negative.

'Suitable for the children?' he repeated. 'What a fantastic idea!
Do you think I should take all this trouble to come and request your
assistance and spend hours of valuable time looking for a book that's
suitable for the children?'

'But, Bruce, if you request my assistance without having the
slightest idea of what book it is, how shall I possibly be able to help?'

'Quite so . . . quite so. Never mind, Edith, don't trouble. If I say
that it's a pity there isn't more order in the house you won't regard
it, I hope, dear, as a reproach in any way. If there were a place for
everything, and everything in its place— However! Never mind. It's
a small matter, and it can't be helped. I know, Edith dear, you were
not brought up to be strictly orderly. Some people are not. I don't
blame you; not in the least. Still, when Dilly grows up I shall be
sorry if—'

'Bruce, it's nothing to do with order. The room is perfectly tidy.
It's a question of your memory. You don't remember the name of the
book.'

'Pardon me, it's not a question of remembering the name; that
would be nothing. Anyone can forget a name. That wouldn't
matter.'

'Oh, then, you mean you don't even know in the least what you
want?'

At this moment Bruce decided it was time to find the book, and
suddenly sprang, like a middle-aged fawn, at the writing-table,
seizing a volume triumphantly.

'There it is—the whole time!' he said, 'staring at you while you
are helplessly looking for it. Oh, Edith, Edith!' he laughed amiably.
'How like a woman that is! And the very book a few inches from
your hand! Well, well, never mind; it's found at last. I hope, dear,
in the future you will be more careful. We'll say no more about it
now.'

Edith didn't point out to Bruce that the book was a novel; that it
was blue; that it belonged to the library, was French, and that it
was still suitable for the children.

'Well, well,' he said, sitting down with the book, which he had never wanted at all, and had never even thought of when he came to the room first, ' well, well, here it is! And now for the point I was going to tell you when I came in.'

' Shall we have tea, dear?' said Edith.

' Tea? Oh, surely not. It's only just four. I don't think it's good for the servants having tea half-an-hour earlier than usual. It's a little thing—yes, I know that, but I don't believe in it. I like punctuality, regularity—oh, well, of course, dear, if you wish it.'

' No, I don't at all! I thought you might.'

' Oh no. I like punctuality, er—and, as a matter of fact, I had tea at the club.'

Laughing, Edith rang the bell.

Bruce lighted a cigarette, first, with his usual courtesy, asking her permission.

' I'll tell you about *that* when Woodhouse has gone,' he said mysteriously.

' Oh, can't you tell me anything about it now? I wouldn't have ordered tea if I'd known that!'

He enjoyed keeping her waiting, and was delighted at her interest. He would have made it last longer, but was unable to bear his own suspense; so he said:

' Before I say any more, tell me: where is Madame Frabelle?'

CHAPTER III

'MADAME FRABELLE'S in her own room. She stays there a good deal, you know. I fancy she does it out of tactfulness.' Edith spoke thoughtfully.

'What does she do there?' Bruce asked with low-toned curiosity, as he stood up and looked in the glass.

'She says she goes there to read. She thinks it bores people to see a visitor sitting reading about the house; she says it makes them get tired of the sight of her.'

'But she can't be reading all those hours, surely?' and Bruce sat down, satisfied with his appearance.

'One would think not. I used to think she was probably lying on the sofa with cold cream on her face, or something of that sort. But she doesn't. Once I went in,' Edith smiled, 'and found her doing Swedish exercises.'

'Good heavens! What a wonderful woman she is! Do you mean to say she's learning Swedish, as well as all the other languages she knows?'

'No, no. I mean physical exercises. But go on, Bruce. I'm getting so impatient.'

Bruce settled himself down comfortably, blew a ring of smoke, and then began slowly:

'I never dreamt, Edith—'

'Oh, Bruce, are you going to tell me everything you never dreamt? We shall take weeks getting to the point.'

'Don't be absurd. I'll get to the point at once then. Look here; I think we ought to give a dinner for Madame Frabelle!'

'Oh, is that all? Of course! I've been wondering that you didn't wish to do it long before now.'

'Have you? I'll tell you why. Thinking Madame Frabelle was a pal, er—a friend—of the Conroys, it stood to reason, don't you see, that she knew everyone in London; or could, if she liked—everyone worth knowing, I mean. Under these circumstances there was no point in—well—in showing off our friends to her. But I found out,

351

only last night '—he lowered his voice—' what do you think? She isn't an intimate friend of Lady Conroy's at all! She only made her acquaintance in the drawing-room of the Royal Hotel two days before she came to London!'

Edith laughed.

' How delightful! Then why on earth did Lady Conroy send her to us with a letter of introduction? Why just us?'

' Because she likes you. Besides, it's just like her, isn't it? And she never said she had known her all her life. We jumped to that conclusion. It was our own idea.'

' And how did you find it out?'

' Why, when you went up to the children and left me alone with Madame Frabelle yesterday evening, she told me herself; perfectly frankly, in her usual way. She's always like that, so frank and open. Besides, she hadn't the slightest idea we didn't know it.'

' I hope you didn't let her think—' Edith began.

' Edith! As if I would! Well, that being so '—he lit another cigarette—' and under the circumstances, I want to ask some people to meet her. See?'

' She seems very happy with us alone, doesn't she? Not as if she cared much for going out.'

' Yes, I know; that's all very well. But I don't want her to think we don't know anyone. And it seems a bit selfish, too, keeping her all to ourselves like this.'

' Who do you want her to meet, dear?'

' I want her to meet the Mitchells,' said Bruce. ' It's only a chance, of course, that she hasn't met them already here, and I've told Mitchell at the Foreign Office a good deal about her. He's very keen to know her. Very keen indeed,' he added thoughtfully.

' And then the Mitchells will ask her to their house, of course?'

' I know they will,' said Bruce, rather jealously. ' Well, I sha'n't mind her going there—once or twice—it's a very pleasant house, you know, Edith. And she likes celebrities, and clever people, and that sort of thing.'

' Mrs Mitchell will count her as one, no doubt.'

' I daresay! What does that matter? So she is.'

' I know she is, in a way; but, Bruce, don't you wonder why she stays here so long? I mean, there's no question of its not being for —well, for, say, interested reasons. I happen to know for a fact that

she has a far larger income for herself alone than we have altogether.
She showed me her bank-book one day.'

' Why?'

' I don't know. She's so confidential, and perhaps she wanted me
to know how she was placed. And—she's not that sort of person—
she's generous and liberal, rather extravagant I should say.'

' Quite so. Still, it's comfortable here, and saves trouble—and she
likes us.'

Bruce again looked up toward the mirror, though he couldn't see
it now.

' Well, *I* don't mind her being here; it's a nice change, but it
seems odd she hasn't said a word about going. Well, about the
dinner. Who else shall we have, Edith? Let it be a small, intimate,
distinguished sort of dinner. She hates stiffness and ceremony. She
likes to have a chance to talk.'

' She does, indeed. All right, you can leave it to me, Bruce. I'll
make it all right. We'll have about eight people, shall we?'

' She must sit next to me, on my left,' Bruce observed. ' And not
lilies of the valley—she doesn't like the scent.'

Madame Frabelle was usually designated between them by the
personal pronoun only.

' All right. But what was the delicate, difficult matter that someone consulted you about, Bruce?'

' Ah, I was just coming to that. . . . Hush!'

The door opened. Madame Frabelle came in, dressed in a violet
tea-gown.

' Tea?' said Edith, holding out a cup.

' Yes, indeed! I'm always ready for tea, and you have such delightful tea, Edith dear!' (They had already reached the point of
Christian names, though Edith always found Eglantine a little difficult to say.) ' It's nice to see you back so early, Mr Ottley.'

' Wouldn't you like a slice of lemon?' said Bruce.

To offer her a slice of lemon with tea was, from Bruce, a tribute
to the lady's talents.

' Oh no! Cream and sugar, please.'

Madame Frabelle was looking very pleasant and very much at her
ease as she sat down comfortably, taking the largest chair.

' I'm afraid that Archie has been bothering you today,' Edith said,
as she poured out tea.

'What!' exclaimed Bruce, with a start of horror.

'Oh no, no, no! Not the least in the world, Mr Ottley! He's a most delightful boy. We were only having some fun together—about my mandolin; that was all!'

(Edith thought of the sounds she had heard on the stairs.)

'I'm afraid I got a little cross. A thing I very seldom do.' Madame Frabelle looked apologetically at Edith. 'But we've quite made it up now! Oh, and by the way, I want to speak to you both rather seriously about your boy,' she went on earnestly. She had a rather powerful, clear, penetrating voice, and spoke with authority, decision, and the sort of voluble fluency generally known as not letting anyone else get a word in edgeways.

'About our boy?' said Bruce, handing the toast to her invitingly, while Edith put a cushion behind her back, for which Madame Frabelle gave a little gracious smile.

'About your boy. Do you know, I have a very curious gift, Mr Ottley. I can always see in children what they're going to make a success of in life. Without boasting, I know you, Edith, are kind enough to believe that I'm an extraordinary judge of character. Oh, I've always been like that. I can't help it. I'll tell you now what you must make of your boy,' she pursued. 'He is a born musician!'

'A musician!' exclaimed both his parents at once, in great astonishment.

Madame Frabelle nodded. 'That boy is a born composer! He has genius for music. Look at his broad forehead! Those grey eyes, so wide apart! I know, just at first one thinks too much from the worldly point of view of the success of one's son in life. But why go against nature? The boy's a genius!'

'But,' ventured Edith, 'Archie hasn't the slightest ear for music!'

'He dislikes music intensely,' said Bruce. 'Simply loathes it.'

'He cried so much over his piano lessons that we were obliged to let him give them up. It used to make him quite ill—and his music mistress too,' Edith said. 'I remember she left the last time in hysterics.'

'Yes, by Jove, I remember too. Pretty girl she was. She had a nervous breakdown afterwards,' said Bruce rather proudly.

'No, dear; you're thinking of the other one—the woman who began to teach him the violin.'

'Oh, am I?'

Madame Frabelle nodded her head with a smile.

'Nothing on earth to do with it, my dear! The boy's a born composer all the same. With that face he must be a musician!'

'Really! Funny he hates it so,' said Bruce thoughtfully. 'But still, I have no doubt—'

'Believe me, you can't go by his not liking his lessons,' assured Madame Frabelle, as she ate a muffin. 'That has nothing to do with it at all. The young Mozart—'

'Mozart? I thought he played the piano when he was only three?'

'Handel, I mean—or was it Meyerbeer? At any rate you'll see I'm right.'

'You really think we ought to force him against his will to study music seriously, with the idea of his being a composer when he grows up, though he detests it?' asked his mother.

Madame Frabelle turned to Edith.

'Won't you feel proud when you see your son conducting his own opera, to the applause of thousands? Won't it be something to be the mother of the greatest English composer of the twentieth century?'

'It would be rather fun.'

'We sha'n't hear quite so much about Strauss, Elgar, Debussy and all those people when Archie Ottley grows up,' declared Madame Frabelle.

'I hear very little about them now,' said Bruce.

'Well, how should you at the Foreign Office, or the golf-links, or the club?' asked Edith.

Bruce ignored Edith, and went on: 'Perhaps he'll turn out to be a Lionel Monckton or a Paul Rubens. Perhaps he'll write comic opera revues or musical comedies.'

'Oh dear, no,' said their guest, shaking her head decidedly. 'It will be the very highest class, the top of the tree! The real thing!'

'Madame Frabelle *may* be right, you know,' said Bruce.

She leant back, smiling.

'I *know* I'm right! There's simply no question about it.'

'Well, what do you think we ought to do about it?' said Edith. 'He goes to a preparatory school now where they don't have any music lessons at all.'

'All the better,' she answered. 'The sort of lessons he would get at a school would be no use to him.'

'So I should think,' murmured Edith.

'Leave it, say, for the moment, and when he comes back for his next holidays put him under a good teacher—a really great man. And you'll see!'

'I daresay we shall,' said Bruce, considerably relieved at the postponement. 'Funny though, isn't it, his not knowing one tune from another, when he's a born musician?'

It flashed across Edith what an immense bond of sympathy it was between Bruce and Madame Frabelle that neither of them was burdened with the slightest sense of humour.

When he presently went out (each of them preferred talking to Her alone, and She also enjoyed a *tête-à-tête* most) Madame Frabelle drew up her chair nearer to Edith and said:

'My dear, I'm going to tell you something. Don't be angry with me, or think me impertinent, but you've been very kind to me, and I look upon you as a real friend.'

'It's very sweet of you,' said Edith, feeling hypnotised, and as if she would gladly devote her life to Madame Frabelle.

'Well, I can see something. You are not quite happy.'

'Not happy!' exclaimed Edith.

'No. You have a trouble, and I'd give anything to take it away.'

Madame Frabelle looked at her with sympathy, pressed her hand, then looked away.

Edith knew she was looking away out of delicacy. Delicacy about what? It was an effort not to laugh; but, oddly enough, it was also an effort not to feel secretly miserable. She wondered, though, what she was unhappy about. She need not have troubled, for Madame Frabelle was quite willing to tell her. She was, indeed, willing to tell anyone anything. Perhaps that was the secret of her charm.

CHAPTER IV

IT was utterly impossible, literally out of the question, that Madame Frabelle could know anything about the one trouble, the one danger, that so narrowly escaped being almost a tragedy, in Edith's life.

It was three years since Bruce, always inclined to vague, mild flirtations, had been positively carried off his feet, and literally taken away by a determined young art student, with red hair, who had failed to marry a friend of his. While Edith, with the children, was passing the summer holidays at Westgate, Bruce had sent her the strangest of letters, informing her that he and Mavis Argles could not live without one another, and had gone to Australia together, and imploring her to divorce him. The complication was increased by the fact that at that particular moment the most charming man Edith had ever met, Aylmer Ross, that eloquent and brilliant barrister, had fallen in love with her, and she had become considerably attracted to him. Her pride had been hurt at Bruce's conduct, but she had certainly felt it less bitterly, in one way, because she was herself so much fascinated by Aylmer and his devotion.

But Edith had behaved with cool courage and real unselfishness. She felt certain that Bruce's mania would not last, and that if it did he would be miserable. Strangely, then, she had declined to divorce him, and waited. Her prophecy turned out correct, and by the time they arrived at their journey's end the red-haired lady was engaged to a commercial traveller whom she met on the boat. By then Bruce and she were equally convinced that in going to Australia they had decidedly gone too far.

So Bruce came back, and Edith forgave him. She made one condition only (which was also her one revenge), that he should never speak about it, never mention the subject again.

Aylmer Ross, who had taken his romance seriously to heart, refused to be kept as *l'ami de la maison*, and as a platonic admirer.

Deeply disappointed—for he was prepared to give his life to Edith
and her children (he was a widower of independent means)—he
had left England; she had never seen him since.

All this had been a real event, a real break in Edith's life. For
the first few months after she suffered, missing the excitement of
Aylmer's controlled passion, and his congenial society. Gradually
she made herself—not forget it—but put aside, ignore the whole
incident. It gave her genuine satisfaction to know that she had made
a sacrifice for Bruce's sake. She was aware that he could not exist
really satisfactorily without her, though perhaps he didn't know it.
He needed her. At first she had endeavoured to remain separated
from him, while apparently living together, from who knows what
feeling of romantic fidelity to Aylmer, or pique at the slight shown
her by her husband. Then she found that impossible. It would make
him more liable to other complications and the whole situation too
full of general difficulties. So now, for the last three years, they had
been on much the same terms as they were before. Bruce had become, perhaps, less patronising, more respectful to her, and she a
shade more gentle and considerate to him, as to a child. For she
was generous and did not forgive by halves. There were moments of
nervous irritation, of course, and of sentimental regret. On the
whole, though, Edith was glad she had acted as she did. But if occasionally she felt her life a little dull and flat, if she missed some of
the excitement of that eventful year, it was impossible for anyone
to see it by her manner.

What *could* Madame Frabelle possibly know about it? What did
that lady really suppose was the matter?

'What do you think I'm unhappy about?' Edith repeated.

Madame Frabelle, as has been mentioned, was willing to tell her.
She told her, as usual, with fluency and inaccuracy.

Edith was much amused to find how strangely mistaken was this
authoritative lady as to her intuitions, how inevitably *à faux* with
her penetrations and her instinctive guesses. Madame Frabelle said
that she believed Edith was beginning to feel the dawn of love for
someone, and was struggling against it. (The struggle of course in
reality had long been over.)

Who was the person?

'I haven't met him yet,' Madame Frabelle said; 'but isn't there a name I hear very often? Your husband is always talking about him; he told me I was to make the acquaintance of this great friend of his. Something tells me it is he. I shall know as soon as I see him. You can't hide it from me!'

Who was the person Bruce was always mentioning to Madame Frabelle? Certainly not Aylmer Ross—he had apparently forgotten his existence.

'Are you referring to—?'

Madame Frabelle looked out of the window and nodded.

'Yes—Mr Mitchell!'

Edith started, and a smile curved her lips.

'It's always the husband's great friend, unfortunately,' sighed Eglantine. 'Oh, my dear' (with the usual cheap, ready-made know-ingness of the cynic), 'I've seen so much of that. Now I'm going to help you. I'm determined to leave you two dear, charming people without a cloud, when I go.'

'You're not thinking of going?'

'Not yet . . . no. Not while you let me stay here, dear. I've friends in London, and in the country, but I haven't looked them up, or written to them, or done anything since I've been here. I've been too happy. I couldn't be bothered. I am so interested in you! Another thing—may I say?—for I feel as if I'd known you for years. You think your husband doesn't know it. You are wrong.'

'Am I really?'

'Quite. Last night a certain look when he spoke of the Mitchells showed me that Bruce is terribly jealous. He doesn't show it, but he is.'

'But—Mrs Mitchell?' suggested Edith. 'She's one of our best friends—a dear thing. By the way, we're asking them to dine with us on Tuesday.'

'I'm delighted to hear it. I shall understand everything then. Isn't it curious—without even seeing them—that I know all about it? I think I've a touch of second sight.'

'But, Eglantine, aren't you going a little far? Hadn't you better wait until you'ye seen them, at least. You've no idea how well the Mitchells get on.'

'I've no doubt of it,' she replied, 'and, of course, I don't know that he—Mr Mitchell, I mean—even realises what you are to him. But I do!'

Edith was really impressed at the dash with which Madame Frabelle so broadly handled this vague theme.

'Wait till you do see them,' she said, rather mischievously, declining to deny her friend's suggestion altogether.

'Odd I should have guessed it, isn't it?' Madame Frabelle was evidently pleased. 'You'll admit this, Edith, from what your husband says I gather you see each other continually, don't you?'

'Very often.'

'Bruce and he are together at the Foreign Office. Bruce thinks much of him, and admires him. With it all I notice now and then a tinge of bitterness in the way he speaks. He was describing their fancy-dress ball to me the other day, and really his description of Mr Mitchell's costume would have been almost spiteful in any other man.'

'Well, but Mr Mitchell is over sixty. And he was got up as a black poodle.'

'Yes; quite so. But he's a fine-looking man, isn't he? And very pleasant and hospitable?'

'Oh yes, of course.'

'On your birthday last week that magnificent basket of flowers came from Mr Mitchell,' stated Eglantine.

'Certainly; from the Mitchells rather. But, really, that's nothing. I think you'll be a little disappointed if you think he's at all of the romantic type.'

'I didn't think that,' she answered, though of course she had; 'but something told me—I don't know why—that there's some strange attraction. . . . I never saw a more perfect wife than you, nor a more perfect mother. But these things should be nipped in the bud, dear. They get hold of you sometimes before you know where you are. And think,' she went on with relish, 'how terrible it would be practically to break up two homes!'

'Oh, really, I must stop you there,' cried Edith. 'You don't think of elopements, do you?'

'I don't say that, necessarily. But I've seen a great deal of life. I've lived everywhere, and just the very households—*ménages*, as we say abroad—that seem most calm and peaceful, sometimes— It would be, anyhow, very dreadful, wouldn't it—to live a double life?'

Edith thought her friend rather enjoyed the idea, but she said:

'You don't imagine, I hope, that there's anything in the nature of an intrigue going on between me and Mr Mitchell?'

'No, no, no—not now—not yet—but you don't quite know, Edith, how one can be carried away. As I was sitting up in my room—thinking—'

'You think too much,' interrupted Edith.

'Perhaps so—but it came to me like this. I mean to be the one to put things right again, if I can. My dear child, a woman of the world like myself sees things. You two ought to be ideally happy. You're meant for one another—I mean you and Bruce.'

'Do you think so?'

'Absolutely. But this—what shall I say?—this fascination is coming between you, and, though you don't realise it, it's saddening Bruce's life; it will sadden yours too. At first, no doubt, at the stage you're in, dear, it seems all romance and excitement. But later on— Now, Edith, promise me you won't be angry with me for what I've said? It's a terrible freedom that I've taken, I know. Really a liberty. But if I were your '—she glanced at the mirror—' elder sister, I couldn't be fonder of you. Don't think I'm a horrid, interfering old thing, will you?'

'Indeed I don't; you're a dear.'

'Well, we won't speak of it any more till after Tuesday,' said Madame Frabelle, ' and take my advice: throw yourself into other things.'

She glanced round the room.

' It's a splendid idea to divert your thoughts; why don't you re-furnish your boudoir?'

Edith had often noticed the strange lack in Eglantine of any sense of decoration. She dressed charmingly, but with regard to surroundings she was entirely devoid of taste. She had the curious provincialism so often seen in cosmopolitans who have lived most of their lives in hotels, without apparently noticing or caring about their surroundings.

Edith made rather a hobby of decoration, and she had a cultured and quiet taste, and much knowledge on the subject. She guessed Madame Frabelle thought her rooms too plain, too colourless. Instead of the dull greys and blues, and surfaces without design, she felt sure her friend would have preferred gorgeous patterns, and even a good deal of gilt. Probably at heart Madame Frabelle's ideal was the crimson plush and stamped leather and fancy ceilings of the lounge in a foreign hotel.

'I rather like my room, you know,' said Edith.

'And so do I. It's very charming. But a change, dear—a change of *entourage*, as we say abroad, would do you good.'

'Well, we must really think that out,' said Edith.

'That's right. And you're not cross?'

'Cross? I don't know when I've enjoyed a conversation so much,' said Edith, speaking with perfect truth.

CHAPTER V

THE Ottleys and Madame Frabelle were in the drawing-room awaiting their guests. (I say advisedly their guests, for no-one could help regarding Madame Frabelle as essentially the hostess, and queen of the evening.) One would fancy that instead of entertaining more or less for the last twelve years the young couple had never given a dinner before; so much suppressed excitement was in the air. Bruce was quiet and subdued now from combined nervousness and pride, but for the few days previous he had been terribly trying to his unfortunate wife; nothing, according to him, could be good enough for the purpose of impressing Madame Frabelle, and he appeared to have lost all his confidence in Edith's undeniable gift for receiving.

The flowers, the menu, the arrangement of the eight people—for the dinner was still small, intimate and distinguished, as he had first suggested—had been subjected to continual and maddening changes in its scheme. Everyone had been disengaged and everyone had accepted—then he wished he had asked other people instead.

When Edith was dressed Bruce put the last touch to his irritating caprices by asking Edith to take out of her hair a bandeau of blue that he had first asked her to put in. Every woman will know what agony that must have caused. The pretty fair hair was waved and arranged specially for this ornament, and when she took it out the whole scheme seemed to her wrong. However, she looked very pretty, dressed in vaporous tulle of a shade of blue which only a faultless complexion can bear.

Edith's complexion was her strong point. When she was a little flushed she looked all the better for it, and when she was pale it seemed to suit her none the worse. Hers was the sort of skin with a satiny texture that improves under bright sunshine or electric light; in fact the more brilliantly it was lighted the better it looked.

Madame Frabelle (of course) was dressed in black, *décolletée*, and with a good deal of jet. A black aigrette, like a lightning conductor, stood up defiantly in her hair. Though it did not harmonise well with the somewhat square and *bourgeoise* shape of her head and face, and appeared to have dropped on her by accident, yet as a symbol of smartness it gave her a kind of distinction. It appeared to have fallen from the skies; it was put on in the wrong place, and it did not nestle, as it should do, and appear to grow out of the hair, since that glory of womanhood, in her case of a dull brown, going slightly grey, was smooth, scarce and plainly parted. Madame Frabelle really would have looked her best in a cap of the fashion of the sixties. But she could carry off anything; and some people said that she did.

Edith had been allowed by her husband *carte blanche* in the decoration of their house.

This was fortunate, as *mise-en-scène* was a great gift of hers; no-one had such a sense as Edith for arranging a room. She had struck the happy mean between the eccentric and the conventional. Anything that seemed unusual did not appear to be a pose, or a strained attempt at being different from others, but seemed to have a reason of its own. For example, she greatly disliked the usual gorgeous *endimanché* drawing-room and dark conventional dining-room. The room in which she received her guests was soft and subdued in colour and not dazzling with that blaze of light that is so trying to strangers just arrived and not knowing their way about a house (or certain of how they are looking). The room seemed to receive them kindly; make them comfortable, and at their ease, hoping they looked their best. The shaded lights, not dim enough to be depressing, were kind to those past youth and gave confidence to the shy. There was nothing ceremonious, nothing chilly, about the drawing-room; it was essentially at once comfortable and becoming, and the lights shone like shaded sunshine from the dull pink corners of the room.

On the other hand, the dining-room helped conversation by its stimulating gaiety and daintiness.

The feminine curves of the furniture, such as is usually kept for the drawing-room, were all pure Louis-Quinze. It was deliciously pretty in its pink and white and pale green.

In the drawing-room the hosts stood by one of those large, old-fashioned oaken fireplaces so supremely helpful to conversation and *tête-à-têtes*. In Edith's house there was never any general conversation except at dinner. People simply made friends, flirted, and enjoyed themselves.

As the clock struck eight the Mitchells were announced. Edith could scarcely control a laugh as Mr Mitchell came in, he looked so utterly unlike the dangerous lover Madame Frabelle had conjured up. He was immensely tall, broad, loosely built, large-shouldered, with a red beard, a twinkle in his eye, and the merriest of laughs. He was a delightful man, but there was no romance about him. Besides, Edith remembered him as a black poodle.

Mrs Mitchell struck a useful note, and seemed a perfect complement to her husband, the ideal wife for him. She was about forty-five, but being slim, animated, and well dressed (though entirely without *chic*), she seemed a good deal younger.

Mr Mitchell might have been any age between sixty and sixty-five, and had the high spirits and vitality of a boy.

It was impossible to help liking this delightful couple; they fully deserved their popularity. In the enormous house at Hampstead, arranged like a country mansion, where they lived, Mr Mitchell made it the object of his life to collect Bohemians as other people collect Venetian glass, from pure love of the material. His wife, with a silly woman's subtlety, having rather lower ideals—that is to say, a touch of the very human vulgarity known as social ambition —made use of his Bohemianism to help her on in her mundane success. This was the principle of the thing. *If things were well done* —and they always were at her house—would not a duke, if he were musical, go anywhere to hear the greatest tenor in Europe? And would not all the greatest celebrities go anywhere to meet a duke?

Next the two young Conistons were announced.

Miss Coniston was a thin, amiable, artistic girl, who did tooling in leather, made her own dresses, recited, and had a pale, good-looking, too well-dressed, disquieting young brother of twenty-two, who seemed to be always going out when other people came in, but was rather useful in society, being musical and very polite. The music that he chose generally gave his audience a shock. Being so young, so pale, and so contemporary, one expected him to sing thin, elusive music by Debussy, Fauré, or Ravel. He seemed never to have heard of these composers, but sang instead threatening songs, such as, ' I'll sing thee Songs of Araby!' or defiant, teetotal melodies, like ' Drink to Me only with thine Eyes!' His voice was good, and

louder and deeper than one would expect. He accompanied himself
and his sister everywhere. She, by the way, to add to the interest
about her, was said to be privately engaged to a celebrity who was
never there. Alice and Guy Coniston were orphans, and lived alone
in a tiny flat in Pelham Gardens. He had been reading for the Bar,
but when the war broke out he joined the New Army, and was now
in khaki.

But the *clou* and great interest of the evening was the arrival of Sir
Tito Landi, that most popular of all Italian composers. With his
white moustache, pink and white complexion, and large bright blue
eyes, his dandified dress, his eyeglass and buttonhole, he had the
fresh, fair look of an Englishman, the dry brilliance of a Parisian,
the *naïveté* of a genius, the manners of a courtier, and behind it all
the diabolic humour of the Neapolitan. He was small, thin and
slight, with a curious dignity of movement.

' Ah, Tito,' cried Bruce cordially. ' Here you are!'
The dinner was bright and gay from the very beginning, even
before the first glass of champagne. It began with an optimistic view
of the war, then, dropping the grave subject, they talked of people,
theatres, books, and general gossip. In all these things Madame
Frabelle took the lead. Indeed, she had begun at once laying down
the law in a musical voice but with a determined manner that gave
those who knew her to understand only too well that she intended
to go steadily on, and certainly not to stop to breathe before the ices.
Sir Tito Landi, fixing his eyeglass in his bright blue eye, took in
Madame Frabelle in one long look, and smiled at her sympathetically.
' What do you think of her?' murmured Edith to Landi.
Hypnotised and slightly puzzled as she was by her guest, she was
particularly curious for his opinion, as she knew him to be the best
judge of character of her acquaintance. He had some of the capri-
ciousness of the spoilt, successful artist, which showed itself, except
to those whom he regarded as real friends, in odd variations of
manner, so that Edith could not tell at all by his being extremely
charming to Madame Frabelle that he liked her, or by his being
abrupt and satirical that he didn't. An old friend and a favourite,
she could rely on what he told her.

'C'est une bonne vieille,' he said. 'Bonne, mais bête!'

'Really?' Edith asked, surprised.

Landi laughed. 'Bête comme ses pieds, ma chère!'

Returning to decent language and conventional tone, he went on with a story he was telling about an incident that had happened when he was staying with some royalties. His stories were short, new, amusing, and invariably suited to his audience. Anything about the Court he saw, at a glance, would genuinely interest Madame Frabelle. Edith was amused as she saw that lady becoming more and more convinced of Landi's importance, and of his respectful admiration.

Long before dinner was over there was no doubt that everyone was delighted with Madame Frabelle. She talked so well, suited herself to everyone, and simply charmed them all. Yet why? Edith was still wondering, but by the time she rose to go upstairs she thought she began to understand her friend's secret. People were not charmed with Eglantine because she herself was charming, but because she was charmed. Madame Frabelle was really as much interested in everyone to whom she spoke as she appeared to be; the interest was not assumed. A few little pretences and affectations she might have, such as that of knowing a great deal about every subject under the sun—of having read everything, and been everywhere, but her interest in other people was real. That was what made people like her.

Young Coniston, shy, sensitive and reserved as he was, had nevertheless told her all about his training at Braintree, the boredom of getting up early, the dampness of the tents, and how much he wanted to be sent to the front. She admired his valour, was interested in his music, and at her persuasion he promised to sing her songs of Araby after dinner.

When the ladies were alone Eglantine's universal fascination was even more remarkable. Mrs Mitchell, at her desire, gave her the address of the little dressmaker who ran up Mrs Mitchell's blouses and skirts. This was an honour for Mrs Mitchell; nothing pleased her so much as to be asked for the address of her dressmaker by a woman with a foreign name.

As to Miss Coniston, she was enraptured with Eglantine. Madame Frabelle arranged to go and see her little exhibition of tooled leather, and coaxed out of the shy girl various details about the celebrity, who at present had an ambulance in France. She adored reciting, and Miss Coniston, to gratify her, offered to recite a poem by Emile Cammaerts on the spot.

As to Mr Mitchell, Madame Frabelle drew him out with more care and caution. With the obstinacy of the mistaken she still saw in Mr Mitchell's friendly looks at his hostess a passion for Edith, and shook her grey head over the blindness of the poor dear wife.

Bruce hung on her words and was open-mouthed while she spoke, so impressed was he at her wonderful cleverness, and at her evident success with his friends.

Later on Landi, sitting in the ingle-nook with Edith, said, as he puffed a cigar:

'Tiens, ma chère Edith, tu ne vois pas quelque chose?'

'What?'

He always talked French, as a middle course between Italian and English, and Edith spoke her own language to him.

'Elle. La Mère Frabelle,' he laughed to himself. 'Elle est folle de ton mari!'

'Oh, really, Landi! That's your fancy!'

He mimicked her. 'Farncy! Farncy! Je me suis monté l'imagination, peut-être! J'ai un rien de fièvre, sans doute! C'est une idée que j'ai, comme ça. Eh bien! Non! Nous verrons. Je te dis qu'elle est amoureuse de Bruce.'

'He is very devoted to her, I know,' said Edith, 'and I daresay he's a little in love with her—in a way. But she—'

'C'est tout le contraire, chère. Lui, c'est moins; il est flatté. Il la trouve une femme intelligente,' he laughed. 'Mais elle! Tu est folle de ne pas voir ça, Edith. Enfin! Si ça l'amuse?'

With a laugh he got up, to loud applause, and went to the little white enamelled piano. There, with a long cigar in his mouth, he struck a few notes, and at once magnetised his audience. The mere touch of his fingers on the piano thrilled everyone present.

He sang a composition of his own, which even the piano-organ had never succeeded in making hackneyed, 'Adieu, Hiver,' and melodious as only Italian music can be. Blue beams flashed from his eyes; he seemed in a dream. Suddenly in the most impassioned part, which he was singing in a composer's voice, that is, hardly any voice, but with perfect art, he caught Madame Frabelle's eye, and gave her a solemn wink. She burst out laughing. He then went on singing with sentiment and grace.

All the women present imagined that he was making love to them, while each man felt that he, personally, was making love to his ideal woman. Such was the effect of Landi's music. It made the most material, even the most unmusical, remember some little romance, some *tendresse*, some sentiment of the past; Landi seemed to get at the soft spot in everybody's heart. All the audience looked dreamy. Edith was thinking of Aylmer Ross. Where was he now? Would she ever see him again? Had she been wise to throw away her happiness like that? She tried to put the thought aside, but she observed, with a smile, that Madame Frabelle looked—and not when he was looking at her—a shade tenderly at Bruce.

Edith remembered what Landi had said: ' Si ça l'amuse?' She found an opportunity to tell him that Madame Frabelle believed in her own intuitions, and had got it into her head that she and Mr Mitchell were attached to one another.

' Naturellement. Elle veut s'excuser; la pauvre.'

' But she really believes it.'

' Elle voit double, alors!' exclaimed Landi.

CHAPTER VI

EDITH and Madame Frabelle had long talks next day over the little dinner-party, and the people of their intimate circle whom she had met. She was delighted with Landi, though a little frightened of him, as most people were when they first knew him, unless he really liked them immensely.

She impressed on Edith to beware of Mr Mitchell.

Bruce, for once, had really been satisfied with his own entertainment, and declared to Edith that Madame Frabelle had made it go off splendidly.

Edith was growing to like her more and more. In a house where Bruce lived it was certainly a wonderful help to have a third person often present—if it was the right person. The absurd irritations and scenes of fault-finding that she had become inured to, but which were always trying, were now shorter, milder, or given up altogether. Bruce's temper was perennially good, and got better. Then the constant illnesses that he used to suffer from—he was unable to pass the military examination and go to the front on account of a neurotic heart—these illnesses were either omitted entirely or talked over with Madame Frabelle, whose advice turned out more successful than that of a dozen specialists.

' An extraordinary woman she is, you know, Edith,' he said. ' You know that really peculiar feeling I sometimes have?'

' Which, dear?'

' You know that sort of emptiness in the feet, and heaviness in the head, and that curious kind of twitching of the eyelids that I get?'

' Yes, I know. Well, dear?'

' Well, Madame Frabelle has given me a complete cure for it. It seems her husband (by the way, *what* a brute he must have been, and what a life that poor woman led! However, never mind that now) had something very much of the same kind, only not quite so bad.'

' Which, dear?'

' How do you mean " Which "? Which what?'

370

'Which peculiar feeling?'

'What peculiar feeling are we talking about?'

'I said, which peculiar feeling did Mr Frabelle have?'

'What are you trying to get at, Edith?' He looked at her suspiciously.

Edith sighed.

'Was it the heaviness in the feet, or the lightness in the head, or was it the twitching of the eyelid which Mr Frabelle used to suffer from?'

'Oh, ah! Yes, I see what you mean. It seemed he had a little of them all. But what do you think she used to do?'

'I haven't the slightest idea.'

'There's some stuff called Tisane—have you ever heard of it?' Bruce asked. 'It's a simple remedy, but a very good thing. Well, he used to use that.'

'Did he bathe his eye with it?'

'Oh, my dear Edith, you're wool-gathering. Do pull yourself together. He drank it, that's what he did, and that's what I'm going to do. Eg—Madame Frabelle would go straight down into the kitchen and show you how to make it if you like.'

'I don't mind, if cook doesn't,' said Edith.

'Oh, we'll see about that. Anyway she's going to show me how to get it made.

'Then there's another thing Madame Frabelle suggested. She's got an idea it would do me a world of good to spend a day in the country.'

'Oh, really? Sounds a good idea.'

'Yes. Say, on the river. She's not been there for years it seems. She thinks she would rather enjoy it.'

'I should think it would be a capital plan,' said Edith.

'Well, how about next Saturday?' said Bruce, thinking he was concealing his eagerness and satisfaction.

'Saturday? Oh yes, certainly. Saturday, by all means, if it's fine. What time shall we start?'

He started at once, but was silent.

'Saturday, yes,' Edith went on, after a glance at him. 'Only, I promised to take the two children to an afternoon performance.'

'Did you though?' Bruce brightened up. 'Rather hard luck on them to disappoint them. Mind you, Edith, I don't believe in *spoiling* children. I don't think their parents should be absolute slaves to them; but, on the other hand, I don't think it's good for them to disappoint them quite so much as that; and, after all—well, a promise to a child!' He shook his head sentimentally. ' Perhaps it's a fad of mine; I daresay it is; but I don't like the idea of breaking a promise to a child!'

' It does seem a shame. Too bad.'

' You agree with me? I knew you would. I've heard you say the same yourself. Well then, look here, Edith; suppose we do it—suppose you do it, I mean. Suppose you go with Archie and Dilly. They're to lunch with my mother, aren't they?'

' Yes, dear. But we were to have fetched them from there and then taken them on to the theatre!'

' Well, do it, then, my dear girl! Stick to your plan. Don't let *me* spoil your afternoon! Gracious heaven! I—I—why, I can quite well take Madame Frabelle myself.' He looked at the barometer. ' The glass is going up,' he said, giving it first a tap and then a slight shake to encourage it to go up higher and to look sharp about it. ' So that's settled, then, dear. That's fixed up. *I*'ll take her on the river. *I* don't mind in the very least. I shall be only too pleased—delighted. Oh, don't thank me, my dear girl; I know one ought to put oneself out for a guest, especially a widow . . . under these circumstances over in England . . . during the war too . . . hang it, it's the least one can do.'

. . . Bruce's murmurings were interrupted by the entrance of the lady in question. He made the suggestion, and explained the arrangement. She consented immediately with much graciousness.

' I dote on the river, and haven't been for years.'

' Now where would you like to go?' he asked. ' What part of the river do you like? How about Maidenhead?'

' Oh, any part. Don't ask me! Anything you suggest is sure to be right. You know far more about these things than I do. But Maidenhead—isn't it just a little commonplace? A little noisy and crowded, even now?'

' By jove, yes, you're quite right. Madame Frabelle's perfectly right, Edith, you know. Well, what about Shepperton?'

' Shepperton? Oh, charming! Dear little town. But it isn't exactly what I call the *river*, if you know what I mean. I mean to say—'

' Well, could you suggest a place?' said Bruce.

' Oh, I'm the worst person in the world for suggesting anything,' said Madame Frabelle. 'And I know so little of the river. But how about Kingston?'

'Kingston? Oh, capital. That would be charming.'

'Kyngestown, as it used to be called' (Madame Frabelle hastened to show her knowledge) 'in the days when Saxon kings were crowned there. Am I wrong or not? Oh, surely yes. . . . Wasn't it Kingston? Didn't great Cæsar cross the river there? And the Roman legions camp upon the sloping uplands?'

Bruce gasped. 'You know everything!' he exclaimed.

'Oh no. I remember a little about the history,' she said modestly. 'Ah, poor, weak King Edwy!'

'Yes, indeed,' said Bruce, though he had no recollection of having heard the gentleman mentioned before. 'Poor chap!'

'Too bad,' murmured Edith.

'How he must have hated that place!' said Madame Frabelle.

'Rather. I should think so indeed.'

'However, *you* won't,' said Edith adroitly changing the subject, seeing her husband getting deeper out of his depth.

Most of the evening Madame Frabelle read up Baedeker, to the immense astonishment of Bruce, who had never before thought of regarding the river from the historical and geographical point of view.

The next day, which was fine, if not warm, the two started off with a certain amount of bustle and a bundle of rugs, Madame Frabelle in a short skirt with a maritime touch about the collar and what she called a suitable hat and a dark blue motor veil. She carried off the whole costume to admiration.

Archie seemed rather bewildered and annoyed at this division of the party.

'But, Mother, we're going out to lunch with grandmother.'

'I know, darling. I'll come and fetch you from there.'

Conventional and restrained as Archie usually was, he sometimes said curious things.

Edith saw by his dreamy expression he was going to say one now.

He looked at her for a little while after his father's departure and then asked:

'Mother!'

'Yes, darling.'

' Is Madame Frabelle a nice little friend for father?'

Edith knew he had often heard her and the nurse or the governess discussing whether certain children were nice little friends for him or Dilly.

' Oh yes, dear, very nice.'

' Oh.'

The cook came in for orders.

' You're going to lunch all alone then, aren't you, Mother?'

' Yes, I suppose I must. I don't mind. I've got a nice book.'

Archie walked slowly to the door, then said in a tone of envious admiration which contained a note of regret:

' I suppose you'll order a delicious pudding?'

She went to fetch the children, who were excited at the prospect of a theatre. The elder Mrs Ottley was a pleasant woman, who understood and was utterly devoted to her daughter-in-law. Fond as she was of her son, she marvelled at Edith's patience and loved her as much as she loved Bruce. Though she had never been told, for she was the sort of woman who does not require to be told things in order to know them, she knew every detail of the sacrifice Edith had once made. She had been almost as charmed by Aylmer Ross as her daughter-in-law was, and she had considered Edith's action nearly sublime. But she had never believed Edith was at that time really in love with Aylmer. She had said, after Bruce's return: ' It mustn't happen again, you know, Edith.'

' What mustn't?'

' Don't spoil Bruce. You've made it almost too easy for him. Don't let him think he can always be running away and coming back!'

' No, never again,' Edith had answered, with a laugh.

Now they never spoke of the subject. It was a painful one to Mrs Ottley.

Today that lady seemed inclined to detain Edith, and make her —as Archie feared—late for the rising of the curtain.

' You really like Madame Frabelle so much, dear?'

' Really I do,' said Edith. ' The more I know her, the more I like her. She's the most good-natured, jolly, kind woman I've ever seen. Landi likes her too. That's a good sign.'

' And she keeps Bruce in a good temper?' said Mrs Ottley slyly.

'Well, why shouldn't she? I'm not afraid of Madame Frabelle,' Edith said, laughing. 'After all, Bruce may be thirty-seven, but she's fifty.'

'She's a wonderful woman,' admitted Mrs Ottley, who had at first disliked her, but had come round, like everyone else. 'Very very nice; and really I do like her. But you know my old-fashioned ideas. I never approve of a third person living with a married couple.'

'Oh—living! She's only been with us about a month.'

'But you don't think she's going away before the end of the season?'

'You can't call it a season. And she can't easily settle down just now, on account of the war. Many of her relations are abroad, and some in the country. She hasn't made up her mind where to live yet. She has never had a house of her own since her husband died.'

'Yes, I see.'

'Do come, Mother!' urged Archie.

'All right, darling.'

'Will I have to take my hat off?' pouted Dilly, who had on a new hat with daisies round it, in which she looked like a baby angel. She had a great objection to removing it.

'Yes, dear. Why should you mind?'

'My hair will be all anyhow if I have to take it off in the theatre,' said Dilly.

'Don't be a silly little ass,' Archie murmured to his sister. 'Why, in some countries women would be sent to prison unless they took their hats off at a play!'

The three reached the theatre in what even Archie called good time. This meant to be alone in the dark, gloomy theatre for at least twenty minutes, no-one present as yet, except two or three people eating oranges in the gallery. He liked to be the first and the last.

Edith was fancying to herself how Madame Frabelle would lay down the law about the history of Kingston, and read portions of the guide-book aloud, while Bruce was pointing out the scenery.

The entertainment, which was all odds and ends, entertained the children, but rather bored her. Archie was learning by heart—which was a way he had—the words of a favourite song now being sung—

> *' Kitty, Kitty, isn't it a pity,*
> *In the city you work so hard,—*
> *With your one, two, three, four, five,*
> *Six, three, seven, five, Gerrard?*
>
> *Kitty, Kitty, isn't it a pity,*
> *That you're wasting so much time?*
> *With your lips close to the telephone,*
> *When they might be close to mine!'*

when Edith's eye was suddenly attracted by the appearance of a boy in khaki, who was in a box to her right. He looked about seventeen, and was tall and good-looking; but what struck her about him was his remarkable likeness in appearance and in movement to Aylmer Ross. Even his back reminded her strongly of her hero. There was something familiar in the thick, broad shoulders, in the cool ease of manner, in the expression of the face. But could that young man— why, of course, it was three years ago! When she parted with Aylmer Ross, Teddy was fourteen; these years made a great difference, and of course all plans had been changed on account of the war. Aylmer, she thought, was too old to have been at the front. The boy must be in the New Army.

She watched him perpetually; she felt a longing to go and speak to him. After a while, as though attracted by her interest, he turned round and looked her straight in the face. How thrilled she felt at this likeness. . . . They were the very last to go out, and Edith contrived to be near the party in the box. She dropped something, and the young man picked it up. She had never seen him, and yet she felt she knew him. When he smiled she could not resist speaking to him.

'Thank you. Excuse me. Are you the son of Mr Aylmer Ross?'

'I am. And I know you quite well by your photograph,' he said in exactly Aylmer's pleasant, casual voice. 'You were a great friend of my father's, weren't you?'

'Yes. Where are you now?'

He was at Aldershot, but was in town on leave.

'And where's your father?'

'Didn't you know? My father's at the front. He's coming over on leave, too, in a fortnight.'

'Really? And are you still at Jermyn Street?'

' Oh yes. Father let his house for three years, but we've come back again. Jolly little house, isn't it?'

' Very. And I hope we shall see you both,' said Edith conventionally.

The boy bowed, smiled and walked away so quickly that Archie had no time for the salute he had prepared.

He was wonderfully like Aylmer.

Edith was curiously pleased and excited about this little incident.

CHAPTER VII

MADAME FRABELLE and Bruce arrived at Waterloo in good time for the 11.10 train, which Bruce had discovered in the A B C.

They wished to know where it started, but nobody appeared interested in the subject. Guards and porters, of whom they inquired, seemed surprised at their questions and behaved as if they regarded them as signs of vulgar and impertinent curiosity. At Waterloo no-one seems to know when a train is going to start, where it is starting from, or where it is going to. Madame Frabelle unconsciously assumed an air of embarrassment, as though she had no responsibility for the queries and excited manner of her companion. She seemed, indeed, surprised when Bruce asked to see the stationmaster. Here things came to a head. There was no train for Kingston at 11.10; the one at that hour was the Southampton Express; and it was worse than useless for Bruce and Madame Frabelle.

'Then the A B C and Bradshaw must both be wrong,' said Bruce reproachfully to Madame Frabelle.

An idea occurred to that resourceful lady. 'Perhaps the 11.10 was only to start on other days, not on Saturdays.'

She turned out to be right. However, they discovered a train at twenty minutes to twelve, which would take them where they wanted, though it was not mentioned, apparently, in any time-table, and could only be discovered by accident by someone who was looking for something else.

They hung about the station until it arrived, feeling awkward and uncomfortable, as people do when they have arrived too early for a train. Meanwhile they abused Bradshaw, and discussed the weather. Bruce said how wonderful it was how some people always knew what sort of weather it was going to be. Madame Frabelle, who was getting sufficiently irritable to be epigrammatic, said that she never cared to know what the weather was going to be; the weather in England was generally bad enough when it came without the added misery of knowing about it beforehand.

Bruce complained that she was too Continental. He very nearly said that if she didn't like England he wondered she hadn't remained in France, but he stopped himself.

At last the train arrived. Bruce had settled his companion with her back to the engine in a corner of a first-class carriage, and placed her rugs in the rack above. As they will on certain days, every little thing went wrong, and the bundle promptly fell off. As she moved to catch it, it tumbled on to her hat, nearly crushing the crown. Unconsciously assuming the expression of a Christian martyr, Madame Frabelle said it didn't matter. Bruce had given her *The Gentlewoman, The World, The Field, Punch,* and *The London Mail* to occupy the twenty-five minutes or so while they waited for the train to start. The journey itself was much shorter than this interval. Knowing her varied interests, he felt sure that these journals would pretty well cover the ground, but he was rather surprised, as he took the seat opposite her, to see that she read first, in fact instantly started, with apparent interest, on *The London Mail.* With a quick glance he saw that she was enjoying. ' What Everybody Wants to Know '—' Why the Earl of Blank looked so surprised when he met the pretty little blonde lady who had been said to be the friend of his wife walking in Bond Street with a certain dark gentleman who until now he had always understood to be her *bête noire,*' and so forth.

As an example to her he took up *The New Statist* and read a serious article.

When they arrived it was fine and sunny, and they looked at once for a boat.

It had not occurred to him before that there would be any difficulty in getting one. He imagined a smart new boat all ready for him, with fresh, gay cushions, and everything complete and suitable to himself and his companion. He was rather irritated when he found instead that the best they could do for him was to give him a broken-down, battered-looking thing like an old chest, which was to be charged rather heavily for the time they meant to spend on the river. It looked far from safe, but it was all they could do. So they got in. Bruce meant to show his powers as an oarsman. He said Madame Frabelle must steer and asked her to trim the boat

In obedience to his order she sat down with a bang, so heavily that Bruce was nearly shot up into the air. Amiable as she always was, and respectfully devoted as Bruce was to her, he found that being on the river has a mysterious power of bringing out any defects of temper that people have concealed when on dry ground. He said to her:

'Don't do that again. Do you mind?' as politely as he could.

She looked up, surprised.

'I beg your pardon, Mr Ottley?'

'Don't do that again.'

'Don't do what? What did I do?'

'Why, I asked you to trim the boat.'

'What did I do? I merely sat down.'

He didn't like to say that she shouldn't sit down with a bump, and took his place.

'If you like,' she said graciously, 'I'll relieve you there, presently.'

'How do you mean—relieve me?'

'I mean I'll row—I'll sit in the stern—row!'

'Perhaps you've forgotten the names of the different parts of a boat. Madame Frabelle?'

'Oh, I think not, Mr Ottley. It's a good while since I was on the river, but it's not the sort of thing one forgets, and I'm supposed to have rather a good memory.'

'I'm sure you have—a wonderful memory—still, where I'm sitting is not the stern.'

There was a somewhat sulky silence. They admired the scenery of the river. Madame Frabelle said she loved the distant glimpses of the grey old palace of the Tudors, and asked him if he could imagine what it was like when it was gay all day with the clanking of steel and prancing horses and things.

'How I love Hampton Court!' she said. 'It looks so quiet and peaceful. I think I should like to live there. Think of the evenings in that wonderful old place, with its panelled walls, and the echo of feet that are no longer there, down the cold, stone corridors—'

Bruce gave a slight laugh.

'Echo of feet that are no longer there? But how could that be? Dear me, how poetical you are, Madame Frabelle!'

'I mean the imaginary echo.'

'Imaginary—ah, yes. You're very imaginative, aren't you, Madame Frabelle? Well, I don't know whether it's imagination or not, but, do you know, I fancy that queer feeling of mine seems to be coming on again.'

' What queer feeling?'

' I told you about it, and you were very sympathetic the other night, before dinner. A kind of emptiness in the feet, and a hollowness in the head, the feeling almost, but not quite, of faintness.'

' It's nearly two o'clock. Perhaps you're hungry,' said Madame Frabelle.

Bruce thought this was not fair, putting all the hunger on to him, as if she had never felt anything so prosaic. Madame Frabelle always behaved as if she were superior to the weaknesses of hunger or sleep, and denied ever suffering from either.

' It may be. I had no breakfast,' said Bruce untruthfully, as though it were necessary to apologise for requiring food to sustain life.

' Nor did I,' said Madame Frabelle hastily.

' Well, don't you feel that you would like a little lunch?'

' Oh no—oh dear, no. Still, I dare say some food would do you good, Mr Ottley—keep you up. I'll come and watch you.'

' But you must have something too.'

' Must I? Oh, very well, just to keep you company.'

They got out very briskly, and, leaving their battered-looking coffin (called ironically the *Belle of the River*), they walked with quick steps to the nearest hotel. Here they found a selection of large, raw-looking cold beef, damp, tired-looking ham, bread, cheese, celery, and dessert in the form of dry apples, oranges, and Brazil nuts that had long left their native land.

Bruce decided that the right thing to drink was shandy-gaff, but, to keep up her Continental reputation, Madame Frabelle said she would like a little light wine of the country.

' Red, white, or blue?' asked Bruce, whose spirits were rising.

She laughed very heartily, and decided on a little red.

They had an adequate, if not exquisite, lunch, then Madame Frabelle said she would like to go over Hampton Court. A tedious guide offered to go with them, but Madame Frabelle said she knew all about the place better than he did, so they wandered through the beautiful old palace.

' Oh, to think of King Charles II's beauties living there—those lovely, languid ladies—how charming they were!' exclaimed Madame Frabelle.

' They wore very low dresses,' said Bruce, who felt rather

sleepy and stupid, and as if he didn't quite know what he was saying.

Madame Frabelle modestly looked away from the pictures.

'How exquisite the garden is.'

He agreed, and they went out and sat, somewhat awkwardly, on an uncomfortable stone seat.

There was a delicious half-hour of real summer sun—'One of those April days that seem a forecast of June,' as Madame Frabelle said.

'How much better it is to be here in the beautiful fresh air than squeezed into a stuffy theatre,' remarked Bruce, who was really feeling a shade jealous of Edith for seeing the revue that he had wished to see.

'Yes, indeed. There's nothing like England, I think,' she said rather irrelevantly.

'How exactly our tastes agree.'

'Do they?'

Her hand was on the edge of the seat. Somehow or other Bruce's had gone over it. She didn't appear to notice it.

'What small hands you have!' he remarked.

'Oh no! I take sixes,' said the lady, whose size was really three-quarters more than that.

He insisted on looking at the grey suède glove, and then examined her rings.

'I suppose these rings have—er—associations for you, Madame Frabelle?'

'Ah!' she said, shaking her head. 'This one—yes, this one—the sapphire recalls old memories.' She sighed; she had bought it in the Brompton Road.

'A present from your husband, I suppose?' said Bruce, with a tinge of bitterness.

'Ah!' she answered.

She thought he was getting a little sentimental, too early in the day, and, with an effort at energy, she said:

'Let's go back to the river.'

They went back, and now Bruce began to show off his rowing powers. He had not practised for a long time, and didn't get along very quickly. She admired his athletic talents, as though he had been a winner of the Diamond Sculls.

'If I'd stuck to it, you know,' he said, rather apologetically, 'I'd have done well in the rowing line. At one time—a good while ago—I thought of going in for Henley, in the Regatta, you know. But with that beastly Foreign Office one can't keep up anything of that sort.'

'I suppose not.'

'My muscle,' said Bruce, sticking out his arm, and hitting it rather hard, 'is fairly good, you know. Not bad for a London man who never has any practice.'

'No indeed.'

'My arm was about seventeen inches round just below the elbow at one time,' Bruce said, 'a few years ago.'

'Just fancy! Splendid!' said Madame Frabelle, who remembered that her waist was not much more a good while ago.

He told her a good many anecdotes of his prowess in the past, until tea-time.

Madame Frabelle depended greatly on tea; anything else she could do without. But a cup of tea in the afternoon was necessary to her well-being, and her animation. She became rather drowsy and absent by four o'clock.

Bruce again suggested their landing and leaving the *Belle of the River*, as they had not thought of bringing a tea-basket.

After tea, which was a great success, they became very cheery and jolly. They went for a walk and then back to their boat.

This was the happiest time of the day.

When they reached the station, about half-past six, they found a disagreeable crowd, pushing, screaming, and singing martial songs. As they got into their first-class carriage about a dozen third-class passengers sprang in, just as the train started. Bruce was furious, but nothing could be done, and the journey back to town was taken with Madame Frabelle very nearly pushed on to his knee by a rude young man who practically sat on hers, smoking a bad cigarette in her face.

They tacitly agreed to say nothing about this, and got home in time for dinner, declaring the day to have been a great success.

Bruce had really enjoyed it. Madame Frabelle said she had; though she had a certain little tenderness, half of a motherly kind, for Bruce, she far preferred his society in a comfortable house. She didn't really think he was the ideal companion for the open air. And he was struck, as he had often been before, by her curious way of contradicting herself in conversation. She took any side and argued in favour of it so long as it was striking or romantic. At one moment she would say with the greatest earnestness, for instance, that divorce should not be allowed. Marriage should be for ever, or not at all. At another moment she would argue in favour of that absurd contradiction in terms known as free love, forgetting that she had completely changed round since earlier in the conversation. This was irritating, but he was still impressed with her infallibility, and Edith remarked more every day how curious that infallibility was, and how safe it was to trust. Whenever Madame Frabelle knew that something was going to happen, it didn't, and whenever she had an intuition that something was going to occur, *then* it was pretty safe. It never would. In the same way she had only to look at a person to see them as they were not. This was so invariable it was really very convenient to have her in the house, for whatever she said was always wrong. One had merely to go by contraries and her prophecies were most useful.

'It's been jolly for you,' Bruce said to Edith, 'having a ripping time in town while I'm taking your visitors about to show them England.'

'You wouldn't have cared for the theatre,' she said. 'But, fancy, I met Aylmer's son there—Aylmer Ross, you know. Aylmer himself is at the front. They have taken their old house again. He means to come back there.'

'Well, I really can't help it,' said Bruce rather fretfully. '*I* should be at the front if it weren't for my neurotic heart. The doctor wouldn't hear of passing me—at least one wouldn't. Any fellow who would have done so would be—not a careful man. However, I don't know that it wouldn't have been just as good to die for my country, and get some glory, as to die of heart trouble here.' He sighed.

'Oh no, you won't,' said Edith reassuringly; 'you look the picture of health.'

'I've got a bit of sunburn, I think,' said Bruce, popping up to look in the glass. 'Funny how I do catch the sun. I asked Dr Pollock about it one day.'

'Really—did you consult him about your sunburn?'

'Yes. What are you smiling at, He said it's caused by the extreme delicacy of the mucous membrane; nothing to be anxious about.'

'I don't think I am anxious; not particularly. And don't worry, my dear boy; it's very becoming,' said Edith.

Bruce patted her head, and gave her a kiss, smiling.

CHAPTER VIII

'We're lunching with the Mitchells today,' said Edith.

'Oh yes. I remember. I'm looking forward to it,' graciously said Madame Frabelle. 'It's a pity your husband can't come, isn't it? Ah, you naughty girl, I don't believe you think so!' Madame Frabelle archly shook her finger at Edith.

'Eglantine, have you really seriously talked yourself into thinking that Mr Mitchell is anything to me?'

'I don't say, dear,' said Madame Frabelle, sitting down comfortably, and bringing out her knitting, 'that you yourself are aware of it. I don't say that you're in love with him, but that he is devoted to you anyone with half-an-eye can see. And some day,' she shook her head, 'some day your interest in him may take you by surprise.'

'It is *your* interest in him that surprises me,' said Edith. 'He's a good friend, and we like him very much. But for anything else!—'

'If so, it's really rather wonderful,' mused Eglantine, 'that you've never had a thought, even the merest dream, beyond your husband; that it has never even occurred to you that anyone else might have suited your temperament better.'

Edith dropped her book, and picked it up again. Her friend thought she saw, whether through stooping or what not, an increase of colour in her face.

'It isn't everyone,' continued Madame Frabelle, 'who would appreciate your husband as you do. To me he is a very charming man. I can understand his inspiring a feeling almost of motherly interest. I even feel sometimes,' she laughed, 'as if it would be a pleasure to look after him, take care of him. I think it would not have been a bad thing for him to have married a woman a little older than himself. But you, Edith, you're so young. You see, you might have made a mistake when you married him. You were a mere girl, and I could imagine some of his ways might irritate a very young woman.'

After a moment she went on: 'I suppose Bruce was very handsome when you married him?'

' Yes, he was. But he hasn t altered much.'

' Yet, as I told you before, Edith, though I think you an ideal wife, you don't give me the impression of being in love with him. I hope you don't take this as an impertinence, my dear?'

' Not at all. And I'm not sure that I am.'

' Yet your mother-in-law told me the other day that you had been such a marvellous wife to him. That you had even made sacrifices. You have never had anything to forgive, surely?'

' Oh no, never,' hastily said Edith, fearing that Mrs Ottley was a little inclined to be indiscreet.

' She told me that Bruce had been occasionally attracted—only very slightly—by other women, but that you were the only person he really cared for.'

' Oh, I doubt if he ever thinks much of anyone else,' said Edith.

A characteristic of the Mitchells' entertainments was that one always met there the people they had met, even for the first time, at one's own house. Here were the Conistons, and Landi, whom Edith was always delighted to see.

It was a large and gay lunch. Edith was placed some distance from Mr Mitchell. Of course there was also a novelty—some lion or other was always at the Mitchells'. Today it consisted of a certain clergyman, called the Rev. Byrne Fraser, of whom Mrs Mitchell and her circle were making much. He was a handsome, weary-looking man of whom more was supposed than could conveniently be said. His wife, who adored him, admitted that though he was an excellent husband, he suffered from rheumatism and religious doubts, which made him occasionally rather trying. There had been some story about him—nobody knew what it was. Madame Frabelle instantly took his side, and said she was sure he had been ill-treated, though she knew nothing whatever about it. She was placed next to him at table and began immediately on what she thought was his special subject.

' I understand that you're very modern in your views,' she said, smiling.

' I !' he exclaimed in some surprise. ' Really you are quite mistaken. I don't think I am at all.'

' Really? Oh, I'm so glad—I've such a worship myself for tradition. I'm so thankful that you have, too.'

'I don't know that I have,' he said.

'It's true, then, what I heard—I felt it was the moment I looked at you, Mr Fraser—I mean, that you're an atheist.'

'A *what?*' he exclaimed, turning pale with horror. 'Good heavens, Madame, do you know what my profession is?'

He seemed utterly puzzled by her. She managed, all the same, somehow or other to lure him into a conversation in which she heartily took his side. By the end of lunch they were getting on splendidly, though neither of them knew what they were talking about.

And this was one of the curious characteristics of Madame Frabelle. Nobody made so many gaffes, yet no-one got out of them so well. To use the lawyer's phrase, she used so many words that she managed to engulf her own and her interlocutor's ideas. No-one, perhaps, had ever talked so much nonsense seriously as she did that day, but the Rev. Byrne Fraser said she was a remarkable woman, who had read and thought deeply. Also he was enchanted with her interest in him, as everybody always was.

Edith thought she had heard Mr Mitchell saying something to the others that interested her. She managed to get near him when the gentlemen joined them in the studio, as they called the large room where there was a stage, a piano, a parquet floor, and every possible arrangement for amusement. Madame Frabelle moved quickly away, supposing that Edith wished to speak to him for his sake, whereas really it was in order to have repeated something she thought she had heard at lunch.

'Did I hear you saying anything about your old friend, Aylmer Ross?' she asked.

'Yes, indeed. Haven't you heard? The poor fellow has been wounded. He was taken into hospital at once, fortunately, and he's getting better, and is going to be brought home almost immediately, to the same old house in Jermyn Street. I think his son is to meet him at the station today. We must all go and see him. Capital chap, Aylmer. I always liked him. He's travelled so much that—even before the war—I hadn't seen him for three years.'

'Was the wound serious?' asked Edith, who had turned pale.

'They were anxious at first. Now he's out of danger. But, poor chap, I'm afraid he won't be able to move for a good while. His leg is broken. I hear he's got to be kept lying down two or three months.'

'Qu'est ce qu'il y a, Edith?' asked Landi, who joined her.

'I've just heard some bad news,' she said, 'but don't speak about it.'

She told him.

'Bien. Du calme, mon enfant; du calme!'

'But, I'm anxious, Landi.'

'Ça se voit!'

'Do you think—'

'Ce ne sera rien. It's the best thing that could happen to him. He'll be all right. . . . I suppose you want to see him, Edith?'

'He may not wish to see me,' said Edith.

'Oh yes, he will. You were the first person he thought of,' answered Landi. 'Why, my dear, you forget you treated him badly!'

'Then, if he'd treated *me* badly he wouldn't care to see me again, you mean?'

'C'est probable,' said Landi, selecting with care a very large cigar from a box that was being handed round. 'Now, be quite tranquil. I shall go and see him directly I leave here, and I'll let you hear every detail. Will that do?'

'Thanks, dear Landi! . . . But even if he wishes to see me, ought I to go?'

'That I don't know. But you will.'

He lighted the long cigar.

N E X T morning Edith, who always came down to breakfast, though somewhat late, found on her plate a letter from Lady Conroy, that most vague and forgetful of all charming Irishwomen. It said:

'M Y D E A R M R S O T T L E Y,

Do excuse my troubling you, but could you give me a little information? Someone has asked me about Madame Frabelle. I know that she is a friend of yours, and is staying with you, and I said so; also I have a sort of idea that she was, in some way, connected with you by marriage or relationship, but of that I was not quite sure. I fancy that it is due to you that I have the pleasure of knowing her, anyhow.

' Could you tell me who she was before she married? What her husband was, and anything else about her? That she is most charming and a very clever woman I know, of course, already. To say she is a friend of yours is enough to say that, but the rest I forget.

' Hoping you will forgive my troubling you, and that you are all very well, I remain, yours most sincerely.

'K A T H L E E N C O N R O Y

' *P.S.*—I began to take some lessons in nursing when I came across a most charming and delightful girl, called Dulcie Clay. Do you happen to know her at all? Her father married again and she was not happy at home, and, having no money, she went in for nursing, seriously (not as I did), but I'm afraid she is not strong enough for the profession. Remember me to Madame Frabelle.'

Edith passed the letter to Bruce.

' Isn't this too delightful?' she said; ' and exactly like her? She sends Madame Frabelle to me with a letter of introduction, and then asks me who she is!'

' Well,' said Bruce, who saw nothing of the absurdity of the situation, ' Lady Conroy is a most charming person. It looks almost as if she wanted to decline responsibility. I wouldn't annoy her for the world. You must give her all the information she wants, of course.'

'But all I know I only know from her.'

'Exactly. Well, tell her what she told you. Madame Frabelle told us candidly she made her acquaintance at the hotel! But it's absurd to tell Lady Conroy *that* back! We *can't*!'

Edith found the original letter of introduction, after some searching, and wrote to Lady Conroy to say that she understood Madame Frabelle, who was no connection of hers, was a clever, interesting woman, who wished to study English life in her native land. She was ' *of good family; she had been a Miss Eglantine Pollard, and was the widow of a well-to-do French wine merchant.*' (This was word for word what Lady Conroy had told her.) She went on to say that she ' *believed Madame Frabelle had several friends and connections in London.*'

'The Mitchells, for instance,' suggested Bruce.

'Yes, that's a good idea. " *She knows the Mitchells very well,*" ' Edith went on writing. ' " *I think you know them also; they are very great friends of ours. Mr Mitchell is in the Foreign Office.*" '

'And the Conistons?' suggested Bruce.

'Yes. " *She knows the Conistons; the nice young brother and sister we are so fond of. She has other friends in London, I believe, but she has not troubled to look them up. The more one sees of her the more one likes her. She is most charming and amiable and makes friends wherever she goes. I don't think I know anything more than this, dear Lady Conroy. Yours very sincerely, Edith Ottley. P.S.—I have not met Miss Dulcie Clay.*" '

Bruce was satisfied with this letter. Edith herself thought it the most amusing letter she had ever written.

'The clergyman whom she met at lunch yesterday, by the way,' said Bruce, 'wouldn't it sound well to mention him?'

Edith good-naturedly laughed, and added to the letter: ' " *The Rev. Byrne Fraser knows our friend also, and seems to like her.*" '

'The only thing is,' said Bruce, after a moment's pause, 'perhaps that might do her harm with Lady Conroy, although he's a clergyman. There have been some funny stories about the Rev. Byrne Fraser.'

'He certainly liked her,' said Edith. 'He wrote her a long letter last night, after meeting her at lunch, to go on with their argument, or conversation, or whatever it was, and she's going to hear him preach on Sunday.'

' Do you feel she would wish Lady Conroy to know that she's a friend of the Rev. Byrne Fraser?' asked Bruce.

' Oh, I think so; or I wouldn't have said it.'

Edith was really growing more and more loyal in her friendship. There certainly was something about Madame Frabelle that everybody, clever and stupid alike, seemed to be attracted by.

Later Edith received a telephone call from Landi. He told her that he had seen Aylmer, who was going on well, that he had begged to see her, and had been allowed by his doctor and nurse to receive a visit from her on Saturday next. He said that Aylmer had been agitated because his boy was going almost immediately to the front. He seemed very pleased at the idea of seeing her again.

Edith looked forward with a certain excitement to Saturday.

A day or two later Edith received a letter from Lady Conroy, saying:

'My Dear Edith,

Thank you so much for your nice letter. I remember now, of course, Madame Frabelle was a friend of the Mitchells, whom I know so well, and like so much. What dears they are! Please remember me to them. I knew that she had a friend who was a clergyman, but I wasn't quite sure who it was. I suppose it must have been this Mr Fraser. She was a Miss Pollard, you know, a very good family, and, as I always understood, the more one knows of her the better one likes her.

' Thanks again for your note. I am longing to see you, and shall call directly I come to London. Ever yours,

'Kathleen Conroy

' P.S.—Madame F's husband was a French wine merchant, and a very charming man, I believe. By the way, also, she knows the Conistons, I believe, and no doubt several people we both know. Miss Clay has gone to London with one of her patients.'

Bruce didn't understand why Edith was so much amused by this letter, nor why she said that she should soon write and ask Lady Conroy who Madame Frabelle was, and that she would probably answer that she was a great friend of Edith's and of the Mitchells, and the Rev. Byrne Fraser.

'She seems a little doubtful about Fraser, doesn't she?' Bruce said.

'I mean Lady Conroy. Certainly she's got rather a funny memory; she doesn't seem to have the slightest idea that she sent her to you with a letter of introduction. Now we've taken all the responsibility on ourselves.'

'Well, really I don't mind,' said Edith. 'What does it matter? There's obviously no harm in Madame Frabelle, and never could have been.'

'She's a very clever woman,' said Bruce. 'I'm always interested when I hear what she has to say about people. I don't mind telling you that I'm nearly always guided by it.'

'So am I,' said Edith.

Indeed Edith did sincerely regard her opinion as very valuable. She found her so invariably wrong that she was quite a useful guide. She was never quite sure of her own judgement until Madame Frabelle had contradicted it.

When Edith went to call on Aylmer in the little brown house in Jermyn Street, she was shown first into the dining-room.

In a few minutes a young girl dressed as a nurse came in to speak to her.

She seemed very shy and spoke in a soft voice.

'I'm Miss Clay,' she said. 'I've been nursing for the last six months, but I'm not very strong and was afraid I would have to give it up when I met Mr Ross at Boulogne. He was getting on so well that I came back to look after him and I shall stay until he is quite well, I think.'

Evidently this was the Dulcie Clay Lady Conroy had mentioned. Edith was much struck by her. She was a really beautiful girl, with but one slight defect, which some people perhaps, would have rather admired—her skin was rather too dark, and a curious contrast to her beautiful blue eyes. As a rule the combination of blue eyes and dark hair goes with a fair complexion. Dulcie Clay had a brown skin, clear and pale, such as usually goes with the Spanish type of brunette. But for this curious darkness, which showed up her ‑dazzling white teeth, she was quite lovely. It was a sweet, sensitive face, and her blue eyes, with long eyelashes like little feathers, were charming in their soft expression. Her smile was very sweet, though she had a look of melancholy. There was something touching about her.

She was below the usual height, slight and graceful. Her hair, parted in the middle, was arranged in the Madonna style in two thick natural waves each side of her face.

She had none of the bustling self-confidence of the lady nurse, but was very gentle and diffident. Surely Aylmer must be in love with her, thought Edith.

Then Miss Clay said, in her low voice:

' You are Mrs Ottley, aren't you? I knew you at once.'

' Did you? How was that?'

A little colour came into the pale, dark face.

' Mr Ross has a little photograph of you,' she said, ' and once when he was very ill he gave me your name and address and asked me to send it to you if anything happened.'

As she said that her eyes filled with tears.

' Oh, but he'll be all right now, won't he?' asked Edith, with a feeling of sympathy for Miss Clay, and a desire to cheer the girl.

' Yes, I think he'll be all right now,' she said. ' Do come up.'

CHAPTER X

I T was a curious thing about Madame Frabelle that, though she was perfectly at ease in any society, and really had seen a good deal of the world, all her notions of life were taken from the stage. She looked upon existence from the theatrical point of view. Everyone was to her a hero or a heroine, a villain or a victim. To her a death was a *dénouement*; a marriage a happy ending. Had she known the exact circumstances in which Edith went to see the wounded hero, Madame Frabelle's dramatic remarks, the obvious observations which she would have showered on her friend, would have been quite unendurable. Therefore Edith chose to say merely that she was going to see an old friend, so as not to excite her friend's irritable imagination by any hint of sentiment or romance on the subject.

During her absence in the afternoon, it happened that Mrs Mitchell had called, with a lady whom she had known intimately since Tuesday, so she was quite an old friend. Madame Frabelle had received them together in Edith's place. On her return Madame Frabelle was full of the stranger. She had, it seemed been dressed in bright violet, and did nothing but laugh. Whether it was that everything amused her, or merely that laughter was the only mode she knew of expressing all her sentiments, impressions and feelings, Madame Frabelle was not quite sure. Her name was Miss Radford, and she was thirty-eight. She had very red cheeks, and curly black hair. She had screamed with laughter from disappointment at hearing Mrs Ottley was out; and shrieked at hearing that Madame Frabelle had been deputed to receive them in her place. Mrs Mitchell had whispered that she was a most interesting person, and Madame Frabelle thought she certainly was. It appeared that Mrs Mitchell had sent the motor somewhere during their visit, and by some mistake it was a long time coming back. This had caused peals of laughter from Miss Radford, and just as they had made up their minds to walk home the motor arrived, so she went away with Mrs Mitchell, giggling so much she could hardly stand.

Miss Radford also had been highly amused by the charming way

the boudoir was furnished, and had laughed most heartily at the
curtains and the pictures. Edith was sorry to have missed her. She
was evidently a valuable discovery, one of their new treasures, a rare
trouvaille of the Mitchells.

Madame Frabelle then told Edith and Bruce that she had
promised to dine with the Mitchells one day next week. Edith was
pleased to find that Eglantine, and also Bruce, who had by now
returned home, were so full of Mrs Mitchell's visit and invitation,
that neither of them asked her a single question about Aylmer, and
appeared to have completely forgotten all about him.

As Madame Frabelle left them for a moment, Edith observed a cloud
of gloom over Bruce's expressive countenance. He said:

'Well, really! Upon my word! This is a bit *too* much! Mind you,
I'm not at all surprised. In fact, I always expected it. But it is a bit
of a shock, isn't it, when you find old friends throwing you over
like this?'

He walked up and down, much agitated, repeating the same thing
in different words: that he had never been so surprised in his life;
that it was what he had always known would happen; that it was a
great shock, and he had always expected it.

At last Edith said: 'I don't see anything so strange about it,
Bruce. It's natural enough they should have asked her.'

'Oh, is it? How would they ever have known her but for us?'

'How could they ask her without knowing her? Besides we went
there last. We lunched with them only the other day.'

'That's not the point. You have missed the point entirely. Unfortunately, you generally do. You have, in the most marked way,
a woman's weakness, Edith. You're incapable of arguing logically. I
consider it a downright slight; no, not so much a slight as an insult
—perhaps injury is the *mot juste*—to take away our guest and not
ask us. Not that I should have gone. I shouldn't have dreamed of
going, in any case. For one thing we were there last; we lunched
there only the other day. Besides, we're engaged to dine with my
mother.'

'Mrs Mitchell knew that; that's why she asked Madame Frabelle
because she would be alone.'

'Oh, how like you, Edith! Always miss the point—always stick
up for everyone but me! You invariably take the other side. How-

ever, perhaps it is all for the best; it's just as well. Nothing would have induced me to have gone—even if I hadn't been engaged, I mean. I'm getting a bit tired of the Mitchells; sick of them. Their tone is frivolous. And if they'd pressed me ever so much, nothing in the world would have made me break my promise to my mother.'

'Well, then, it's all right. Why complain?'

Bruce continued, however, in deep depression till they received a message from the Mitchells, asking Edith if she and her husband couldn't manage to come, all the same, if they were not afraid of offending the elder Mrs Ottley. They could go to Bruce's mother at any time, and the Mitchells particularly wanted them to meet some people tomorrow night—a small party, unexpectedly got up.

'Of course you won't go,' said Edith to Bruce from the telephone. 'You said you wouldn't under any circumstances. I'll refuse, shall I?'

'No—no, don't! Certainly not! Of course I shall go. Accept immediately. They're quite right, it *is* perfectly true we can go to my mother any other day. Besides, I don't think it's quite fair to old friends like the Mitchells to throw them over when they particularly want us and ask us as a special favour to them, like this.'

'You don't think, perhaps, that somebody else has disappointed them, and they asked us at the last minute, to fill up?' suggested Edith, to whom this was perfectly obvious.

Bruce was furious at this suggestion.

'Certainly not!' he exclaimed. 'The idea of such a thing. As if they would treat *me* like that! Decidedly we will go.'

'All right,' she said, 'just as you wish. But your mother will be disappointed.'

Bruce insisted. Of course the invitation was accepted, and once again he was happy!

And at last Edith was able to be alone, and to think over her meeting with Aylmer. A dramatic meeting under romantic circumstances between two people of the Anglo-Saxon race always appears to fall a little flat; words are difficult to find. When she went in, to find him looking thin and weak, pale under his sunburn, changed and worn, she was deeply thrilled and touched. It brought close to her the simple, heroic manner in which so many men are calmly risking their lives, taking it as a matter of course, and as she knew for a fact that he was forty-two and had gone into the New Army at the very beginning of the war, she was aware he must have strained a point in order to join. She admired him for it.

He greeted her with that bright expression in his eyes and with the smile that she had always liked so much, which lighted up like a ray of sunshine the lean, brown, somewhat hard, face.

She sat down by his side, and all she could think of to say was: 'Well, Aylmer?'

He answered: 'Well, Edith! Here you are.'

He took her hand, and she left it in his. Then they sat in silence, occasionally broken by an obvious remark.

When he had left three years ago both had parted in love, and Aylmer in anger. He had meant never to see her again, never to forgive her for her refusal to use Bruce's escapade as a means of freeing herself, to marry him. Yet now, when they met they spoke the merest commonplaces. And afterwards neither of them could ever remember what had passed between them during the visit. She knew it was short, and that it had left an impression that calmed her. Somehow she had thought of him so much that when she actually saw him again her affection seemed cooler. Had she worn out the passion by dint of constancy? That must be strange. Unaccountably, touched as she was at his wishing to see her just after he had nearly died, the feeling now seemed to be more like a warm friendship, and less like love.

The little nurse had seen her out. Edith saw that she had been crying. Evidently she was quite devoted to Aylmer, and, poor girl, she probably regarded Edith as a rival. But Edith would not be one, of that she was determined. She wondered whether their meeting had had the same effect on Aylmer. She thought he had shown more emotion than she had.

'He will be better now,' Dulcie Clay had said to her at the door. 'Please come again, Mrs Ottley.'

Edith thought that generous.

It seemed to her that Dulcie was as frank and open as a child. Edith, at any rate, could read her like a book. It made her feel sorry for the girl. As Edith analysed her own feelings she wondered why she had felt no jealousy of her—only gratitude for her goodness to Aylmer.

All her sensations were confused. Only one resolution was firm in her mind. Whether he wished it or not, they should never be on the terms they were before. It could only lead to the same ending—to unhappiness. No; after all these years of separation, Edith would be his friend, and only his friend. Of that she was resolved.

CHAPTER XI

'LADY CONROY,' said Bruce thoughtfully, at breakfast next day, 'is a very strict Roman Catholic.'

Bruce was addicted to volunteering information, and making unanswerable remarks.

Madame Frabelle said to Edith in a low, earnest tone:

'Pass me the butter, dear,' and looked attentively at Bruce.

'I sometimes think I shouldn't mind being one myself,' Bruce continued; 'I should rather like to eat fish on Fridays.'

'But you like eating fish on Thursdays,' said Edith.

'And Mr Ottley never seems to care very much for meat.'

'Unless it's particularly well cooked—in a particular way,' said Edith.

'Fasts,' said Madame Frabelle rather pompously, 'are meant for people who like feasts.'

'How true!' He gave her an admiring glance.

'I should not mind confessing, either,' continued Bruce, 'I think I should rather like it.'

(He thought he was having a religious discussion.)

'But you always do confess,' said Edith, 'not to priests, perhaps, but to friends; to acquaintances, at clubs, to girls you take in to dinner. You don't call it confessing, you call it telling them a curious thing that you happen to remember.'

'He calls it conversing,' said Madame Frabelle. She then gave a slight flippant giggle, afterwards correcting it by a thoughtful sigh.

'The Rev. Byrne Fraser, of course, is very High Church,' Bruce said. 'I understood he was Anglican. By the way, was Aylmer Ross a Roman Catholic?'

'I think he is.'

Bruce having mentioned his name, Edith now told him the news about her visit to their friend. Bruce liked good news—more, perhaps, because it was news than because it was good—yet the incident seemed to put him in a rather bad temper. He was sorry for Aylmer's illness, glad he was better, proud of knowing him, or, indeed, of knowing anyone who had been publicly mentioned; and jealous of the admiration visible in both Edith and Madame Frabelle. This medley of feeling resulted in his taking up a book and saying:

' Good heavens! Again I've found you've dog's-eared my book, Edith!'

' I only turned down a page,' she said gently.

' No, you haven't; you've dog's-eared it. It's frightfully irritating, dear, how you take no notice of my rebukes or my comments. Upon my word, what I say to you seems to go in at one ear and out at the other, just like water on a duck's back.'

' How does the water on a duck's back get into the dog's ears?— I mean the duck's ears. Oh, I'm sorry. I won't do it again.'

Bruce sighed, flattened out the folded page and left the room with quiet dignity, but caught his foot in the mat. Both ladies ignored the accident.

When he had gone, Madame Frabelle said:

' Poor Edith!'

' Bruce is only a little tidy,' said Edith.

' I know. My husband was dreadfully untidy, which is much worse.'

' I suppose they have their faults.'

' Oh, men are all alike!' exclaimed Madame Frabelle cynically.

' Only some men,' said Edith. ' Besides, to a woman—I mean, a nice woman—there is no such thing as men. There is a man; and either she is so fond of him that she can talk of nothing else, however unfavourably, or so much in love with him that she never mentions his name.'

' Men often say women are all alike,' said Madame Frabelle.

' When a man says that, he means there is only one woman in the world, and he's in love with her, and she is not in love with him.'

' Men are not so faithful as women,' remarked Madame Frabelle, with the air of a discovery.

' Perhaps not. And yet—well, I think the difference is that a man is often more in love with the woman he is unfaithful to than with the woman he is unfaithful with. With us it is different. . . . Madame Frabelle, I think I'll take Archie with me today to see Aylmer Ross. Tell Bruce so, casually; and will you come with me another day?'

' With the greatest pleasure,' said Madame Frabelle darkly, and with an expressive look. (Neither she nor Edith had any idea what it expressed.)

Edith found Aylmer wonderfully better. The pretty little nurse with the dark face and pale blue eyes told her he had had a peaceful night and had bucked up tremendously. He was seated in an arm-chair with one leg on another chair, and with him was Arthur Coniston, a great admirer of his.

It was characteristic of Aylmer, the moment he was able, to see as many friends as he was allowed. Aylmer was a very gregarious person, though—or perhaps because—he detested parties. He liked company, but hated society. Arthur Coniston, who always did his best to attract attention by his modest, self-effacing manner, was sitting with his handsome young head quite on one side from intense respect for his host, whom he regarded with the greatest admiration as a man of culture. and a judge of art. He rejoiced to be one of the first to see him, just returned after three years' absence from England, and having spent the last three months at the front.

Arthur Coniston (also in khaki), who was a born interviewer, was anxious to know Aylmer's impression of certain things over here, after his long absence.

' I should so very much like to know,' he said, ' what your view is of the attitude to life of the Post-Impressionists.'

Aylmer smiled. He said : ' I think their attitude to life, as you call it, is best expressed in some of Lear's Nonsense Rhymes : " *His Aunt Jobiska said, ' Everyone knows that a pobble is better without his toes.' " '*

Archie looked up in smiling recognition of these lines, and Edith laughed.

' Excuse me, but I don't quite follow you,' said young Coniston gravely.

' Why, don't you see? Of course, Lear is the spirit they express. A portrait by a post-Impressionist is sure to be " *A Dong with a luminous nose.*" And don't you remember, " *The owl and the pussy-cat went to sea in a beautiful pea-green boat* "? Wouldn't a boat painted by a Post-Impressionist be pea-green?'

' Perfectly. I see that. But—why the pobble without its toes?'

' Why, the sculptor always surrenders colour, and the painted form. Each has to give up something for the limitation of art. But the more modern artist gives up much more—likeness, beauty, a few features here and there—a limb now and then.'

' Ah yes. I quite see what you mean. Like the statuary of Rodin or Epstein. One sees really only half the form, as if growing out of the sketchy sculpture. And then there's another thing—I hope I'm not wearying you?'

' No, indeed. It's great fun: such a change to hear about this sort of thing again.'

' The Futurists?' asked Arthur. ' What is your view of them?'

' Well, of course, they are already past. They always were. But I should say their attitude to life is that of the man who is looking at the moon reflected in a lake, but can't see it; he sees the reflection of a coal-scuttle instead.'

' Ah yes. They see things wrong, you mean. They're not so real. not so logical, as the Post-Impressionists.'

' Yes, the Futurist is off the rails entirely, and he seems to see hardly anything but railways. But all that noisy nonsense of the Futurists always bored me frightfully,' Aylmer said. ' Affectation for affectation, I prefer the pose of depression and pessimism to that of bullying and high spirits. When the affected young poet pretended to be used up and worn out, one knew there was vitality under it all. But when I see a cheerful young man shrieking about how full of life he is, banging on a drum, and blowing on a tin trumpet, and speaking of his good spirits, it depresses me, since naturally it gives the contrary impression. It can't be real. It ought to be but it isn't. If the noisy person meant what he said, he wouldn't say it.'

' I see. The modern *poseurs* aren't so good as the old ones. Odle is not so clever as Beardsley.'

' Of course not. Beardsley had the gift of line—though he didn't always know where to draw it—but his illustrations to Wilde's work were unsuitable, because Beardsley wanted everything down in black and white, and Wilde wanted everything in purple and gold. But both had their restraints, and their pose was reserve, not flamboyance.'

' I think you mean that if people are so sickening as to have an affectation at all, you would rather they kept it quiet,' said Edith.

' Exactly! At least, it brings a smile to one's lips to see a very young man pretend he is bored with life. I have often wondered what the answer would be from one of these chaps, and what he

would actually say, if you held a loaded pistol to his head—I mean
the man who says he doesn't think life worth living.'

'What do you think he would say?' asked Coniston.

'He would scream: "Good heavens! What are you doing? Put
that down!"' said Edith.

'She's right,' said Aylmer. 'She always is.'

Dulcie came in and brought tea.

'I hope we're not tiring him,' Edith asked her.

'Oh no. I think it does him good. He enjoys it.'

She sat down with Archie and talked to him gently in the corner.

'After living so much among real things,' Coniston was saying,
'one feels half ashamed to discuss our old subjects.'

However, he and Aylmer continued to talk over books and
pictures, Coniston hanging on his lips as though afraid of missing
or forgetting a word he said.

Presently Edith told Aylmer about their new friend, Madame
Frabelle. He was very curious to see her.

'What is she like?' he asked. 'I can't imagine her living with you.
Is she a skeleton at the feast?'

'A skeleton!' exclaimed Coniston. 'Good heavens—no! Quite
the contrary.'

'A skeleton who was always feasting would hardly remain one
long,' suggested Edith.

'Anyhow,' said Aylmer, 'the cupboard is the proper place for a
skeleton.'

Archie had joined the group round Aylmer. Edith sat in a corner
for some time, chatting with Dulcie. They arranged that Bruce was
to call the next day, and Edith and Madame Frabelle the day after.

When they went away Archie, who had listened very closely to
the conversation, said:

'What a lot of manners Mr Coniston has! What did he mean by
saying that Spanish painters painted a man in a gramophone?'

Edith racked her brain to remember the sentence. Then she said,
with a laugh:

'Oh yes, I know! Mr Coniston said: "The Spanish artists painted
—to a man—in monochrome." I can't explain it, Archie. It doesn't
matter. Why did you leave Miss Clay and come back to us?'

'Why, I like her all right, but you get tired of talking to women.
I get bored with Dilly sometimes.'

' Then you're looking forward to going back to school?'

' I shall like the society of boys of my own sex again,' he said grandly.

' You're not always very nice to Dilly, Archie. I've noticed when anything is given to her, you always snatch at it. You must remember Ladies first.'

' Yes, that's all very well. But then Dilly takes it all, and only gives me what's left.'

Archie looked solemn.

CHAPTER XII

'EDITH,' said Bruce, next morning, with some importance of manner, 'I've had a letter from Aylmer—Aylmer Ross, you know—asking me, *most* particularly, to call on him.'

'Oh, really,' said Edith, who knew it already, as she had asked him to write to Bruce.

'He wants me to come at half-past four,' said Bruce, looking over the letter pompously. 'Four-thirty, to the minute. I shall certainly do it. I sha'n't lose a minute.'

'I'm afraid you'll have to lose a few minutes,' said Edith. 'It's only ten o'clock.'

Bruce stared at her, folded up the letter, and put it in his pocket. He thought it would be a suitable punishment for her not to see it.

Obviously he was not in the best of humours. Not being sure what was wrong, Edith adopted the simple plan of asking what he meant.

'What do I mean!' exclaimed Bruce, who, when his grievances, were vague, relied on such echoes for his most cutting effects. 'You ask me what I mean? Mean, indeed!' He took some toast and repeated bitterly: 'Ah! You may well ask me what I mean!'

'May I? Well, what were the observations you didn't approve of?'

'Why . . . what you said. About several minutes being lost before half-past four.'

'Oh, Bruce dear, I didn't mean any harm by it.'

'Harm, indeed!' repeated Bruce. 'Harm! It isn't a question of actual harm. I don't say that you meant to injure me, nor even, perhaps, to hurt my feelings. But it's a way of speaking—a tone—that I think extremely *déplacé*, from you to me. Do you follow me, Edith? From *you* to *me*.'

'That's a dark saying. Well, whatever I said I take it back, if you don't like it. Will that do?'

Bruce was mollified, but wouldn't show it at once.

'Ah,' he said, 'that's all very well. These sort of things are not

so easily taken back. You should think before you speak. Prevention
is better than cure.'

'Yes, and a stitch in time saves nine—though it doesn't rhyme.
And it's no good crying over spilt milk, and two heads are better
than one. But, really, Bruce, I didn't mean it.'

'What didn't you mean?'

'Good heavens, I really don't know by now! I'm afraid I've
utterly forgotten what we were talking about,' said Edith, looking
at the door with some anxiety.

She was hoping that Madame Frabelle would soon come down
and cause a diversion.

'Look here, Edith,' said Bruce, 'when an old friend, an old
friend of yours and mine, and at one time a very intimate friend—
next door to a brother—when such a friend as that has been
wounded at the front, fighting for our country—and, mind you, he
behaved with remarkable gallantry, for it wasn't really necessary for
him to go, as he was beyond the age—well, when a friend does a
thing like that, and comes back wounded, and writes, with his own
hand, asking me to go and see him—well, I think it's the least I can
do! I don't know what *you* think. It seems to *me* the right thing. If
you disagree with me I'm very sorry. But, frankly, it appears to me
that I ought to go.'

'Who could doubt it?'

'Read the letter for yourself,' said Bruce, suddenly taking it out
of his pocket and giving it to her. 'There, you see. " Dear Ottley,"
he says.'

Here Bruce went to her side of the table and leant over her, reading the letter aloud to her over her shoulder, while she was reading
it to herself.

'"DEAR OTTLEY,—If you could look in tomorrow about
half-past four, I should be very glad to see you. Yours sincerely,
AYLMER ROSS." Fairly cordial, I think, isn't it? Or not? Perhaps you think it cold. Would you call it a formal letter?'

Bruce took the letter out of her hand and read it over again to
himself.

'Very nice, dear,' said Edith.

'So I thought.' He put it away with a triumphant air.

Edith was thinking that the writing was growing stronger. Aylmer
must be better.

'I say, I hope it isn't a sign he's not so well, that he wants to see me. I don't call it a good sign. He's depressed. He thinks I'll cheer him up.'

'And I'm sure you will. Ah, here's Madame Frabelle.'

'I'm afraid I'm a little late,' said their guest, with her amiable smile.

'Oh dear, no—not at all, not at all,' said Bruce, who was really much annoyed at her unpunctuality. 'Of course, if you'd been a minute later I shouldn't have had the pleasure of seeing you at all before I went to the office—that's all. And what does that matter? Good heavens, *that's* of no importance! Good gracious, this is Liberty Hall, I hope—isn't it? I should be very sorry for my guests to feel tied in any way—bound to be down at any particular time. Will you have some coffee? Edith, give Madame Frabelle a cup of coffee. Late? Oh dear, no; certainly not!' He gave a short, ironical laugh.

'Well, I think I'm generally fairly punctual,' said Madame Frabelle, beginning her breakfast without appearing to feel this sarcasm. 'What made me late this morning was that Archie and Dilly came into my room and asked me to settle a kind of dispute they were having.'

'They regard you quite as a magistrate,' said Edith. 'But it was too bad of them to come and bother you so early.'

'Oh no. Not at all. I assure you I enjoy it. And, besides, a boy with Archie's musical talents is bound to have the artistic temperament, you know, and—well—of course, we all know what that leads to—excitement; and finally a quarrel sometimes.'

'If he were really musical I should have thought he ought to be more harmonious,' Edith said.

'Oh, by the way, Edith, did you consult Landi about him?' Bruce inquired. 'You said you intended to.'

'Oh yes, I did. Landi can see no sign of musical genius yet.'

'Dear, dear!' said Bruce.

'Ah, but I am convinced he's wrong. Wait a few years and you'll find he'll agree with me yet,' said Madame Frabelle. 'I'm not at all sure, either, that a composer like Landi is necessarily the right person to judge of youthful genius.'

'Perhaps not. And yet you'd think he'd know a bit about it, too! I mean to say, they wouldn't have made him a baronet if he didn't understand his profession. Excuse my saying so, won't you?'

' Not at all,' she answered. ' It doesn't follow. I mean it doesn't follow that he's right about Archie. Did he try the boy's voice?' she asked Edith.

' Very much.'

' How?'

' Well, he asked Archie to sing a few notes.'

' And did he?'

' Yes, he did. But they weren't the notes Landi asked him to sing.'

' Oh!'

' Then Landi played him two tunes, and found he didn't know one from the other.'

' Well, what of that?'

' Nothing at all. Except that it showed he had no ear, as well as no voice. That is all.'

Madame Frabelle would never own she was beaten.

' Ah, well, well,' she said, shaking her head in an oracular way. ' You wait!'

' Certainly. I shall.'

' By the way, I may be a little late for dinner tonight. I'm going to see an old friend who's been wounded in the war,' Bruce told Madame Frabelle proudly.

It had always been something of an ordeal to Edith when she knew that Aylmer and Bruce were alone together. It was a curious feeling, combined of loyalty to Bruce (she hated him to make himself ridiculous), loyalty to Aylmer, and an indescribable sense of being lowered in her own eyes. When they seemed friendly together it pained her self-respect. Most women will understand the sensation. However, she knew it had to be, and would be glad when it was over.

CHAPTER XIII

THE next evening Bruce came in, holding himself very straight, with a slightly military manner. When he saw his wife he just stopped himself from saluting.

'That's a man!' he exclaimed. 'That's a splendid fellow.'

Edith didn't answer.

'You don't appreciate him. In my opinion Aylmer Ross is a hero.'

'I hope he's better?'

'Better! *He* would say so, anyhow. Ah, he's a wonderful chap!' Bruce hummed Tipperary below his breath.

Edith was surprised to find herself suffering no less mental discomfort and irritation while Bruce talked about Aylmer and praised him than she used to feel years ago. It seemed as if three years had passed and altered nothing. She answered coldly. Bruce became more enthusiastic. He declared that she didn't know how to value such a fine character. 'Women,' he repeated, 'don't know a hero when they see one.'

Evidently if Bruce had had his way Aylmer would have been covered with D S O's and V C's; nothing was good enough for him.

On the other hand, if Edith had praised Aylmer, Bruce would have been the first to *débiner* his actions, undervalue his gifts, and crab him generally.

Edith was not one of those women, far more common than is supposed, who consider themselves aggrieved and injured when a discarded lover consoles himself with someone else. Nor was she one of the numerous people who will not throw away what they no longer want for fear someone else will pick it up. She had such a strong sympathy for Dulcie Clay that she had said to herself several times she would like to see her perfectly happy. Edith was convinced that the nurse adored her patient, but she was not at all sure that he returned the admiration. Edith herself had only seen him alone once, and on that occasion they had said hardly anything to each other. He had been constrained and she had been embarrassed. The

410

day that Arthur Coniston was there and they talked of pictures, Aylmer had given her, by a look, to understand that he would like to see her again alone, and she knew perfectly well, even without that, that he was longing for another *tête-à-tête*.

However, the next day Edith went with Madame Frabelle.

This was a strangely unsatisfactory visit. Edith knew his looks and every tone of his voice so well that she could see that Aylmer, unlike everybody else, was not in the least charmed with Madame Frabelle. She bored him; he saw nothing in her.

Madame Frabelle was still more disappointed. She had been told he was brilliant; he said nothing put commonplaces. He was supposed to be witty; he answered everything she said literally. He was said to be a man of encyclopædic information; but when Madame Frabelle questioned him on such subjects his answers were dry and short; and when she tried to draw him out about the war, he changed the subject in a manner that was not very far from being positively rude.

Leaving them for a moment, Edith went to talk to Dulcie.

'How do you think he's getting on?' she said.

'He's getting well; gradually. He seems a little nervous the last day or so.'

'Do you think he's been seeing too many people?'

'He hasn't seen more than the doctor has allowed. But, do you know, Mrs Ottley, I think it depends a great deal who the people are.'

She waited a moment and then went on in a low voice:

'You do him more good than anyone. You see, he's known you so long,' she added gently, 'and so intimately. It's no strain—I mean he hasn't got to make conversation.'

'Yes, I see,' said Edith.

'Mr Ross hasn't any near relations—no mother or sister. You seem to take their place—if you understand what I mean.'

Edith thought it charmingly tactful of her to put it like that.

'I'm sure *you* take their place,' Edith said.

Dulcie looked down.

'Oh, of course, he hasn't to make any effort with me. But then *I* don't amuse him, and he wants amusement, and change. It's a great bore for a man like that—so active mentally, and in every way—to have to lie perfectly still, especially when he has no companion but me. I'm rather dull in some ways. Besides, I don't know anything about the subjects he's interested in.'

'Don't talk nonsense,' said Edith, smiling. 'I should imagine that just to look at you would be sufficient.'

'Oh, Mrs Ottley! How can you?'

She turned away as if rather pained than pleased at the compliment.

'I haven't very high spirits,' she said. 'I'm not sure that I don't sometimes depress him.'

'On the contrary; I'm sure he wouldn't like a breezy, restless person bouncing about the room and roaring with laughter,' Edith said.

She smiled. 'Perhaps not. But there might be something between. He will be able to go for a drive in a week or two. I wondered whether, perhaps, you could take him out?'

'Oh yes; I dare say that could be arranged.'

'I have to go out all tomorrow afternoon. I wondered whether you would come and sit with him, Mrs Ottley?'

'Certainly I will, if you like.'

'Oh, *please* do! I know he's worrying much more about his son than anybody thinks. You see, the boy's really very young, and I'm not sure he's strong.'

'I suppose neither of them told the truth about their age,' said Edith. 'It reminds one of the joke in *Punch*: " Where do you expect to go if you tell lies? To the front." '

Miss Clay gave a little laugh. Then she started. A bell was heard ringing rather loudly.

'I'll tell him you're coming tomorrow, then,' she said.

They returned to Aylmer's room.

He was looking a little sulky. He said as Edith came in:

'I thought you'd gone without saying good-bye. What on earth were you doing?'

'Only talking to Miss Clay,' said Edith, sitting down by him. 'How sweet she is.'

'Charming,' said Madame Frabelle. 'Wonderfully pretty, too.'

'She's a good nurse,' said Aylmer briefly. 'She's been awfully good to me. But I do hope I sha'n't need her much longer.' He spoke with unnecessary fervour.

'Oh, Mr Ross!' exclaimed Madame Frabelle. 'I'm sure if I were a young man I should be very sorry when she had to leave me!'

' Possibly. However, you're not a young man. Neither am I.'

There was a moment's silence. This was really an exceptional thing when Madame Frabelle was present. Edith could not recall one occasion when Eglantine had had nothing to say. Aylmer must have been excessively snubbing. Extraordinary! Wonder of wonders! He had actually silenced Madame Frabelle!

All Aylmer's natural politeness and amiability returned when they rose to take their leave. He suddenly became cordial, cheery and charming. Evidently he was so delighted the visitor was going that it quite raised his spirits. When they left he gave Edith a little reproachful look. He did not ask her to come again. He was afraid she would bring Madame Frabelle.

' Well, Edith, I thoroughly understand your husband's hero-worship for that man,' said Madame Frabelle (meaning she thoroughly misunderstood it). ' I've been studying his character all this afternoon.'

' Do tell me what you think of him!'

' Edith, I'm sorry to say it, but it's a hard, cold, cruel nature.'

' Is it really?'

' Mr Aylmer Ross doesn't know what it is to feel emotion, sentiment, or tenderness. Principle he has, perhaps, and no doubt he thinks he has great self-control, but that's only because he's absolutely incapable of passion of any kind.'

Edith smiled.

' I see you're amused at my being right again. It *is* an odd thing about me, I must own. I never make a mistake,' said Madame Frabelle complacently.

As they walked home, she continued to discourse eloquently on the subject of Aylmer. She explained him almost entirely away.

There was nothing Madame Frabelle fancied herself more on than physiognomy. She pointed out to Edith how the brow showed a narrow mind, the mouth bitterness. (How extraordinarily bored Aylmer must have been to give that impression of all others, thought her listener.) And the eyes, particularly, gave away his chief characteristic, the thing that one missed most in his personality.

' And what is that?'

' Can't you see?'

' No, I don't think I can.'

'He has no sense of humour!' said Madame Frabelle triumphantly.

After a few moment's pause, Edith said:

'What do you think of Miss Clay?'

'She's very pretty—extremely pretty. But I don't quite like to say
what I think of her. I'd rather not. Don't ask me. It doesn't concern me.'

'As bad as that? Oh, do tell me. You're so interesting about
character, Eglantine.'

'Dear Edith, how kind of you. Well, she's very, very clever, of
course. Most intellectual. A remarkable brain, I should say. But
she's deep and scheming; it's a sly, treacherous face.'

'Really, I can't see that.'

Madame Frabelle put her hand on Edith's shoulder. They had
just reached the house.

'Ah, you don't know so much of life as I do, my dear.'

'I should have said she is certainly not at all above the average
in cleverness, and I think her particularly simple and frank.'

'Ah, but that's all put on. You'll see I'm right some day. However, it doesn't matter. No doubt she's a very good nurse.'

'Don't abuse her to Bruce,' said Edith, as they went in.

'Certainly not. But why do you mind?'

'I don't know; I suppose I like her.'

Madame Frabelle laughed. 'How strange you are!'

She lowered her voice as they walked upstairs, and said:

'To tell the real truth, she gave me a shiver down the spine.
I believe that girl capable of anything. That dark skin with those
pale blue eyes! I strongly suspect she has a touch of the tar-
brush.'

'My dear! Nonsense. You can't have looked at her fine little
features and her white hands.'

'Why is she so dark?'

'There may have been Italian or Spanish blood in her family,'
said Edith, laughing. 'It's not a symptom of crime.'

'There may, indeed,' replied Madame Frabelle in a tone of deep
meaning, as they reached the door of her room. 'But, mark my
words, Edith, that's a dangerous woman!'

An event had occurred in the Ottley household during their

absence. Archie had brought home a dog and implored his mother to let him keep it.

'What sort of dog is it?' asked Edith.

'Come and look at it. It isn't any particular *sort*. It's just a dog.'

'But, my dear boy, you're going to school the day after tomorrow, and you can't take it with you.'

'I know; but I'll teach Dilly to look after it.'

It was a queer, rough, untidy-looking creature; it seemed harmless enough; a sort of Dobbin in *Vanity Fair* in the canine world.

'It's an inconsistent dog. Its face is like a terrier's, and its tail like a sort of spaniel,' said Archie. 'But I think it might be trained to a bloodhound.'

'You do, do you? What use would a bloodhound be to Dilly?'

'Well, you never know. It might be very useful.'

'I'm afraid there's not room in the house for it.'

'Oh, Mother!' both the children cried together. 'We *must* keep it!'

'Was it lost?' she asked.

Archie frowned at Dilly, who was beginning to say, 'Not exactly.'

'Tell me how you got it.'

'It was just walking along, and I took its chain. The chain was dragging on the ground.'

'You stole it,' said Dilly.

Archie flew at her, but Edith kept him back.

'Stole it! I didn't! Its master had walked on and evidently didn't care a bit about it, poor thing. That's not stealing.'

'If Master Archie wants to keep a lot of dogs, he had better take them with him to school,' said the nurse. 'I don't want nothing to do with no dogs, not in this nursery.'

'There's only one thing to be done, Archie; you must take care of it for the next day or two, and I shall advertise in the paper for its master.'

'Oh, mother!'

'Don't you see it isn't even honest to keep it?'

Archie was bitterly disappointed, but consoled at the idea of seeing the advertisement in the paper.

'How can we advertise it? We don't know what name it answers to.'

'It would certainly be difficult to describe,' said Edith.

They had tried every name they had ever heard of, and Dilly declared it had answered to them all, if answering meant jumping rather wildly round them and barking as if in the very highest spirits, it certainly had.

'It'll be fun to see my name in the paper,' said Archie thoughtfully.

'Indeed you won't see your name in the paper.'

'Well, I found it,' said Archie rather sulkily.

'Yes; but you had no right to find it, and still less to bring it home. I don't know what your father will say.'

Bruce at once said that it must be taken to Scotland Yard. Dilly cried bitterly, and said she wanted it to eat out of her hand, and save her life in a snowstorm.

'It's not a St Bernard, you utter little fool,' said her brother.

'Well, it might save me from drowning,' said Dilly.

She had once seen a picture, which she longed to realise, of a dog swimming, holding a child in its mouth. She thought it ought to be called Faithful or Rover.

All these romantic visions had to be given up. Madame Frabelle said the only thing to do was to take it at once to the Battersea Dogs' Home, where it would be 'happy with companions of its own age'. Immediately after dinner her suggestion was carried out, to the great relief of most of the household. The nurse said when it had gone that she had 'known all along it was mad, but didn't like to say so.'

'But it took such a fancy to me,' said Archie.

'Perhaps that was why,' said Dilly.

The children were separated by force.

CHAPTER XIV

F o r a woman who was warm-hearted, sensitive and thoughtful, Edith had a singularly happy disposition. First, she was good-tempered; not touchy, not easily offended about trifles. Such vanity as she had was not in an uneasy condition; she cared very little for general admiration, and had no feeling for competition. She was without ambition to be superior to others. Then, though she saw more deeply into things than the generality of women, she was not fond of dwelling on the sad side of life. Very small things pleased her, while trifles did not annoy her. Hers was not the placidity of the stupid, fat, contented person who never troubles about other people. She was rather of a philosophical turn, and her philosophy tended to seeing the brighter side. Where she was singularly fortunate was that though she felt pleasure deeply—a temperament that feels pain in proportion—her suffering, though acute, seldom lasted long. There was an elasticity in her disposition that made her rebound quickly from a blow.

Her affections were intense, but she did not suffer the usual penalty of love—a continual dread of losing the loved object. If she adored her children and was thankful for their health and beauty, she was not exactly what is called an anxious mother. She thought much about them, and was very determined to have her own way in anything concerning them. That, indeed, was a subject on which she would give way to no-one. But as she had so far succeeded in directing them according to her own ideas, she was satisfied. And she was very hopeful. She could look forward to happiness, but troubles she dealt with as they arose.

Certainly, after the first few months of their marriage, Bruce had turned out a disappointment. But now that she knew him, knew the worst of him, she did not think it bad. He had an irritating person-ality. But most people had to live with someone who was a little irritating; and she was so accustomed to his various ways and weak-nesses that she could deal with them unmoved, almost mechanically. She did not take him seriously. She would greatly have preferred, of course, that he should understand her, that she could look up to him and lean on him. But as this was not so, she made the best of it, and managed to be contented enough. Three years ago she had not even known she could be deeply in love.

She had loved Aylmer Ross. But even at that time, when Bruce gave her the opportunity, by his wild escapade with Miss Argles, to free herself and marry Aylmer—her ideal of divine happiness at the time—somehow she could not do it. She had a curious sense of responsibility towards Bruce, which came in the way.

Often since then she had had regrets; she had even felt it had been a mistake to throw away such a chance. But she reflected that she would have regrets anyhow. It would have worried her to know that Bruce needed her. For all that, she knew he did, if unconsciously. So she had made up her mind to content herself with a life which, though peaceful, was certainly, to her temperament, decidedly incomplete.

Edith had other sources of happiness more acute than that of the average. She took an intense and keen enjoyment in life itself. Everything interested her, amused her. She was never bored. She so much enjoyed the mere spectacle of life that she never required to be the central figure. When she had to play the part of a mere spectator it didn't depress her; she could delight in society and in character as if at a theatre. On the other hand, as she had a good deal of initiative and a strong personality, she could also revel in action, in playing a principal part. Under a quiet manner her courage was daring and her spirit high. Unless someone or something was actively tormenting her, to an extent quite insupportable, she was contented, even gay.

Her past romance with Aylmer had naturally opened to her a source of delight that she knew nothing of before.

Since she had seen him again she scarcely knew how she felt about it. This day she was to see him again alone, because he wished it, and because Dulcie Clay had begged her to gratify the wish.

Why was it, she asked herself, that the little nurse desired they should be alone together? It was perfectly clear, to a woman with Edith's penetration, that Dulcie was in love with Aylmer. Also, she was equally sure that the girl believed Aylmer to be devoted to her, Edith. Then it must be the purest unselfishness. Dulcie probably, she thought, loved him with a kind of hopeless worship. She had seen him ill and weak, she pitied him, she wanted him to be happy. In return for this generosity Edith felt a generous kindness for her, a sympathy that she would never have believed she could feel at seeing such a beautiful girl on those rather intimate terms with Aylmer.

It must mean, simply, that Edith knew Aylmer cared for her still. A look was enough to convince her that at least he still took a great and deep interest in her. And she wanted to come to an understanding with him, or she could have avoided a *tête-à-tête*.

During the three years he had been away the feeling had calmed down, but the ideal was still there, and the memory. Whenever Bruce was maddening—which was fairly often—when she heard music, when she saw beautiful scenery, when she was reading a romantic book, when any other man admired her, Aylmer was always in her thoughts.

When Edith saw him again she was not sure that she had not worn out her passion by dwelling on it. But that might easily be caused by the mere *gêne* of the first two or three meetings. There is a shyness, a sort of coldness, in meeting again a person one has passionately loved. To see the dream in flesh and blood, the thought made concrete, once more brings poetry down to prose. Then the terms they met on now were changed. He was playing such a different part. Instead of the strong, determined man who had voluntarily left her, refusing to know her as a friend, and reproaching her bitterly for playing with him, as he called it, here was a broken invalid, a pathetic figure who appealed to entirely different sentiments. There is naturally something maternal in a woman's feeling to a sick man. There was also the halo that surrounds the wounded hero. He was not ill through weakness, but through strength and courage.

She found herself thinking of him day and night, but it was in a different way. It might be because he had not yet referred to their past love affair.

Edith dressed with unusual care to go and see him today. Even if a woman wishes to discourage or to break off all relations with a man, she doesn't, after all, wish to leave a disagreeable impression.

Her prettiness and charm—of which she was modestly but confidently aware, by her experience of its effect—was a great satisfaction. It was remarkably noticeable today. In front of the glass Edith hesitated between her favourite plain sailor hat and a new black velvet toque, which shaded her eyes, contrasting with the fair hair of which very little showed, and giving her an aspect of dashing yet discreet coquetry. She looked younger in the other sailor hat (so she decided when she put it on again) and more as she used to look. Which was the more attractive? She decided on novelty, and went out, finally, in the toque.

Of course only another woman could have appreciated the remarkable fact that she could wear at thirty-five such a small hat and yet look fresh. Certainly a brim was more flattering to most women of her age, but the contour of Edith's face was still as youthful as ever; she had one of those clearly shaped oval faces that are not disposed to growing thick and broad, or to haggardness. The oval might be a shade wider than it was three years ago; that was all the more becoming; did it not make the features look smaller?

As she went out she laughed at herself for giving so much thought to her appearance. It was as though she believed she was going to play an important part in the chief scene of a play.

Once dressed, as usual she lost all self-consciousness, and thought of outside things.

Miss Clay was out, as she had told Edith she would be, and the servant showed her in.

She saw at once that Aylmer, also, had been looking forward to this moment with some excitement. He, too, had dressed with special care; and she knew, without being told, that orders had been given to receive no other visitors.

He was sitting in an arm-chair, with the bandaged leg on the other chair, a small table by his side laid for tea. Even a kettle was boiling (no doubt to avoid interruption). It was his old brown library, where she had occasionally seen him with others in the old days. But this was literally the first time she had seen him in his own house alone.

It was essentially a man's room. Comfortable, but not exactly luxurious; very little was sacrificed to decoration.

There were a few very old dark pictures on the walls. The room was crammed with books in long, low bookcases. On the mantelpiece was a pewter vase of cerise-coloured carnations.

An uncut *English Review* was in his hand, but he threw it on the floor with a characteristic gesture as she came in.

'You look very comfortable,' said Edith, as she took her seat in the arm-chair placed for her.

He answered gravely, speaking in his direct, quick way, with his sincere manner:

'It was very good of you to come.'

'Shall I pour out your tea?'

'Yes. Let's have tea and get it over.'

She laughed, took off her gloves, and he watched her fingers as they occupied themselves with the china, as though he were impatient for the ceremony to be finished.

While she poured it out and handed it to him he said not a word. She saw that he looked pale and seemed rather nervous. Each tried to put the other at ease, more by looks than words. Edith saw it would worry him to make conversation. They knew each other well enough to exchange ideas without words.

He had something to say and she would not postpone it. That would irritate him.

'There,' said Aylmer, giving a little push to the table. 'Do you want any more tea?'

'No, thanks.'

'Well—do you mind coming a little nearer?'

She lifted the little table, put it farther behind his chair, placed the arm-chair closer to him by the fire, and sat down again. He looked at her for some time with a serious expression. Then he said, rather abruptly and unexpectedly:

'What a jolly hat!'

'Oh, I *am* glad you like it!' exclaimed Edith. 'I was afraid you'd hate it.'

For the first time they were talking in their old tone, she reflected.

'No, I like it—I love it.' He lowered his voice to say this.

'I'm glad,' she repeated.

'And I love *you*,' said Aylmer as abruptly, and in a still lower voice.

She didn't answer.

'Look here, Edith. I want to ask you something.'

'Yes.'

He seemed to have some difficulty in speaking. He was agitated.

'Have you forgotten me?'

'You can see I haven't, or I wouldn't be here,' she answered.

'Don't fence with me. I mean, really. Are you the same as when I went away?'

'Aylmer, do you think we had better talk about it?'

'We must. I must. I can't endure the torture of seeing you just like anybody else. You know I told you—' He stopped a moment.

'You told me you'd never be a mere friend,' she said. 'But everything's so different now!'

'It isn't different; that's where you're wrong. You're just the same, and so am I. Except that I care for you far more than I ever did.'

'Oh, Aylmer!'

'When I thought I was dying I showed your little photograph to Miss Clay. I told her all about it. I suppose I was rather mad. It was just after an operation. It doesn't matter a bit; she wouldn't ever say a word.'

'I'm sure she wouldn't.'

'I had to confide in somebody,' he went on. 'I told her to send you back the photograph, and I told her that my greatest wish was to see you again.'

'Well, my dear boy, we have met again! Do change your mind from what you said last! I mean when you went away.' She spoke in an imploring tone.

'Do you wish to be friends, then?'

She hesitated a moment, then said: 'Yes, I do.'

CHAPTER XV

A F T E R a moment's pause he said: 'You say everything's changed. In a way it is. I look at things differently—I regard them differently. When you've been up against it, and seen life and death pretty close, you realise what utter rot it is to live so much for the world.'

Edith stared. 'But . . . doesn't it make you feel all the more the importance of principle—goodness and religion, and all that sort of thing? I expected it would, with you.'

'Frankly, no; it doesn't. Now, let us look at the situation quietly.'

After an agitated pause he went on:

'As far as I make out, you're sacrificing yourself to Bruce. When he ran away with that girl, and begged you to divorce him, you could have done it. You cared for me. Everything would have been right, even before the world. No-one would have blamed you. Yet you wouldn't.'

'But that *wasn't* for the world, Aylmer; you don't understand. It was for myself. Something *in* me, which I can't help. I felt Bruce needed me and would go wrong without me—'

'Why should you care? Did he consider you?'

'That isn't the point, dear boy. I felt as if he was my son, so to speak—a sort of feeling of responsibility.'

'Yes, quite. It was quixotic rubbish. That's my opinion. There!'

Edith said nothing, remembering he was still ill.

'Well,' he went on, 'now, he *hasn't* run away from you. He's stayed with you for three years; utterly incapable of appreciating you, as I know he is, bothering you to death.'

'Oh, Aylmer!'

'Don't I know him? You're wasting and frittering yourself away for nothing.'

'The children—'

'Don't you think I'd have looked after the children better than he?'

'Yes, I do, Aylmer. But he *is* their father. They may keep him straight.'

'I consider you're utterly wasted,' he said. 'Well! He's stuck to you, apparently, for these last three years (as far as *you* know), and now I'm going to ask you something entirely different, for the last time. When I was dying, or thought I was, things showed themselves clearly enough, I can tell you. And I made up my mind if I lived to see you, to say this. Leave Bruce, with me!'

She stared at him.

'In six weeks, when he's tired of telling his friends at the club about it, he'll make up his mind, I suppose, if you insist, or even without, to divorce you. But do you suppose he'll keep the children? No, my dear of course he won't. You'll *never* have to leave them. I would never ask you that. Now listen!' He put his hand over hers, not caressingly, but to keep her quiet. 'He'll want to marry again, won't he?'

'Very likely,' she answered.

'Probably already he's in love with that woman What's-her-name—Madame Frabelle—who's staying with you.'

Edith gave a little laugh.

'Perhaps he's in love with her already,' continued Aylmer.

'Quite impossible!' said Edith calmly.

'She's a very good sort. She's not a fool, like the girl. She'd look after Bruce very well.'

'So she would,' answered Edith.

'Bruce will adore her, be under her thumb, and keep perfectly 'straight', as you call it—as straight as he ever would. Won't he?'

She was silent.

'You'll get the children then, don't you see?'

'Yes. With a bad reputation, with a cloud on my life, to bring up Dilly!'

He sighed impatiently, and said: 'You see, you don't see things as they really are, even now. How could *you* ever possibly hurt Dilly? You're only thinking of what the world says, now.

'Hear me out,' he went on. 'Is this the only country? After the war, won't everything be different? Thank goodness, I'm well provided for. You needn't take a farthing. Leave even your own income to Bruce if you like. You know I've five thousand a year now, Edith?'

' I didn't know it. But that has nothing on earth to do with it,' she answered.

' Bosh! It has a *great* deal to do with it. I can afford to bring your children up as well as Teddy, my boy. We can marry. And in a year or two no-one would think any more about it.'

' You bewilder me,' said Edith.

' I want to. Think it over. Don't be weak. I'm sorry, dear, to ask you to take the blame on your side. It's unfair; but after all, perhaps, it's straighter than waiting for an opportunity (which you could easily get in time) of finding Bruce in the wrong.'

Her face expressed intense determination and disagreement with his views.

' Don't answer me,' he said, ' think—'

' My dear boy, you must let me answer you. Will you listen to me?'

' Go on, Edith. I'll always listen to you.'

' You don't realise it, but you're not well,' she said.

He gave an impatient gesture.

' How like a woman! As soon as I talk sense you say I'm not well. A broken leg doesn't affect the brain, remember.'

' No, Aylmer; I don't mean that. But you've been thinking this over till you've lost your bearings, your sense of proportion. . . .'

' Rot! I've just got it! That's what you mean. It comes to this, my dear girl '—he spoke gently. ' Of course, if you don't care for me, my suggestion would be perfectly mad. Perhaps you don't. Probably you regard our romance as a pretty little story to look back on.'

' No, I don't, unless—'

' I won't ask you straight out,' he said. ' I don't suppose you know yourself. But, if you care for me, as I do for you '—he spoke steadily —' you'll do as I ask.'

' I might love you quite as much, and yet not do it.'

' I know it's a big thing. It's a sacrifice, in a way. But don't you see, Edith, that if you still like me, your present life is a long, slow sacrifice to convention, or (as you say) to a morbid sense of responsibility?'

She looked away with a startled expression.

' Well, *do* you love me?' he said rather impatiently, but yet with his old charm of tenderness and sincerity. ' I have never changed.

As you know, after the operation, when they thought I was practically done in—it may seem a bit mad, but I was really more sane than I have ever been—I told Dulcie Clay all about it.'

She stopped him. 'I know you did, my dear, and I don't blame you a bit. She's absolutely loyal. But now, listen. Has nothing occurred to you about her?'

'Nothing, except that I'm hoping to get rid of her as soon as possible.'

'She's madly in love with you, Aylmer.'

He looked contemptuous.

'She's a dear girl,' said Edith. 'I feel quite fond of her.'

'Really, I don't see how she comes in. You *are* perverse, Edith!'

'I'm not perverse. I see things.'

'She's never shown the slightest sign of it,' said Aylmer. 'I think it's your imagination. But even if it's not, it isn't my business, nor yours.'

'I think it is, a little.'

'If you talk like that, I'll send her away today.'

'Oh, Aylmer! how ungrateful of you to say such a thing! She's been an angel.'

He spoke wearily. 'I don't want *angels*! I want *you*!' He suddenly leant forward and took her hands.

She laughed nervously. 'What a compliment.'

Then she disengaged herself and stood up.

Aylmer sighed. 'Now you're going to say, Ought you to talk so much? What is your temperature? Oh, women *are* irritating, even the nicest, confound them!'

Edith was unable to help laughing.

'I'm afraid I *was* going to say something like that.'

'Now, are you going to say you won't answer me for fear it will excite me?'

'Don't talk nonsense,' said Edith. '*I* take you seriously enough. Don't worry!'

He looked delighted.

'Thank heaven! Most women treat a wounded man as if he were a sick child or a lunatic. It's the greatest rot. I'm nearly well.'

Edith looked round for his tonic, but stopped herself.

'Are you going now?' he asked.

'No, Aylmer. I thought of stopping a few minutes, if you don't mind.'

'Shall we talk of something else,' said Aylmer satirically, 'to divert my thoughts? Hasn't it been lovely weather lately?'

She smiled and sat down again.

'Would you like to know how soon the war will be over?' he went on. 'Oddly enough, I really don't know!'

'Are you going back when you've recovered?' she asked abruptly.

'Of course I'm going back; and I want to go back with your promise.' Then he looked a little conscience-stricken. 'Dear Edith, I don't want to rush you. Forgive me.'

They both sat in dead silence for five minutes. He was looking at the black velvet toque on the fair hair, over the soft eyes. She was staring across at the cherry-coloured carnations in the pewter vase on the mantelpiece.

As has been said, they often exchanged ideas without words.

He remarked, as she glanced at a book: 'Yes, I have read *A Life of Slavery*. Have you? Do you think it good?'

'Splendid,' Edith answered; 'it's a labour of hate.'

He laughed.

'Quite true. One can't call it a labour of love, though it was written to please the writer—not the public.'

'I wonder you could read it,' said Edith, 'after what you've been through.'

'It took my thoughts off life,' he said.

'Why? Isn't it life?'

'Of course it is. Literary life.'

Edith looked at the clock.

'When am I going to see you again?' he asked in a rather exhausted voice.

'Whenever you like. What about taking you out for a drive next week?'

'Right.'

'I'll think over what you said,' said Edith casually as she stood up.

'What a funny little speech. You're *impayable*! Oh, you are a jolly girl!'

'"Jolly" girl,' repeated Edith, not apparently pleased. 'I'm thirty-five, with a boy at school and a growing girl of seven!'

P*

'You think too much of the almanac. I'm forty-one, with a son at the front.'

'How on earth did you get your commissions?'

'In the usual way. Teddy and I told lies. He said he was eighteen and I said I was thirty-nine.'

'I see. Of course.'

He rang the bell.

'Will you write to me, dear Edith?'

'No. I'll come and see you, Aylmer.'

'Are you going to bring Archie, Bruce, or Madame Frabelle?'

'Neither.'

'Do leave Madame Frabelle at home.'

'Though you don't like her, you might pronounce her name right! She's such a clever woman.'

'She's an utter fool,' said Aylmer.

'Same thing, very often,' said Edith. 'Don't worry. Good-bye.'

She went away, leaving him perfectly happy and very hungry.

Hardly had she gone when Miss Clay came in and brought him some beef-tea on a tray.

CHAPTER XVI

To Edith's joy, as they entered the Mitchell's huge, familiar drawing-room, the first person she saw was her beloved confidant, Sir Tito Landi. This was the friend of all others whom she most longed to see at this particular moment.

The extraordinary confidence and friendship between the successful Italian composer and Edith Ottley needs, perhaps, a word of explanation. He was adored equally in the artistic and the social worlds, and was at once the most cynical of Don Juans and the most unworldly of Don Quixotes. He was a devoted and grateful friend, and a contemptuous but not unforgetful enemy.

It was not since his celebrity that Edith had first met him; she had known him intimately all her life. From her earliest childhood she had, so to speak, been brought up on Landi; on Landi's music and Landi's views of life. He had been her mother's music teacher soon after he first made a name in London; and long before he was the star whose singing or accompanying was a rare favour, and whose presence gave a *cachet* to any entertainment.

How many poor Italians—yes, and many people of other nationalities—had reason to bless his acquaintance! How kind, how warm-hearted, how foolishly extravagant on others was Landi! His brilliant cleverness, which made him received almost as an Englishman among English people, was not, however, the cleverness of the *arriviste*. Although he had succeeded, and success was his object, no-one could be less self-interested, less pushing, less scheming. In many things he was a child. He would as soon dine at Pagani's with a poor sculptor, or a poor and plain woman who was struggling to give lessons in Italian, as with the most brilliant hostess in London. And he always found fashion and ceremony a bore. He was so great a favourite in England that he had been given that most English of titles, a knighthood, just as though he were very rich, or political, or a popular actor. In a childish way it amused him, and he was pleased with it. But though he was remarkable for his courtly tact, he loved most of all to be absolutely free and Bohemian, to be

429

quite natural among really sympathetic, witty, or beautiful friends.

He liked to say what he thought, to go where he wished, and to make love when he chose, not when other people chose. He had long been a man with an assured position, but he had changed little since he was twenty-one, and arrived from Naples with only his talent, his bright blue eyes, his fair complexion, his small, dignified figure and his daring humour. Yet the music he wrote indicated his sensitive and deeply feeling nature, and though his conversation could hardly be called other than cynical, nor his jokes puritanical, there was always in him a vein of genuine—not sentimental, but perhaps romantic—love and admiration for everything good; good in music, good in art, good in character. He laid down no rules of what *was* good. 'Tout savoir c'est tout pardonner' was perhaps his motto. But he was very unexpected; that was one of his charms. He would pass over the most extraordinary things—envious slights, small injuries, things another man would never forgive. On the other hand, he retained a bitter memory, not at all without its inclination for repayment, for other trifles that many would disregard.

Ever since she was a child Edith had been his special favourite. He loved the privilege of calling her Edith, of listening to her confidences, of treating her with loving familiarity. It was a joke between them that, while he used formerly to say, 'Cette enfant! Je l'ai vue en jupe courte, vous savez!' he had gradually reached the point of declaring, 'Je l'ai vue naître!' almost with tears in his eyes.

This explains why Landi was the only creature to whom Edith could tell everything, and did. Must not all nice people have a confidant? And no girl or woman friend—much as they might like her, and she them—could ever take the place of Landi, the wise and ever-sympathetic.

There was something in his mental attitude that was not unfeminine, direct and assertive as he was. He had what is generally known as feminine intuition, a quality perhaps even rarer in women than in men.

Tonight the persistently hospitable Mrs Mitchell had a large party. Dressed in grey, she was receiving her guests in the big room on the ground floor, and tactfully directing the conversation of a crowd of various and more or less interesting persons.

It was one of those parties that had been described as a Russian Salad, where one ran an equal risk—or took an equal chance—of being taken to dinner by Charlie Chaplin or Winston Churchill, and where society and the stage were equally well represented. Young officers on leave and a few pretty girls filled the vacancies.

As Bruce, Edith and Madame Frabelle came in together, Landi went straight to Edith's side.

Looking at her through his eyeglass, he said, as if to himself, in an anxious tone:

' Elle a quelquechose, cette enfant; oui, elle a quelquechose,' and as the last guest had not arrived he sat down thoughtfully by her on the small sofa.

' Yes, Landi, there is something the matter. I'm longing to tell you about it. I want your advice,' said Edith, smiling.

' Tout se sait; tout se fait; tout s'arrange,' sententiously remarked Landi, who was not above talking oracular commonplaces at times.

' Oh, it isn't one of *those* things, Landi.'

' Not? Are you sure? Don't be sad, Edith. Be cheerful. Tiens! Tiens! Tiens! How excited you are,' he went on, as she looked at him with perfect composure.

' You will think I have reason to be excited when I tell you.'

He smiled in an experienced way.

' I'll sit next to you at dinner and you shall tell me everything. Tiens! La vieille qui voit double!' He bowed politely as Madame Frabelle came up.

' Dear Sir Tito, *what* a pleasure to see you again! Your lovely songs have been ringing in my ears ever since I heard them!'

' Where did you hear them? On a piano-organ?' he asked.

' You're too bad! Isn't he naughty? No, when you sang here last.'

Mr Mitchell came up, and Madame Frabelle turned away.

' Dieu merci! La pauvre! Elle me donne sur les nerfs ce soir,' said Landi. ' I shall sit next to you whether the cards are placed so or not, Edith, and you'll tell me everything between the soup and the ices.'

' I will indeed.'

' Madame Meetchel,' he said, looking round through his eyeglass, ' is sure to have given you a handsome young man, someone who ought to drive Bruce wild with jealousy, but doesn't, or . . . or . . .'

' Or some fly-blown celebrity.'

'Sans doute!'

The door opened and the last guest appeared. It was young
Coniston (in khaki), who was invariably asked when there was to
be music. He was so useful.

He approached Landi at once.

'Ah, cher maître, quel plaisir!' he said with his South Kensington accent and his Oxford manner. (He had been a Cambridge
man.)

'C'est vrai?' asked Landi, who had his own way of dismissing a
person in a friendly way.

Coniston began talking to him of a song. Landi waved him off
and went up to Mrs Mitchell, said something which made her laugh
and blush and try to hit him with her fan—the fan, the assault and
the manner were all out of date, but Mrs Mitchell made no pretence
at going with the times—and his object was gained.

Sir Tito took Edith in to dinner.

CHAPTER XVII

A s they found their places at the long table (Sir Tito had exchanged cards, as though he meant to fight a duel with Edith's
destined partner) of course the two turned their backs to one
another. On her other side was Mr Mitchell. When Madame
Frabelle noticed this, she gave Edith an arch shake of the head,
and made a curious warning movement with her hand. Edith
smiled at her in astonishment. She had utterly forgotten her friend's
fancy about the imaginary intrigue supposed to be going on between her and Mr Mitchell, and she wondered what the gesture
meant. Sir Tito also saw it, and, turning round to Edith, said in a
low voice:

'Qu'est-ce-qu'elle a, la vieille?'

'I really don't know. I never understand signs. I've forgotten the
code, I suppose!'

Mr Mitchell, after a word to the person he had taken down,
gladly turned to Edith. He always complained that the host was
obliged to sit between the oldest and the most boring guests. It was
unusual for him to have so pretty a neighbour as Edith. But he was
a collector: his joy was to see a heterogeneous mass of people,
eating and laughing at his table. For his wife there were a few
social people, for him the Bohemians, and always the younger
guests.

'Not bad—not bad, is it?' he said, looking critically round down
the two sides of the table, while his kind pink face beamed with
hospitable joy.

'You've got a delightful party tonight.'

'What I always say is,' said Mr Mitchell; 'let them enjoy
themselves! Dash it, I hate etiquette.' He lowered his voice. 'Bruce
is looking pretty blooming. Not so many illnesses lately has
he?'

'Not when he's at home,' said Edith.

'Ah! At the F O the dear fellow does, I'm afraid, suffer a good
deal from nerves,' said Mr Mitchell, especially towards the end of

the day. About four o'clock, I mean, you know! You know old
Bruce! Good sort he is. I see he hasn't got the woman I meant him
to sit next to, somehow or other. I see he's next to Miss Coniston.'

'Oh, he likes her.'

'Good, good. Thought she was a bit too artistic, and high-
browed, as the Americans say, for him. But now he's used to that
sort of thing, isn't he? Madame Frabelle, eh? Wonderful woman.
No soup, Edith: why not?'

'It makes me silent,' said Edith; 'and I like to talk.'

Mitchell laughed loudly. 'Ha ha! Champagne for Mrs Ottley.
What are you about?' He looked up reprovingly at the servant. Mr
Mitchell was the sort of man who never knows, after twenty years'
intimate friendship, whether a person takes sugar or not.

Edith allowed the man to fill her glass. She knew it depressed Mr
Mitchell to see people drinking water. So she only did it surrepti-
tiously, and as her glass was always full, because she never drank
from it, Mr Mitchell was happy.

A very loud feminine laugh was heard.

'That's Miss Radford,' said Mr Mitchell. 'That's how she always
goes on. She's always laughing. She was immensely charmed with
you the day she called on you with my wife.'

'Was she?' said Edith, who remembered she herself had been out
on that occasion.

'Tremendously. I can't remember what she said: I think it was
how clever you were.'

'She saw Madame Frabelle. I wasn't at home.'

'Ha ha! Good, very good!' Mr Mitchell turned to his other
neighbour.

'Eh bien,' said Sir Tito, who was waiting his opportunity. 'Com-
mence!'

At once Edith began murmuring in a low voice her story of
herself and Aylmer, and related today's conversation in Jermyn
Street.

Sir Tito nodded his head occasionally. When he listened most
intently, he appeared to be looking round the table at other people.
He lifted a glass of champagne and bowed over it to Mrs Mitchell;
then he put his hand to his lips and blew a kiss.

'Who's that for?' Edith asked, interrupting herself.

'C'est pour la vieille.'

'Madame Frabelle! Why do you kiss your hand to her?'

'To keep her quiet. Look at her: she's so impressed, and thinks it so wicked, that she's blushing and uncomfortable. I've a splendid way, Edith (pardon), of silencing all these elderly ladies who make love to me. I don't say "Ferme!" I'm polite to them.'

Edith laughed. Sir Tito was not offended.

'Yes, you needn't laugh, my dear child. I'm not old enough yet pour les jeunes; at any rate, if I am they don't know it. I'm still pursued by the upper middle-age class, with gratitude for favours to come (as they think).'

'Well, what's your plan?'

He giggled.

'I tell Madame Frabelle, Madame Meetchel, Lady Everard—first, that they have beautiful lips; then, that I can't look at them without longing to kiss them. Lady Everard, after I said that, kept her hand before her face the whole evening, so as not to distract me, and drive me mad. Consequently she couldn't talk.'

'Do they really believe you?'

'Evidemment! . . . I wonder,' he continued mischievously, as he refused wine, 'whether Madame Frabelle will confess to you to-night about my passion for her, or whether she will keep it to herself?'

'I dare say she'll tell me. At least she'll ask me if I think so or not.'

'Si elle te demande, tu diras que tu n'en sais rien! Well, I think . . .'

'What?'

'You must wait. Wait and see. Really, it's impossible, my dear child, for you to accept an invitation for an elopement as if it were a luncheon-party. Not only that, it's good for Aylmer to be kept in doubt. Excellent for his health.'

'Really?'

'When I say his health, I mean the health and strength of his love for you. You must vacillate, Edith. Souvent femme varie. You sit on the fence, n'est-ce-pas? Well, offer the fence to him. But, take it away before he sits down. Voilà!'

Edith laughed. 'But then this girl, Miss Clay, she's always there. And I like her.'

'What is her nationality?'

'How funny you should ask that! I think she must be of Spanish descent. She's so quiet, so religious, and has a very dark complexion. And yet wonderful light blue eyes.'

'Quelle histoire! Qu'est-ce-que ça fait?'

'The poor girl is mad about Aylmer. He doesn't seem to know it, but he makes her worse by his indifference,' Edith said.

'Why aren't you jealous of her, ma chère? No, I won't ask you that—the answer is obvious.'

'I mean this, that if I can't ever do what he wishes, I feel she could make him happy; and I could bear it if she did.'

'Spanish?' said Landi, as if to himself. 'Olé! olé! Does she use the castanets, and wear a mantilla instead of a cap?'

'How frivolous and silly you are. No, of course not. She looks quite English, in fact particularly so.'

'And yet you insist she's Spanish! Well, my advice is this. If he has a secret alliance with Spain, you should assume the Balkan attitude.'

'Good gracious! What's that?'

'We're talking politics,' said Landi, across the table. 'Politics, and geography! Fancy, Meetchel, Mrs Ottley doesn't know anything about the Balkans!'

'Ha, very good,' said Mitchell. 'Capital. What a fellow you are!' He gave his hearty, clubbable laugh. Mr Mitchell belonged to an exceptionally large number of clubs and was a favourite at all. His laugh was the chief cause of his popularity there.

'Il est fou,' said Landi quietly to Edith. 'Quel monde! I don't think there are half-a-dozen sane people at this table.'

'Oh, Landi!'

'And if there are, they shouldn't by rights be admitted into decent society. But the dear Meetchels don't know that; it's not public. I adore them both,' he went on, changing his satirical tone, and again apparently drinking the health of Mrs Mitchell, who waved her hand coquettishly from the end of the long table.

'Now listen, my child. Don't see Aylmer for a little while.'

'He wants me to take him out for a drive.'

'Take him for a drive. But not this week. How Madame Frabelle loves Bruce!' he went on, watching her.

'Really, Landi, I assure you you're occasionally as mistaken as she is. And *she* thinks I'm in love with our host.'

'That's because *elle voit double.* I don't.'

'What makes you think . . .'

'I read between the lines, my dear—between the lines on Madame Frabelle's face.'

'She hasn't any.'

'Oh, go along,' said Landi, who sometimes broke into peculiar English which he thought was modern slang. Raising his voice, he said: 'The dinner is *exquis—exquis,*' so that Mr Mitchell could hear.

'I can't help noting what you've eaten tonight, Landi, though I don't usually observe these things,' Edith said. 'You've had half-a-tomato, a small piece of vegetable marrow, and a sip of claret. Aren't you going to eat anything more?'

'Not much more. I look forward to my coffee and my cigar. Oh, how I look forward to it!'

'You know very well, Landi, they let you smoke cigarettes between the courses, if you like.'

'It would be better than nothing. We'll see presently.'

'Might I inquire if you live on cigars and coffee?'

'No,' he answered satirically; 'I live on eau sucré. And porreege. I'm Scotch.'

'I can't talk to you if you're so silly.'

'You'll tell me the important part on the little sofa upstairs in the salon,' he said. 'After dinner. Tonight, here, somehow, the food and the faces distract one—unless one is making an acquaintance. I know you too well to talk at dinner.'

'Quite true. I ought to take time to think then.'

'There's no hurry. Good heavens! the man has waited four years; he can wait another week. Quelle idée!'

'He's going back,' said Edith, 'as soon as he's well. He wants me to promise before he goes.'

'Does he! You remind me of the man who said to his wife: "Good-bye, my dear, I'm off to the Thirty Years' War." It's all right, Edith. We'll find a solution, I have no fears.'

She turned to Mr Mitchell.

The rest of the evening passed pleasantly. Alone with the women, Madame Frabelle was the centre of an admiring circle, as she lectured on 'dress and economy in war-time,' and how to manage

a house on next to nothing a year. All the ladies gasped with
admiration. Edith especially was impressed; because the fact that
Madame Frabelle was a guest, and was managing nothing, did not
prevent her talking as if she had any amount of experience on the
subject, although, by her own showing she had been staying at
hotels ever since the war began, except the last weeks she had spent
with the Ottleys.

The men soon joined them.

A group of war valetudinarians, amongst whom Bruce was not
the least emphatic, told each other their symptoms in a quiet
corner. They described their strange shiverings down the spine; the
curious fits of hunger that came on before meals; the dislike to
crossing the road when there was an accident; the inability to
sleep, sometimes taking the form of complete insomnia for as much
as twenty minutes in the early morning. They pitied each other
cordially, though neither listened to the other's symptoms, except in
exchange for sympathy with their own.

'The war has got on my nerves; I can't think of anything else,'
Bruce said. 'It's an *idée fixe*. I pant for the morning when the
newspaper's due, and then I can't look at it! Not even a glance!
Odd, isn't it?'

The Rev. Byrne Fraser, who gave his wife great and constant
anxiety by his fantasies, related how he had curious dreams—the
distressing part of which was that they never came true—about the
death of relatives at the front. Another man also had morbid fancies
on the subject of the casualty list, and had had to go and stay at a
farm so as to 'get right away from it all'. But he soon left, as he
had found, to his great disappointment, that his companions there
were not intellectual, and could not even talk politics or discuss
literature. And yet they went in (or so he had heard) for 'intensive
culture'! ...

Presently Sir Tito played his Italian march. The musical portion
of the party, and the unmusical alike, joined in the chorus. Then
the party received a welcome addition. Valdez, the great composer,
who had written many successful operas and had lived so much
abroad that he cared now for nothing but British music, looked in
after a patriotic concert given in order to help the unengaged professionals. Always loyal to old friends, he had deserted royalty itself
tonight to greet Mrs Mitchell and was persuaded by adoring ladies

to sing his celebrated old song, 'After Several Years.' It pleased and thrilled the audience even more than Landi's 'Adieu Hiver'. Indeed, tonight it was Valdez who was the success of the evening. Middle-aged ladies who had loved him for years loved him now more than ever. Young girls who saw him now for the first time fell in love, just as their mothers had done, with his splendid black eyes and commanding presence, and secretly longed to stroke at least every seventh wave of his abundant hair. When Edith assured him that his curls were 'like a flock of goats on Mount Gilead' he laughed, declared he was much flattered at the comparison, and kissed her hand with courtly grace.

Young Mr Cricker, who came because he wasn't asked, insisted on dancing like Nijinsky because he was begged not to, but his leaps and bounds were soon stopped by a few subalterns and very young officers on leave, who insisted, with some fair partners, on dancing the Fox Trot to the sound of a gramophone.

For a few moments on the little sofa Edith managed to convey the rest of her confidence to Landi. She pointed out how hurried, how urgent, how pressing it was to give an answer.

'He wants a war elopement, I see,' said Landi. 'Mais ça ne se fait pas!'

'Then what am I to say?'

'Rien.'

'But, Landi, you know I sha'n't really ever . . .'

'Would it give you pleasure to see him married to the Spanish girl?'

'She's not exactly Spanish—she only looks it. Don't laugh like that!'

'I don't know why, but Spain seems always to remind me of something ridiculous. Onions—or guitars.'

'Well, I shouldn't mind her nearly so much as anyone else.'

'You don't mind her,' said Landi. 'Vous savez qu'il ne l'épouse pas? What would you dislike him to do most?'

'I think I couldn't bear anyone else to take my place exactly,' admitted Edith.

'C'est ça! you don't want him to be in love with another married woman with a husband like Bruce? Well, my dear, he won't. There is no other husband like Bruce.

Landi promised to consider the question, and she arranged to go and see him at his studio before seeing Aylmer again.

As they went out of the house Miss Coniston ran after Madame Frabelle and said eagerly:

'Oh, do tell me again; you say *soupe à la vinaigre* is marvellously nourishing and economical. I can have it made for my brother at our flat?'

'Of course you can! It costs next to nothing.'

Arthur Coniston came up.

'And tastes like nothing on earth, I suppose?' he grumbled in his sister's ear. 'You can't give me much less to eat than you do already.'

'Oh, Arthur!' his sister said. 'Aren't you happy at home? I think you're a pessimist.'

'A pessimist!' cried Mitchell, who was following them into the hall. 'Oh, I hate pessimists! What's the latest definition of them? Ah, I know; an optimist is a person who doesn't care what happens as long as it doesn't happen to him.'

'Yes,' said Edith quickly, 'and a pessimist is the person who lives with the optimist.'

'Dear, dear. I always thought the old joke was that an optimist looks after the eyes, and a pessimist after the feet!' cried Madame Frabelle as she fastened her cloak.

'Why, then, he ought to go to a cheer-upadist!' said Mr Mitchell. And they left him in roars of laughter.

CHAPTER XVIII

DULCIE CLAY, in her neat uniform of grey and white, with the scarlet cross on the front of her apron, was sitting in the room she occupied for the moment in Aylmer's house in Jermyn Street. It was known as ' the second best bedroom '. As she was anxious not to behave as if she were a guest, she used it as a kind of boudoir when she was not in attendance.

It was charmingly furnished in the prim Chippendale style, a style dainty, but not luxurious, that seemed peculiarly suited to Dulcie.

She was in the window-seat—not with her feet up, no cushions behind her. Unlike Edith, she was not the kind of woman who rested habitually; she sat quite upright in the corner. A beautiful little mahogany table was at her right, with a small electric lamp on it, and two books. One of the books was her own choice, the other had been lent to her by Aylmer. It was a volume of Bernard Shaw. She could make neither head nor tail of it, and the prefaces, which she read with the greatest avidity, perplexed her even more than the books themselves. Every now and then a flash of lightning, in the form of some phrase she knew, illumined for a second the darkness of the author's words. But soon she closed the thick volume with the small print and returned to *The Daisy Chain*.

Dulcie was barely one-and-twenty. She carried everywhere in her trunk a volume called *The Wide, Wide World*. She was never weary of reading this work with the comprehensive title; it reminded her of schooldays. It was comforting, like a dressing-gown and slippers, like an old friend. Whether she had ever thoroughly understood it may be doubted. If any modern person nowadays were to dip into it, he would find it, perhaps, more obscure than George Meredith at his darkest. Secretly Dulcie loved best in the world, in the form of reading matter, the feuilletons in the daily papers. There was something so exciting in that way they have of stopping at a thrilling moment and leaving you the whole day to think over what would come next, and the night to sleep over it.

441

She preferred that; she never concentrated her mind for long on a story, or any work of the imagination. She was deeply interested in her own life. She was more subjective than objective—though, perhaps, she had never heard the words. Unconsciously she dealt with life only as it related to herself. But this is almost universal with young girls who have only just become conscious of themselves, and of their importance in the world; have only just left the simple objectiveness of the child who wants to look at the world, and have barely begun to feel what it is to be an actor rather than a spectator.

Not that any living being could be less selfish or vain, or less of an egotist than Dulcie. If she saw things chiefly as they were related to herself, it was because this problem of her life was rather an intricate one. Her position was not sufficiently simple to suit her simple nature.

Her mother, who had been of Spanish descent, had died young; her father had married again. He was the sort of man who always married again, and if his present wife, with whom he was rather in love, had passed away he would have undoubtedly married a third time. Some men are born husbands; they have a passion for domesticity, for a fireside, for a home. Yet, curiously, these men very rarely stay at home. Apparently what they want is to have a place to get away from.

The new stepmother, who was young and rather pretty, was not unkind, but was bored and indifferent to the little girl. Dulcie was sensitive; since her father's second marriage she had always felt in the way. Whether her stepmother was being charming to her husband, or to some other man—she was always charming to somebody—Dulcie felt continually that she was not wanted. Her father was kind and casual. He told everyone what he believed, that his second wife was an ideal person to bring up his little daughter.

Therefore it came upon him as a surprise when she told him she was grown up, and still more that she wished to leave home and be a nurse. Mrs Clay had made no objection; the girl rather depressed her, for she felt she ought to like her more than she did, so she 'backed up' with apparent good nature the great desire to go out and do something.

Dulcie had inherited three hundred a year from her mother. Her father had about the same amount of his own to live on. He believed that he added to it by mild gambling, and perhaps by talking a good deal at his club of how he had been born to make a fortune but had had no luck. His second wife had no money.

Dulcie, therefore, was entirely independent. No obstacles were placed in her way—the particular form that her ambition took was suggested by the war, but in any case she would have done something. She had taken the usual means of getting into a hospital.

Gentle, industrious, obedient and unselfish, she got on well. Her prettiness gained her no enemies among the women as she was too serious about her work at this time to make use of her beauty by attracting men. Yet Dulcie was unusually feminine; she had a natural gift for nursing, for housekeeping, for domesticity. She was not artistic and was as indifferent to abstractions and to general ideas as the ideal average woman. She was tactful, sweet, and, she had been called at school, rather a doormat. Her appearance was distinguished and she was not at all ordinary. It is far from ordinary, indeed it is very rare, to be the ideal average woman. She took great interest in detail; she would lie awake at night thinking about how she would go the next day to a certain inexpensive shop to get a piece of ribbon for one part of her dress to match a piece of ribbon in another part—neither of which would ever be seen by any human being.

Such men as she saw liked and admired her. Her gradual success led her to being sent abroad to a military hospital. She inspired confidence, not because she had initiative, but because one knew she would do exactly as she was told, which is, in itself, a great quality. At Boulogne she made the acquaintance at once of Aylmer, and of the *coup de foudre*. She worshipped him at first sight. So she thought herself fortunate when she was allowed to come back to London with him. Under orders she continued her assiduous attention. Everyone said she was a perfect nurse.

Occasionally she went to see her father. He greeted her with warmth and affection, and told her all about how, on account of racing being stopped, he was gradually becoming a pauper. When she began telling him of the events in which she was absorbed he answered by giving her news of the prospects for the Cambridgeshire. In the little den in the house in West Kensington, where he lived, she would come in and say in a soft voice:

'Papa dear, you know I sha'n't be able to stop much longer.'

'Much longer where?'

'Why, with my patient, Mr Ross—Mr Aylmer Ross.'

'Sha'n't you? Mind you, my dear, there are two good three-year-olds that are not to be sneezed at.' He shook his head solemnly.

It had never occurred to Dulcie for a moment to sneeze at three-year-olds. She hardly knew what they were.

'But what do you advise for me, papa?'

'My dear child, I can't advise. You can't select with any approach to confidence between Buttercup and Beautiful Doll. Mind you, I'm very much inclined to think that More Haste may win yet. Look how he ran in August, when nobody knew anything about him!'

'Yes, I know, papa, but—'

She gave it up.

'Go and see your mother, dear; go and ask her about it,' and he returned to the racing intelligence.

Strange that a man who had not enough to live on should think he could add to his income by backing losers. Still, such was Mr Clay's view of life. Besides, he was just going out; he was always just going out.

She would then go and see her stepmother, who greeted her most affectionately.

Dulcie only kept half her little income for herself at present, a considerable advantage to a woman like Mrs Clay, who declared she was 'expected to dress up to a certain standard, though, of course, simply during war-time.' She would kiss the girl and drag her up to her bedroom to show her a new coat and skirt, or send the general servant up to bring down the marvellously cheap little tea-gown that had just come home.

Both her parents, it will be seen, were ready enough to talk to her, but they were not prepared to listen. All the warmth and affection that she had in her nature very naturally was concentrated on her patient.

Dulcie now sat in the window-seat, wondering what to do. She was sadly thinking what would happen when the time came for her to leave.

In her mind she knew perfectly well that what several people had said was true: the profession she had chosen was too arduous for her physical strength. Besides, now she could not bear the idea of nursing anyone else after Aylmer. She was trying to make up her mind to take something else—and she could not think what.

A girl like Dulcie Clay, who has studied only one thing really thoroughly, could be fitted only to be a companion either to children, whom she adored, or to some tedious elderly lady with fads. She knew she would not do for a secretary; she had not the education nor the gift for it.

The thought of going back to the stepmother who showed so clearly her satisfaction and high spirits in having got rid of her, and of being again the unwanted third in the little house in West Kensington, was quite unbearable.

She had told much of her position to Edith, who was so sympathetic and clever. It would have been a dream of hers, a secret dream, to teach Edith's little girl, whom she had once seen, and loved. Yet that would have been in some ways rather difficult. As she looked out of the window, darkened with fog, she sighed. If she had been the governess at Edith's house, she would be constantly seeing Aylmer. She knew, of course, all about Aylmer's passion. It would certainly be better than nothing to see him sometimes. But the position would have been painful. Also, she disliked Bruce. He had given her one or two looks that seemed rather to demand admiration than to express it; he had been so kind as to give her a few hints on nursing; how to look after a convalescent; and had been exceedingly frank and kind in confiding to her his own symptoms. As she was a hospital nurse, it seemed to him natural to talk rather of his own indisposition than on any other subject. Dulcie was rather highly strung, and Bruce got terribly on her nerves; she marvelled at Edith's patience. But then Edith. . . . No, she could not go to the Ottleys.

Her other gift—a beautiful soprano voice—also was of hardly any use to her, as she was now placed. When she sang she expressed herself more completely than at any other time, but that also she had not been taught thoroughly; she had been taught nothing thoroughly.

A companion! Though she had not absolutely to earn her living, and kept only half of her little inheritance for herself, what was to become of her? Well, she wouldn't think about it any more that day. At any rate Aylmer talked as though she was to remain some time longer.

When he had returned suddenly to the house in Jermyn Street, a relative had hastily obtained for him the necessary servants; his former valet was at the front; they were all new to him and to his ways, and he had no housekeeper. Dulcie did the housekeeping— could she take that place in his house? No, she knew that she was too young, and everyone else would have said she was too pretty. Only as a nurse would it be correct for her to be his companion.

And from fear of embarrassing him she was hardly ever with him alone. She thought he was abrupt, more cool to her since their return, and guessed the reason; it was for fear of compromising her. How angelic of him; what a wonderful man—how fortunate his first wife must have been. And the boy, Teddy—the charming boy so like his father, whom she had only seen for a day or two before he left to go out. Teddy's presence would help to make it more difficult for her to remain.

In that very short time the boy had distinctly shown her by his marked attention how much he admired her. He thought her lovely. He was devoted to music and she had sung to him.

Aylmer also liked music, but apparently did not care to hear her sing. On the occasion that she did, it seemed to irritate him. Indeed, she knew she was merely the most amateurish of musicians, and could just accompany herself in a few songs, though the voice itself was a rare gift. . . . How perfect Aylmer had been! . . . There was a sharp ring. She closed the book, turned out the little electric lamp and went downstairs.

She was looking ideally pretty in the becoming uniform, but uniforms are always becoming, whatever the uniforms or the people may be. The reason of this is too obscure to fathom. One would say that to dress to suit oneself would be more becoming to men and women. Yet, in fact, the limitation and the want of variety in this sort of dress had a singular attraction. However, if she had chosen it to suit her, nothing could have been more becoming. The severity of the form, the dull colour, relieved by the large scarlet cross, showed off to the greatest advantage her dense dark hair, her Madonna-like face and the slim yet not angular lines of her figure. Dulcie's beauty was of a kind that is thrown into relief by excessive plainness of dress.

CHAPTER XIX

A s she came in, Aylmer looked at her with more observation than usual, and he acknowledged to himself that she was pretty— remarkably pretty, quite a picture, as people say, and he liked her, as one likes a confidante, a reliable friend. He trusted her, remembering how he had given himself away to her that dreadful day in the Boulogne hospital. . . . And she had another quality that pleased him immensely; she was neither coquettish nor affected, but simple and serious. She appeared to think solely of her duties, and in Aylmer's opinion that was just what a nurse should do.

But Edith's remark that Dulcie was madly in love with him had made a certain impression on his mind. Indeed, everything Edith said, even a merely trivial observation, was of importance to Aylmer. Edith wouldn't have said that unless she meant it. If it was true, did it matter? Aylmer was very free from vanity and masculine coquetry. He had a good deal of pride and great self-respect. Like almost every human being who is superior to the average, he didn't think ill of himself; there were things that he was proud of. He was proud, secretly, of having gone into the army and of having been wounded. It made him feel he was not on the shelf, not useless and superannuated. He took a certain pride also in his judgement, his excellent judgement on pictures and literature. Perhaps, even, having been a spoilt only child, he was privately proud of some of his faults. He knew he was extravagant and impatient. The best of everything was barely good enough for Aylmer. Long before he inherited the property that had come to him a year ago he had never been the sort of young man who would manage on little; who would, for example, go to the gallery by Underground or omnibus to see a play or to the opera. He required comfort, elbow-room, ease. For that reason he had worked really hard at the Bar so as to have enough money to live according to his ideas. Not that he took any special interest in the Bar. His ideal had always been—if it could be combined—to be either a soldier or a man of leisure, devoted to sport, literature and art.

Now he had asserted himself as a soldier, and he meant to go back. But he looked forward to leisure to enjoy and indulge his favourite tastes, if possible, with the only woman he had ever been deeply in love with.

He was particularly attractive to women, who liked his strong will and depth of feeling, his assertive manner and that feeling of trust that he inspired. Women always know when a man will not treat them badly. Teddy's mother, his first wife, he had really married out of pity.

When she died everyone regarded it as a tragedy except himself. He still worshipped his mother, whose little miniature he kept always by him, and he had always fancied that Edith resembled her. This was simply an *idée d'amoureux*, for there was no resemblance. His mother, according to the miniature, had the dark hair and innocent expression that were the fashion at the time, while Edith was fair, with rather dark eyebrows, grey eyes and the mouth and chin characteristic of Burne-Jones's and Rossetti's pictures. But though she might be in appearance a Burne-Jones, she was very modern. His favourite little photograph of her that he had shown, in his moment of despair, to Dulcie, showed a charming face, sensuous yet thoughtful, under a large hat. She had fur up to her chin, and was holding a muff; it was a snapshot taken the winter before they had parted.

Aylmer worshipped these two women: his dead mother and the living woman whom he had never given up entirely. How unlike were both the types to Dulcie Clay, with her waved Madonna hair, dark skin, large, clear blue eyes, softened by eyelashes of extraordinary length. Her chin was very small, her mouth fine, rather thin; she had a pathetic expression; one could imagine her attending, helping, nursing, holding a child in her arms, but not his intellectual equal, guiding and directing like his mother; and without the social brilliance and charm of Edith.

Seeing him looking at her with a long, observant look, Dulcie became nervous and trembled slightly. She waited for him to speak.

'Come here, Miss Clay. I want to speak to you.'

Instantly she sat down by him.

' I wanted to say—you've been most awfully kind to me.'

Dulcie murmured something.

' I'm nearly well now—aren't I?'

' Dr Wood says you can go out driving next week.'

' Yes; but I don't mean that. I mean, I'm well in myself?'

He spoke quickly, almost impatiently.

' The doctor says you're still suffering from nervous shock,' she answered in a toneless voice, professionally.

' Still, very soon I sha'n't need any attendance that a valet or a housekeeper couldn't give me, shall I?'

' No, I suppose not.'

' Well, my dear Miss Clay—of course, I shall hate you to go,' he said politely, ' but don't you think we ought to be thinking—'

He stopped.

She answered:

' Of course I'll go whenever you and Dr Wood think it right.'

' You see,' he went on, ' I know I shall need a housekeeper, especially when Teddy comes back. He's coming back on leave next week '—Aylmer glanced at the telegram in his hand—' and, well—'

' You don't think I could—'

' Of course you would make a splendid housekeeper,' he laughed. ' You are already, but—'

She didn't wish to make him uncomfortable. Evidently he was thinking what she knew herself. But she was so reluctant to go.

' Don't you think I could remain here for a little while?' she said modestly. ' To do the housekeeping and be useful? You see, I've nowhere to go really.'

' But, my dear girl, excuse me, don't you see you're rather too— young. It would be selfish of me to let you.'

He wished to say that it would be compromising, but a certain consciousness prevented his saying it. He felt he would be ridiculous if he put it into words.

' Just as you like. How soon do you think I ought to go?'

Though she tried not to show it, there was a look almost of despair in her face. Her eyes looked startled, as if trying not to shed tears.

He was very sorry for her, but tried to hide it by a cool and impatient manner.

' Well, shall we say in about a fortnight?'

' Certainly.' She looked down.

' I shall miss you awfully,' he said, speaking more quickly than usual to get it over.

She gave a very small smile.

' Er—and then may I ask what you're thinking of doing next?'

' That was just what I was thinking about,' she answered rather naïvely. ' There are so few things I can do.'

Then fearing this sentence sounded like begging to remain, she hastily added:

' And of course if I don't go home I might be a companion or look after children.'

' I wonder if Mrs Ottley—' began Aylmer. ' She has a dear little girl, and I've heard her say she would soon want someone.'

' Dilly?' said Dulcie, with a slight smile.

' Yes, Dilly.'

There was a moment of intense awkwardness between them. Then Dulcie said:

' I'm afraid that wouldn't quite do. I'm not clever enough.'

' Oh, rot. You know enough for a child like that. I shall speak to Mrs Ottley about it.'

' It's very, very kind of you, but I would rather not. I think I shall try to be a companion.'

' What's the name of that woman,' Aylmer said good-naturedly, ' that Irish woman, wife of one of the Cabinet Ministers, who came to the hospital at Boulogne and wanted to have lessons?'

' Lady Conroy,' Dulcie answered.

' Yes, Lady Conroy. Supposing that she needed a secretary or companion, would you dislike that?'

' Oh, no, I should like it very much.'

' Right. I'll get Mrs Ottley to speak to her about it. She said she was coming to London, didn't she?'

' Yes. I got to know her fairly well,' said Dulcie. ' She's very charming.'

' She's celebrated for her bad memory,' Aylmer said, with a smile. ' She declares she forgets her own name sometimes. Once she got into a taxi and told the man to drive home. When he asked where that was, she said it was his business to know. She had forgotten her address.'

They both laughed.

'I'll go tomorrow,' said Dulcie, 'and see my stepmother, if you don't want me in the afternoon. Or, perhaps, the day you go for a drive would be better.'

'Tell me, Miss Clay, aren't you happy at home?'

'Oh, it isn't that. They don't want me. I'm in the way. You see, they've got used to my being out of the house.'

'But, excuse me—you don't earn your own living really?'

'No, that isn't really necessary. But I don't want to live at home.'

Her face showed such a decided distaste to the idea that he said no more.

'You're looking very well today,' Dulcie said.

He sighed. 'I feel rather rotten. I can't read, can't settle to anything.'

She looked at him sympathetically. He felt impelled to go on.

'I'm a bit worried,' he continued.

'About your son?'

'No, not about him so much, though I wish he would get a flesh wound and be sent back,' his father said, laughing. 'But about myself.'

She looked at him in silence.

'You know—what I told you.'

She made no answer, looking away to give him time to speak.

'I've made a suggestion,' he said slowly. . . . 'If it's accepted it'll alter all my life. Of course I shall go out again. But still it will alter my life.'

Suddenly, overpowered by the longing for sympathy, he said to himself aloud.

'I wonder if there's a chance.'

'I don't know what it is,' she murmured, but instinctively she had guessed something of it.

'I don't want to think about it any more at present.'

'Shall I read to you?'

'Yes, do.'

She quietly arranged a pillow behind him and took up a newspaper.

He often liked her to read to him; he never listened to a word of it, but it was soothing.

She had taken up 'This Morning's Gossip' from *The Daily Mail*, and she began in the soft, low, distinct voice reading from The Rambler:

'Lord Redesdale says that when Lord Haldane's scheme for a Territorial Army was on foot he took it to the—'

Aylmer stopped her.

'No—not that.'

'Shall I read you a novel?'

'I think I should like to hear some poetry today,' he answered.

She had taken up a pretty, tiny little book that lay on his table, called *Lyrists of the Restoration*, and began to read aloud:

> *'Phyllis is my only joy,*
> *Faithless as the winds or seas,*
> *Sometimes cunning, sometimes coy,*
> *Yet she never fails to please.'*

'Oh, please, stop,' Aylmer cried.

She looked up.

'It tinkles like an old-fashioned musical-box. Try another.'

'What would you like?' she asked, smiling.

He took up a French book and passed it to her.

'You'll think I'm very changeable, but I should like this. Read me the beginning of *Là-Bas*.'

And she began.

He listened with his eyes closed, lulled by the curious technique, with its constant repetitions and jewelled style, charmed altogether. She read French fluently enough.

'That's delightful,' he said, but he soon noticed she was stumbling over the words. No, it was not suitable for her to read. He was obstinate, however, and was determined she should read him something.

So they fell back on *Northanger Abbey*.

CHAPTER XX

LADY CONROY had arrived home in Carlton House Terrace, complaining of a headache. She remained on the sofa in her sitting-room for about five minutes, during which time she believed she had been dozing. In reality she had been looking for her glasses, dropping her bag and ringing the bell to send a servant for a handkerchief.

She was a handsome woman of thirty-eight, with black hair turning a little grey, grey Irish eyes and a wonderfully brilliant complexion. She must have been a remarkably good-looking girl, but now, to her great vexation, she was growing a little too fat. She varied between treatments, which she scarcely began before she forgot them, and utter indifference to her appearance, when she declared she was much happier, letting herself go in loose gowns, and eating everything of which she had deprived herself for a day or two for the sake of her figure.

Lady Conroy had often compared herself to the old woman who lived in a shoe, because of her large family. Her friends declared she didn't remember how many children she had. She loved them, but there were certainly weeks when she didn't see the younger ones, for she was constantly absorbed in various different subjects. Besides, she spent most of her life in looking for things.

She was hopelessly careless and had no memory at all.

Suddenly she glanced at the watch on her wrist, compared it with the splendid Empire clock on the mantelpiece, and went with a be-wildered look to the telephone on her writing-desk. Having gone through a considerable amount of torture by calling up the wrong number and absently ringing off as soon as she had got the right one, she at last found herself talking to Edith.

'Oh, is that you, dear? How lucky to catch you! Yes. . . . Yes. . . . I came back yesterday. Dying to see you. Can't you come round and see me? Oh, you've got on your hat; you were just coming? Of course, I forgot! I knew I had an appointment with someone! How soon will you be here? . . . In a quarter of an hour? Good!

Could you tell me the time, dear? . . . Four o'clock, thanks. My watch is wrong, and they've never wound the clock up all the time I've been away. Good-bye. Don't be long. . . . How soon did you say you could come? . . . Oh, about a quarter of an hour! Do hurry! . . . I say, I've something very particular to tell you. It's about . . . Oh, I'm detaining you. Very well. I see. Au revoir.'

As she waited for her visitor, Lady Conroy walked round the room. Nearly everything on which she cast her eye reminded her of a different train of thought, so that by the time Edith was announced by the footman she had forgotten what she wanted to tell her.

' How sweet you look, dear!' cried Lady Conroy, welcoming her most affectionately. ' How dear of you to come. You can't think how I was longing to see you. Can you tell me what day it is?'

' Why, it's Thursday,' Edith said, laughing. ' Don't you remember? You wired to me to come and see you today.'

' Of course; so I did. But, surely, I didn't ask you to come on Thursday?'

' I assure you that you did.'

' Fancy! How stupid of me! Thursday is my day at home. Dear, dear, dear. I forgot to tell Standing; there will be no proper tea. Oh, I've brought such a nice French maid—a perfect wonder. She knows everything. She always knows what I want. One moment, dear; I'll ring for her and give her orders. Wait a minute, though.' She took Edith's hand and patted it affectionately. ' Nobody knows I've come back; it'll be all right. We sha'n't have any visitors. I'm bursting with news to tell you.'

' And I'm longing to hear what it is.'

Lady Conroy's charming, animated face became blank. She frowned slightly, and a vague look came into her eyes—the pathetic look of someone who is trying to remember.

' Wait a minute—what is it? Oh yes. You know that woman you introduced me to at Dieppe?'

' What woman?'

' Don't you know, dear? Good heavens, it was you who introduced her—you ought to know.'

' Do you mean Madame Frabelle?' asked Edith, who was accustomed to Lady Conroy, and could follow the drift of her mind.

'Capital! That's it. How wonderful of you! Yes, Madame Frabelle. How do you like her?'

'Very much. But I didn't introduce her to you. You sent her to me.'

'Did I? Well, it's very much the same. Look here, Edith dear. This is what I want to ask you. I remember now. Oh, do you mind ringing the bell for me? I must tell Marie about the tea, in case people call.'

Edith obeyed.

'You see, dear,' went on her hostess, 'I've undertaken a terrific number of things— Belgian refugees, weekly knitting, hundreds of societies—all sorts of war work. Well, you know how busy I am, even without all that, don't you? Thank heaven the boys are at school, but there are the children in the nursery, and I don't leave them—at least hardly ever—to their nurse. I look after them my-self—when I think of it. Oh, they've grown such heavenly angels— too sweet! And how's your pet, Dilly?'

'Very well. But do go on.'

'How right of you to keep me to the point, darling. That's where you're such a comfort always. Do you mind passing me my glasses? Thanks.'

She put them on and immediately took them off. She only needed them for reading.

'Oh yes. I wanted to consult you about something, Edith.'

The footman came in.

'Oh, Standing, send Marie to me at once. . . . Bother the man, how he keeps worrying! Well, Edith dear, as I've got all this tre-mendous lot of work to do, I've made up my mind, for the sake of my health, I simply must have a sort of secretary or companion. You see?'

'I quite see. You spoke of it before.'

'Well, how do you think that woman you introduced to me, Madame Frabelle—how do you think she would—? Oh, Marie, today's my day at home; isn't it, Edith?'

'Today is Thursday,' said Edith.

'Thursday! Oh, my dear. Thursday's not my day at home. Well, anyhow, never mind about that. What was I saying, Marie?'

Marie remained respectfully waiting, with a tight French smile on her intelligent face.

'Oh, I know what it was. Marie, I want you to look after certain things for me here—anyhow, at present. I want you to tell the cook that I want tea at four o'clock. Oh no, it's half-past four—well, at five. And there's something I particularly want for tea. What is it?' she asked, looking at Edith. Immediately answering herself she said: 'I know, I want muffins.'

'Madame want "nuffing"?' said Marie.

'No, no, no! Don't be so stupid. It's an English thing, Marie; you wouldn't understand. Something I've forgotten to tell the cook about. It's so cosy I always think in the winter in London. It always cheers me up. You know, what is it? . . . I know—muffins—*muffins!*' she said the word carefully to the French maid.

Edith came to the rescue.

'Tell the cook,' she said, 'for madame, that she wants some muffins for tea.'

'Oh, oui. Ah, oui, bien, madame. Merci, madame.'

As the maid was going away Lady Conroy called out:

'Oh, tell the cook it doesn't matter. I won't have them today.'

'Bien, madame.'

Edith was already in a somewhat hilarious mood. Lady Conroy didn't irritate her; she amused her almost more than any friend she had. Besides, once she could be got to concentrate on any one subject, nobody was more entertaining. Edith's English humour delighted in her friend's Irish wit.

There was something singularly Irish in the way Lady Conroy managed to make a kind of muddle and untidiness all round her, when she had been in a room a minute or two. When she had entered the room, it was a fine-looking apartment, rather sparsely furnished, with very little in it, all severest First Empire style. There were a few old portraits on striped pale green walls, and one large basket of hot-house flowers on a small table. Yet, since her entrance, the room already looked as if several people had been spending the week in it without tidying it up. Almost mechanically Edith picked up her bag, books, newspaper, cigarettes and the glasses.

'Well, then, you don't think Madame Frabelle would do?' said Lady Conroy.

'My dear Lady Conroy, Madame Frabelle wouldn't dream of going as a companion or secretary. You want a young girl. She's about fifteen years older than you are and she's staying with me as my guest. I shouldn't even suggest such a thing.'

' Why not? It wouldn't be at all a hard place.'

' No, I know. But she doesn't want a place. She's very well off, remember.'

' Good heavens, she can't have much to do then if she's only staying with you,' said Lady Conroy.

' Oh, she has plenty of engagements. No, I shouldn't advise Madame Frabelle. But I do know of someone.'

' Do you? Oh, darling Edith, how sweet of you. Oh, just ring the bell for me, will you?'

Edith rang.

' I want to send for Marie, my maid, and tell her to order some muffins for tea. I forgot to tell the cook.'

' But you have already ordered and countermanded them.'

' Oh, have I?—so I have! Never mind, don't ring. It doesn't matter. Who do you know, dear?'

Standing appeared in answer to the bell.

' What do you want, Standing? You mustn't keep bothering and interrupting me like this. Oh, tea? Yes, bring tea. And tell Marie I sha'n't want her after all.'

Lady Conroy leant back against her cushions and with a sigh went on:

' You see, I'm in the most terrible muddle, dear Edith. I don't know where to turn.'

She turned to her writing-table and opened it.

' Look at this, now,' she said rather triumphantly. ' This is all about my war work. Oh no, it isn't. It's an advertisement from a washer-woman. Gracious, ought I to keep it, do you think? No, I don't think I need.'

She folded it up and put it carefully away again.

' Don't you think yourself I need someone?'

' Yes, I do. I think it would be very convenient for you to have a nice girl with a good memory to keep your things in order.'

' That's it,' cried Lady Conroy, delighted, as she lit a cigarette. ' That's it—someone who will prevent me dropping cigarette ash all over the room and remember my engagements and help me with my war work and write my letters and do the telephoning. That's all I shall want. Of course, if she could do a little needlework—

No, no, that wouldn't do. You couldn't expect her to do brain-work as well as needlework.'

Edith broke in.

' Do you remember mentioning to me a girl you met at Boulogne —a nurse called Dulcie Clay?'

' Perfectly well,' answered Lady Conroy, puffing away at her cigarette, and obviously not speaking the truth.

Edith laughed.

' No, my dear, you don't. But it doesn't matter. Well, this girl has been nursing Mr Aylmer Ross, and he doesn't need her any more—at least he won't after next week. Would you see her and judge for yourself? You might try her.'

' I'm sure I shall if I take her. I'm afraid I'm a trying person. I try everyone dreadfully. Oh, by the way, Edith, I met such a perfect angel coming over. He was a wounded soldier. He belongs to the Black Watch. Doesn't the name Black Watch thrill you? He's in the Irish Guards, so, of course, my heart went out to him.'

' The Irish Guards as well?'

' Oh no. That was another man.'

She put her hand to her forehead.

' I'm worrying you, dear, with my bad memory. I'm so sorry. Well, then, you'll see Madame Frabelle for me?'

' I will if you like, but not as a companion. It's Miss Clay.'

' Miss Clay,' repeated Lady Conroy. ' Ah, here's tea. Do you take milk and sugar. Edith?'

' Let me pour it out,' said Edith, to whom it was maddening to see the curious things Lady Conroy did with the tea-tray. She was pouring tea into the sugar basin, looking up at Edith with the sweetest smile.

' I can't stay long,' Edith went on. ' I'm very sorry, dear, but you remember I told you I'm in a hurry. . . . I've an appointment at Landi's studio.'

' Landi? And who is that?'

' You know him—the composer—Sir Tito.'

' Oh, darling Sir Tito! Of course I do know him!' She smiled reminiscently. ' Won't you have anything to eat, dear? Do have a muffin! Oh, bother, there are none. I wonder how it is cook always forgets? Then you're going to send Madame Frabelle to see me the day after tomorrow?'

Edith took both her hands and shook them, laughing, as she stood up.

' I will arrange to send Miss Clay to see you, and if you like her, if you don't mind waiting about ten days or a fortnight, you might engage her. It would be doing her a great kindness. She's not happy at home.'

' Oh, poor girl !'

' And she went as a nurse,' continued Edith, ' chiefly because she couldn't think of anything else to do. She isn't really strong enough for nursing.'

' Isn't she? How sad, poor girl. It reminds me of a girl I met at Boulogne. So pretty and nice. In very much the same position really. She also wasn't happy at home—'

' This is the same girl,' said Edith. ' You wrote to me about her.'

' Did I? Good heavens, how extraordinary ! What a memory you've got, Edith. Well, then, she's sure to do.'

' Still, you'd better have an interview,' said Edith. ' Don't trouble to ring. I must fly, dear. We'll soon meet again.'

Lady Conroy followed her to the door into the hall, pouring forth questions, sympathy and cheerful communications about the charming young man in the Black Watch. Just before Edith escaped her friend said :

' Oh, by the by, I meant to ask you something. Who *is* Madame Frabelle?'

CHAPTER XXI

S I R T I T O lived in a flat in Mayfair, on the second floor of a large corner house. On the ground floor was his studio, which had two entrances. The studio was a large, square, white room, containing a little platform for pupils. A narrow shelf ran all the way round the dado; this shelf was entirely filled with the most charming collection of English and French china, little cottages, birds and figures. Above the shelf was a picture-rail, which again was filled all the way round with signed photographs of friends. Everything in the room was white, even the piano was *laqué* white, and the furniture, extremely luxurious and comfortable, was in colour a pale and yet dull pink. A curtain separated it from another smaller room, which again had a separate entrance into the hall on the left, and, through a very small dressing-room, led into the street on the right side.

Sir Tito was waiting for Edith, spick, span and debonair as always (although during the war he had discarded his button-hole). He was occupied, as he usually was in his leisure time, not in playing the piano or composing, but—in making photograph frames! This was his hobby, and people often said that he took more pleasure in the carving, cutting out, gumming and sticking together of these objects than in composing the melodies that were known and loved all over the world.

As soon as Edith came in he showed her a tiny frame carved with rosebuds.

'Regarde,' he said, his eyes beaming. 'Voilà! C'est mignon, n'est-ce-pas? On dirait un petit cœur! Ravissante, hein?' He gazed at it lovingly.

'Very sweet,' said Edith, laughing. 'Who is it for?'

'Why, it's for your *mignonne*, Dilly. I've cut out a photograph of hers in the shape of a heart. Gentil, n'est ce pas?'

He showed it to her with childish pleasure. Then he put all traces of the work carefully away in a drawer and drew Edith near to the fire.

'I've just a quarter of an hour to give you,' said Sir Tito, suddenly turning into a serious man of business. And, indeed, he always had many appointments, not a few of which were on some subject connected with love affairs. Like Aylmer, but in a different way, Sir Tito was always being consulted, but, oddly enough, while it was the parents and guardians usually who went to Aylmer, husbands worried about their wives, mothers about their children; to the older man it was more frequently the culprit or the confidant himself or herself who came to confide and ask for help and advice.

Edith said:

'The dreadful thing I've to tell you, Landi, is that I've completely changed.'

'Comment?'

'Yes. I'm in love with him all over again.'

'C'est vrai?'

'Yes. I don't know how and I don't know why. When he first made that suggestion, it seemed wild—impossible. But the things he said—how absolutely true it is. Landi, my life's been wasted, utterly wasted.'

Landi said nothing.

'I believe I was deceiving myself,' she went on. 'I've got so accustomed to living this sort of half life I've become almost abrutie, as you would say. I didn't realise how much I cared for him. Now I know I always adored him.'

'But you were quite contented.'

'Because I made myself so; because I resolved to be satisfied. But, after all, there's something in what he says, Landi. My life with Bruce is only a makeshift. Nothing but tact, tact, tact. Oh, I'm so tired of tact!' She sighed. 'It seems to me now really too hard that I should again have such a great opportunity and should throw it away. You see, it is an opportunity, if I love him—and I'm not deceiving myself now. I'm in love with him. The more I think about it the more lovely it seems to me. It would be an ideal life, Landi.'

He was still silent.

She continued:

'You see, Aylmer knows so well how much the children are to me, and he would never ask me to leave them. There's no question of my ever leaving them. And Bruce wouldn't mind. Bruce would be only too thankful for me to take them. And there's another thing—though I despised the idea at the time, there's a good deal in it. I mean that Aylmer's well off, so I should never be a burden. He would love to take the responsibility of us all. I would leave my income to Bruce; he would be quite comfortable and independent. Oh, he would take it. He might be a little cross, but it wouldn't last, Landi. He would be better off. He'd find somebody—someone who would look after him, perhaps, and make him quite happy and comfortable. You're shocked?'

'Ça ne m'étonne pas. It's the reaction,' said Landi, nodding.

'How wonderful of you to understand! I haven't seen him again, you know. I've just been thinking. In fact, I'm surprised at myself. But the more I reflect on what he said, the more wonderful it seems. . . . Think how he's cared for me all this time!'

'Sans doute. You know that he adores you. But, Edith, it's all very well—you put like that—but could you go through with it?'

'I believe I could now,' she answered. 'I begin to long to. You see, I mistook my own feelings, Landi; they seemed dulled. I thought I could live without love—but why should I? What is it that's made me change so? Why do I feel so frightened now at the idea of losing my happiness?'

'C'est la guerre,' said Sir Tito.

'The war? What has that to do with it?'

'Everything. Unconsciously it affects people. Though you yourself are not fighting, Aylmer has risked his life, and is going to risk it again. This impresses you. To many temperaments things seem to matter less just now. People are reckless.'

'Is it that?' asked Edith. 'Perhaps it is. But I was so completely deceived in myself.'

'I always knew you could be in love with him,' said Landi. 'But wait a moment, Edith—need the remedy be so violent? I don't ask you to live without love. Why should a woman live without the very thing she was created for? But you know you hate publicity—vulgar scandal. Nobody loathes it as you do.'

'It doesn't seem to matter now so much,' Edith said.

'It's the war.'

'Well, whatever's the cause, all I can tell you is that I'm begin-

ning to think I *shall* do it! I want to! . . . I can't bear to refuse
again. I haven't seen him since our talk. I changed gradually, alone,
just thinking. And then you say—'

'Many people have love in their lives without a violent public
scandal,' he repeated.

'Yes, I know. I understand what you mean. But I hate deceit,
Landi. I don't think I could lead a double life. And even if I would,
he wouldn't!'

She spoke rather proudly.

'Pauvre garçon!' said Sir Tito. 'Je l'admire.'

'So do I,' said Edith. 'Aylmer's not a man who could shake
hands with Bruce and be friends and deceive him. And you know,
before, when I begged him to remain . . . my friend . . . he simply
wouldn't. He always said he despised the man who would accept
the part of a tame cat. And he doesn't believe in Platonic friendship: Aylmer's too honest, too *real* for that.'

'But, Edith, oh, remember, before,' said Landi taking her hand,
'even when Bruce ran away with another woman, you couldn't
bear the idea of divorce.'

'I know. But I may have been wrong. Besides, I didn't care for
him as I do now. And I'm older now.'

'Isn't this rather sudden, my dear?'

'Only because I've let myself go—let myself be natural! Oh,
do encourage me—give me strength, Landi! Don't let me be a
coward! Think if Aylmer goes out again and is killed, how miserable I should feel to have refused him and disappointed him—for
the second time!'

'Wait a moment, Edith. Suppose, as you say, he goes out again
and is killed, and you *haven't* disappointed him, what would your
position be then?'

She couldn't answer.

'How is it your conscientiousness with regard to Bruce doesn't
come in the way now? Why would it ruin him less now than
formerly?'

'Bruce doesn't seem to matter so much.'

'Because he isn't fighting?' asked Sir Tito.

'Oh no, Landi! I never thought of that. But you know he always
imagines himself ill, and he's quite all right really. He'll enjoy his
grievance. I *know* he won't be unhappy. And he's older, and he's

not tied to that silly, mad girl he ran away with. And besides, *I'm*
older. This is probably *my* last chance!'

She looked at Landi imploringly, as if begging his permission.

He answered calmly: 'Écoute, chérie. When do you see him
again?'

'I'm to take him for a drive tomorrow.'

'My dear Edith, promise me one thing; don't undertake anything
yet.'

'But why not?'

'You mustn't. This may be merely an impulse; you may change
again. It may be a passing mood.'

'I don't think it is,' said Edith. 'Anyhow, it's my wish at present.
It's the result of thinking, remember—not of his persuasion.'

'Go for a drive, but give him no hope yet.' He took both her
hands. 'Make no promise, except to me. Don't I know you well? I
doubt if you could do it.'

'Yes, I could! I could go through *anything* if I were determined,
and if I had the children safe.'

'Never mind that for the present. Live for the day. Will you
promise me that?'

She hesitated for a moment.

Then he said:

'Really, dear, it's too serious to be impulsive about. Take
time.'

'Very well, Landi. I promise you that.'

'Then we'll meet again afterwards and talk it over. I'll come
and see you.'

'Very well. And mustn't I tell him anything? Not make him a
little bit happy?'

'Tell him nothing. Be nice to him. Enjoy your drive. Put off all
decision at present.'

He looked at her. Her eyes were sparkling, her colour, her expression were deepened. She looked all animation, with more life
than he had ever seen in her. . . . Somehow the sight made his
heart ache a little, a very little.

Poor girl! Of course she had been starving for love, and hidden
the longing under domestic interests, artistic, social, but human. But
she deserved real love, a real lover. She was so loyal, so true
herself.

'Tiens! You look like a lamp that has been lighted,' said Sir Tito, chuckling a little to himself. 'Eh, bien!—and the pretty nurse? Does she still dance the Cachuca? I know I'm old-fashioned, but it's impossible for me not to associate everything Spanish with the ridiculous. I think of guitars, mantillas, sombreros, or—what else is it? Ah, I know—onions.'

'She isn't even Spanish, really!'

'Then why did you deceive me?' said Landi, a shade absently, with a glance at his watch and another in the mirror.

'She can't remain with Aylmer. She knows it herself. I'm trying to arrange for her to become a companion for Lady Conroy.'

He laughed.

'You are more particular about her being chaperoned than you were last week.'

'Landi, Aylmer will never care for her. She's a dear, but he won't.'

'Tu ne l'a pas revu? Lui—Aylmer?'

'No, but he's written to me.'

'Oh, for heaven's sake, my child, burn the letters! I daresay it won't be difficult; they are probably all flames already.'

'I did have one lovely letter,' said Edith.

She took it out of her dress. He glanced at it.

'Mon Dieu! To think that a pupil of mine drives about in a taxi-cab with compromising letters in her pocket! Non, tu est folle, véritablement, Edith.'

To please him she threw it into the fire, after tearing a small blank piece of the paper off, and putting this unwritten-on scrap back in the bodice of her dress. As she hurried away, she again promised him not to undertake anything, nor to allow Aylmer to overpower her prudent intention during their drive.

'What time do you start? I think I shall come too,' said Sir Tito, pretending to look at his engagement-book.

He burst out laughing at her expression.

'Ah, I'm not wanted! Tiens! If you're not very careful *one* person will go with you, I can tell you. And that will be Madame Frabelle.'

'No, she won't. Indeed not! It's the last day of Archie's holidays.'

'He's coming with you?'

'On the front seat, with the chauffeur,' said Edith.

There was a ring at the bell. He lifted the curtain and caressingly but firmly pushed her through into the other room.

Sir Tito had another appointment.

CHAPTER XXII

W H I L E this drama was taking place in the little house in Sloane Street, Madame Frabelle, who lived for romance, and was always imagining it where it didn't exist, was, of course, sublimely unconscious of its presence. She had grown tired of her fancy about Edith and Mr Mitchell, or she made herself believe that her influence had stopped it. But she was beginning to think, much as she enjoyed her visit and delighted in her surroundings, that it was almost time for her at least to *suggest* going away.

She had made Edith's friends her own. She was devoted to Edith, fonder of the children than anyone except their grandmother, and strangely, considering she was a visitor who gave trouble, she was adored by the servants and by everyone in the house, with the single exception of Archie.

She was carrying on a kind of half-religious flirtation with the Rev. Byrne Fraser, who was gradually succeeding in making her very high church. Sometimes she rose early and left the house mysteriously. She went to Mass. There was a dreamy expression in her eyes when she came back. A slight perfume of incense, instead of the lavender water that she formerly affected, was now observable about her.

She went to see the 'London Group' and the 'New English' with young Coniston, who explained to her all he had learnt from Aylmer, a little wrong; while she assured him that she knew nothing about pictures, but she knew what she liked.

She bought book-bindings from Miss Coniston, and showed her how to cook macaroni and how to make cheap but unpalatable soup for her brother. And she went to all the war concerts and bazaars got up by Valdez, to meetings for the Serbians arranged by Mrs Mitchell and to Lady Conroy's Knitting Society for the Refugees. She was a very busy woman. But it was not these employments that were filling her mind as she sat in her own room, looking seriously at herself in the glass. Something made her a little preoccupied.

She was beginning to fear that Bruce was getting too fond of her.

The moment the idea occurred to her, it occurred to Bruce also. She had a hypnotic effect on him; as soon as she thought of anything he thought of it too. Something in her slight change of manner, her cautious way of answering, and of rustling self-consciously out of the room when they were left alone together, had this effect. Bruce was enchanted. Madame Frabelle thought he was getting too fond of her! Then, he must be! Perhaps he was. He certainly didn't like the idea at all of her going away and changed the subject directly she mentioned it. He had always thought her a very wonderful person. He was immensely impressed by her universal knowledge and agreeable manners and general charm. Still, Madame Frabelle was fifteen years older than Bruce, and Bruce himself was no chicken. Although he was under forty, his ideal of himself was that he liked only very young girls. This was not true. But as he thought it was, it became very much the same thing. As a matter of fact, only rather foolish girls were flattered at attentions from Bruce. Married women preferred spirited bachelors, and attractive girls preferred attractive boys. In fact, Bruce was not wanted socially, and he felt a little bit out of it among the men through not being among the fighters. The fact that he told everyone that he was not in khaki because he was in consumption didn't seem to make him more interesting to the general public. His neurotic heart bored his friends at the club. In fact there was not a woman, even his mother, except Madame Frabelle, who cared to listen to his symptoms. That she did so, and with sympathy, was one of her attractions.

But as long as she had listened to them in a sisterly, friendly way, he regarded her only as a friend—a friend of whom he was very proud, and whom he respected immensely. As has been said, she impressed him so much that he did not know she bored him. When she began rustling out of the room when they were left alone, and looking away, avoiding his eye when he stared at her absently, things were different, and he began to feel rather flattered. Of course it would be an infernal shame, and not the act of a gentleman, to take advantage of one's position as a host by making love to a fascinating guest. But there was so much sympathy between them! It is only fair to say that the idea would never have occurred to Bruce unless it had first occurred to Madame Frabelle.

If a distinguished-looking woman in violet velvet leaves the room five minutes after she's left alone with one—even though she has grey hair—it naturally shows that she thinks one is dangerous. The result of it all was that when Bruce heard Edith was taking Aylmer for a drive, he apologised very much indeed for not going with her. He said, frankly, much as he liked Aylmer, wounded heroes were rather a bore. He hoped Aylmer would forgive him. And Madame Frabelle had promised to take him to the Oratory. She disapproved of his fancy of becoming a Catholic; she was not one herself, though she was extremely high, and growing daily higher, but the music at the Oratory on that particular day was very wonderful, and they agreed to go there. And afterwards—well, afterwards they might stroll home, or—go and have tea in Bond Street.

It was the last day of Archie's holidays, and though it was rather cold his mother insisted on taking him with her.

Aylmer tried to hide the shade that came over his face when he saw the boy, but remembering that he had undertaken to be a father to him, he cheered up as soon as Archie was settled.

It was a lovely autumn day, one of those warm Indian-summer days that resemble early spring. There is the same suggestion of warmer sunshine yet to come; the air has a scent as of growing things, the kind of muffled hopes and suppressed excitement of April is in the deceptive air. This sort of day is dangerous to charming people not in their very first youth.

In high spirits and beyond the speed limit they started for Richmond.

CHAPTER XXIII

A WEEK later Aylmer and his son were sitting looking at each other in the old brown library. Teddy had come over for ten days' leave from somewhere in France. Everyone, except his father, was astonished how little he had changed. He seemed exactly the same, although he had gone through strange experiences. But Aylmer saw a different look in his eyes. He looked well and brisk—perhaps a little more developed and more manly; his shoulders, always rather thick and broad, seemed even broader, although he was thinner. But it was the expression of the eyes that had altered. Those eyes had *seen things*. In colour pale blue, they had a slightly strained look. They seemed paler. His sunburn increased his resemblance to his father, always very striking. Both had large foreheads, clearly cut features and square chins. Aylmer was, strictly speaking, handsomer. His features more refined, more chiselled. But Teddy had the additional charm of extreme youth—youth with the self-possession and ease that seemed, as it were, a copy—as his voice was an echo—of his father. The difference was in culture and experience. Teddy had gone out when he was just on the point of going to Balliol, yet seemed to have something of the Oxford manner, characteristic of his father—a manner suave, amiable, a little ironical. He had the unmistakable public-school look and his training had immensely improved his appearance.

Aylmer was disappointed that the very first thing his son insisted on doing was to put on evening clothes and go to the Empire. That was where the difference in age told. Aylmer would not have gone to the Empire fresh from the fighting line. He made no objection, and concealed the tiniest ache that he felt when Teddy went out at once with Major Willis, an elder friend of his. Quite as old, Aylmer thought to himself, as *he* was. But not being a relative, he seemed of the same generation.

The next evening Teddy spent at home, and sat with his father, who declared himself to be completely recovered, but was still not allowed to put his foot to the ground, Miss Clay was asked to sing to them. Her voice, as has been said, was a very beautiful one, a clear, fine soprano, with a timbre rare in quality, and naturally thrilling. She had not been taught well enough to be a public success perhaps, but was much more accomplished than the average amateur.

Teddy delighted in it. She sang all the popular songs—she had a way that was almost humorous of putting refinement into the stupidest and vulgarest melody. And then she sang some of those technically poor but attaching melodies that, sung in a certain way, without sickening sentimentality or affectation, seem to search one's soul and bring out all that there is in one of romance.

She looked very beautiful, that Aylmer admitted to himself, and she sang simply and charmingly; that he owned also. Why did it irritate him so intensely to see Teddy moved and thrilled, to see his eyes brighten, his colour rise and to see him obviously admiring the girl? When she made an excuse to leave them Teddy was evidently quite disappointed.

The next day Aylmer limped down to the library. To his great surprise he heard voices in the room Dulcie used for her sitting-room. He heard Teddy begging her to sing to him again. He heard her refuse and then Teddy's voice asking her to go out to tea with him.

Aylmer limped as loudly as he could, and they evidently heard him, but didn't mind in the least. He didn't want Miss Clay to stop at home. He was expecting Edith.

'Hang it, let them go!' he said to himself, and he wondered at himself. Why should he care? Why *shouldn't* she flirt with the boy if she liked, or rather—for he was too just not to own that it was no desire of hers—why shouldn't the boy make up to her? Whatever the reason was, it annoyed him.

Annoyance was soon forgotten when Mrs Ottley was announced.

Since their drive to Richmond there had been a period of extraordinary happiness and delight for Edith. Not another word had been said with reference to Aylmer's proposal. He left it in abeyance, for he saw to his great joy and delight that she was becoming her old self, more than her old self.

Edith was completely changed. The first thing she thought of now in the morning was how soon she should see him again. She managed to conceal it well, but she was nervous, absent, with her eyes always on the clock, counting the minutes. When other people were present she was cool and friendly to Aylmer, but when they were alone he had become intimate, delightful, familiar, like the time, three years ago, when they were together at the seaside. But her mother-in-law had then been in the house. And the children. Everything was so conventional. Now she was able to see him alone. Really alone. . . . His eyes welcomed her as she came in. Having shut the door quietly, she reached his chair in a little rush.

'Don't take off your hat. I like that hat. That was the hat you wore the day I told you—'

'I'm glad it suits me,' she said, interrupting. 'Does it really? Isn't it too small?'

'You know it does.'

He was holding her hand. He slowly took off the glove, saying: 'What a funny woman you are, Edith. Why do you wear grey gloves? Nobody else wears grey gloves.'

'I prefer white ones, but they won't stay white two minutes.'

'I like these.'

'Tell me about Teddy. Don't, Aylmer!'

Aylmer was kissing her fingers one by one. She drew them away.

'Teddy! Oh, there's not much to tell.' Then he gave a little laugh. 'I believe he's fallen in love with Miss Clay.'

'Has he really? Well, no wonder; think how pretty she is.'

'I know. Is she? I don't think she's a bit pretty.'

'She's to see Lady Conroy tomorrow, you know,' Edith said, divining an anxiety or annoyance in Aylmer on the subject.

'Yes. Will it be all right?'

'Oh yes.'

'Well, Teddy's going back on Monday anyway, and I certainly don't need a nurse any more. Headley will do all I want.'

Headley was the old butler.

'What scent do you use, Edith?'

'I hardly ever use any. I don't care for scent.'

'But lately you have,' he insisted. 'What is it? I think I like it.'

'It's got a silly name. It's called Omar Khayyám.'

'I thought it was Oriental. I think you're Oriental, Edith. Though you're so fair and English-looking. How do you account for it?'

'I can't think,' said Edith.

'Perhaps you're a fair Circassian,' said he. 'Do you think your-self you're Oriental?'

'I believe I am, in some ways. I like lying down on cushions. I like cigarettes, and scent, and flowers. I hate wine, and exercise, and cricket, and bridge.'

'That isn't all that's needed. You wouldn't care for life in a harem, would you?' He laughed. 'You with your independent mind and your cleverness.'

'Perhaps not exactly, but I can imagine worse things.'

'I shall take you to Egypt,' he said. 'You've never been there, have you?'

'Never.' Her eyes sparkled.

'Yes, I shall take you to see the Sphinx. For the first time.'

'Oh, you can't. You're looking very well, Aylmer, wonderfully better.'

'I wonder why? You don't think I'm happy, do you?'

'I am,' said Edith.

'Because you're a woman. You live for the moment. I'm anxious about the future.'

'Oh, oh! You're quite wrong. It's not women who live for the moment,' said Edith.

'No, I don't know that the average woman does. But then you're not an average woman.'

'What am I?'

'You're Edith,' he answered, rather fatuously. But she liked it, She moved away.

'Now that's awfully mean of you, taking advantage of my wounded limb.'

She rang for tea.

'And that's even meaner. It's treacherous,' he said, laughing.

She sat down on a chair at a little distance.

'Angel!' he said, in a low, distinct voice.

'It is not for me to dictate,' said Edith, in a tone of command, · but I should think it more sensible of you not to say these things to me—just now.'

The servant came in with tea.

CHAPTER XXIV

JUST before Archie went back to school he made a remark that impressed Edith strangely. Quite dressed and ready to start, as he was putting on his gloves, he fell into one of his reveries. After being silent for some time he said:

'Mother!'

'Yes, darling?'

'Why doesn't father fight?'

'I told you before, darling. Your father is not very strong.'

'Mother!'

'Yes, dear?'

'Is Aylmer older than father?'

'Yes. Aylmer's four years older. Why?'

'I don't know. I wish I had a father who could fight, like Aylmer. And I'd like to fight too, like Teddy.'

'Aylmer hasn't any wife and children to leave. Teddy's eighteen; you're only ten.'

'Mother!'

'Yes, dear?'

'I wish I was old enough to fight. And I wish father was stronger. . . . Do you think I shall ever fight in this war?'

'Good heavens, dear! I hope it isn't going to last seven years more.'

'I wish it would,' said Archie ferociously. 'Mother!'

'Yes, darling?'

'But what's the *matter* with father? He seems quite well.'

'Oh, he isn't very well. He suffers from nerves.'

'Nerves! What's nerves?'

'I think, darling, it's time for us to start. Where's your coat?'

She drove him to the station. Most of the way he was very silent. As she put him in the train he said.

'Mother, give my love to Aylmer.'

'All right, dear.'

He then said:

'Mother, I wish Aylmer was my father.'
'Oh, Archie! You mustn't say that.'

But she never forgot the boy's remark. It had a stronger influence on her action later than anything else. She knew Archie had always had a great hero-worship for Aylmer. But that he should actually prefer him to Bruce!

She didn't tell Aylmer that for a long time afterwards.

Before returning to the front Teddy had become so violently devoted to Miss Clay that she was quite glad to see him go. She received his attentions with calm and cool friendliness, but gave him not the smallest encouragement. She was three years older, but looked younger than her age, while Teddy looked much older, more like twenty-two. So that when on the one or two occasions during his ten days' leave they went out together, they didn't seem at all an ill-assorted couple. And whenever Aylmer saw the two together, it created the greatest irritation in him. He hardly knew which vexed him more—Dulcie for being attractive to the boy, or the boy for being charmed by Dulcie. It was absurd—out of place. It displeased him.

A day or two after Teddy's departure Dulcie went to see Lady Conroy, who immediately declared that Dulcie was extraordinarily like a charming girl she had met at Boulogne. Dulcie convinced her that she was the same girl.

'Oh, how perfectly charming!' said Lady Conroy. 'What a coincidence! *Too* wonderful! Well, my dear, I can see at a glance that you're the very person I want. Your duties will be very, *very* light. Oh, how light they will be! There's really hardly anything to do! I merely want you to be a sort of walking memorandum for me,' Lady Conroy went on, smiling. 'Just to recollect what day it is, and what's the date, and what time my appointments are, and do my telephoning for me, and write my letters, and take the dog out for a walk, and *sometimes* just hear my little girls practise, and keep my papers in order. Oh, one can hardly say exactly—you know the sort of thing. Oh yes! and do the flowers,' said Lady Conroy, glancing round the room. 'I always forget my flowers, and I won't let Marie do them, and so there they are—dead in the vases! And I do like a few live flowers about, I must say,' she added pathetically.

Dulcie said she thought she could undertake it.

'Well, then, won't you stay now, and have your things sent straight on? Oh, do! I do wish you would. I've got two stalls for the St James's tonight. My husband can't come, and I can't think of anybody else to ask. I should love to take you.'

Dulcie would have enjoyed to go. The theatre was a passion with her, as with most naïve people. She made some slight objection which Lady Conroy at once waved away. However, Dulcie pointed out that she must go home first, and as all terms and arrangements absolutely suited both parties, it was decided that Dulcie should go to the play with her tonight and come the next day to take up her duties.

She asked Lady Conroy if she might have her meals alone when there were guests, as she was very shy. A charming little sitting-room, opening out of the drawing-rooms, was put at her disposal.

'Oh, certainly, dear; always, of course, except when I'm alone. But you'll come when I ask you, now and then, won't you? I thought you'd be very useful sometimes at boring lunches, or when there were too many men—that sort of thing. And I hear you sing. Oh, that will be delightful! You'll sing when we have a few tedious people with us? I adore music. We'll go to some of those all-British concerts, won't we? We must be patriotic. Do you know it's really been my dream to have a sweet, useful, sympathetic girl in the house. And with a memory too! Charming!'

Dulcie went away fascinated, if slightly bewildered. It was a pang to her to say good-bye to Aylmer, the more so as he showed, in a way that was perfectly obvious to the girl, that he was pleased to see her go, though he was as cordial as possible.

She had been an embarrassment to him of late. It was beginning to be what is known as a false position, since Headley the butler could now look after Aylmer. Except for a limp, he was practically well.

Anyone who has ever nursed a person to whom they are devoted, helped him through weakness and danger to health again, will understand the curious pain she felt to see him independent of her, anxious to show his strength. Still, he had been perfect. She would always remember him with worship. She meant never to love anyone else all her life.

When she said good-bye she said to him:

'I do hope you'll be very happy.'

He laughed, coloured a little, and said as he squeezed her hand warmly:

'You've been a brick to me, Miss Clay. I shall certainly tell you if I ever am happy.'

She wondered what that meant, but she preferred to try to forget it.

When Dulcie arrived, as she had been told, at a quarter to eight, dressed in a black evening dress (she didn't care to wear uniform at the theatre), she found Lady Conroy, who was lying on the sofa in a tea-gown, utterly astonished to see her.

'My dear! you've come to dine with me after all?'

'No, indeed. I've dined. You said I was to come in time to go to the play.'

'The play? Oh! I forgot. I'm so sorry. I've sent the tickets away. I forgot I'd anyone to go with me. I'm afraid it can't be helped now. Are you very disappointed? Poor child. Well, dear, you'll dine with me, anyhow, as you've come, and I can tell you all about what we shall have to do, and everything. We'll go to the theatre some other evening.'

Dulcie was obliged to decline eating two dinners. She had not found it possible to get through one—her last meal at Aylmer's house. However, as she had no idea what else to do, she remained with Lady Conroy. And she spent a very pleasant evening.

Lady Conroy told her all about herself, her husband, her children and her friends. She told her the history of her life, occasionally branching off on to other subjects, and referring to the angel she had met on a boat who was in the Black Watch, and who, Dulcie gathered, was a wounded officer. Lady Conroy described all the dresses she had at present, many that she had had in former years, and others that she would like to have had now. She gravely told the girl the most inaccurate gossip about such of her friends as Dulcie might possibly meet later. She was confidential, amusing, brilliant and inconsequent. She appeared enchanted with Dulcie, whom she treated like an intimate friend at sight. And Dulcie was charmed with her, though somewhat confused at her curious memory. Indeed, they parted at about eleven the best possible friends; Lady Conroy insisting on sending her home in her car.

Dulcie, who had a sensitive and sensible horror of snobbishness, felt sorry to know that her father would casually mention that his daughter was staying with the Conroys in Carlton House Terrace, and that her stepmother would scold her unless she recollected every dress she happened to see there. Still, on the whole she felt cheered.

She had every reason to hope that she would be as happy as a companion, in love without hope of a return, could be under any circumstances.

CHAPTER XXV

MADAME FRABELLE and Edith were sitting side by side in Edith's boudoir. Madame Frabelle was knitting. Edith was looking at a book. It was a thin little volume of essays, bound by Miss Coniston.

'What is the meaning of this design?' Edith said. 'It seems to me very unsuited to Chesterton's work! Olive-green, with twirly things on it!'

'I thought it rather artistic,' answered Madame Frabelle.

'It looks like macaroni, or spaghetti. Perhaps the idea was suggested by your showing her how to cook it,' said Edith, laughing.

Madame Frabelle looked gravely serene.

'No—I don't think that had anything to do with it.'

'How literal you are, Eglantine!'

'Am I? I think you do me injustice, Edith dear,' returned the amiable guest with a tinge of stateliness as she rolled up her wool.

Edith smiled, put down her book, looked at the clock and re-arranged the large orange-coloured cushion behind her back. Then she took the book up again, looked through it and again put it down.

'You're not at all—forgive me for saying so—not the least bit in the world restless today, Edith darling, are you?' said Madame Frabelle in a calm, clear, high voice that Edith found quite trying.

'Oh, I hope not—I think not.'

'Ah, that's well,' and Madame Frabelle, with one slight glance at her hostess, went on knitting.

'I believe I miss Archie a good deal,' said Edith.

'Ah, yes, you must indeed. I miss the dear boy immensely myself,' sympathetically said Madame Frabelle. But Edith thought Madame Frabelle bore his loss with a good deal of equanimity, and she owned to herself that it was not surprising. The lady had been very good to Archie, but he had teased her a good deal. Like the Boy Scouts, but the other way round, he had almost made a point of worrying her in some way or other every day. Edith could never persuade him to change his view of her.

He said she was a fool.

Somehow, today Edith felt rather pleased with him for thinking so. All women are subject to moods, particularly, perhaps, those who have a visitor staying with them for a considerable time. There are moments of injustice, of unfairness to the most charming feminine guest, from the most gentle hostess. And also there are, undoubtedly, times when the nicest hostess gets a little on one's nerves.

So—critical, highly strung—Madame Frabelle was feeling today. So was Edith. Madame Frabelle was privately thinking that Edith was restless, that she had lost her repose, that her lips were redder than they used to be. Had she taken to using lip salve too? She was inclined to smile, with a twinkle in her eye, at Madame Frabelle's remarks, a shade too often. And what was Edith thinking of at this moment? She was thinking of Archie's remarks about Madame Frabelle. That boy had genius!

But there would be a reaction, probably during, or immediately after, tea-time, for these two women were sincerely fond of one another. The irritating fact that Edith was eighteen years younger than her guest made Eglantine feel sometimes a desire to guide, even to direct her, and if she had the disadvantage in age she wanted at least the privilege of gratifying her longing to give advice.

The desire became too strong to be resisted The advantage of having something to do with her hands while she spoke was too great a one not to be taken advantage of. So Madame Frabelle said:

'Edith dear.'

'Yes?'

'I've been wanting to say something to you.'

Edith leant forward, putting her elbows on her knees and her face on her hands, and said:

'Oh, *do* tell me, Eglantine. What is it?'

'It is simply this,' said the other lady, calmly continuing her knitting. . . . 'Very often when one's living with a person, one doesn't notice little things a comparative stranger would observe. Is that not so?'

'What have you observed? What's it about?'

'It is about your husband,' said Madame Frabelle.

'What! Bruce?' asked Edith.

'Naturally,' replied Madame Frabelle dryly.

'What have you observed about Bruce?'

'I have observed,' replied Madame Frabelle, putting her hand in the sock that she was knitting, and looking at it critically, her head on one side, 'I have observed that Bruce is not at all well.'

'Oh, I'm sorry you think that. It's true he has seemed rather what he calls off colour lately.'

'He suffers,' said Madame Frabelle, as if announcing a great discovery, 'he suffers from Nerves.'

'I know he does, my dear. Who should know it better than I do? But—do you think he is worse lately?'

'I do. He is terribly depressed. He says things to me sometimes that—well, that really quite alarm me.'

'I'm sorry. But you mustn't take Bruce too seriously, you know that.'

'Indeed I don't take him too seriously! And I've done my best either to change the subject or to make him see the silver lining to every cloud,' Madame Frabelle answered solmenly, with a shake of her head.

'I think what Bruce complains of is the want of a silver lining to his purse,' Edith said.

'You are jesting, Edith dear.'

'No, I'm not. He worries about money.'

'But only incidentally,' said Madame Frabelle. 'Bruce is really worried about the war.'

'Naturally. But surely— I suppose we all are.'

'But Mr Ottley takes it particularly to heart,' said Madame Frabelle, with a kind of touching dignity.

Edith looked at her in a little surprise Why did she suddenly call Bruce 'your husband' or 'Mr Ottley'?

'Why this distant manner, Eglantine?' said Edith, half laughing. 'I thought you always called him Bruce.'

'I beg your pardon; yes, I forgot. Well, don't you see, Edith dear, that what we might call his depression, his melancholy point of view, is—is growing worse and worse?'

Edith got up, walked to the other end of the room, rearranged

some violets in a copper vase and came back to the sofa again.
Madame Frabelle followed her with her eyes. Then Edith said,
picking up the knitting:

'Take care, dear, you're losing your wool. Yes; perhaps he *is*
worse. He might be better if he occupied his mind more.'

'He works at the Foreign Office from ten till four every day,' said
Madame Frabelle in a tone of defence; 'he looks in at his club,
where they talk over the news of the war, and then he comes home
and we discuss it again. . . . Really, Edith, I scarcely see how much
more he could do!'

'Oh, my dear, but don't you see all the time he doesn't *do* anything?—anything about the war, I mean. Now both you and I do
our little best to help, in one way or another. You especially, I'm
sure, do a tremendous lot; but what does Bruce do? Nothing, except
talk.'

'That's just it, Edith. I doubt if your husband is in a fit state of
health to strain his mind by any more work than he does already.
He's not strong, dear; remember that.'

'Of course, I know; if he were all right he wouldn't be here,' said
Edith. 'I suppose he really does suffer a great deal.'

'What was it again that prevented him joining?' asked Madame
Frabelle, with sympathetic tenderness.

'Neurotic heart,' answered Edith. Though she tried her very
utmost she could not help the tone of her voice sounding a little dry
and ironical. Of course, she did not in the least believe in Bruce's
neurotic heart, but she did not want Madame Frabelle to know
that.

'Ah! ah! that must cause him a great deal of pain, but I think
so far his worst symptoms are his nervous fears. Look at last night,'
continued Madame Frabelle, and now she put down her knitting
and folded it into her work-basket. 'Last night, because there was
no moon, and it wasn't raining, and fairly clear, Mr Ott—Bruce
had absolutely made up his mind there would be a Zeppelin raid.
It was his own idea.'

'Not quite, dear. Young Coniston, who is a special constable,
rang up and told him that there was a chance of the Zeppelins last
night.'

'Well, perhaps so. At any rate he believed it. Well, instead of
being satisfied when I told him that I had got out my mask, that

I saw to the bath being left half-filled with water, helped your husband to put two large bags of sand outside his dressing-room— in spite of all that, do you know what happened in the middle of the night?'

'I'm afraid I don't,' said Edith. 'Since Archie went back to school I have had Dilly in my room, and we both slept soundly all night.'

'Did you? I fancied I saw a light in your room.'

This was quite true. Edith was writing a very long letter.

'Ah, perhaps.'

'Well, at three o'clock in the morning, fancy my surprise to hear a knock at my door!'

'I wonder I didn't hear a knock at mine,' said Edith.

'Your husband was afraid to disturb the little girl. Most considerate, I thought. Well, he knocked at my door and said that he was unable to sleep, that he felt terribly miserable and melancholy, in fact was wretched, and that he felt on the point of cutting his throat. . . . Don't be frightened, dear. I don't mean that he really *meant* it,' said Madame Frabelle, putting her hand on Edith's.

'Poor fellow! But what a shame to disturb you.'

'I didn't mind in the least. I was only too pleased. Well, what do you think I did? I got up and dressed, went down to the library and lighted the fire, and sat up for half-an-hour with your husband trying to cheer him up!'

'Did you really?' Edith smiled. 'It was very sweet of you, Eglantine.'

'Not at all; I was only too glad. I made a cup of tea, Bruce had a whisky and soda, we had a nice talk, and I sent him back quite cheerful. Still, it just shows, doesn't it, how terribly he takes it all?'

'Rather hard on you, Eglantine; quite improper too,' laughed Edith as she rang the bell.

Madame Frabelle ignored this remark.

'If I could only feel at all that I've done a little good during my stay here, I shall be quite satisfied.'

'Oh! but you mustn't dream yet of—' began Edith.

There was a ring at the bell.

'Why, here is Bruce, just in time for tea.'

Edith went to meet him in the hall. Although he came in with his key, he invariably rang the bell, so that the maid could take his coat and stick.

'Hallo, Edith,' he said, in a rather sober tone. 'How are you? And where is Madame Frabelle?'

CHAPTER XXVI

B R U C E came in with a rather weary air, and sat down by the fire. Madame Frabelle was presiding at the tea-table.

'How are you feeling, Bruce?' Edith asked.

'Oh, pretty rotten. I had a very bad night. How are you, Madame Frabelle?'

'Oh, very well. Tea?'

'Poor Bruce!' said Edith kindly. 'Oh, and poor Madame Frabelle,' she added, with a smile.

Bruce gave Madame Frabelle a slightly reproachful look as he took a cup of tea from her.

'I've been telling Edith,' said that lady in a quiet, dignified way.

'What about?'

'About last night,' said Madame Frabelle, passing Bruce the buttered toast without looking at him, as if avoiding his glance.

'I'm really very much ashamed of it,' said Bruce. 'You can't think how kind she was to me, Edith.'

'I'm sure she was,' said Edith.

'Oh, you won't have a bad night like that again,' said Madame Frabelle cheerily.

'I'm sure I hope not.' He gave a dark, despairing look, and sighed. 'Upon my word, if it hadn't been for her I don't know what I would have done.' He shook his head and stroked his back hair.

Suddenly Edith felt intensely bored. Madame Frabelle and Bruce were looking at each other with such intense sympathy, and she knew they would repeat in different words what they had said already. They were so certain to go over the same ground again and again! . . . Edith felt she was not wanted. But that didn't annoy her.· She was merely thinking of an excuse to get away from them.

'By the way, how's Aylmer, Edith?' asked Bruce.

'Getting on well. I believe he's been ordered out of town.'

'To the seaside? For God's sake don't let him go to the east coast!'

'The east coast is quite as safe as any other part of England, I think.' said Madame Frabelle.

'Oh, he'll take his chance,' Edith replied.

'I expect he'll miss *you*, my dear,' said Bruce. 'You've been so jolly good to him lately.'

'Naturally,' said Madame Frabelle, a little quickly, very smoothly, and with what Edith thought unnecessary tact. 'Naturally. Anyone so kind-hearted as Edith would be sure to try and cheer up the convalescence of a wounded friend. Have a *foie-gras* sandwich, Edith?'

Edith felt an almost irresistible desire to laugh at something in the hospitable, almost patronising tone of her guest.

'Oh, Edith likes going to see him,' said Bruce to Madame Frabelle. 'So do I, if it comes to that. We're all fond of old Aylmer, you know.'

'I know. I quite understand. You're great friends. Personally, I think Mr Ross has behaved splendidly.' Madame Frabelle said this with an air of self-control and scrupulous justice.

'You don't care very much about him, I fancy,' said Bruce with the air of having made a subtle discovery.

She raised one eyebrow slightly. 'I won't say that. I see very excellent points in him. I admit there's a certain coldness, a certain hard reserve about his character that— Well, frankly, it doesn't appeal to me. But I hope I am fair to him. He's a man I respect. . . . Yes, I respect him.'

'But he doesn't amuse you—what?' said Bruce.

'The fact is, he has no sense of humour,' said Madame Frabelle.

'Fancy your finding that out now!' said Bruce, with a broad smile. 'Funny! Ha ha! Very funny! Do you know, it never occurred to me! But now I come to think of it—yes, perhaps that's what's the matter with him. Mind you, I call him a jolly, cheery sort of chap. Quite an optimist—a distinct optimist. You never find Aylmer depressed.'

'No, not depressed. It isn't that. But he hasn't got— You won't either of you be angry with me for what I say, will you?'

'Oh no, indeed.'

' You won't be cross with me, Edith? Perhaps I ought not to say it.'

' Yes, do tell us,' urged Edith.

' Well, what I consider is the defect in Aylmer Ross is that he has brains, but no temperament.'

' Excellent!' cried Bruce. ' Perfectly true. Temperament! That's what he wants!'

Edith remembered hearing that phrase used in her presence to Madame Frabelle—not about Aylmer, but about someone else. It was very characteristic of Madame Frabelle to catch up an idea or a phrase, misapply it, and then firmly regard it as her own.

Bruce shook his head. ' Brains, but no temperament! Excellent!'

' Mind you, that doesn't prevent him being an excellent soldier,' went on Madame Frabelle.

' Oh dear, no. He's done jolly well,' said Bruce. ' I think I know what she means—don't you, Edith?'

' I'm sure she does,' said Edith, who had her doubts. ' I don't know that I do quite know what people mean when they say other people haven't got temperament. The question is—what is temperament?'

' Oh, my dear, it's a sort of—a something—an atmosphere—a sympathy. What I might call the magnetism of personality!'

' That's right!' said Bruce, passing his cup for another cup of tea. ' Aylmer's hard, hard as nails.'

' Hasn't he got the name of being rather warm-hearted and impulsive, though?' suggested Edith.

' Oh, he's good-natured enough,' said Bruce. ' Very generous. I've known him to do ever so many kind things and never let a soul except the fellow he'd helped know anything about it.'

' You don't understand me,' said Madame Frabelle. ' I don't doubt that for a moment. He's a generous man, because he has a sense of duty and of the claims of others. But he has the effect on me—'

' Go on, Eglantine.'

' Frankly, he chills me,' said Madame Frabelle. ' When I went to see him with Edith, I felt more tired after a quarter of an hour's talk with him than I would—' She glanced at Bruce.

' Than you would after hours with Landi, or Bruce, or Byrne Fraser, or young Coniston,' suggested Edith.

'That's what I mean. He's difficult to talk to.'

'I have no doubt you're right,' said Edith.

'Well, she generally is,' said Bruce. 'The only thing is she's so infernally deep sometimes, she sees things in people that nobody else would suspect. Oh, you do, you know!'

'Oh, do I?' said Madame Frabelle modestly.

'Yes, I think you do,' said Edith, who by this time felt inclined to throw the tea-tray at her guest. The last fortnight Edith's nerves had certainly not been quite calm. Formerly she would have been amused at the stupidity of the conversation. Now she felt irritated, bored and worried, except when she was with Aylmer.

There was a moment's silence. Bruce leant back and half shut his eyes. Madame Frabelle softly put a cushion behind his shoulder, putting a finger on her lip as she looked at Edith.

Edith suddenly got up.

'You won't think it horrid of me, Bruce? I've got to go out for a few minutes.'

'Oh no, no, no!' said Bruce. 'Certainly not. Do go, my dear girl. You'll be back to dinner?'

'Dinner? Of course. It isn't a quarter to six.'

Her eyes were bright. She looked full of elasticity and spirit again.

'I quite forgot,' she said, 'something that I promised to do for Mrs Mitchell. And she'll be disappointed if I don't.'

'I know what it is,' said Madame Frabelle archly. 'It's about that Society for the Belgians,'—she lowered her voice—'I mean the children's *lingerie*!'

'That's it,' said Edith gratefully. 'Well, I'll fly—and be back as soon as I can.'

Bruce got up and opened the door for her.

'For heaven's sake don't treat me with ceremony, my dear Edith,' said Madame Frabelle.

She made a little sign, as much as to say that she would look after Bruce. But she was not very successful in expressing anything by a look or a gesture. Edith had no idea what she meant. However, she nodded in return, as if she fully comprehended, and then ran up to her room, put on her hat, and, too impatient to wait while the servant called a cab, walked as quickly as possible until she met one near the top of Sloane Street. It was already very dark.

'Twenty-seven Jermyn Street,' said Edith as she jumped in.

Ten minutes later she was sitting next to Aylmer.

'Only for a second; I felt I must see you.'

'Fool! Angel!' said Aylmer, beaming, and kissing her hand.

'Bruce is too irritating for words today. And Madame Frabelle makes me sick. I can't stand her. At least today.'

'Oh, Edith, don't tell me you're jealous of the woman! I won't stand it! I sha'n't play.'

'Good heavens, no! Not in the least. But her society's so tedious at times. She has such a pompous way of discovering the obvious.'

'I do believe you object to her being in love with Bruce,' said Aylmer reproachfully. 'That's a thing I will *not* stand.'

'Indeed I don't. Besides, she's not. Who could be? . . . And don't be jealous of Bruce, Aylmer. . . . I know she's very motherly to him, and kind. But she's the same to everyone.'

They talked on for a few minutes. Then Edith said:

'Good-bye. I must go.'

'Good-bye,' said Aylmer.

'Oh! Are you going to let me go already?' she asked reproachfully.

She leant over him. Some impulse seemed to draw her near to him.

'You're using that Omar Khayyám scent again,' he said. 'I wish you wouldn't.'

'Why? you said you liked it.'

'I do like it. I like it too much.'

She came nearer. Aylmer gently pushed her away.

'How unkind you are!' she said, colouring a little with hurt feeling.

'I can't do that sort of thing,' said Aylmer in a low voice. 'When once you've given me your promise—but not before.'

'Oh, Aylmer!'

'I won't rush you. You'll see I'm right in time, dear girl.'

'You don't love me!' suddenly exclaimed Edith.

'But that's where you're wrong. I do love you. And I wish you'd go.'

She looked into his eyes, and then said, looking away:

'Are you really going out of town?'

'I'm ordered to. But I doubt if I can stand it.'

'Well, good-bye, Aylmer dear.'

'Fiend! Are you going already? Cruel girl!'

'Why you've just sent me away!'

'I can stand talking to you, Edith. Talking, for hours. But I can't stand your being within a yard of me.'

'Thank you so much,' she said, laughing, and arranging her hat in front of the mirror.

He spoke in a lower voice:

'How often must I tell you? You know perfectly well.'

'What?'

'I'm not that sort of man.'

'What sort?'

After a moment's pause he said:

'I can't kiss people.'

'I'm very glad you can't. I have no wish for you to kiss *people*.'

'I can't kiss. I don't know how anyone can. I can't do those things.'

She pretended not to hear, looked round the room, took up a book and said:

'Will you lend me this, Aylmer?'

'No, I'll give it you.'

'Good-bye.'

'Good-bye, darling,' said Aylmer, ringing the bell.

The butler called her a cab, and she drove to Mrs Mitchell's.

When she got to the door she left a message with the footman to say she hadn't been able to see about that matter for Mrs Mitchell yet, but would do it tomorrow.

Just as she was speaking Mr Mitchell came up to the door.

'Hallo, hallo, hallo!' he cried in his cheery, booming voice. 'Hallo, Edith! How's Bruce?'

'Why, you ought to know. He's been with you today,' said Edith.

'He seems a bit off colour at the Foreign Office. Won't you all three come and dine with us tomorrow? No party. I'm going to ring up and get Aylmer. It won't hurt him to dine quietly with us.'

'We shall be delighted,' said Edith.

Mr Mitchell didn't like to see her go, but as he was longing to tell his wife a hundred things that interested them both, he waved his hand to her, saying:

'Good-bye. The war will be over in six months. Mark my words! And then won't we have a good time!'

'Dear Mr Mitchell!' said Edith to herself as she drove back home in the dark.

CHAPTER XXVII

L A N D I was growing rather anxious about his favourite, for it was quite obvious to him that she was daily becoming more and more under the spell. Curious that the first time she should have found the courage to refuse, and that now, after three years' absence and with nothing to complain of particularly on the subject of her husband, she should now be so carried away by this love.

She had developed, no doubt. She was touched also, deeply moved at the long fidelity Aylmer had shown. He was now no longer an impulsive admirer, but a devotee. Even that, however, would not have induced her to think of making such a break in her life if it hadn't been for the war. Yes, Sir Tito put it all down to the war. It had an exciting, thrilling effect on people. It made them reckless. When a woman knows that the man she loves has risked his life, and is only too anxious to risk it again—well, it's natural that she should feel she is also willing to risk something. Valour has always been rewarded by beauty. And then her great sense of responsibility, her conscientiousness about Bruce—no wonder that had been undermined by his own weak conduct. How could Edith help feeling a slight contempt for a husband who not only wouldn't take any chances while he was still within the age, but positively imagined himself ill. True, Bruce had always been a *malade imaginaire*; like many others with the same weakness, his valetudinarianism had been terribly increased by the anxiety and worry of the war. But there was not much sympathy about for it just now. While so much real suffering was going on, imaginary ills were ignored, despised or forgotten.

Bruce hated the war; but he didn't hate it for the sake of other people so much as for his own. The interest that the world took in it positively bored him—absurd as it seems to say so, Edith was convinced that he was positively jealous of the general interest in it! He had great fear of losing his money, a great terror of Zeppelins; he gave way to his nerves instead of trying to control them. Edith knew his greatest wish would have been, had it been possible, to get right away from everything and go and live in Spain or America, or somewhere where he could hear no more about the war. Such a point of view might be understood in the case, say, of a great poet, a great artist, a man of genius, without any feeling of patriotism, or even a man beyond the age; but Bruce—he was the most ordinary and average of human beings, the most commonplace Englishman of thirty-seven who had ever been born; that Bruce should feel like that did seem to Edith a little—contemptible; yet she was sorry for him, she knew he really suffered from insomnia and nerves, though he looked a fine man and had always been regarded as a fair sportsman. He had been fair at football and cricket, and could row a bit, and was an enthusiastic golfist; still, Edith knew he would never have made a soldier. Bruce wanted to be wrapped up in cotton wool, petted, humoured, looked up to and generally spoilt.

But what Sir Tito felt most was the thought of his favourite, who had forgiven her husband that escapade three years ago, now appearing in an unfavourable light. She had been absolutely faithful to Bruce in every way, under many temptations, and he knew she was still absolutely faithful. Aylmer and Edith were neither of them the people for secret meetings, for deception. It was not in her to *tromper* her husband while pretending to be a devoted wife, and it was equally unlike Aylmer to be a false friend.

Landi was too much of a man of the world to have been particularly shocked, even if he had known they had both deceived Bruce. Privately, for Edith's own sake he almost wished they had. He hated scandal to touch her; he thought she would feel it more than she supposed. But, after all, he reflected, had they begun in that way it would have been sure to end in an elopement, with a man of Aylmer's spirit and determination. Aylmer, besides, was far too exclusive in his affections, far too jealous, ever to be able to endure to see Edith under Bruce's thumb, ordered about, trying to please him; and indeed Landi was most anxious that they should not be alone too much, in case, now that Edith cared for him so much, his feelings would carry him away. . . . Yes, if it once went too far the elopement was a certainty.

Would the world blame her so very much? That Bruce would let her take the children Landi had no doubt. He would never stand the bother of them; he wouldn't desire the responsibility; his pride might be a little hurt, but on the whole Sir Tito shrewdly suspected, as did Edith herself, that there would be a certain feeling of relief. Bruce had become such an egotist that, though he would miss Edith's devotion, he wouldn't grudge her the care of the children. Aylmer had pledged her his faith, his whole future; undoubtedly he would marry her and take the children as his own; still, Edith would bear the brunt before the world.

This Sir Tito did not fancy at all, and instinctively he began to watch Bruce. He felt very doubtful of him. The man who had flirted with the governess, who had eloped with the art student—was it at all likely that he was utterly faithful to Edith now? It was most unlikely. And Edith's old friend hoped that things would be adjusted in fairness to her.

He knew she would be happy with Aylmer. Why should she not at thirty-five begin a new life with the man she really cared for— a splendid fellow, a man with a fine character, with all his faults, who felt the claims of others, who had brains, pluck, and a sense of honour?

But Aylmer was going out again to the front. Until he returned again, nothing should be done. They should be patient.

CHAPTER XXVIII

D u l c i e had now been settled down with Lady Conroy for about a week. She found her luxurious life at Carlton House Terrace far more congenial than she had expected. Her own orderly ways were obviously a great comfort to her employer, and though Lady Conroy turned everything to chaos as soon as Dulcie had put it straight, still she certainly had a good effect on things in general. She had a charming sitting-room to herself, and though she sometimes sighed for the little Chippendale room with the chintzes, at Jermyn Street, she was on the whole very contented. Lady Conroy was a delightful companion. She seldom pressed Dulcie to come down to meals when there were guests. Occasionally she did so, but so far the only person Dulcie had met more than once was Valdez, the handsome composer, who was trying so hard, with the help of Lady Conroy and his War Emergency Concerts, to assist such poor musicians as were suffering from the war, and at the same time to assert the value of British music.

Dulcie had been immensely struck by the commanding appearance and manner of Valdez, known everywhere as a singer, a writer of operas and a favourite of foreign royalties.

Landi she had often met at Aylmer's, but, privately, she was far more impressed by Valdez; first, he was English, though, like herself, of Spanish descent, and then he had none of the *méchanceté* and teasing wit that made her uncomfortable with Landi. He treated her with particularly marked courtesy, and he admired her voice, for Lady Conroy had good-naturedly insisted on her singing to him. He had even offered, when he had more time, to give her a few lessons. Lady Conroy told her a hundred interesting stories about him and Dulcie found a tinge of romance about him that helped to give piquancy to her present life.

Dulcie was very much afraid of Lord Conroy, though he didn't appear to notice her. In his own way he was as absent-minded as his wife, to whom he was devoted, but whose existence was entirely independent of his.

Lord Conroy had his own library, his own secretary, his own suite of rooms, his own motor, he didn't even tell his wife when he intended to dine out, and if he occasionally spoke to her of the strained political situation which now absorbed him, it certainly wasn't when Dulcie was there. With his grey beard and dark eyebrows, and absent, distinguished manner, he was exactly what Dulcie would have dreamed of as an ideal Cabinet Minister. He evidently regarded his wife, despite her thirty-eight years and plumpness, almost as a child, giving her complete freedom to pursue her own devices, admiring her appearance, and smiling at her lively and inconsequent conversation; he didn't seem to take her seriously. Dulcie was particularly struck by the fact that they each had their own completely distinct circle of friends, and except when they gave a party or a large dinner these friends hardly met, and certainly didn't clash.

As everyone in the house had breakfasts independently, and as Dulcie didn't even dine downstairs unless Lady Conroy was alone, she saw very little of the man whom she knew to be a political celebrity, and whose name was on almost everybody's lips just now. She heard from his wife that he was worried and anxious, and hoped the war wouldn't last much longer.

There were no less than seven children, from the age of twelve downwards. Two of these lived in the schoolroom with the governess, one boy was at school, and the rest lived in the nursery with the nurse. One might say there were five different sets of people living different lives in different rooms, in this enormous house. Sometimes Dulcie thought it was hardly quite her idea of home life, a thing Lady Conroy talked of continually with great sentiment and enthusiasm, but it was pleasant enough. Since she was here to remember engagements and dates everything seemed to go on wheels.

One day, feeling very contented and in good spirits, she had gone to see her father with an impulse to tell him how well she was getting on. Directly the door was opened by the untidy servant Dulcie felt that something had happened, that some blow had fallen. Everything looked different. She found her father in his den surrounded by papers, his appearance and manner so altered that the first thing she said was:

'Oh, papa! what's the matter?'

Her father looked up. At his expression she flew to him and threw her arms round him. Then, of course, he broke down. Strange that with all women and most men it is only genuine sympathy that makes them give way. With a cool man of the world, or with a hard, cold, heartless daughter who had reproached him, Mr Clay would have been as casual as an undergraduate.

At her sweetness he lost his self-control, and then he told her everything.

It was a short, commonplace, second-rate story, quite trivial and middle-class, and *how* tragic! He had gambled, played cards, lost, then fallen back on the resource of the ill-judged and independent-minded—gone to the professional lenders. Mr Clay was not the sort of man who would ever become a sponge, a nuisance to friends. He was far too proud, and though he had often helped other people, he had never yet asked for help. In a word, the poor little house was practically in ruins, or rather, as he explained frankly enough (giving all details), unless he could get eighty pounds by the next morning his furniture would be sold and he and his wife would be turned out. Mr Clay had a great horror of a smash. He was imprudent, even reckless, but had the sense of honour that would cause him to suffer acutely, as Dulcie knew. Of course she offered to help; surely since she had three hundred a year of her own she could do something, and he had about the same. . . . The father explained that he had already sold his income in advance. And her own legacy had been left so that she was barred from anticipation. Dulcie, who was practical enough, saw that her own tiny income was absolutely all that the three would have to live on until her father got something else, and that bankruptcy was inevitable unless she could get him eighty pounds in a day.

'It's so little,' he said pathetically, ' and just to think that if Blue Boy hadn't been scratched I should have been bound to— Well, well, I know. I'm not going to bet any more.'

She made him promise to buck up, she would consult her friends. . . . Lady Conroy would perhaps be angelic and advance her her salary. (Of course she loathed the idea when she had been there only a week of being a nuisance and— But she must try.) It was

worth anything to see her father brighten up. He told her to go and
see her stepmother.

Mrs Clay received her with the tenderest expressions and poured
out her despairs and her troubles; she also confided in Dulcie that
she had some debts that her husband knew nothing of and must
never know. If only Dulcie could manage to get her thirty pounds
—surely it would be easy enough with all her rich friends!—it
would save her life. Dulcie promised to try, but begged her not
to bother so much about dress in future.

' Of course I won't, darling! You're a pet and an angel. *Darling*
Dulcie! The truth is I adore your father. And he always told me
that he fell in love with me because I looked so smart! I was so
terrified of losing his affection by getting dowdy, don't you see?
Besides, he doesn't take the slightest notice what I wear, he never
knows what I've got on! Always betting or absorbed in the Racing
Intelligence; it's really dreadful.'

Dulcie promised anything, at least to do her best, if only Mrs
Clay would be kind, sweet to her father.

' Don't scold him, don't reproach him,' she begged. ' I'm sure he'll
be terribly ill unless you're very patient and sweet to him. And I
promise he shall never know about your debts.'

Mrs Clay looked at her in wonder and gratitude. The real reason
Dulcie took on herself the wife's separate troubles and resolved to
keep them from her father was that she felt sure that if he reproached his wife she would retort and then there would be a miserable state of feud in the house, where at least there had been peace
and affection till now. Dulcie couldn't endure the idea of her father
being made unhappy, and she thought that by making her stepmother under an obligation to her, she would have a sort of hold
or influence and could make her behave well and kindly to her
husband. Dulcie hadn't the slightest idea how she was going to do
it, but she would.

She never even thought twice about giving up her income to her
father. She was only too delighted to be able to do it. And she
believed that his pride and sense of honour might really even
make him stop gambling. And then there was *some* chance of happiness for the couple again.

Dulcie had really undertaken more of a sacrifice for her stepmother, whom she rather disliked, than for her father, whom she adored, but it was for his sake. She left them cheered, grateful, and relying on her.

When she got home to her charming room at Carlton House Terrace she sat down, put her head in her hands and began to think. She had undertaken to get a hundred and ten pounds in two days.

How was she to do it? Of course she knew that Aylmer Ross would be able and willing, indeed enchanted, to come to the rescue. He was always telling her that she had saved his life.

She would like to get his sympathy and interest, to remind him of her existence.

But she was far too much in love with him still to endure the thought of a request for money—that cold douche on friendship! She would rather go to anyone in the world than Aylmer.

What about Edith Ottley? Edith had been kindness itself to her; it was entirely through Edith that she had this position as secretary and companion at a salary of a hundred a year which now would mean so much to her.

She admired Edith more than any woman she knew; she thought her lovely, elegant, clever, fascinating and kindness itself. Yet she would dislike to ask Edith even more than Aylmer. The reason was obvious. Edith was her rival. Of course it was not her fault. She had not taken Aylmer away from her, she was his old friend, but the fact remained that her idol was in love with Edith. And Dulcie was so constituted that she could ask neither of them a favour to save her life.

Lady Conroy then. . . . But how awkward, how disagreeable, how painful to her pride when she had been there only a week and Lady Conroy treated her almost like a sister! . . . There was a knock at the door.

'Come in!' said Dulcie, surprised. No-one ever came to her little sitting-room at this hour, about half-past five. Who could it be? To her utter astonishment and confusion the servant announced Mr Valdez.

Dulcie was sitting on the sofa, still in her hat and coat, her eyes red with crying, for she had utterly given way when she got home.

She was amazed and confused at seeing the composer, who came calmly in, holding a piece of music in his hand.

' Good morning, Miss Clay. Please forgive me. I hope I'm not troubling you? They told me Lady Conroy was out but that you were at home and up here; and I hoped—' He glanced at the highly decorated little piano. This room had been known as the music-room before it was given to Dulcie.

' Oh, not at all,' she said in confusion, looking up and regretting her crimson and swollen eyes and generally unprepared appearance.

He immediately came close to her, sat down on a chair opposite her sofa, leant forward and said abruptly, in a tone of warm sympathy:

' You are distressed. What is it, my child? I came up to ask you to play over this song. But I shall certainly not go now till you've told me what's the matter.'

' Oh, I can't,' said Dulcie, breaking down.

He insisted:

' You can. You shall. I'm sure I can help you. Go on.'

Whether it was his personality which always had a magnetism for her, or the reaction of the shock she had had, Dulcie actually told him every word, wondering at herself. He listened, and then said cooly:

' My dear child, you're making a mountain out of a molehill. People mustn't worry about trifles. Just before the war I won a lot of money at Monte Carlo. I simply don't know what to do with it. Stop!' he said, as she began to speak. ' You want a hundred and ten pounds. You shall have it in half-an-hour. I shall go straight back to Claridge's in a taxi, write a cheque, get it changed—for you won't know what to do with a cheque, or at any rate it would give you more trouble—and send you the money straight back by my servant or my secretary in a taxi.' He stood up. ' Not another word, my dear Miss Clay. Don't attach so much importance to money. It would be a bore for you to have to bother Lady Conroy. I understand. Don't imagine you're under any obligation; you can pay it me back just whenever you like and I shall give it to the War Emergency Concerts. . . . Now, *please*, don't be grateful. Aren't we friends?'

' You're too kind,' she answered.

He hurried to the door.

'When my secretary comes back she will ask to see you. If any-one knows you have a visitor say I sent you the music or tickets for the concert. Good-bye. Cheer up now!'

In an hour from the time Valdez had come in to see her, father and stepmother had each received the money. The situation was saved.

Dulcie marvelled at the action and the manner in which it was done. But none who knew Valdez well would have been in the least surprised. He was the most generous of men, and particularly he could not bear to see a pretty girl in sincere distress through no fault of her own. It was Dulcie's simple sincerity that pleased him. He came across very little of it in his own world. That world was brilliant, distinguished, sometimes artistic, sometimes merely *mondain*. But it was seldom sincere. He liked that quality best of all. He certainly was gifted with it himself.

From this time, though Valdez still encouraged Dulcie to sing and occasionally accompanied her, the slight tinge of flirtation vanished from his manner. She felt he was only a friend. Did she ever regret it? Perhaps, a little.

CHAPTER XXIX

'B R U C E , said Edith, 'I've just had a letter from Aylmer, from Eastcliff.'

' Oh yes,' said Bruce. ' Got him off to the seaside at last, did they?'

It was a Sunday afternoon. Bruce was sitting in a melancholy attitude on a sofa in Edith's boudoir; he held *The Weekly Dispatch* in his hand, and was shaking his head over a pessimistic article when his wife came in.

Bruce was always depressed now, and if he felt a little more cheerful for a moment he seemed to try and conceal it. No doubt his melancholy was real enough, but it was also partly a pose and a profession. Having undertaken to be depressed, he seemed to think it wrong to show a gleam of brightness. Besides, on Sundays Madame Frabelle usually listened to him; and this afternoon she had gone, unaccompanied, to hear the Rev. Byrne Fraser preach. Bruce felt injured.

He had grown to feel quite lost without her.

' He's very dull there,' said Edith.

' I dare say he is,' he answered. ' I'm sure *I* should feel half inclined to cut my throat if I were alone, with a game leg, at a place like that. Besides, they've had the Zepps there already once. Just the place for them to come again.'

' He's very bored. But he's much better, and he's going back to the front in a fortnight.'

' In a fortnight! Good heavens! Pretty sharp work.'

' It is, indeed. He's counting the hours till he can get off.'

Bruce, sighing, lighted his cigarette.

' I wondered if you'd mind, Bruce, if I went down for the day to see him?'

' Mind! Oh *dear*, no! Of course, go. I think it's your duty, poor old chap. I wondered you didn't run down for the weekend.'

' I didn't like to do that,' she said.

' Why on earth not?' said Bruce. ' Hard luck for a poor chap with no-one to speak to. Going back again; so soon too.'

502

'Well, if you don't mind I *might* go down tomorrow for a couple of days, and take Dilly.'

'Do,' said Bruce eagerly; 'do the kid good.'

Edith looked at him closely.

'Wouldn't you miss her, now that Archie's at school too? Wouldn't the house seem very quiet?'

'Not a bit!' exclaimed Bruce with emphatic sincerity. 'Not the least bit in the world! At least, of course, the house *would* seem quiet, but that's just what I like. I *long* for quiet—yearn for it. You don't half understand my condition of health, Edith. The quieter I am, the less worried, the better. Of course, take Dilly. *Rather!* I'd *like* you to go!'

'All right. I'll go tomorrow morning till Tuesday or Wednesday. But wouldn't it seem the least bit rude to Madame Frabelle? She talks of going away soon, you know.'

'Oh, *she* won't mind,' said Bruce decidedly. 'I shouldn't bother about her. We never treat her with ceremony.'

When, a little bit later, Madame Frabelle came in (with a slight perfume of incense about her, and very full of a splendidly depressing sermon she had heard), she heartily agreed with Bruce. They both persuaded Edith to run down on the Monday and stay till Wednesday evening at least.

'Perhaps we shall never meet again,' said Bruce pleasantly, as Edith, Dilly and the nurse were starting; 'either the Zeppelins may come while you're away, or they may set your hotel at Eastcliff on fire. Just the place for them.'

'Well, if you want me you've only to telephone, and I can be back in a little more than an hour.'

Madame Frabelle accompanied Edith to the station. She said to her on the way:

'Do you know, Edith, I'm half expecting a telegram which may take me away. I have a relative who is anxious for me to go and stay with her, an aunt. But even if I did go, perhaps you'd let me come back to you after?'

Edith assented. Somehow she did not much believe either in the telegram nor the relative. She thought that her friend talked like that so as to give the impression that she was not a fixture; that she was much sought after and had many friends, one or two of whom might insist on her leaving the Ottleys soon.

Aylmer was at the little Eastcliff station to meet them. Except that he walked with the help of a stick, he seemed well, and having put Dilly, the nurse and the luggage in a cab, he proposed to Edith to walk to the hotel.

' This *was* angelic of you, Edith. How jolly the child looks!—like a live doll.'

' You didn't mind my bringing her?'

' Why, I'm devoted to her. But, you know, I hope it wasn't done for any conventional reasons. Headley and I are in the Annexe, nearly half-a-mile from you.'

' I know,' said Edith.

' And when you see the people here, my dear, nobody on earth that counts or matters!—people whom you've never seen before and never will again. But I've been counting the minutes till you came. It really isn't a bad little hole.'

He took her down to a winding path covered in under trees, which led to the sea by steps cut in the rock. They sat down on a bench. The sea air was fresh and soothing.

' This is where I sit and read—and think about you. Well, Edith, are you going to put me out of my suspense? How much longer am I to suffer? Let me look at you.'

She looked up at him. He smiled at what he saw.

' It'll be rather jolly to have two days or so here all to ourselves,' he said, ' but it will be far from jolly unless you give me that promise.'

' But doesn't the promise refer to after you come back again?' she said in a low voice.

' I don't ask you to come away until I'm back again. But I want you to promise before that you will.'

Nothing more was said on the subject at the time, but after dinner, when Dilly had been put to bed, it was so warm that they could come out again, and then she said:

' Aylmer, don't worry yourself any more. I mean to do it.'

' You do!'

He looked at her ecstatically.

' Oh, Edith! I'm too happy! Do you quite realise, dear, what it is? . . . I've been waiting for you for four years. Ever since that night I met you at the Mitchells'. Do you know that before the war, when I came into that money, I was wild with rage. It seemed

so wasted on me. I had no use for it then. And when I first met
you I used to long for it. I hated being hard up. . . . The first time
I had a gleam of hope was when they told me I'd got over the
operation all right. I couldn't believe my life would be spared for
nothing. And now—you won't change your mind again?'

Edith convinced him that she would not. They sat hand in hand,
perhaps as near perfect happiness as two human beings can be. . . .

'We shall never be happier than we are now,' said Edith in a
low voice.

'Oh, sha'n't we?' he said. 'Rubbish! Rot! What about our life
when I come back again?—every dream realised!'

'And yet your going to risk it,' said Edith.

'Naturally; that's nothing. I shall come back like a bad penny,
don't you worry. Edith, say you mean it, *again.*'

'Say I mean what?'

'Say you love me, you'll marry me. You and the children will
belong to me. You won't have any regrets? Swear you won't have
any regrets and remorse!'

'I never will. You know, Aylmer, I am like that. Most women
know what they want till they've got it, and then they want something else! But when I get what I want I don't regret it.'

'I know, my darling sensible angel! . . . Edith, to think this
might have happened three years ago!'

'But then I *would* have had regrets.'

'You only thought so,' he answered. 'I should have made you
forget them very soon! Don't you feel, my dear, that we're made
for each other? I know it.'

'Aylmer, how shall I be able to bear your going out again? It
will be like a horrible nightmare. And perhaps all we've both gone
through may be for nothing!'

'No, now I've got your promise everything will be all right. . . .
I feel I shall come back all right. . . . Look here, darling, you need
not be unhappy with Bruce. We're not going to deceive him. And
when I come back, we'll tell him. Not till then. There is really no
need.'

They walked together to the Annexe, which was entered by a
small flight of stone steps from the garden. Here Aylmer had a little
suite of rooms. Edith went into the sitting-room with him and
looked round.

'It's ten o'clock and you're here for your health! Call Headley and go to bed, there's a good boy.'

He held both her hands.

'I mustn't ask you to stay.'

'*Aylmer!* With Dilly here! And Bruce let me come down to look after you! He was quite nice about it.'

'All right, dear, all right. . . . I know. No. I'm looking forward to when I come back. . . . Go, dear, go.'

Edith walked very slowly down the steps again. He followed her back into the garden.

'And suppose—you didn't come back,' she said in a very low voice.

Aylmer glanced round: there was no-one in the garden.

'I'm on my honour here,' he said. 'Go, dear, go. Go in to Dilly.' He gave her a little push.

'One kiss,' said Edith.

He smiled.

'Darling girl, I've told you before that's a thing I can't do. I really oughtn't to be alone with you at all until we're quite free. . . .'

'But I feel we're engaged,' said Edith simply. 'Is it wrong to kiss your fiancée?'

'Engaged? Of course we're engaged. Wrong? Of course it's not wrong! Only . . . I *can't!* Haven't got the self-command. . . . I do believe you're made of ice, Edith—I've often thought so.'

'Yes,' said Edith, 'I dare say you're right.'

Aylmer laughed.

'Nonsense! Good night, my darling—don't catch cold. And, Edith.'

'Yes, Aylmer?'

'I'll meet you here at nine o'clock tomorrow morning.'

'Yes, Aylmer.'

'Then you'd better go back in the afternoon. It won't do for you to stay another night here. Oh, Edith, how happy we *shall* be!'

He watched her as she walked across the garden and went into the hotel at the front door. Then he went indoors.

The next day Edith, Dilly and the nurse went back to London early in the afternoon.

CHAPTER XXX

E D I T H , during the short journey home, sat with a smile on her lips, thinking of a little scene she had seen before leaving Eastcliff from the hall, known as the lounge, of the hotel. She had watched Dilly, beaming with joy, playing with a particularly large air-ball, bright rose colour, that Aylmer had bought her from a well-known character of the place, a very old woman, who made her living by the sale of these old-fashioned balloons. Dilly was enchanted with it. She had said to Aylmer when the old woman passed with a quantity of them. 'They look like flowers; they ought to have a pretty scent,' which amused him immensely. As she held it in her hand, pressing it with her tiny finger, a tragedy happened. The air-ball burst. Edith could hardly help laughing at seeing Dilly's expression. It was despair—gradual horror—shock, her first disillusion! Then as tears were welling up in the large blue eyes—she was saying: 'Oh, it's dead!'—Edith saw Aylmer snatch the collapsed wreck from the child's hand and run as fast as he could (which was not very fast, and only when leaning on a stick) after the old woman. . . . He caught her as she turned the corner, brought back a pink and a blue air-ball and gave them to Dilly, one for each hand. The child beamed again, happier than at first, threw her arms round his neck and kissed him. How touched and delighted Edith was! Would Bruce *ever* have done such a thing? Aylmer had so thoroughly appreciated the little drama of joy, disillusion and consolation shown in the expression in Dilly's lovely little face. Had anything been wanting to Edith's resolution this small incident would have decided it.

When they arrived home, a day sooner than they were expected, the servant told Edith at the door that Madame Frabelle had gone away.

'Gone without seeing me?'

'Yes, madam. A telegram came for her and she left last night. Here is a letter for you, madam.'

Edith ran into the dining-room and tore it open.

'MY DEAREST EDITH (it said),

'To my great regret a wire I half expected came, and I was compelled to leave before your return, to join my relative, who is ill. I can't tell you how sorry I am not to say good-bye and thank you for your dear kind hospitality. But I'll write again, a long letter. I hope also to see you later. I will give you my address next time.

'May I say one word? I can't say half enough of my gratitude for your kindness and friendship, but, apart from that, may I mention that I fear your husband *is very unwell indeed*, his nerves are in a terrible state, and I think his condition is more serious than you suppose. He should be humoured in everything, not worried, and allowed to do whatever he likes. Don't oppose any of his wishes, dear. I say this for your and his own good. Don't be angry with him or anybody. Never think me wanting in gratitude and friendship.

'Truly, I am still your affectionate friend,

'EGLANTINE.'

What a strange letter. How like her to lay down the law about Bruce! It irritated Edith a little, also it made the future seem harder.

About four o'clock Landi called unexpectedly. He always came just when Edith wanted him most, and now she confided in him and told him of her promise to Aylmer.

He approved of their resolution to wait till Aylmer returned from the front and to have nothing on their conscience before. He was indeed much relieved at the postponement.

'And how is the Spanish girl?' he asked. 'How does she get on with Lady Conroy?'

'Oh, all right. She's not Spanish at all. She had rather a blow last week, poor girl. Her father nearly went bankrupt; she was quite in despair. It seems your friend Valdez came to the rescue in the most generous way, and she's immensely grateful.'

'He helped her, did he?' said Landi, smiling.

'He seems to have behaved most generously and charmingly. Do you think he is in love with her, Landi?'

'Very likely he will be now.'

'And she—she adores Aylmer. Will she fall in love with Valdez out of gratitude?'

'C'est probable. C'est à espèrer. . . . Enfin—mais toi, mon enfant?'

'And where is Madame Frabelle?' asked Landi.

Edith looked at the postmark.

'Apparently she's at Liverpool, of all places; but she may be going somewhere else. I haven't got her address. She says she'll write.'

'C'est ça. . . . When does Aylmer return to the front?'

'He goes before the Board tomorrow and will know then.'

That evening, when Bruce came in, Edith was struck by his paleness and depression; and she began to think Madame Frabelle was right; he must be really ill. Then, if he was, could she, later, be so cruel as to leave him? She was in doubt again. . . .

'Very bad news in the evening papers,' he said.

'Is it so bad?'

'Edith,' said Bruce, rather solemnly, without listening, 'I want to speak to you after dinner. I have something serious to say to you'.

'Really?'

'Yes, really.'

Edith wondered. Could Bruce suspect anything? But apparently he didn't, since he spoke in a very friendly way of Aylmer, saying that he hoped he wouldn't stop away long. . . .

The dinner passed in trivial conversation. She described East-cliff, the hotel, the people. Bruce appeared absent-minded. After dinner she went to join him in the library, where he was smoking, and said:

'Well, Bruce, what is it you have to say to me?'

'Good heavens,' said Bruce, looking at his writing-desk, 'if I've spoken of this once I've spoken of it forty times! The inkstand is too full!'

'Oh! I'm so dreadfully sorry,' said Edith, feeling the strangeness of Bruce's want of sense of proportion. He had, as it seemed, to speak to her about some important matter. Yet the inkstand being too full attracted his attention, roused his anger! She remembered he had said these very words the day he came back from his elope-ment with the art student.

Edith looked round the room, while Bruce smoked. And so she had really made up her mind! She *meant* to leave him! Not that she intended to see Aylmer again now, except once, perhaps, to say good-bye.

But still, she really intended to change her whole life when he returned again. She felt rather conscience-stricken, but was glad when she looked at Bruce that there had never been anything as yet but Platonic affection between her and Aylmer, which she could have no cause to blush for before Bruce. And how grateful she felt to Aylmer for his wonderful self-control. Thanks to that, she could look Bruce in the face. . . . Bruce was speaking.

'Edith,' he said with some agitation, 'I wish to tell you something.'

She saw he looked pale and nervous.

'What is it, Bruce?' she asked kindly.

'It's this,' he said in a somewhat pompous tone, 'I am in a very strange condition of health. I find I can no longer endure to live in London; I must get away from the war. The doctor says so. If I'm to keep sane, if I'm not to commit suicide, I must give up this domestic life.' She stared at him. 'Yes, I'm sorry, I've tried to endure it,' he went on. 'I can't stand the responsibility, the anxiety of the children and everything. I'm—I'm going away.'

She said nothing, looking at him in silence.

'Yes. I'm going to America. I've taken my passage. I'm going on Friday. . . . I thought of leaving without telling you, but I decided it was better to be open.'

'But, Bruce, do you mean for a trip?'

He stood up and looked at her full in the face.

'No, I don't mean for a trip. I want to live in America.'

'And you don't want me to come too?'

'No, Edith; I can't endure married life any longer. It doesn't suit me. Three years ago I offered you your freedom and you refused to take it; I offer it you again now. You are older, you are perfectly fit to manage your life and the children's without me. I must be free—free to look after my health and to get away from everything!'

'You mean to leave us altogether then?' said Edith, feeling unspeakably thankful.

'Exactly. That's just what I do mean.'

'But will you be happy—comfortable—alone in America?'

He walked across the room and came back.

'Edith, I'm sorry to pain you, but I shall not be alone.'

Edith started, thinking of Madame Frabelle's letter . . . from Liverpool! Evidently they were going away together.

'Of course I give up the Foreign Office and my salary there, but you have some money of your own, Edith; it will be enough for you and the children to live quietly. And perhaps I shall be able to afford to send you part of my income that my father left me when I get something to do over there,' he added rather lamely.

'You mean to get something to do?'

'Yes; when I'm strong enough. I'm very ill—very.'

There was a long pause, then Edith said kindly:

'Have you any fault to find with me, Bruce?'

'Edith, you are a perfect mother,' he said in a peculiar tone which sounded to Edith like an echo of Madame Frabelle. 'I've no fault to find with you either as a wife. But I'm not happy here. I'm miserable. I implore you not to make a scene. Don't oppose me; forgive me—on account of my health. This will save my life.'

If he only knew how little she wished to oppose him! She stood up.

'Bruce, you shall do exactly as you like!'

He looked enchanted, relieved.

'I hope you will be happy and well, and I shall try to be. May I just ask—is Madame Frabelle going to America?'

'Edith, I will not deny it. We mean to throw in our lot together! Look out! You'll have the inkstand over!' She had moved near the writing-table.

Edith stopped herself from a hysterical laugh.

'You won't mind if I go down to the club for an hour?'

'Certainly not.'

'And, Edith—say what you can to my mother, and comfort her. Tell her it's to save my going off my head, or committing suicide. Will you say that?'

'I will,' she replied.

Five minutes later the door banged. Bruce had gone to the club. He hadn't told her he had taken a room there, and the same evening he sent up for his luggage. He did not wish to see Edith again.

Just before he went out, as if casually for an hour at the club, Edith had said:

'Would you like to come and see Dilly asleep?'

It had occurred to her that at least he had been frank and honest, and for that he deserved to see Dilly again.

'Edith, my nerves won't stand scenes. I'd better not. I won't see her.'

'Oh, very well!' she cried indignantly. 'I offered it for your sake. I would rather you *didn't* see her.'

'Try not to be angry, Edith. Perhaps—some day—'

'No. Never.'

'You would never let me come back again to see you all?'

'Never. Never.'

'Edith.'

'Yes.'

'Oh! nothing. You needn't be so cross. Remember my health.'

'I do,' said Edith.

'And—Edith.'

'Yes, Bruce?'

'Don't forget about that inkstand, will you? It's always filled just a little too full. It's—it's very awkward. . . . Remember about it, won't you?'

'Yes. Good night.'

'Good night.'

And Bruce went to the club.

The next day Edith felt she could neither write nor telephone to Aylmer. Just once—only once, for a long time—she must see him.

She confided in Landi, who invited them both to tea at his studio for once only and was urgent in impressing patience on them.

When Edith arrived with this thrilling piece of news to announce she found Aylmer alone in the pretty white studio. Landi was expected back every moment from a lesson at a pupil's house.

Aylmer was beaming with joy. 'Oh, my dear!' he cried, 'I'm not going away at all! They won't have me! They've given me an appointment at the War Office.'

'Oh, Aylmer! How wonderful! I know now—I couldn't have borne your going out again—now.'

He put his arm round her. Ah! this, she felt, was real love—it wrapped her round, it lifted her off her feet.

'But now, Aylmer, we mustn't meet, for a long time.'

'But, why not? What is it? Something has happened!'

'Aylmer, I needn't keep my promise now.'

'What do you mean?'

'Aylmer, Bruce wants to leave me. He's going to leave me—to desert me. And the children, too.'

'What! Do you mean— Do you mean—like before?'

'Yes. But this time he won't come back. And he wants me to divorce him. And—this time— I shall!'

'Edith! And do you mean—will he want to marry again?'

'Yes, of course! And she'll take care of him—he'll be all right.'

'Oh, Edith!' exclaimed Aylmer. 'Thank heaven for Madame Frabelle!'

ADA LEVERSON

(1862–1933), was the daughter of Zilla and Samuel Beddington. Her mother was a pianist and music lover (Paderewski used to play to her), and her father invested in London property. At the age of nineteen Ada married Ernest Leverson, an inveterate gambler who worked in the City; they had two children.

Ada Leverson began contributing sketches to *Punch* and other periodicals: one in particular attracted the attention of Oscar Wilde and in 1892 they met, becoming devoted friends. He called her his 'Sphinx' and introduced her to fashionable nineties society: Aubrey Beardsley, Walter Sickert, John Singer Sargent, Mrs Patrick Campbell and Max Beerbohm all became *habitués* of her salon. During his trial in 1895 Wilde was sheltered by the Leversons, living in their little boy's nursery where he dined and received calls amidst rocking-horses and golliwogs. On his release from prison two years later, Ada was the first to visit him: he greeted her with the words 'Sphinx, how marvellous of you to know exactly the right hat to wear at seven o'clock in the morning to meet a friend who has been away.'

Ada Leverson published two stories in *The Yellow Book*, in 1895 and 1896 (the former being accompanied by a portrait-drawing of her by Sickert), but it was not until 1905 that she began writing novels. By now Wilde and many of her old friends were dead and, bankrupt, her husband had fled to Canada. She published six classic comedies of manners: *The Twelfth Hour* (1907), *Love's Shadow* (1908), *The Limit* (1911), *Tenterhooks* (1912), *Bird of Paradise* (1914) and *Love at Second Sight* (1916). She also wrote a memoir of Oscar Wilde, published as *The Last First Night* in the *Criterion* in 1926.

In her later years Ada Leverson's friends included Harold Acton, William Walton and the Sitwells with whom she wintered abroad, in Florence and Amalfi. She died of pneumonia in London shortly after one of these Italian sojourns.